Zoë Marriott says of *FrostFire*: "Most stories spark to life when the main character starts to talk in my head. *FrostFire* arrived with three characters talking, all at once. Frankly, they gave me a heck of a headache until I figured out just who they were and how they'd got into this mixed-up love/hate situation. Each of them had their own journey and their own heartbreak to overcome. At its core, *FrostFire* is a story about the thin, thin line between good and evil, and how sooner or later each of us has to decide on which side we're going to make our stand."

Zoë lives in North East Lincolnshire with her two cats, named Echo and Hero, and the Devil Hound, otherwise known as Finn.

FrostFire is Zoë's fourth book.

Books by the same author

The Swan Kingdom
Daughter of the Flames
Shadows on the Moon

Frostfire

ZOË MARRIOTT

WALKER
BOOKS

First published 2012 by Walker Books Ltd
87 Vauxhall Walk, London SE11 5HJ

2 4 6 8 10 9 7 5 3 1

Text © 2012 Zoë Marriott
Cover photograph © 2012 Trigger Image/Alamy

This book has been typeset in Berkeley

Printed and bound in Great Britain by Clays Ltd, St Ives plc

British Library Cataloguing in Publication Data:
a catalogue record for this book is available from the British Library

ISBN 978-1-4063-1814-2

www.walker.co.uk

This book is dedicated to Wonder Editor Annalie Grainger
and Super Agent Nancy Miles, with the deepest gratitude.
I'm not quite sure how, but you got me through it!

"*That I should love a bright particular star,*
And think to wed it, he is so above me:
In his bright radiance and collateral light
Must I be comforted, not in his sphere."
—Shakespeare, *All's Well That Ends Well*

In my dreams, the wolves come for me. I hear their voices echoing from the far-off mountains and the frost-bright stars. They sing of the hunt, and hot blood spilled on snow, and the scent of their prey's fear on the wind. My fear.

I am running. Always running. Shadowy fields blur past my eyes, the jagged skeletons of trees, frozen rivers marked in stark black by the unforgiving starlight. My bare feet sink into the snow, and the cold burns them. Breath crystallizes in the air before me. My heartbeat throbs through my body.

But no matter how swiftly I flee, they are always just behind me.

Prologue

The first time the Wolf took me I was eight.

Before that I had thought I was normal. Even though the other children taunted me sometimes, calling me "Fatherless", "Nameless", their words didn't touch me, because they were not true. I had a father. He was the great hunter who had fallen to the fangs of the Demon Wolf before I was born. Everyone knew his name. I was proud to be the daughter of Garin Aeskaar.

I did not know then – no one knew – that he had left me much more than his name and his legend when he died.

I broke a pot that morning. The heat burned through the cloth as I made to pass the earthenware bowl to my mother, and singed my palm. I dropped the bowl, splattering the strong-smelling herbal mixture over the packed dirt floor. Shards of red pottery flew everywhere.

My mother's hand struck out, and the right side of my face went numb.

"Useless, clumsy girl," she said, eyes narrowing to icy black holes in her face. "You're just like your father... No, don't try to tidy up! You'll only make it worse. Get out. Go on! Get out of my sight!"

I went at a run, belly turning over with a sick mixture of shame and defiance. My clumsiness had wasted a morning's work and caused a mess, and I was sorry. But as the numbness wore off and the whole right side of my face ached and my hand stung, my guilt turned to anger. It wasn't fair, because it had been an accident. And it would be useless to ask for any of Ma's burn salve on the blister, or a bruise compress for my face. She never wasted those things on us. She sold them and hoarded the money in the hollow leg of the wobbly stool under the window.

The sunlight was bright enough to make my tearful eyes water even more, but the air was cold. I rubbed at the goose pimples on my bare forearms as my feet crunched on the frozen ground. Spring rain the day before had turned the village paths to churned-up mud, but the night had brought frost, and turned the squelching, foul-smelling mess into hard swirls of earth that dug into the thin soles of my boots as I walked between the squat, beehive-shaped houses.

I hurried past Elder Gallen's house, where his wife was cursing their nanny goat in the front yard, and slowed down as I neared the blacksmith's. Hot, iron-stinking air billowed out of the smithy, with the occasional burst of orange sparks. The rhythmic noise of metal bashing against metal was like music.

On a normal morning I would have lingered there, enjoying the warmth on my skin, watching Eilik the smith pound the glowing iron into useful shapes on his anvil. But I could already feel my face swelling up. He would see.

Eilik wouldn't ask questions. He never did. But I would see that look in his kind eyes, the look that made me squirm. So I kept on, skirting the blacksmith's yard and Elder Rangar's broken cart, which was waiting for its new wheel, and went into the trees.

It was quiet in the forest. A kind of companionable quiet. Birds called, bushes rustled, the wind played in the tops of the trees. None of them paid me any mind, and I liked it that way. I kilted my skirt up into my belt and wandered a little way, crunching through rotting yellow winter grass, letting my hands brush the rough red and grey bark of the towering trees.

I reached the little clearing where me and some of the other village children sometimes played in the summer, and sat down on a fallen log. Gingerly, I felt my face. The skin was hot and puffy, tender under my fingers. All except for one place. I traced the puckered curve of the scar. It was always cold, that place. Even when the bruise darkened my skin, the mark would stand out like a spray of white wax on my cheek. No matter how many times Ma hit it, the scar never got red, never got hot. Never went away.

It had been a part of me for as far back as I could remember. And for as far back as I could remember, Ma had hated it. She hated it when the villagers took to calling me "Frost" *because of it. She was the only one who carried on calling me by my real name, Saram.*

Saram meant "sorrow". That was what she wanted me called.

I reached into my shirt and pulled out the leather thong that hung around my neck. At the end of the leather was a sharp, curving tooth, the size of my index finger and marked with fine yellow-brown lines. A wolf's tooth. A tooth from the wolf that had killed Garin Aeskaar. My father.

When I was little, before I started to grow so big and clumsy like my da, and Ma's temper got so uncertain, I had asked her many times about the scar on my face. When had I got it? How did it happen? She only ever answered once. She said: "A wolf did it."

And when I asked, "What wolf?" she said, "The Demon Wolf."

That was the first time she hit me.

My father and the Demon Wolf had killed each other before I was born. The Wolf could never have bitten me. But I liked to pretend that it had for the same reason that I wore its tooth around my neck. It made me feel closer to my father. I imagined sometimes what things would have been like if the Wolf had not killed him; if Ma had not left my father's home in the North – where the grey eyes I got from him would have been normal – and made us live here in this village with people who whispered and looked at me sideways. But mostly I imagined that one day I would be strong enough to take his great axe, with its double-blades, down from its resting place above the mantel.

One day I would be as strong as my father had been.

My fingers clenched on the tooth, and I relished its sharpness. One day no one would hit me any more.

"Oh, look! It's Frost Eyes!"

I groaned under my breath and stuffed the tooth back under my shirt. Ulem Gallen.

"What are you doing out here, Fatherless?" I felt a shock of real fear when I heard the second voice. That was Marik Ersk, Ulem's best friend. "Who said you could come into our forest?"

I stood up and turned to face them, blood tingling. Ulem was bad enough on his own, but at least he was slow and stupid and he got bored easily. Marik was something different. He had hated me and Ma since we hadn't managed to save his mother from the fever last winter. He couldn't hurt Ma – but with Ulem on his side he'd made hunting me into a sport. I'd had a black eye, pulled hair, kicked shins and ripped clothes from them, and there was nothing I could do to stop it. Ulem's father was in charge of the village. No one would take my side over his.

They were coming at me from opposite sides of the clearing. I swallowed hard, my gaze darting everywhere as I searched for a gap in the trees.

"Get away," I said. I wanted the words to come out strong and angry, but they sounded thin and weak. I tried again. "Leave me alone!"

"Listen to that!" Marik said mockingly. "Giving orders. We don't have to do what a stupid fatherless girl tells us. You're nothing. No one has to listen to you."

Ulem laughed. It was mean, flat laughter and it made his cheeks flush an ugly red. His small eyes were gleaming with excitement. "Your da died just to get away from you! Even your ma calls you Saram. No one wants you, Frost Eyes."

"Maybe we should do everyone a favour and get rid of her," Marik whispered, creeping closer.

I could hear Ma's voice hissing in my head: Don't fight them. Don't annoy them. Stay quiet. Stay out of their way. We can't upset the elders. Be a good girl and stay out of trouble.

How, Ma? How am I supposed to get away without fighting now?

I sucked in a deep breath, turned towards Marik — and ran. I shoved past him, shrugging off the hand that tried to grab the back of my shirt, and leaped down a shallow slope. They shouted angrily behind me. For a moment, I thought I'd made it.

Then my foot went into a hole. My ankle turned. I toppled over, hands scrabbling uselessly at the undergrowth. I shoved myself back up, ignoring the throb from my leg — but it was too late. Ulem and Marik were at the top of the slope behind me and I'd never climb up the other side with this ankle. I was trapped.

Marik's eyes were angry and cold, the way they'd been

every day since the priests had lit his ma's funeral fire. He had a rock in his hand.

I cried out with pain as it bounced off my chest. I clutched the bruised spot, anger driving Ma's cautious voice from my head. "You throw rocks at girls now? Coward!"

In answer, he stooped and hurled a piece of fallen wood. I jerked aside, but I couldn't avoid the stone that Ulem threw at the same time. It smashed into my shoulder. I felt something crack and I screamed – but the sound was cut off as another missile slammed into my sore cheek. The pain made me dizzy. I fell to my knees, angry, frightened gasps choking me.

Don't fight them. Stay quiet. Stay out of their way.

Something warm slid down my face. Warmer than tears. It dripped on to the back of my hand, where my fist was clenched in the dirt.

It was red.

Somewhere near by, a wolf began to howl.

I stared down at the gleaming, scarlet drops on my hand. Rocks and clods of frozen mud and branches were still falling down on me. I couldn't feel them any more. A deep, convulsive shudder moved down my spine, making my muscles twitch. The skin under the droplet of blood began to change. Silvery-white patterns like scars – like frost – curled across the brown skin.

Shivers quaked my body. I was cold.

So cold.

The wolf was howling. Closer now. It was coming.

Didn't Ulem and Marik hear it? They should be running. Why weren't they running?

The howling drowned out everything else. It hummed through my bones, made my sight blur and my teeth chatter. But Marik and Ulem still couldn't hear it.

Only me.

And I realized: It wasn't out there. It was inside. The wolf was inside me.

Do not fear, my daughter, it howled.

I am here.

I will protect you.

Nine years later...

One

My mouth tasted of dust and iron.

The cool white mists that rolled down the mountain slopes in the early morning had burned away, and the sun was directly overhead. Now and again, a sudden, blinding flash of light would pierce the silvery-blue-leaf canopy, dazzling me. I had learned to walk with eyelids half closed. My hips and feet ached like a half-healed bruise. Sweat itched at the small of my back, in the bends of my knees and elbows. Waving strands of dark hair had worked free of the braid pinned up around my head and clung damply to my skin no matter how often I tried to brush them back.

I'd been walking a long time.

I was blowing hair out of my face again when the dry earth gave way beneath my left boot. I lurched sideways and snatched at the waxy tree roots thrusting out of the hillside to drag myself away from the edge. The path was dangerously narrow and winding. If I tumbled off, it was a very long fall down the steep layers of terraces into the river I could hear thundering below. I'd likely never get the chance to climb back up again.

I regained my footing, then sighed tiredly, letting go of the roots to shake red soil from my hands. The first few times the path had betrayed me, my heart had pounded and my fingers had shaken, but I was too weary to get excited about these brushes with death any more.

The bush ahead of me rustled.

I froze.

Something was shifting in the foliage. Something big.

A bandit? No. The bush wasn't big enough.

Animal, then. Leopard?

I couldn't outrun a leopard.

My feet felt as if they had rooted into the crumbling earth. I swallowed hard, and slowly, slowly, *slowly* reached back for my father's axe, which was secured across the top of my pack—

A massive blue pheasant burst out of the bush. The fan-shaped copper tail nearly grazed my face as the bird flew upwards, filling the air with a frantic beating of wings that seemed to mock my speeding heartbeat. As it disappeared into the trees, my hand fell limply from the axe. Just a bird. Just a bird.

I squeezed my eyes shut, taking deep, careful breaths

as the world swam around me. *Too weary to be excited by brushes with death? Oh, Father – the lies I tell.*

My stomach rumbled loudly, and I let out a weak laugh. My stomach cared nothing for fear. I scrubbed my face roughly with dusty hands. Then, turning off the path, I clambered up the slope until I found a thick clump of glossy purple shrubs that would hide me from anyone passing below. I sank down into the shelter of the leaves and shrugged off my leather pack. My shoulders crunched with the movement. I groaned, stretching out aching legs and rotating my feet in their heavy boots. From my new vantage point above the path, I could see the bright glint of water through the trees. The River Mesgao. Not far now. I just had to follow the river and it would take me where I needed to go. My blood surged with hope and longing – and fear.

I had come such a very long way.

Out of habit, I reached for Da's axe first. Untying the hide straps that held it across the top of the pack, I took a moment to check the blades over. The axe was precious, and not just because it was nearly all I had left of my father. If I could not offer to split logs, bring down rotted outbuildings and drag out stubborn stumps, there would be no reason for anyone to offer me a bite of food or a night's stay in their hayloft. I could not rely on luck or the mercy of strangers. Both were uncertain at best.

When I was satisfied that the axe was in good

condition, I opened my pack and looked at the contents with resignation. I'd traversed the foothills and crossed into Ruan through the low passes of the great Subira range as soon as the winter ice had thawed. Offers of employment had been scarce in the two weeks since. This part of the world seemed mostly inhabited by gnarled, bone-hard shepherds and goatherds who looked as if they had grown up out the red earth and grey rock of their mountain home. They stared at me, towering over them with my big awkward hands and feet, and my foreign-looking eyes and axe, and shook their heads wordlessly, faces a mixture of suspicion and scorn. Even if they did need my help, they had little to offer in return. My food supplies were dwindling rapidly. All I had left now was a small package of dried mutton, tough and chewy, and the remains of a block of sharp white goat's cheese. I'd had earned the cheese two days ago, climbing down into a ravine to retrieve a strayed nanny goat.

I put away the meat, which would last longer, and slowly ate the cheese, trying to make each bite last as long as possible. I licked the white crumbs from my fingers and washed it down with a gulp of tepid liquid from a half-full waterskin. Unless I came across a farmstead or a village where I could trade labour for food soon, I would have to stop for a day or two and set up traps to snare fresh meat. I shrugged restlessly at the thought of the wasted time.

I needed to keep moving. I needed to find the Goddess in the Fire.

The quiet was shattered by a loud *Maaah*, followed by the tinny ring of a bell. I jumped and pressed a hand to my heart. After a moment, I heard the familiar clomping noise of hoofed feet growing closer. I put away my water-skin and closed up my pack, giving my hands a moment to steady. *Calm down. No one wants to hurt you here. And this herd might bring a shepherd who requires your strong back.*

I leaned forward and peered cautiously through the leaves. There were four shaggy-coated goats with impressive horns ambling up the path, their goatherd behind them.

He was dark-skinned, darker than me, with a bright red cap crammed down over unruly black curls. I guessed he was probably a year or two older than my own seventeen; square and burly and fit-looking, he moved lightly over the uneven ground, guiding his flock with a wooden quarterstaff. I grimaced. He would need no help from me. Anyway, I made it a practice to avoid young men, especially lone ones. Knotted-up old fellows with grey hair and bent backs were safer.

I waited impatiently for him to move on. His steps were slow and his path meandering, as if he were lost in his own thoughts.

There in the cool, shadowy cave made by the leaves, I could feel my eyelids growing heavy. I was tired from my weeks of travel. In a moment I'd be falling asleep and wasting half a day. I forced my eyes wide in an effort to stave off the sleepiness – and saw a glint of light in the scrub below the path.

A cold shiver moved over my skin. My gaze skittered across the hillside, tracking the glint. Polished metal, moving stealthily through the undergrowth. The shape was unmistakeable.

A knife.

Now that I knew it was there, I could see bits and pieces of the man carrying it. He was thin and ragged-looking and wearing dented, mismatched armour. He had very pale skin and yellow hair – both were greasy and streaked with dirt. And he wasn't alone. There was another man hiding behind a tree further down the path. That one held a sword.

Before crossing into the mountains I had done a day's labour at a border farm and stayed the night in their hay-loft. The farmer's wife had warned me that the Rua hills were infested with rebels who had been banished by the Rua queen after the civil war. The men had been soldiers once. Now they were thieves and bandits. But even with-out this warning, I'd met enough people in my life who wanted to do me harm to recognize the eager tension in these men's bodies, the grimness on their faces.

They were going to ambush the goatherd. Steal his animals. Kill him.

Stay quiet. Don't fight. Stay out of trouble.

This was none of my business. The goatherd was a stranger. He was nothing to me. He wouldn't care about my fate if our positions were reversed.

Stay out of trouble. Don't fight.

I squeezed my eyes shut. It didn't help. The images were inside my head, and I could not escape them. I saw my mother's face: cold as clay, eyes milky and opaque, blood and foam dried around her mouth. The body of a teenage boy, sprawled on fallen leaves, his face destroyed. I saw my own hands, smeared with blood. Priests holding the unlit torches, their faces cold and righteous. Two boys, faces sneering, stones flying through the air. I saw my past.

I saw death.

Fine tremors shook my body as I stared down at the goatherd's cheerful red hat.

Stay out of trouble.

I can't. I can't. I can't.

I can't watch him die.

I'm the only hope he's got.

My fingers fumbled with the sackcloth-wrapping around the axe. The goatherd was almost beneath me now. The bandit ahead of him was rocking forward, making ready to move.

The goatherd stopped. Turning back, he grabbed the horns of one of his animals that had strayed up the slope. As he dragged it back down onto the path, the bandit stepped out from behind the tree, sword raised.

Father, protect them.

Keep my blood from spilling

A scream of terror and defiance ripped from my throat. I crashed out of the bush and charged down the hillside, hitting the path with a bone-shaking thud. The bandit staggered back in shock. I swung my father's axe wildly. It hit the bandit's blade with a grating *clang* that nearly deafened me. The sword was dashed from the man's hands. As he stared at his empty fists, I kicked out as hard as I could. My heavy boot drove straight into the soft tissue between his legs.

The bandit doubled over, retching. I whacked him on the back of the head with the iron langet of the axe, cringing at the meaty thud. He collapsed onto the path.

I stood gasping for a split second, stunned by what I had done. Then I turned and seized the goatherd's arm. "Run!"

I tried to tow him forward, but it was like tugging the limb of a tree. He was no taller than me, but his muscles outweighed me. I couldn't budge him, and he just gawked at me, open-mouthed.

"Are you a halfwit?" I shrieked. "Come on!"

I yanked at his arm with all my might – and felt the path dissolve under my heel again. I stumbled back, releasing the goatherd as I pinwheeled my arms, desperate to retain my balance. The goatherd, finally provoked into movement, reached out and caught my wrist, as if to pull me back.

Instead, he was dragged over the edge with me as the earth I was standing on disintegrated. We hit the slope. The goatherd let go of my wrist as I rolled over and over; brush and vines whipped across my exposed skin and clouds of dry earth billowed up around me. I clung desperately to Da's axe as the blades whirled dangerously close to my face.

The pick of the axe snagged on a giant, pale root and my fall was halted with a jolt that nearly ripped my arm from its socket. I looked down to see my feet dangling out into space. The river glinted below.

Coughing out a mouthful of dirt, I inched my other arm up to grab the root and, grunting with effort, heaved myself up onto my feet. I freed my axe, keeping a strong grip on the root. Then I looked around for the goatherd.

He was just above me, straightening up on a small plateau scooped out of the hillside. He was covered in grazes and dirt, and he had lost his red cap, but the staff was still in his right hand. He stared down at me, and I noticed for the first time that his eyes were a pale greenish shade that looked odd against his dark skin.

"Get up here." His voice was low and rough.

The hand he held out was trembling. *Anger, or fear?* I hesitated for a second, looking at those odd, cold eyes. But his hand looked strong enough, and he had no reason to hurt me right now. I reached out and let him haul me up over the lip of the plateau. As soon as I was on level ground he dropped my fingers.

"Arian!" someone shouted. It was a male voice: deep and commanding. There was a skittering noise of small stones falling and a movement in the bushes, as if someone was climbing down. "Hello! Are you hurt? What's happening down there?"

"I'm not injured," the goatherd called back. "Did you get the other one?"

"No, he disappeared as soon as you went over the edge. Is she all right?"

"Who cares? The whole thing's ruined now, thanks to this – this idiot."

I felt my jaw drop. "I just saved your life."

"You? You couldn't save your own backside with both hands." He shot me a look of cold anger. I flinched, hands clenching on my axe haft.

He ignored me and craned his neck, apparently looking for the man who had called out to him. Something was wrong here. Where had this other person come from? There hadn't been anyone else on the path. Only me, the goatherd and the bandits. Was this some kind of trap? And if so, for whom?

I started to edge sideways, eyes searching the hillside for handholds. Whatever was going on, I didn't want to be caught in the middle of it. I turned just as a bandit swarmed up onto the plateau, knife in hand.

His face was twisted with rage. His eyes were fixed on the goatherd's back. "Rua *scum!*"

Without thinking, I threw myself forward, thrusting my axe up like a shield. The bandit's long blade hit one of the metal langets and sheered sideways with a screech. Sunlight sizzled from the edge of the knife, blinding me. Pain flared across the back of my hand.

Black dots danced in my vision as it cleared. I stared at the red drops welling up on my skin.

The bandit turned on me, his knife slicing down in a vicious arc.

A wooden staff capped with silver knocked the knife from the bandit's hand, and then whirled around and swept his legs out from under him. The man toppled off the edge of the plateau with a hoarse cry and disappeared down the slope below.

"Clumsy," the goatherd said gruffly. "You let him get you."

He reached out as if to touch my hands that were still curled, white-knuckled, around the haft of the axe.

"No." I choked the word out and stumbled backwards. I dropped the axe, still staring at the blood. The sweat was turning to ice on my skin. My next breath clouded in the air. "Don't."

"Let me see," he snapped.

"Get away!" The words warped and changed in my

mouth, emerging as a snarl. "Run!"

The bushes stirred overhead, and a second man, taller than the first, dropped down lightly onto the plateau, unsheathed broadsword in hand. He wore brightly polished plate armour and a helm that obscured most of his features. A pair of dark, glittering eyes flicked to my face, and he swiftly sheathed the sword.

"What's wrong? I thought you said she wasn't hurt."

Inside me – in the cold place – a piercing, lonely cry rang out. It filled my ears. The men's lips were still moving, but I could no longer hear either of them.

All I could hear was the Wolf.

The colours were slowly leaching out of my vision. I blinked, and the world was blue and grey and silver. The only red left was the bright liquid spilling from my hand. The second man moved slowly towards me, his hands lifting in a calming gesture. I tried to back away again – but there was nowhere for me to go.

No. I begged silently. *Not now. I'm so close. Please…*

The connection between me and my body shattered.

Sound rushed back. Vision sharpened. Muscles tensed.

The Wolf's lips peeled back over its teeth as it scented blood.

Two

I didn't dare open my eyes.

My skull throbbed in time with my heartbeat. I was stiff and bone-deep sore. There was a maddening itch from the wound on my right hand. But the worst thing was the shame churning in my belly. Tears squeezed out from under my eyelids and slid down my face.

Oh, Father. It happened again.

There was a tiny squeak, as of leather. My eyes snapped open. Teardrops blurred my sight. There was a man sitting on a low stool next to me.

The goatherd.

The shabby, voluminous robes were gone. Instead he wore a fine linen shirt, unlaced at the throat, soft leather breeches and polished boots. And there was a sword at his waist. As I watched, his fingers tightened on the weapon.

I looked up into his face, and froze like a rabbit facing

a leopard. Those green eyes were flat and cold and more menacing than a shouted death threat. When he looked away I breathed a sigh of relief – until I saw that his jaw was marked with four deep, distinct claw marks.

"She's awake," he called out, standing.

I tried to take in as much information about my surroundings as I could. It was dim, but I could see that the walls were planed wooden planks, the roof low and unplastered. It was a small space, and there were no windows. The only light came from a narrow opening high up in the roughly cut iron-bolted door. The room smelled of straw and livestock. Like a barn.

My chest started to tighten. I forced myself to concentrate on what I could hear. Voices. Some distant, some closer. Birdsong. Jingling and heavy stamping that grew louder and than faded away – horses being led. The ringing noise of metal being beaten into shape.

It was too familiar. All of it. It reminded me … reminded me…

Stop it. Stop thinking about it!

The door swung open. Late-afternoon sunlight flooded the room, and my eyes watered still more as I squinted at the man standing silhouetted against the light.

"I hope you're ready to answer some questions, my would-be assassin," the silhouette said. I recognized his voice. It was the second man on the hillside, the one with dark eyes. "I have to confess, I'm not feeling very patient."

I tried to raise my hands to shield my face from the sun, so that I could see him properly – and felt the weight of metal encircling my wrists. Thick iron manacles bound my hands together.

The fear I had been desperately suppressing broke free and ripped through me with claws of ice. The iron chains clanked as my body began to shake. In an instant, I was eight years old again and locked up in Elder Gallen's barn. I could hear the priests chanting outside, and smell the smoke.

Father, help me.

I surged to my feet, abused muscles screaming, head filled with the roar of fire.

The goatherd stepped hastily towards me. I threw my full weight at him, ramming him into the wall. The little wooden structure shuddered with the impact. The goatherd grunted, breath driven out of him. I pushed him away and dived towards the open door.

The silhouette put one arm out in a horrible imitation of an embrace. I slammed the manacles down, not caring if I broke his wrist. But he was too quick. He whipped his arm back and wrapped it around my shoulders instead, his other arm going around my waist, so that I was crushed against him, just inches from freedom.

I bucked and squirmed. His arms were like iron, stronger even than the cuffs on my wrists. Distantly, I was aware of his voice rumbling as he spoke to me, but

I couldn't make out the words. All I knew was that I had to get away before the priests came and lit the fire.

My eyes took in everything outside the cell. It was surrounded by canvas tents of all shapes and sizes, their walls streaked with green and yellow and blue paint. *Some kind of camp?* Beyond the tents I could see the forest and the mountains. I had to get to them: get away, hide. I had to run until no one could find me.

The silhouette took a step back. He was trying to drag me back inside.

I screamed. It was a high-pitched shriek, like a rabbit in a snare.

"Calm down," he said. "For the Mother's sake, stop fighting."

Stop fighting. Stay quiet. Stay out of trouble.

I jerked forward with every bit of strength I had, and felt his grip around my shoulders slip. At the same moment, my legs were swept out from under me and I crashed backwards. My head hit something with enough force to make my vision flare with black and silver spots. Then the black and silver faded and everything went white again.

I hear their voices in the wind. In the movement of water. In the rustle of the leaves. No matter what I dream, they are there. They hide beneath the surface. Watching. Waiting. The world of my dreams always grows colder. The dream sun always sets. And when the stars come out, I must run...

Three

Afterwards – after it happened – I always pretended that I couldn't remember anything. I pretended that the Wolf had stolen my mind as well as my body. But it wasn't true. I was still there. Held back by walls of ice, unable to speak or so much as twitch a finger, I watched it all happen.

I remember the Wolf leaping up the slope towards Ulem and Marik and the shock and sudden fear on their faces. I remember it clawing and kicking and hitting until they were both down; until the noise of their screams brought the whole village running; until Elder Gallen and two other men dragged the Wolf – dragged me – off the boys, still howling and fighting.

I remember every moment of the Wolf's attack. And I remember how good it felt.

I tried to tell myself that it was only the Wolf's pleasure I experienced, the Wolf's exultation in pain and violence. But *that was a lie too. A part of me had enjoyed what the Wolf did with my body. A part of me had wanted to hurt those boys. Had wanted to hurt them as much as they had hurt me.*

Looking back, a part of me still does.

The men took the chains from a plough shear and wrapped them around the Wolf's arms and legs. They dragged it through the village and threw it into Elder Gallen's little barn and left it there.

For a long time, the Wolf fought the chains. It was not strong enough to break them, though, not then. Finally, I suppose its strength gave out. The Wolf stopped struggling and fell asleep.

And I woke up.

"Her skull is intact, but she's going to be very sorry for herself when she wakes up. Did you really have to hit her this hard, especially so soon after the last time?" The voice was female. It sounded old, and a little grumpy – like someone who was used to being in charge.

"I told you; I didn't hit her. She hit her own head on the door." That was the goatherd: words sharp edged, like flint.

"After you kicked her legs from under her. Yes."

There was a short pause and then a different voice, the voice of the man who had caught me and told me to stop fighting. "She *was* trying to escape, Livia. Arian was just doing his job."

"I think she's coming around," said the woman. "Holy Mother, she's only a child. Can't be any more than sixteen."

"Sev ... seventeen..." I mumbled. My lips felt thick and dry.

"Oh? Well, that's still a baby to me, my girl. Open your eyes now."

I struggled to obey her, reacting to the tone just as I always had to my mother's no-nonsense commands. I winced from the light, then sighed as someone put something wet and cool on my forehead. It smelled of herbs – plants that I had known the names of once, before my mother had realized what I was and banned me from her stillroom. There had been no point in remembering their names after that.

A woman was leaning over me. She was pale-skinned but deeply tanned; the fine wrinkles around her eyes and mouth placed her age in the mid-sixties. Iron-grey hair straggled from an untidy knot at the nape of her neck. There was a funny mark on one side of her face, a blueish smudge that curved around her left eye onto one bony cheekbone. A tattoo. I squinted, trying to focus on it. Stars. Tiny flowers. A rabbit – no, a hare, staring up at the stars above one grey brow.

"That's my healer's mark you're gawping at," the woman said briskly. "If you can see enough to gawp, your eyes are most likely all right."

"Where…?" My voice ran out and turned into a dry cough. My head throbbed and I groaned weakly.

"Here." The second man spoke again. "Let her drink this."

The woman brought a wooden cup to my lips. I sipped and then gasped as heat spread down my throat and into my belly. My head began to clear a little. I managed to whisper, "Thank you."

"Well, you were right, Lieutenant," the woman said, arching an eyebrow. "She's a fierce berserker assassin, all right. I should never have got you to unlock those manacles."

Unlock the manacles? I lifted my hands – arm muscles twitching feebly – and went weak with relief when I realized the chains were gone. I also saw that my wounded hand had been neatly bandaged with a clean cloth.

"Where am I?" I croaked.

"You're at the royal hill-guard encampment and back in the cell you tried to escape from about ten minutes ago," the healer said. "I'm Livia, and these other two are Captain Luca and his lieutenant, Arian." She patted my arm, then began to stand, grunting with the effort.

"Don't go," I whispered, clutching at her hand. She was my only protection against these two strange men. I didn't want to be alone with them.

The woman's face softened, but she shook her head.

"Sorry, child. I've done all I can for you. Just tell the truth and I'm sure everything will be well. And no more running about for a while, understand? You'll do yourself in next time."

The healer cast me a look that I thought was meant to be reassuring and then went to the door. I closed my eyes against the glare of the sun, and when I opened them again she was gone, the door shut behind her. The goatherd had positioned himself against it, as if to ensure I did not try to run again. The other man was taking the healer's place on the stool next to the mattress. He laced long, sinewy fingers together and leaned forward, clearly waiting for me to speak.

Even when he was sitting, I could see that he was taller than the other one, though not as bulky; his long limbs folded up gracefully in the limited space. He looked as if he were in his late teens, maybe twenty at most. His skin was pale, lightly tanned, and he had very long hair. Longer than mine, even. It was the rich dark-gold of blossom honey, streaked with lighter shades, and had been drawn back from his broad forehead into a simple braid. The gleaming rope of it fell over one muscled shoulder. His face was heart-shaped, with a sharp, determined chin and a thin blade of a nose. If the goatherd was a leopard, ruthless and rippling with muscle, then this one was a bird of prey. Beautiful and deadly.

It was unbelievable. This man – with the goatherd's

help — had actually brought the Wolf down. Without killing it. Without killing me.

I realized that he was staring at me just as intensely as I was at him, a thoughtful frown pulling at his brow. A shaft of light from the barred opening in the door fell across his eyes. They were like deep, still water — so blue that in certain lights they might almost look black.

"Admiring your handiwork?" he asked.

His voice was deep for a young man, and deceptively gentle. My gaze followed his pointing finger to his forehead where, I now saw, there was a red, puffy area exactly matching the shape of my own knuckles.

"It was a good hit," he continued. "Not many people can get past my guard. What I'd like to know is why. Why save Arian twice and then turn on us? What are you?"

I couldn't speak. My heart jumped wildly, and each deafening beat forced the air from my lungs. *What are you?* How could I answer that? I didn't know myself.

He sighed. "Silence is not a good policy. If you refuse to answer my questions, I'll be forced to assume the worst. Although if you are an assassin, you employed a very odd strategy today."

I tried to answer — to deny the accusation — but my throat tightened on the words, nearly choking me. *Say something! Say anything!*

"Odd or not, it nearly worked," the goatherd chimed

in. "You're lucky you didn't succeed, girl. Luca stopped me from finishing the job earlier, but if it were up to me, you would already be dead."

I could see, in the blank iciness of his eyes, that he was telling the truth.

"I'm n–not an assassin," I managed to stutter, forcing the words out. "I d–didn't want to hurt anyone. I was just trying to help."

"We didn't ask for your help," the goatherd said sharply.

"People shouldn't have to be asked! I thought the bandits were going to kill you! I couldn't just sit by and watch." I looked back at the other man – Luca. "Th–Then suddenly *you* were there. I thought I'd walked into the middle of a trap. I'm sorry I attacked you – but I p–panicked. I thought I was defending myself."

The dark-blue eyes narrowed thoughtfully. "The trap wasn't meant for you. We were trying to find the lair of some bandits who've been kidnapping the locals and selling them as slaves over the border and … other places. It was unfortunate that you stumbled into it. Where do you come from?"

There was no point in lying. "Uskaand."

"You're a long way from Uskaand," the goatherd said, disbelief evident. "Who were you travelling with?"

"N–No one. I was alone. *Am* alone." The words were stark and painful; I hated him for making me say them.

"Why are you in Ruan?" Luca asked.

I opened my mouth, then closed it again, my gaze travelling warily between the two men. "My ma died last winter. I don't have anyone else. She used to talk about Ruan and the Goddess in the Fire. I had nowhere else to go, so I came here."

"The Goddess in the Fire? Do you mean the Holy Mother?" Luca asked.

"The G–Goddess in the Fire," I repeated stubbornly.

"And you came a thousand miles, alone, to seek a bedtime story your mother told you." The goatherd shook his head. "You honestly expect us to swallow that?"

"It's the truth."

The light rippled over Luca as he stood up, showing colours like a tiger's eye stone in his long plait. "You've been through a lot today. I'll talk to you again tomorrow – after you've eaten and slept. Maybe then your story will make more sense."

"You're going to k–keep me locked up here?" I demanded between gritted teeth. "I didn't do anything wrong. You can't—"

"We have every right to hold you," Luca said. "You attacked us."

"I t–told you. I was afraid! I panicked!"

"You didn't fight like a panicked young girl. You fought like some kind of wild animal, and you howled like one too. You're hiding something. It's the hill guards' job to keep these mountains safe. I don't believe it would be safe to let you go without knowing the truth as to why you're here and what you intend to do."

"I'm n–not lying. I just want to go on my way. Let me go!"

"I'm sorry." He did look sorry, just for a second, then his back straightened.

He left the cell without another word.

The goatherd closed the door behind the other man and moved silently to the foot of the mattress to look down at me. One of his hands was clenched on his sword hilt, the knuckles yellow-red with the force of his grip.

"If you carry on lying, eventually he'll give up and march you down to the elders in Mesgao."

"I'm not ly—"

He cut me off. "Once the elders have you locked up you're no problem of mine, and I don't care what you do. But while you're in this camp I won't be taking my eyes off you for a single second. If you do anything, anything at all, to make me suspect you intend to harm him a second time, I will execute you. Immediately, and without warning. Luca won't like that – but he's an honourable man. I'm not. Bear it in mind."

He turned, ripped the door open and went out. I heard the grating sound of a rough iron lock sliding into place on the outside. It took me a few seconds to be able to breathe again.

Shaking, I curled up on my side, making myself into as small a target as I could. The herbal compress slipped off my forehead, but I didn't try to hold it on. My hands went to my chest, where the familiar pointed shape of the wolf tooth made a hard lump under my shirt. I clutched it through the coarse material.

Oh, Father. I have to get away. I have to get to the Goddess. Before I kill someone again.

Four

I was kneeling on the mattress, searching the wooden planks of the cell wall for cracks or weaknesses, when I heard the sound of approaching footsteps. A shadow moved over the golden bar of light cast by the narrow opening in the door, turning the cell cold and dark. There was a sharp knock, then an impatient voice. "Do you want to eat or not?"

I heaved myself to my feet just as a wooden tray was thrust through the opening. It tipped forward, and I had to lunge across the little space to grab it before it fell.

"Wasting good food on bad rubbish," the man on the other side of the door muttered. His footsteps were heavy as he stomped away, letting the light back into the cell.

I looked down at the tray, expecting to see stale bread and mouldy cheese, if I was lucky. Instead, I found a clay plate of neatly sliced flatbreads and a small bowl of some kind of yellow peas. There was another bowl filled with what I guessed must be meat stew, although it was a strange red colour, and a cup of water. Everything save the water was steaming faintly. They had even given me a spoon.

No wonder the man had been annoyed. Surely normal prisoners did not eat like this. Perhaps Livia had intervened on my behalf. For a moment, the thought warmed me, then I shook it away. *Stupid.* It did not matter who had ordered the food. I could not afford to feel gratitude towards anyone here. Not if I was to survive.

The smells coming from the tray were spicy and unfamiliar but good. I turned to sit on the mattress, and felt my foot slip down into a depression in the floor. I wobbled, and only just managed to save the tray. Here was something...

Immediately my hunger faded to the back of my mind. I put the food and water out of the way on the bedding and knelt down. The tips of my fingers skated over the ground, exploring the corner of the cell where the ground dipped. My own shadow made it impossible to see anything, but it didn't matter. I knew what I could feel. A gap under the planks of the wall that was just big enough for the first and second joints of my fingers.

My breath sped up in excitement. Maybe an animal had tried to burrow its way in, or perhaps a recent flood had reformed the earth. But however it had happened, the gap was there.

Trepidation held me still for a long moment. What if

they caught me trying to escape again? What if they had left this gap here on purpose as a kind of test? I ruthlessly stepped on these fears. I couldn't let them make me weak. If I stayed I was sure to die – or kill. The only way to avoid that was to run.

And now I had a way out of this prison.

I looked around determinedly. I needed a digging tool. The bucket in the corner was too splintered and old. *The stool?* No, that would be too easily missed if I smashed it up. My eyes fell on the large, crude metal spoon on the tray of food. It was the next best thing to a spade. But if it were missing when someone returned for the tray, they would notice. It was the sort of thing jailers paid attention to – it was why there was no knife.

I would have to hide the theft of the spoon in a larger misdeed, something that would make them so angry that no one would realize the spoon was gone until it was too late.

I let myself drink the water. My throat was painfully dry, and I had no way of knowing when I might get more. Besides, no one would miss it once I was done. Then I allowed myself two mouthfuls of the peas, two of the stew, and two small pieces of flatbread. The spices in the food burned my mouth, but it was the best thing I had tasted in weeks, maybe months. My stomach cramped painfully, making hollow noises as it begged for more. I ignored it.

Regret made my limbs slow and heavy as I took the tray to the door. One by one, I shoved everything out of the narrow opening. I heard the thick clay plate and pots smash as they hit the earth and the splatter of the wasted food. I was about to put the tray out too – but, after weighing it in my hand, instead broke it into splinters under my foot, keeping one corner intact, and then threw the remaining pieces out. It would make a good scoop.

With my eyes on the wall, where the rectangle of sunlight from the slot in the door would warn me if someone approached, I dragged my mattress away from the other wall. Then I sat on it, so I was blocking the corner of the cell from view and pulled the leather thong from around my neck. I quickly kissed the smooth curve of the wolf fang.

"I beg your pardon, Father," I whispered.

Taking a firm grip on the tooth – the bandage wrapped around my fingers helped – I began to hack at the rock-hard surface of the earth under the gap. The first few inches of dirt were almost impossible to break into. Sweat dripped down my forehead. I gritted my teeth and stabbed harder, the menace of the goatherd's last words echoing in my mind. He'd make me suffer a lot worse than this.

The serrated underside of the tooth dug into my thumb, and the bandage around my hand began to flap loose. My head protested the activity by sending spikes of pain through my skull and into my eyes.

The earth dimpled. Then cracked.

With a sigh of relief, I wiped the crumbs of soil off the tooth and hung the leather thong back around my neck, tucking it safely down under my shirt again. I had to stop and flex my stiff fingers for a few moments before I was able to pick up the spoon.

Grunting with effort, I worked the thin edge of the spoon's bowl down into the crack I had made, prising away the top layer of dirt to get at the softer, looser stuff beneath. After a few minutes the handle of the spoon was digging painfully into the sore spot on my thumb. I stopped with a muttered oath. I couldn't afford to get a blister. It would slow me down. After considering for a moment, I unravelled the bandage from around my fingers and rewrapped it tightly around the spoon's handle. I tested the grip and nodded in satisfaction. *Good.*

The wound the bandit had made on my hand was a sore red line that itched furiously as I worked, but just like the rumbling of my stomach and the threat of splinters from the underside of the wall, I ignored it. I knew that by tomorrow it would have scabbed over and in another day it would be gone completely, leaving no mark behind. I healed fast. Very fast. And I never scarred. It had been that way since the Wolf first took me. If the hill guards had realized just how quickly I would recover, they would have been a lot more cautious about taking those manacles off.

I managed to clear a foot-long section of hard earth from the corner of the cell. I had shoved the chunks of dirt under the thin, straw-filled mattress. It bulged strangely, but the bedding was lumpy anyway, so I hoped no one would notice. Then I heard footsteps. I hastily shoved my digging tools under the mattress and huddled into a ball in front of the hole I had dug as the light from the opening in the door disappeared. The air filled with an outraged cursing as someone caught sight of the mess I had made. I kept my head down and waited for him to go away. There was more swearing and banging, as he bad-temperedly cleaned up the wasted food and ruined pottery. When the noises stopped, I waited another minute, just to be sure he wasn't coming back, and then I got to work again.

By the time the rectangle of sunlight had slid across the wall to sit above my head, the gap was large enough that I could fit one arm and my shoulder through it. In the opening I saw tall grass and undergrowth, as well as the piles of dark earth that I had scooped up and out of the cell. If anyone decided to take a walk around the back of the prison, I would be dead. The thought only made me work faster.

I had stopped to pick a splinter from the back of my hand when the sunlight died out of the cell again. I frowned. No footsteps had approached. Had a cloud moved over the sun?

I jumped like a spring hare when Luca's voice came through the door.

"I'm told you don't care for our food," he said. "Any particular reason?"

I shrank deeper into the corner of the cell, using my body to conceal as much of the gap as I could.

I heard a faint thud – as if he had let his head fall against the door. When he spoke again his voice was softer. "You must feel like death dragged through a ditch right now. But you'll only make yourself feel worse by refusing to eat. If I send more food, will you throw it out again?"

Was I supposed to believe that he cared? Maybe he thought he could trick me. I clutched my digging tools to my chest.

"I don't even know your name," he muttered, as if he were speaking to himself. "How can you reason with someone when you don't know their name? Listen. We don't want to harm you. You're not in danger in this camp."

I will execute you. Immediately, and without warning...

I squeezed myself into a tighter ball.

"We are the royal hill guard. Do you understand what that means? We follow and enforce the reia's law. That means no torturing prisoners. It means everyone gets a fair trial. We risk our lives patrolling these mountains to keep the local people safe from the Sedorne bandits. We're the good ones. You don't need to be frightened of us."

There was a long pause. Was he expecting a response? What did he want me to say?

The good ones? As far as I had seen, the world was divided into people who were trying to kill you now and people who hadn't tried yet. What did good and bad have to do with it?

"All right. I'll leave you be for now. Here."

There was a soft flumping noise. I peeked over my shoulder to *see* that he had shoved a folded blanket through the gap in the door. A leather waterskin followed, landing on the blanket with a wet slosh. I stared incredulously.

"Think about what I've said. If you tell me the truth, I can try to help you. We're only enemies if you choose to make it so."

His shadow moved away from the door. I listened for footsteps, but there were none. The man really was as silent as a bird of prey. I'd best remember that.

I waited a count of sixty before I stood, went to the door and peered out of the gap. One or two people were passing by, intent on their own business; there was no sign of Luca or his goatherd guardian.

I picked up the blanket and waterskin and checked them over carefully. The blanket was thick, double-woven wool, grey and soft with washing. The waterskin was well sealed, with no drips, and full.

Luca had just given me everything I needed to make my escape a success. This was too easy. Why would he give me these things? Not out of kindness. Not when the Wolf and I had attacked him and his man twice now. It made no sense. But he already had me locked up: luring me out only to chase me down again made no sense either.

No, it must be that these hill guards wanted me alive for more questioning. They thought I was a spy – someone with valuable information, perhaps. It was unlucky for them that I didn't intend to wait around until they realized they were wrong.

By the time night fell, my shoulders, arms and back were quivering with tiredness. My fingers no longer had the strength to grasp the digging implements. Blisters were rising up on both my palms, and I had been forced to re-bandage my right hand and use the damp herbal compress Livia had made on the left.

But the gap under the wall was big enough for me to squeeze through.

I moved the mattress again, kicking and shoving at it with my feet so that it sat askew across the floor, hopefully concealing as much of the mess I had made as possible. Then I arranged myself on top of it and lay still, gingerly opening and closing my hands to try and work some strength back into them.

Someone walked past the cell and shone a lamp in. I tensed as I followed the path of their eyes in my imagination.

They moved on. I waited as long as I could bear, listening to the noises of the camp change with the darkness. When everything had been peaceful for some time, I went to the door and peered out again.

The camp was still under the cold blue starlight. I couldn't see anyone near by, but that didn't mean there was no one there – it was just too dark to be sure. I couldn't afford to delay any longer, though. I needed to put the furthest possible distance between me and these people before sunrise.

I took the waterskin and blanket and pushed them out of the gap. Then I flattened myself against the dusty earth, pressing my belly and shoulders down and turning my face sideways. The rough wooden planks ripped out hairs from my braid and scraped my ear and cheek as I wriggled through the gap. I could feel the seams of my shirt strain across my back. The sensation of the wall pressing down on me, trapping me against the dirt, made me feel sick. I sucked in a deep breath, making myself as thin as possible – and popped out on the other side.

I lay face down in the dirty hollow I had made until the panic had passed away and my heart had slowed a little. Then I pulled myself into a crouch and looked around.

I couldn't believe my luck. My cell was at the end of a long, single-storey building, and immediately behind it rose a little hill, covered in scrubby grass, weeds and bushes. I could be out of the camp and under cover in moments. I draped the blanket over one shoulder, put the strap of the waterskin across my body to hold the blanket in place and crept up the slope.

The sound of water reached my ears around halfway up. My heart sank. By the time I got to the top of the hill it was obvious why the prison had been built here. It wasn't a hill at all. It was the edge of a ravine.

The river cut a winding channel through the rock at the bottom of a sheer, forty-foot drop. The tree cover on the other side of the ravine might as well have been a hundred miles away.

If I wanted to escape, I would need to head the other way. And it was no good trying to skirt the camp – that was where the sentries would be.

I had to go *through* the campsite.

I remembered the goatherd's icy eyes and the hand clenching his sword hilt, and shivered. If he caught me running he would have all the excuse he needed. I would be dead before the Wolf had time to ascend.

Make sure he doesn't catch you, then, I told myself as I headed back down the slope. I pressed myself into the shelter of the prison wall, judging the distance to the nearest tent. *And stop wasting time.* I took a deep breath and ran flat out for the canvas wall, dropping down into a crouch when I reached it, heart thundering. No shouts. No arrows. Good so far.

The thump and slosh of the waterskin against the small

of my back seemed deafening as I scuttled, crablike, from shadow to shadow, zigzagging through the outer ring of tents. Only the brilliance of the starlight allowed me to avoid tent pegs driven into the earth, casually abandoned camp chairs, washing pails and kicked-over campfires. But that same brilliance would betray me in an instant if anyone happened to glance my way.

When I reached the edge of the camp, I stopped for a moment, huddling in the grass against the wall of a small tent to catch my breath. Beyond this tent, there was an open area where the ground climbed gently towards the forest. I had to make it across that emptiness to get away. All it would take was one sentry to glance up at the wrong moment and—

I imagined the arrows thudding into my back and shivered again.

I found myself straining to hear something, any noise at all, from the camp. Whenever I had come across groups of soldiers in Uskaand they had been noisy, rowdy men, needing little excuse to shout, swear and brawl. This camp seemed eerily quiet in comparison. None of the tents even had a lamp burning in them as far as I could see.

Enough hesitating, I told myself. *Go. Go now!*

My muscles bunched in readiness for the last burst of speed I would need to see me away. But instead of running I froze.

Someone was singing. The deep golden voice echoed

and carried through the still night air, until it seemed that he might be standing right beside me. The song was hauntingly familiar. It was an old folk song – a song that my ma had hummed all her life. Sometimes, when I was very small, she had sung it to me at night as she tucked me into bed.

> "Farewell, my love, our time has come,
> Long though I might to stay;
> Our time has come, my one true love,
> The world calls me away…"

Slowly other voices, male and female, began to join the first. The sweet, sad notes of a wood flute wove in among them, and a drum took up the slow rhythm of the melancholy song.

My scalp prickled. But it wasn't fear this time. Longing was what I felt now, longing and loneliness, like a lost wolf listening to a strange pack howling in the night. Close by, so close, but utterly untouchable. A family I could never be a part of.

I lifted my gaze to the frosty stars, letting their light fill my eyes and remind me that sometimes it is better to be alone. Safer. For everyone. I took a firm grip on my blanket and waterskin, and ran from the hill-guard camp into the darkness.

I look back. Always. I cannot help myself.

The wolves are rivulets of darkness streaming over the snow, like blood, black in the starlight. Silver teeth flash. Silver eyes spark. They know I am looking.

They raise their faces to the moon, and their high, eerie song fills the night. The wolves call to me. They call my name.

And they have my father's voice.

Five

The villagers left me in the barn in chains for two days. No one would cross the threshold to bring me food or water. When the thirst became too great, and the burning tightness of my throat threatened to close it forever, I managed to drag myself close enough to the wall to lick the moisture from the green mould that grew there, though the taste of it made me retch.

The barn was near the centre of the village and the square of frozen, churned-up earth they called a green. It was where the elders went to pass judgement on village matters. The whole village gathered there that first day to debate what to do with me. The law prohibited the killing of children under the age of twelve without a special dispensation from a priest of Askaan. Elder Gallen ordered a messenger on a fast horse to ride to the nearest town, find the temple there and bring a priest back, urgently.

I listened to my mother plead for mercy. I was only a child, she said, only a girl. She offered to leave the village and take me with her. She begged to be allowed to bring me food and care for my injuries. A few others – including Eilik the blacksmith – sided with her, but the elders overruled them.

I was mad, they said. No one must go near me until the priest had come.

The messenger returned the next day. I heard the commotion as he – and the men he had brought – arrived. I was nearly too faint with thirst and hunger and the cold to care. But somehow all the bruises and pains I had acquired the day before didn't hurt as much as I had expected. I rolled painfully through the straw and muck until I could press my eye to a chink in the wooden wall of the barn.

A golden-robed priest of Askaan, with a white beard and a stern, fatherly face, dismounted from a golden horse. He handed the reins to Elder Gallen, who stared at them as if he had never seen leather before.

There was another man with the messenger. A slight, slim man. His head was bald, and it gleamed in the early morning sun, but he looked young, not even as old as my mother. His face was smooth and unlined, and his eyes, although I could not see their exact colour at that distance, seemed dark and grim. His robe was black, and so was his horse. He was a priest of the Other.

That was when I really began to believe that I would die.

The two priests directed tables and chairs to be brought out to the centre of the village. They wanted to question everyone.

Ulem and Marik were forced to leave their beds to testify that I had howled like a wolf and foamed at the mouth, while my eyes had glowed with an unearthly light – and I had attacked without provocation and tried to bite out their throats. They questioned my mother too. Had I shown signs of madness before? Had I ever spoken strange languages or blasphemed; shown any desire to eat raw meat?

Ma denied it all, but I could hear in their voices that they did not believe her.

They stopped for a midday meal. The smells of cooking meat and vegetables should have made me drool, but my mouth was too dry even for that. My cramping stomach made me curl into as tight a ball as I could with the chains wrapped around me.

At the end of the day, as the light coming through the chink in the wall turned orange, the priests ordered the barn to be opened. Elder Gallen did not like that. He said I was too dangerous. When the holy men insisted, he offered to give them a pitchfork each, just to be safe. They refused that too.

Slowly, creakingly, the barn door was pushed back.

I heard my mother cry out and the sounds of a struggle, as if someone were holding her back. I could not see her.

The priest of Askaan took a few steps towards me, then he backed away, putting up his hand to cover his mouth. The barn stank, not just of animal dung but of my own. I had fouled myself. I had had no choice in the matter, but the shame did what the fear had not the power to do. It broke me. I began to cry silently, my body shaking with painful sobs.

"They gave you quite a beating, didn't they, child?"

I squinted up at the man who had spoken. His voice was mild and kind. It was the priest of the Other. He crouched beside me, apparently unaffected by the smell, and took my chin in his hand, turning my face gently towards him to examine me. His fingers were dry and cool.

He gave me a sad smile. Then he stood and left the barn. The priest of Askaan followed gratefully, and the doors were slammed shut again, sending splinters, hay and dust showering down on me.

Outside, the two priests conferred in hushed voices. I could not see them, or hear what they were saying through the hole in the wall, and after a few minutes they moved back to the green.

The priest of Askaan took out the Holy Book and read a blessing from it.

Then the priest of the Other passed judgement. "The girl has been possessed by a demon of the Other. I believe she is too young to have voluntarily taken the demon in – it is a tragedy probably brought about by her upbringing. Fatherless children are always particularly vulnerable. She must be cleansed. And the village too."

"How?" Elder Gallen asked.

"With fire, Elder," the priest of the Other said. "With fire."

The blanket, tied around my shoulders as a makeshift cloak now, was no protection against the bitter chill that had crept into my bones as I laboured up the shaly mountain slope towards my destination. My hands were raw from clawing at the rough surface for handholds, and my skin felt chapped and brittle. I was distantly aware of these things, but none of them were pressing enough to break my concentration on the place I had come so far to reach. The place I had lied, stolen and fought to get to.

I had finally arrived.

But something was terribly wrong. The cold inside me was a hundred times deeper than the chill of the mountain. What I was staring at was not the sacred place my mother had rambled about in her sickness – a place where the holy people were healers and warriors and where no one in need was ever turned away. This was not the home of the Goddess in the Fire.

This was a viper's nest.

I stared at the towering outer wall of the structure. From my hiding place on the hillside, I could see that what must once have been an impenetrable stone barrier was now little more than a series of rotting masonry teeth. The gaps in the wall were filled with sections of sharpened wooden stakes, forming a seven-foot palisade with a single pair of rough wooden gates. Men in mismatched, dented armour, their pale hair greasy and unwashed, their skin streaked with dirt, moved freely through these gates. They brought in goats, sheep, carts loaded with grain, barrels of what looked like ale and other produce.

And they brought people.

People with dark skin. People with blood and bruises and tracks of tears on their faces. People whose hands were lashed behind their backs and who were kicked, punched or whipped if they fell or tried to resist.

On the other side of the wall I could see women and children with fair hair and pale skin dressed in fine clothes. They were laughing, playing, gossiping. Men in neat, lacquered armour with strangely peaked helmets casually patrolled the inner wall of the keep. The dark-skinned ones toiled: chopping wood, digging trenches and scrubbing clothes, backs hunched as if waiting for a blow.

Slaves.

If there had been anything in my stomach I would have vomited.

This was where the bandits brought their stolen goods and their stolen people. This was the home of the rebels that Luca had spoken of. Whatever holy place had been here once was long gone. There was no Goddess in the Fire. There was no help for me in Ruan. There was no help for me anywhere.

Almost without realizing what I was doing, I began the climb back down the mountain, desperate to escape the biting cold and the sight of my shattered hopes.

It had taken me nearly a full day to reach the ridge. I was down again in half the time, so despairing was I that

I didn't even think to test my handholds, or to search for a safe path. Somewhere in the back of my mind I knew I was acting dangerously; I could fall and be seriously hurt, or even die. The Wolf only forced its superior strength and reflexes on me if others shed my blood – if there was a chance for it to fight and kill. A careless stumble off a cliff wouldn't rouse it.

But all I cared about was getting away.

The slope of the land became more gentle. Scrubby bush changed to grey, stunted trees and twisted shrubs, and then to the towering greenery of the hill forest. I walked on aimlessly, my eyes passing over everything without making sense of it.

I don't know when I began to shake. I only noticed at all because despite walking on almost level ground, my feet started to slip and scuff. My vision blurred. I realized I was gasping for breath. I stopped and stared at the green and blue arches of the trees around me, at the sunlight turning the air to gold, at the moss and the rich dark earth.

Where am I? Where am I going?

Stones and broken twigs crunched beneath me as I sat down in the dirt.

I'll never get the Wolf out of me. I'll never be free.

I fumbled with the wolf tooth, nearly choking myself as I pulled the leather thong over my head, and squeezed the hard, familiar shape between my hands.

Father. Father, please help me. Tell me what to do.

"You've come a long way just to sit muttering to yourself."

I jumped up, the wolf tooth flying from my hands. It landed in the dirt a couple of feet away. Instinctively, I made a grab for it, but Luca got there first, scooping the necklace up and looking at it thoughtfully. "A wolf fang? Why would you wear something like this around your neck?"

He looked up at me, his expression mildly curious. The sun made his eyes glow with a golden inner light, like the sky just before dawn, when the world hesitates on the brink of waking.

He was not wearing armour, but a wide leather strap crossed his chest diagonally and the hilt of a sword protruded over his left shoulder. Two more leather straps across his shoulders supported a massive canvas pack that probably weighed as much as I did. A pair of long knives were strapped to the outside of one muscular leather-clad thigh.

He had come prepared to kill.

I backed away, stumbling in my haste. I caught at the trunk of a nearby tree to halt my fall. "You followed me."

"No, I tracked you. That's slightly different. You went up to the House of God, didn't you?"

I couldn't take my eyes off the wolf tooth that dangled so casually from his long-fingered hand. I had lost

Da's axe. The tooth was all I had left. All I had of Garin Aeskaar.

"Why did you go there? To collect payment for the attempt on mine and Arian's life? Or was there another reason?"

I took another step back. What would it matter if I had my father's wolf tooth if I was dead?

"Answer me!" He raised his voice slightly, and my gaze snapped back to his face. "Why did you go to the rebel base?"

My nerve broke. I wrenched the blanket from my shoulders and threw it in Luca's face.

I crashed into the trees about a foot from where he stood, careening downhill, ducking and swerving, thin branches whipping and scratching at my skin, roots catching at my boots, stones turning under my feet. The air rasped in my lungs and my mouth tasted of copper.

I could escape if I kept going. Luca was taller than me; he was broader and weighed down with weapons and a pack that would catch in the branches and slow him down. I just had to put a good enough distance between us. Then I could hide.

A flock of birds flew up ahead of me with piercing squawks. I leaped back, skidding to a halt. And realized something. There were no sounds of pursuit.

Could I have lost him so easily?

No. What had he said? He hadn't *followed* me. He had *tracked* me.

He was still tracking me.

An icy droplet of sweat crawled down my back like a many legged insect.

In Uskaand I had hunted birds and squirrels for the pot and set snares for rabbits and foxes. I knew how to move quietly through the forest. But this man ... this man was silent. More silent than any human had a right to be. I had never even heard his footsteps. He was somewhere in the trees. And he was coming for me.

I moved hesitantly now, placing each foot with care, cupping the waterskin to my side so that the few meagre mouthfuls of water I had left would make no telltale sound. A twig snapped somewhere uphill. I spun round, my eyes searching for something, anything that might betray my pursuer's location.

There was nothing there. The only thing that moved was the wind among the leaves. I breathed out slowly, turned—

—and found myself face to face with Luca.

A long scratch marred one cheek, and there was a leaf in his neatly plaited hair. He lifted an eyebrow. "I never really liked hide and seek."

I yelled, jolting backwards. My boot snagged in a trailing vine and I went down hard, landing on my right hip with a jarring impact that knocked the wind out of me. I scrabbled at the dirt, trying to push myself up.

A strong hand closed around my wrist and pulled me gently, inexorably, into a sitting position. Another hand rubbed my back vigorously, fingers pressing into the ridge of my spine. "Breathe. Just breathe. That's it. You'll be all right."

I tried to shrug his hand away, tried to yank my arm free. "Get off," I gasped. "Get away."

Luca's grip tightened. I tensed, anxiety tightening my belly as I waited for the hand on my back to move lower, to pull at my clothes. I got ready to bite, scratch and scream if I had to. Anything to get away.

He just continued to rub briskly. He smelled clean, like soap and leather and warm skin, and something else, something … sweet. *Honeysuckle?* His hands held onto me, but not hard enough to bruise. And he was warm, and I was so very cold.

"When was the last time you ate a decent meal?" he asked quietly. "Your ribs are sharp enough to cut my hand. You're nothing but bones and hair." He ignored my reflexive jerk away from him in the way an oak tree ignores a songbird alighting on a branch. "Why did you go to the House of God? Tell me the truth."

I tugged at my wrist again. "Ma made me promise to go there. She made me swear, before she died. I had to find the Goddess in the Fire. But the Goddess is gone, if she was ever there, and now the holy place is filled with bandits and slaves, and I don't know what to do. I don't know what to do. I don't know—"

"All right," he interrupted softly. "It's all right. I understand."

"No, you don't!" I shrieked, and from somewhere a little strength came back to me, and I began to fight, shoving and kicking. *"I don't know what to do!"*

He let me struggle. As abruptly as it had flared, the burst of anger died. I felt the burning heat of tears sliding down my cheeks and turned my head away from him, putting my free hand up to hide my face. His hand loosened on my wrist, but he didn't let go and he didn't say anything.

"I'm not an assassin," I mumbled after a few minutes. "I don't care if you believe me any more. String me up if you want."

"You have a definite liking for the dramatic, don't you? Who in the Mother's name ever mentioned stringing you up?"

"Your lieutenant," I said. "'Immediately, and without warning'."

He groaned, releasing my wrist at last and sitting back. Cold air stung my side where he had been pressed against me.

"Suddenly digging your way out of the cell and fleeing in the night makes a lot more sense. I'm sorry he threatened you – but I promise that was all it was, a threat. Arian would never hurt a prisoner, especially not an unarmed girl."

I rubbed my face into the crook of my elbow to wipe away my tears and hide the disbelief in my face. That goatherd had meant every word he'd said. It had not been a threat, but an oath.

"I can see you don't believe me," Luca said dryly. "But you'll just have to take my word for it."

No, I won't.

I surged to my feet – and fell over as a tide of dizziness swept my legs from under me.

Luca caught me before I hit the ground. He eased me back to sit on the forest floor again, and this time he kept a firm grip on the back of my shirt.

"The problem with making grand gestures with your food," he said, calmly, "is that eventually you just get too hungry to run away any more."

Six

The fire crackled merrily, flickering with vivid blue and yellow and purple lights. I had thought only driftwood made those shades in flame. Perhaps there was something special in the woods here. Something special in the earth. The pulsing colours were strangely absorbing. I felt as though I was being drawn in...

I tore my eyes away with a gasp and pulled my knees up to my chest, shuffling backwards so that I was braced against one of the large boulders ringing the clearing Luca had dragged me to.

He was sat cross-legged by the fire, humming tunelessly to himself as he stirred the contents of a small tin pot. He had filled it with water from a little stream near the tumbled rocks and then poured some kind of fine cereal grains into it, before adding dried peas and meat and what I thought were dried apricots, as well as pinches of colourful stuff from little paper packets. The smell was luscious – warm and spicy. I was sure he must be able to hear the strangled noises my stomach was making. *Damn him.*

Night was drawing in and turning the patches of sky I could see through the trees to a dull slate-grey. Firelight gilded Luca's face and made his eyes glow with those strange, half-seen traces of gold. His long braid fell forwards over his shoulder in a sort of liquid slither, and he shrugged it back – a graceful, absent-minded gesture that made me all the more aware of my own dirty hair and grimy body.

Using the edge of a blanket to shield his hand, he took the metal cooking pot from the framework of long twigs he had built to hold it over the fire. He ladled some of the spiced grains onto a small wooden dish, added a round of flatbread and held everything out to me.

"Normally I'd ask if you were hungry, but I already know the answer. Please don't try to break this bowl, or dig with the spoon. I need to use them after you."

I glared at him, wishing I had the willpower to throw the meal back in his face. But I didn't. My hands shook as I reached out. I would probably have dropped the food if Luca hadn't shaped my fingers carefully around the smooth curve of the wood.

"Watch out," he said, his fingers slipping away from mine. "It's hot."

I withdrew quickly to my corner, digging the spoon into the food and blowing on it carefully before taking a mouthful. The favours were wonderful – sweet, hot and savoury all at once. The strange grain was soft, and the peas, apricots and pieces of meat, plumped up by the cooking liquids, were juicy. I burned my tongue on the next spoonful and didn't care.

"I take it that it's edible?" He was grinning.

I stopped eating, my fingers tightening on the spoon. Then I recognized the look in his eyes. It was a look Ma sometimes had when one of her herbal recipes came out perfectly, first try. He wasn't mocking me – he was just proud that he had made something good. I tore off some of the bread. "It's delicious. Thank you."

He looked down at his hands, and I thought I saw a hint of red in his cheeks. It might just have been the glow of the fire.

I scraped the last grains off the plate with a piece of bread then knelt up to hold the dish and spoon out to him, snatching my hand away as soon as his long fingers brushed against mine. Despite his tan, his hand looked the colour of bone next to mine – and I wasn't even accounted particularly dark-skinned back home, not with a Northern father.

"You're pale," I muttered as I sat back.

His eyebrows went up. He poured the remainder of the food from the cooking pot onto the wooden plate, took another piece of bread from his pack and began to eat, without wiping the eating things first. Something twisted under my breastbone. My mother had boiled everything I had touched before using it herself.

"Was I meant to hear that? Is it an insult where you come from?" he asked, after a mouthful or two. He didn't sound offended, only interested.

"It's not an insult. It's just … those rebels I saw at that place—"

"The House of God."

I jerked my shoulder impatiently. "They all had pale skin like yours. They were using the dark-skinned ones like … like cattle. The bandits that attacked the goatherd – I mean, Arian – they were pale too. He's dark-skinned and the pale ones attacked him. It makes sense. People always hurt people who are different. But you don't fit. You look like them. Why aren't you with them?"

He stared at me. His eyes seemed very dark, and for a moment I thought I really had offended him. Then he shook his head and the fire made his eyes bright again. "You don't know anything about Ruan, do you? I can't believe you came all the way here without the faintest idea what you were walking into. Did you even hear about the war in Uskaand?"

"Of course we did," I said, folding my arms. "So there was a war? What's that got to do with it?"

He studied my face. "What do you know about Mad King Abheron?"

"Not much," I admitted. "Not much that's real. When I was little the other children used to tell stories about him. Silly stories. If you were bad, he might come sneaking into your house in the night and roast you in the fire and eat you – that sort of thing."

Luca let out a snort of laughter, but it wasn't a happy laugh. "Those stories aren't as silly as you might think. Abheron was the king of Sedra, our neighbouring country. But he couldn't hold onto power there. When he was inches away from being deposed he came to Ruan, supposedly to ask his brother-in-law, the rei – that's the title of the Rua leader – for sanctuary. Instead, Abheron set fire to the royal palace, murdered his sister and her husband and all their children except one – who escaped – and took the throne of Ruan for himself."

Suddenly the shadows in the trees around us seemed darker. "That's…"

"Mad?" Luca put in helpfully. "Yes. Hence his nickname. After he'd killed the Rua royal family he brought his Sedorne noblemen here. Things were getting a bit uncomfortable for them back home as well. They occupied Ruan for ten years and those were not happy years for the Rua people, believe me. Then Abheron's niece Zahira – the one surviving member of the Rua royal family – managed to defeat him. She took the throne back and married Lord Sorin, who was a Sedorne, and they tried to make us all one united people. But some of the Sedorne noblemen had got used to treating the Rua like … like property, like beasts of burden. They weren't going to change their ways, not on the word of a Rua leader. There were assassination attempts, skirmishes, and finally a war that lasted about a year. At the end of it, Reia Zahira rounded up all the rebels and marched them over the border, back to Sedra."

"That's not much of a punishment," I said scornfully. "Sending them back home."

"It was the worst thing she could have done to them, short of death. Sedra is a republic now. Those noblemen forfeited everything – lands, titles, money – when they left to follow Abheron. She sent them home with nothing but the clothes on their back, and when they got to the border they had to beg to be allowed into their own country. I doubt many of those exiles are still alive.

"But that's where the reia's plan went wrong. A group of the rebels broke away from the main body of the army before her men could catch them. They escaped, taking their soldiers, families, supporters and servants with them. They had been stripped of their lands here, but rather than face returning to Sedra, they fled to these mountains and dug in. They're trying to establish a new territory of their own here, far away from the reia's seat of power. They bribe local merchants to bring them goods, or attack and rob foreign trade caravans that use the mountain passes. They send out splinter groups of low-ranking men to steal from local farmers and villagers. Lately they've begun kidnapping too: taking slaves for themselves and to sell over the border in Sedra. Officially, slavery was outlawed in Sedra years ago, but the authorities there don't seem to be able to enforce it."

"So the pale-skinned ones, they're Sedorne?"

"That's right."

"And the dark-skinned people are Rua?"

"Yes."

"But that means you're Sedorne. You're still on the wrong side."

"It's not about skin colour. Didn't you hear me say that the reia *married* a Sedorne? There are far more of us who consider ourselves Rua first and Sedorne a distant second, than those who believe we're innately superior because our parents came from over the border. The reia and the king have many loyal Sedorne subjects. The rebels aren't rebels because they've got pale skin and light hair. They're rebels because they are violent, corrupt and hungry for power."

A breeze stirred in the leaves overhead. The fire stretched as if it were reaching for the wind, sending sparks spiralling upwards. I followed them with my eyes. Through the interlacing branches of the trees I could make out the distant lights of the stars. I shivered.

"And you're here to try and capture them."

"Yes. After two years of sending regular army patrols up here and finding nothing, the reia created the hill guard. A permanent force of well-armed, well-trained soldiers who could make the mountains their home, keep the passes safe for trade, protect the local people and, eventually, find and capture the rebel leaders."

"You have found them. They're in that place." I remembered the prosperous, well-fed faces of the Sedorne and the bruised, despairing ones of the kidnapped Rua. "Why haven't you done anything?"

"Because we've only recently discovered their base. We never even thought to look at those ruins. Frankly, we spent the first year in these mountains fighting so hard for our own lives that we hardly had time to look anywhere. Groups of bandits attacked us constantly, and any energy and resources left over went into trying to save local people from being murdered and kidnapped. It's taken a lot of work to establish ourselves. There was a time, not long ago, when you wouldn't have been able to cross into these mountains without being attacked at once. Some very brave men and women have given their lives for that cause in the past year."

"But you know they're there now! Why are you still letting them live there? They were dragging captives in all trussed up. They were hurting them. You have to help them!"

Luca smiled. There was still a line of tension between his eyebrows, but his voice was somehow different when he spoke again. "I know we do. We just don't have enough men right now to take the fortress the rebels have made. I've sent a message to the king and reia asking for reinforcements, and when the new men arrive, we'll march on the House of God, and take it back from the rebels. I promise."

I realized he was trying to reassure me. I shifted uncomfortably as I felt the odd tug in my chest again. I cast about for something to distract myself. Something to stop him looking at me like that, as if I'd said just the right thing and he was proud of me. It was an illusion. A trick of the firelight, or my imagination. It wouldn't do to believe in it.

"Why would the rebels go there anyway? I thought it was supposed to be a holy place. Aren't they afraid of getting cursed?"

Luca shrugged. "It was a holy place, but it was ruined years ago. It's been deserted ever since. There was talk of rebuilding it, but the reia could never find the money. I imagine the rebels went there because it offered more shelter than the bare mountains." He hesitated, then went on: "There's a legend about the House of God. There was supposed to be a hidden room somewhere in the building. A chamber that contained a Sacred Flame, like a ... a portal to the Holy Mother. The legend says that those who had the courage to walk into the Fire would be able to speak to Her directly. If they pleased the Mother, She might give them gifts: healing, or blessings. They say that Reia Zahira was horribly injured in the fire that killed the rest of her family. One of her servants brought her to the House of God and put her in the Sacred Flame. And she was not only healed, but received the Mother's blessing. They say that's why she won out against King Abheron, when everyone thought she was mad to try. It's possible the rebels went to the House of God thinking that if they could find the Flame, it would grant them some special advantage. More likely it would have sent them all mad, though, or charred them to a cinder. But that's the rebels for you. They're arrogant enough to think they can take whatever they want."

I barely heard his last few sentences. *A Sacred Flame.*

I remembered the dry, painful rasp of my mother's voice, rambling as she lay on her deathbed.

"It was a sacred place, a secret place. A goddess was there. The Goddess in the Fire. Some who walked into the fire went mad. Others were burned up. But some were healed. You could be healed. You're already mad, aren't you, Saram? Better to be dead than alive with that thing inside you. If only you could find the Goddess in the Fire, you could be saved…

"I'm too weak to make that journey. I've always been too weak. Too afraid. After your father died… He shouldn't have left me. He never should have gone that day…" Her fingers

had felt like the fragile skeleton of a bird resting in my palm.
"When I'm gone, you mustn't stay here, Saram. Promise me.
Don't stay here like I did. Make the journey. Go to the moun-
tains. Find the holy place and the Goddess. Promise me."

"Yes, Ma," I had whispered, as her hand had slipped away
from mine. "I promise."

"You recognize that legend, don't you?" Luca said,
breaking into my thoughts. "That was what you meant by
the Goddess in the Fire. How on earth could you have
known about that when you didn't even know the difference between Rua and Sedorne?"

I swallowed dryly. "Ma's parents died when she was
young. There was a herbwoman visiting the village at the
time. Stela, she was called. She was from Ruan and barely
spoke any Uskaandian, but she tried to ease their suffering.
After my grandparents had died, Ma's aunt and uncle
couldn't afford to pay Stela for the nursing she'd done, and
they didn't want Ma around anyway, so they gave her to the
herbwoman as a servant. Only Stela … she wasn't like that.
She treated Ma like her own child, and they went travelling together, all over Uskaand. Ma translated for her and
assisted her, and eventually taught her Uskaandian. Stela
taught Ma healing, and lots of old songs and stories, and
how to read and write and speak Rua like a native."

"And your mother taught you?" Luca asked. "Your
accent is very good."

I shrugged awkwardly. "When Ma got sick, she

remembered the story about the Goddess in the Fire and made me promise to come here. She made me promise to find the Goddess. I had to keep my promise."

"You must have loved your mother very much."

I looked at the blue, purple and yellow fire. *Must I? She didn't love me. I don't think she taught me how...* Automatically, I put my hand to my chest. But the wolf tooth wasn't there. It was still in Luca's pocket. My fingers closed on air and clenched into a fist.

"Why did your mother make you promise that? Why did she want you to find the Goddess in the Fire?"

My hand clenched tighter – until it shook. I looked through the fire at his face. It was full dark now, and the shadows made his eyes look black. I didn't know this man. Why had I told him all this? He had no right to know about me. He'd tricked it out of me.

"Why did they send you out here to fight the rebels?" I shot back. "You're young to be in command, aren't you? Was it to get rid of you? Did you do something wrong?"

He blinked, seemingly speechless for a moment, and I felt a vicious stab of satisfaction. "No," he answered at last. "I suppose they sent me because they knew they could trust me."

"Why's that?"

"There are two reasons," he said, voice flat and expressionless now. "For a start, Lord Sorin, the man who married the reia and became king, is my cousin."

"Oh," I said faintly. I looked at him sat comfortably in the dirt, with a wooden spoon in his hand, and swallowed. "What's the other reason?"

"The leader of the rebels is a man called Ion Constantin. The king knows I'll never rest until he's brought to justice. It's my duty and no one else's. Ion Constantin is my brother. He murdered my family."

Seven

I sat in silence, eyes fixed on the man who slept across from me. The banked remains of last night's campfire produced only the slightest of heat-ripples to interfere with my view. Luca lay on his back, one arm folded beneath his head, the other draped across his flat belly, fingers slightly curled. His breathing was deep and even.

The pale gold light of dawn filtering through the leaves cast a strange glow on his still face. He looked unreal, like a creature from a children's story. A wood glim, maybe, in mortal guise, ensnaring girls with his unearthly beauty. Wood glims lured their victims into the forest, and when the girls lay down beneath the branches and died of love, their bodies provided sustenance to the tree roots and kept the wood glim immortal. Luca's face would have ensured his existence was a long one.

I sighed at my own uncharacteristic flight of fancy.

Luca was a mere mortal man. And I wasn't going to be ensnared by him, or anyone. I was leaving, right now.

I just had one thing to do first.

With as much care as if I moved across the thin crust of a frozen lake, I circled the fire and crouched beside my sleeping captor. His shirt had twisted up in the night, and my necklace now lay over his heart. The collar of his shirt gaped open, showing the golden skin of his throat and the fine blonde hair there; it was so soft that even my shallow breaths disturbed it. Blood pulsed strongly in the hollow at the base of his neck. My fingers hovered in the air above his chest.

"Are you usually this heavy a sleeper?" I whispered, voice almost soundless. "Or do you really trust me not to stab you while you dream?" I wanted the words to be mocking. Somehow they were not.

Get on with it. I slid my forefinger into his pocket, and touched leather.

He sighed. My gaze shot to his face. His eyelids, with their long wheat-coloured lashes, flickered, but did not open. I slid a second finger into his pocket. His skin was warm, even through the linen. I could feel the shape of his muscle under my fingers.

I insinuated my finger through the leather thong and drew it up, my fingers pressing gently into Luca's chest. He made a low noise. I froze, checking his face again. His eyes were still closed, but he was frowning a little now, his lips parted slightly. The pulse at his throat seemed faster. I stayed as still as a rock, not daring even to breathe as I watched him. He sighed once more, shifted his head on his arm, and lay quietly.

He was asleep. He had to be asleep.

I pulled the wolf tooth free with a last, careful tug. The relief at having it in my hand again was nearly equalled by the relief of not having woken Luca. I sat back on my heels and dropped the thin leather necklace over my head. I picked up the blanket and waterskin and put them on as before, with the blanket over my shoulder and the strap of the waterskin diagonally across my body. For a moment, I hesitated, looking around the clearing. Then I was annoyed with myself. *Why are you waiting? You haven't forgotten anything. You haven't got anything to forget.*

I walked out of the clearing, forcing myself to concentrate on moving silently so that I could not look back.

For a little while my success in having escaped Luca, twinned with last night's meal in my belly, made me feel cheerful, even light-hearted. I smiled as I moved through the white wisps of mist that rose up from the moist forest floor and listened to birdsong with pleasure. But the further I got from the clearing, the more my mood darkened.

Nothing had changed since yesterday.

I still had nowhere to go and no way to support myself. If I had been free, really free, I would have taken my chances, walked to the nearest town and tried to find work. But how could I, like this? In a town or city there were always dozens of people around. All it would take was an overly eager young man in his cups who couldn't take no for an answer, a cut-throat who thought I was an easy target, or some foolish girl with long nails who didn't like foreigners. One nick, one drop of blood, and the Wolf would rampage, killing anyone it saw.

I had been careful in my travels to stay out of densely populated areas; to find work for one or two days and then move on before I could cause trouble. The less people near me, the less people at risk. But without my father's axe I was just another unskilled wanderer, and a female at that. What farmer or crofter would want to hire me?

And I couldn't live out here alone. When I had lost my pack I had lost my snares, my knives for cleaning game, my greased groundsheet. The first snow – the first leopard or bear – would finish me off. The same was true of trying to cross back into Uskaand. The Wolf was much faster and stronger than a man, but it was not invincible – not while clothed in my mortal flesh.

I cursed myself for believing my mother's stories, for letting her words convince me that there was hope in Ruan. There was no hope, here or anywhere. And now I was worse off than ever.

I had been walking for half an hour, lost in the bitterness of my thoughts, when I felt my senses sharpen. A warning. I wrinkled my nose as I picked up the scent on the air. It was one I hated, but knew well. Death.

Two men lay just ahead of me in a hollow in the ground. They were tangled together, clothes stained with dirt and blood. The earth near by was marked with ruts where their bodies had been dragged and then rolled.

My instincts told me to run, *now*, run far and run fast. But although I could see the dull dead eyes of one of the men, the other had his face hidden in the dirt. I had to make sure he was beyond help. I forced myself to take the last few steps towards the bodies. I eased down onto one knee and caught the shoulder of the man whose face I could not see. I could feel the warmth of his skin through his shirt. Maybe…?

I turned him over. The sight of his face made me jerk away with a cry. Savage cuts gaped, forming crude cross shapes on both his cheeks. He was middle-aged, pale-skinned, with mousy-coloured hair. And he was most definitely beyond anyone's help.

Now that I was closer, I could see that the other was only a boy, no more than thirteen, with olive skin and dark curly hair. Despite the differences in colouring, the two looked enough alike to be related. They had both been stabbed, but only the older man had been mutilated.

The blood on the bodies was still wet.

This had only just happened. The killers could still be here. Right here, watching.

I jumped to my feet and pelted up out of the hollow.

I rounded the vast trunk of a twisted tree and ploughed head first into a warm, solid chest. Large hands came up to catch my shoulders and steady me, and a familiar honeysuckle scent rose around me. I managed to bite off the shriek before it left my lips.

"In a rush?" Luca asked. "Did you suddenly decide you didn't want to run away after all?"

I looked up at him. His expression went from mocking to serious in a heartbeat. He shoved me behind him and took a step forward, searching the forest with his eyes. "What happened? Are you all right?"

I rubbed both hands over my face, wiping away cold sweat. The panic that had gripped me was easing. "I found some bodies. They were murdered not long ago."

Luca swore under his breath. "Show me."

Reluctantly I led him down into the hollow, staying close to him as he knelt beside the men.

"You were right. These men were murdered within the last hour. Maybe even less."

"Why would anyone do that?" I asked, my voice shaking. "This one's only a child. And why cut up the other one's face?"

Luca bowed his head, concealing his expression. "To Sedorne, the cross is the mark of a traitor. Over the border they used to burn it on with a hot branding iron. Rebels did this."

I turned away hastily and spat out a mouthful of bile,

coughing and choking as it burned my throat. I wiped my lips on the back of my sleeve, but stayed facing away from him as I asked, "The older one … he's Sedorne, isn't he?"

"It was *because* he was Sedorne," Luca said, grim sorrow in his voice. "From his clothes I'd say he was a farmer, probably heading down to Mesgao to sell live-stock. This boy is most likely his son. Bandits killed him and his boy for their animals, but they marked the man's face because he'd made a peaceful life here and settled with a Rua woman. The boy has dark skin, you see. To the rebels that's treachery. Holy Mother, help me, if we'd just arrived here a little earlier…"

I made myself look at the bodies again. It was wrong to turn from them. What had happened to them was not their fault.

"We should bury—" I stopped abruptly. "Luca, look." I took the farmer's hand, trying to ignore the eerie warmth of the flesh as I peeled back the dead fingers to reveal a torn fragment of pink cloth. It was embroi-dered with white flowers. "This isn't from either of their clothes. They had someone else with them. A girl."

Luca swore again, and this time he didn't keep his voice down. He climbed to his feet, took two quick steps and then paced back the other way. His hands had doubled up into shaking fists. "Those sons of whores. They took her."

"You said this happened less than an hour ago – she could still be alive, couldn't she?"

"They wouldn't have bothered taking her away if they didn't intend to have some fun with her. Yes. She's probably alive. She's probably wishing she wasn't."

"You could save her. You could go after them, get her back." I stared up at him. "But ... you're not going to, are you? Why? Why not? Isn't that your job? You can't just let them get away!"

His jaw clenched. His eyes flashed to me and then back down to the ground.

"It's because of me," I said numbly. "You don't trust me. You think I'll run away."

"Won't you?" He met my eyes now, fury and frustration warring with pain in the dark blue.

I looked at the tiny scrap of fabric in my hand. *They wouldn't have bothered taking her away if they didn't intend to have some fun with her...*

"If you go after them, I won't run. I promise. I'll do whatever you say. Just ... help her. Please."

Out of the corner of my eye, I saw Luca's fists unclench slowly. He sucked in a deep breath. "All right. But you'll have to come with me. We probably don't have much time."

I stood up, my hand closing around the torn piece of cloth. "Then we should go now."

We followed the deep drag marks uphill at a trot until we reached a narrow trail. The earth was marked by the attack that had taken the farmer and his son's lives.

Thick, sticky drops of blood gleamed on the leaves and the churned-up dirt. I saw sheep tracks and several distinct sets of footprints.

"There were *two* women here," Luca said, tracing the shapes in the dirt. "And four bandits. They must have thought this was their lucky day. The farmer didn't stand a chance. They headed uphill from here."

Luca moved faster now; he was almost flying through the trees ahead of me, and yet somehow he barely made any noise. I winced at every twig that snapped under my foot, every leaf I disturbed, and at my own wheezing.

You have to tell him. Warn him now, before it's too late.

"If something happens," I panted. "If—if I get cut—"

"I won't let anything happen to you." He didn't even glance back at me.

"You don't understand. It's you I'm worried about. You and those girls."

Luca's pace slowed, and then stopped completely. I stumbled to a halt and bent over at the waist, waterskin sloshing as I put my hands on my knees, trying to get my breath back.

"If I get cut," I said, staring at the rich green of the moss under my boots. "If you see any blood on me at all, run. Just get the girls and run."

"You're going to have to explain yourself a bit better than that. You just promised you wouldn't try to get away—"

A snort popped out of my lips. "*You're* the one that will be running, not me."

"What are you talking about? We don't have time for riddles!" he said, exasperated.

I straightened up and looked him in the eye. "I'll go insane. If I am attacked and if any of my blood is spilled, I'll lose control. It won't be me any more, do you under-stand?"

"Not really, no."

I made a noise somewhere between a laugh and a sob. So much effort spent trying to keep my secret and now he didn't even seem to be listening. I fought a craven impulse to leave it there. But I knew all too well that I couldn't be around people without bringing death. That was my curse. If I wanted to avoid hurting someone – maybe even Luca – I *had* to make him understand. And once he understood, it would only be a matter of time before he handed me over to the priests. I was on bor-rowed time now.

"I call it the Wolf," I said slowly, forcing the words out. "If my blood is spilled in battle, in anger, it takes over. It will attack anyone. Anyone within reach. Friend or foe. It's *killed* people before. So if you see me get in-jured – if you see blood – you have to get away and take those girls with you, or I … it might turn on you."

Luca stared at me. "That's what happened to you be-fore, isn't it? You tried to save Arian, but you got cut, and then you couldn't control yourself any more. The way you fought – the howling and snarling..."

"I know what that makes me," I said wearily, avoiding the look of fear and disgust that I knew would be in his eyes. "I know what comes next. But I just want to do one good thing before ... before that. I want to help save these women, and I can't do that unless you promise me that if you see me bleeding, you will run and not look back."

"We don't have time for this," he said, not annoyed this time but thoughtful. "I'm not going to make any promises, but I will be careful, and I'll make sure I don't put anyone in danger who can't defend themselves."

"Luca—"

"This isn't a debate. Now come on."

He started running again. I followed, and within a few moments, I was too breathless to say any more.

Eight

By the time Luca halted again my blood was thundering in my ears like a river in full flood. His arm flew out to motion me to stillness, then he dropped to the ground and crept ahead of me, bellying through the undergrowth.

I got down on my hands and knees and tried to copy his movements, placing my hands only where his had been. Leaf mould and dirt squelched through my fingers and dampened the legs of my breeches as I squirmed after him until I fetched up against a large, mossy boulder.

The smell of woodsmoke teased my nose. I could hear sheep calling restlessly and the low murmur of male voices. Luca, peering around the edge of the boulder, gave me a nod. *This is it.* I peered between the leaves.

A few feet away there was a rock outcrop that jutted above a crevice in the side of the mountain to create a deep natural shelter. Two Sedorne men – alike enough to be brothers, both heavily muscled and with reddish hair – sat in front of the cave on either side of a small fire. A large haunch of meat was cooking there, dripping strong-smelling fat into the fire and sending out a plume of bluish smoke. I sniffed again. Venison. Despite everything, my stomach rumbled.

One of the men turned the meat occasionally with a stick while his brother rooted through a leather bag, pulling out cloths and jars and setting them beside him in an untidy pile. The spoils of their attack on the farmer and his family.

A third man sat a little way from the others. This one was older, with thinning iron-grey hair. He was cleaning dried brown stains off his hands with a rag.

In the shadow of the rock shelter, behind a makeshift wicker fence that contained a small flock of sheep, were two Rua women. One of them looked middle-aged. The smaller one was no older than fourteen, I thought. The girl's face was streaked with dirt and tears, and the woman's left eye and nose were bruised and swelling. Both were gagged and their hands were bound with rope, but their feet were free. Given the chance, they could run.

"I wish Birkin'd hurry up with his washing," the older man grumbled, picking at the brownish stains under his fingernails. "Never saw nothing to be squeamish about in a little blood. Why's he always got to scrub himself down so well?"

"That's just Birkin," one of the brothers said, empty-ing out the last items from the leather bag. "And if you've any sense you'll wait for him like he told us to."

"I'm waiting, aren't I?" The older man turned his head to look at the women. "Don't see why he's worried, myself. The younger one might be worth something to Constan-tin, but the old bitch isn't going to whet his appetite."

The girl whimpered through her gag and I felt Luca stiffen beside me. *Constantin*. The leader of the rebels. His brother. I flicked a glance at him and saw his eyes blaz-ing, like a night sky in the instant after a lightning strike.

Hesitantly, I touched his elbow, looking for instruc-tion. He indicated with a whirl and point of his finger that he would circle the camp uphill. An emphatic jab of his finger first at me and then at the ground signalled that I was to stay put. He shrugged off his loaded pack, then readjusted the strap of his sword across his chest and rotated his neck, stretching carefully.

I wanted to protest that I could help. But I had just told him about the Wolf. Even if he trusted me not to run, I couldn't expect him to trust me not to hurt anyone. I nodded resignedly. Luca frowned at me, then twisted around and pulled one of the long knives from the sheath at his thigh. He reversed it and offered the hilt to me.

I stared at it, disbelieving. He sighed, seized my hand and thrust the hilt into it. *Stay here*, he mouthed. I nodded again, weighing the costly leather-wrapped steel hilt in my palm. The blade was leaf-shaped and finely honed. Despite the terrible situation, I felt a tiny smile tugging at my lips. He did trust me – at least enough to allow me to defend myself.

Luca's hand was still cupped warmly around the back of mine. For a brief moment his long fingers entwined with mine around the handle of the knife, and squeezed. *Be careful*, he mouthed.

I nodded again. *You too.*

He released me and wriggled out of sight. I fixed my eyes on the captive women huddled in darkness, and gritted my teeth. *Just hang on a little longer. He's coming to save you.*

Luca stepped into the clearing. He took off one of the brother's heads with a single sweep of his sword. I swallowed a cry at the brutal swiftness of the death. The other brother yelled, dropped his handful of stolen items, and went for a sword that was leaning against the rock next to him. Before he could reach it, Luca's sword flashed again. The man's yell turned into a strange hiccuping noise. He crumpled inches away from where I was crouched. A long rivulet of blood crept across the dirt and moss towards me, and I inched away.

"Birkin!" the third man shouted as Luca rushed at him. The man's sword, dull with dried blood, flicked up to deflect Luca's. "Birkin! Get out here!"

This older man was faster and warier than the two brothers. He didn't try to attack or escape; he merely concentrated on avoiding Luca as he carefully manoeuvred around the fire. "Birkin!" he yelled again.

Luca's body seemed to blur. He flew into a kick that forced the bandit away from the fire towards the rocks. The Rua women were already on their knees, struggling with the ropes, their eyes fixed on the fighting.

Come on, I urged them mentally. *Come on, you can do it.*

Something crashed through the trees behind me. I whipped around.

A gigantic man, bulging with oversize muscles, stood directly in front of me. His long blonde hair was damp and hung in disarray around his freshly scrubbed face. In one hand he held a drying cloth and a bar of soap. In the other was a broadsword. His pale eyes glittered with fury.

He took a step towards me. I leaped up, pushing off from the boulder – and tripped over the body of the bandit Luca had just killed. I fell headlong into the clearing, almost landing in the fire. My hair sizzled. I rolled, and the haunch of meat went flying in a spray of hot fat as I scrambled to my feet, still clutching the knife.

Birkin's sword jabbed towards my belly. I dodged, slashing wildly with Luca's knife. Birkin didn't even flinch. It must have been painfully obvious that I had no idea what I was doing, and his reach was a foot longer than mine. I couldn't get near him. I spun away from another slash of his sword. He was going to nick me eventually. And when that happened…

I flicked a panicked glance at Luca and saw him wrenching his sword free of the grey-haired bandit's chest. I felt a spurt of relief. Then Birkin came at me with a roar, his sword flying down in a two-handed slash that would gut me like a pig.

Something I had no name for – not fear, not even anger – shivered through my body, cold as ice. I screamed defiance, my body moving of its own volition. His blade sliced the air where I had been a moment before. My knife flashed twice.

Two long lines of blood appeared on Birkin's chest, crossing his heart. He reeled backwards. His foot went into the fire and he roared as he jerked his leg out of the burning logs. He landed on one knee, still clutching his sword.

The older Rua woman, arms trailing pieces of rope, rose up behind him. The great haunch of venison was in her hands. She brought it down on the back of Birkin's head with a dull *smack*. Once. Twice. A third time. The bandit's eyes rolled up in his skull. The sword fell from his fist. He slumped into the dirt.

She stood over him, chest heaving. The deer's leg bone was gripped so tightly in her hands that her fingers seemed the same colour. She lifted her weapon again.

Luca stepped past me, jamming his sword back into its sheath, blood and all. He held his palms up in a peaceful gesture, attracting the woman's attention. "You're safe now," he said. "You're safe. You can stop."

The young girl, gag still in her mouth, scrambled out from under the ledge and ran towards her mother. A sob rattled the older woman's frame, and she dropped the venison leg. Putting her arms around the girl, she pulled the gag gently away from her daughter's face.

"They killed my husband," she said softly, her voice broken. "They killed my boy."

"We know," Luca said. "We found them. I'm so sorry."

The girl turned her face into her mother's shoulder and cried.

The rest of that day took on a strange quality for me. It felt as though I had been given another person's part in some grand play. I knew what to say and what to do, but I kept waiting for the real actor to come and push me out into my proper role again.

Luca and I rolled the bodies of the dead bandits to one side of the clearing and stoked up the fire for the shivering women – Mala and her daughter, Crina – to sit by. He took small clay pots with wax stoppers from his seemingly bottomless pack, along with bandages, and I helped the women clean and anoint their cuts and bruises, and wrapped Crina's sprained ankle. My fingers moved briskly and skilfully, my mother's training not quite forgotten, it seemed.

Meanwhile, Luca did a rather less neat job of bandaging the still-unconscious Birkin's wounds, and then trussed him hand and foot to a nearby tree.

"I'll have someone come by to collect him later," he said, when I caught his eye.

"What if a bear or a big cat smells the blood and finds him?"

Luca shrugged. "He's got plenty of daylight left. And any predators will go for the dead meat first. I have more important things to see to at the moment."

We herded the sheep out of the bandit's corral and followed Mala and Crina back to their farmstead, a small piece of land scooped out of the hillside. It didn't take long to reach. The family had been ambushed almost on their own threshold. Two dark-haired boys, about the same age as me – twins, I thought, though not identical – came running to meet us as soon as we were within sight of the small house. They must have been left in charge of the farm by their parents. I saw their handsome faces blanch with horrified realization as they saw the state of their mother and sister, and looked in vain for their father and brother. Once we had the livestock safely shut in the family's barn, the two young men went out with Luca to find and bury the bodies of their murdered kinfolk. I was left with the grieving women.

Mala urged me to sit in one of the wooden chairs by the fire. She bustled about, her voice brisk and slightly too high-pitched as she offered me tea and honey cake. Crina sat in the chair opposite, rocking ever so slightly, hands clamped on her knees. Her fingers twitched and strained, as if she were still struggling against the ropes that had left their mark on her wrists.

This morning Mala and Crina had set out to market as a normal family with their own cares and preoccupations. By noon they had been plunged into a world of blood and screaming and unimaginable terror. Now they were home again. But it was not the same home. It would never be the same again; nothing would ever be the same for them again, because they had had been changed forever by what had happened. Their family had been shattered as easily as a clay cup is smashed by a careless child. Darkness and mourning had filled the void left behind by those they had loved.

Luca and the twins returned a couple of hours later, mud-streaked and weary. I was relieved when one of them immediately urged their mother to sit and drink some of the tea she had made, while the other one draped a blanket around Crina and whispered gently to her until her tense hands uncurled from their straining grip on her knees. They would take care of their mother and sister, these two. They were good boys.

Luca had spoken to me about good people. He had said that he and his men were the "good ones". I had scorned his words, telling myself there was no such thing as good people, or bad. Remembering the sickening, careless cruelty of the bandits who had caused this family's heartbreak, I knew now that was a lie. I had clung to the untruth because it was easier than admitting to myself what I feared. The thing I had always feared, in my heart.

That I was not one of the good ones.

Luca leaned tiredly against the frame of the open door. Warm sunlight streamed in around him. "Mala, I will send to Mesgao today for an elder and a namoa to come here as soon as possible," he said. "You'll get a widow's purse from the Crown. It's not a fortune, but it will help."

Mala winced from the word "widow". She nodded wordlessly, eyes lowered.

"Thank you," one of the twins said on his mother's behalf. He turned his grave eyes to me. "And thank you. Captain Luca told us that you were the one who found my father and Abhay, that you were the one who realized Mother and Crina had been taken. They would be dead were it not for you. We'll never be able to repay you, but we won't ever forget what you've done."

I looked helplessly at Luca, but the sun was too bright. I could not see his expression. Why had he told them that? He of all people knew I was no heroine.

"What is your name?" Crina asked, suddenly stirring in the muffling folds of her blanket. "We must add you to our nightly prayers. It's the least we can do when – when you've been so kind."

I hesitated, feeling Luca's attention like a heavy weight on the back of my neck.

"Frost," I said, finally. "My name is Frost Aeskaar."

"Do not run, daughter."

Their voices — a dozen versions of my father's voice — are sorrowful. I stumble through the snow, pressing my hands over my ears. It slows me down, and it does not block out the wolf-song, but it is all I can do.

"Do not run. We only wish to help you."

"Leave me alone," I scream, my voice shrill and trembling. "You are not my father."

"Daughter," the wolves cry. "Wait for us."

But it is a lie. When they catch me, I know they will devour me whole.

I dig my blistered toes into the snow and run faster.

Nine

I shuddered and shook with cold. My own breath nearly blinded me: spreading out silvery-white like a constellation before my eyes. I barely heard Elder Gallen arguing with the priests.

"We can build a pyre on the edge of the forest," he pleaded. "Burning a whole building in the centre of the village is too dangerous."

"Far more dangerous to allow a demon-tainted girl to walk out of the barn and infect others on her way to her death," the priest of the Other said calmly.

"But – it is my barn! The expense of rebuilding—"

"Is but a small price to pay to keep your people safe," the priest of Askaan said. "My beard, man! You have housed a monster in that place! How could you put good cattle in there now? They would sicken. Their flesh would turn black, their milk to poison."

That silenced the elder. No one raised any more objections. My mother's shouts had faded into the distance. Someone had dragged her away. Probably Eilik.

Footsteps scurried past the barn. I imagined the villagers running back to their homes. I imagined the people I had known all my life – the faces I had smiled at or nodded to every day – hurriedly shutting themselves into their houses. I imagined them turning from the windows and putting their hands over their ears to block out the sound of the priests' chanting.

I wished I could put my hands over my ears. But I could not. The men's voices, solemn and sincere, echoed through the barn as they circled it. I imagined the priest of the Other smiling his sad smile and shuddered more. My shivers made the chains clink, almost drowning out the chatter of my teeth. Gradually their voices faded away.

Soon I saw the flames. The smoke drifted up towards the roof, curling and twisting there like a living creature. I coughed and choked, gasping for air. Fire licked at the walls with long red tongues. Heat drummed against my skin, but it did not warm me. I was so cold; I thought the ice would kill me before the fire did, and I was glad.

There was a crash behind me. My body, weighed down by the chains, jerked involuntarily as a panel of the wall fell in. Cold air whooshed into the barn. The fire roared.

A large, square figure, face muffled in cloth, charged into the gap waving a hammer in one hand and a chisel in the other. He ran towards me through the smoke. I cringed away.

Someone had decided fire was too merciful.

The figure leaned over me. The cloth dripped icy cold water on my face, making me flinch. I recognized the kind eyes and singed eyebrows above the cloth. Eilik.

He jammed his chisel into one of the chains and smashed his hammer down. Three times he did this. On the final strike, the chains loosened and fell away.

"Come on, girl!" he shouted over the crackle and hiss of the fire. "Before the roof falls in!"

He grabbed my arms and pulled me to my feet. My muscles cramped and twitched and I nearly fell. He hefted me into his arms as if I weighed nothing, as if I did not stink of dirt and urine and mould. His hands were as warm as the air that gushed out of his smithy.

Pressing my face into his chest, he ran with me out into the darkness, carrying me away from the burning barn, through the outskirts of the village, to the edge of the forest where the light was blue and faint. Under the trees, two pale shapes waited. I recognized Dolla, my mother's mule. She was weighed down with bags and boxes that had been haphazardly strapped to her saddle. And next to Dolla, my mother. She stepped forward as Eilik heaved me up onto Dolla's back with a grunt of effort. I lay there, gasping for air, breathing in the clean horse-scent of Dolla's mane, soaking up the warmth of her broad back. She shifted under me, but made no noise. Good girl.

Ma reached out. Not to me, but to Eilik. Her hand looked very white against his tanned forearm.

"Thank you," she whispered.

"I need no thanks," he said gruffly. He turned his face towards me, but I could not see his expression in the dark. "'Tis nothing but fear that made a child's fight into a nightmare. They see their own demons in the dark. I see only a little girl. You go on and start again, far away where they cannot find you." A moment later he was gone.

"Ma," I whispered. My voice crackled and hissed, like the fire. I reached out to her. Wanting comfort, wanting anything to help wipe the horror of what had just happened from my mind.

She shrugged my hand away. "Don't." Her voice was low and broken.

As she led Dolla into the forest, I began to shiver again.

Luca's hand rested lightly on the centre of my back, guiding me through the farmyard and out onto the dust track that led away from Mala and Crina's house. The heat of his sun-drenched skin soaked through my shirt, almost burning me. I took a deep breath to steady myself. With each step I tried to work up the courage to ask him what would happen to me now: how did they deal with people like me here? I couldn't find the strength. The words clogged up in my throat like dry, stale breadcrumbs. I had promised to go with him and not to run away again, and I would keep that promise, even if every muscle in my body was quivering with the desire to flee. But that was all the bravery I had in me.

I was surprised when Luca stopped and seated himself on the low stone wall at the border of the family's farm. From here, I could see the whole property, including the two new mounds of dark earth under the trees to one side of the house. Each one was crowned with a ring of white stones. The graves of the farmer and his son. *Nicu and Abhay.*

"Sit down," Luca said, gesturing to a fallen log with one hand while he shrugged his pack off and set it on the ground with the other.

I obeyed, watching him warily as he unbuckled the strap that held his scabbard to his back. He sighed and stretched, then laid the sheathed sword across his knees.

"So, I've learned your name at last," he said. Almost casually, he drew his sword from its scabbard.

Fear stopped my mouth. My hands wanted to reach for my wolf tooth, but I kept them clasped tightly before me. I had to keep still, or I would break and run.

He won't hurt me, I tried to reassure myself. *He'll make it quick, I know he will.*

Luca had a folded square of soft cloth in one hand now and was attacking the blood stains on his blade with it. "In fact, I feel as if I've learned a great deal about you today. For example, I know that you're not the type to cut a man's throat in his sleep. No matter how easy he makes it for you."

I gasped as I realized his meaning, outrage overcoming fright. "You were awake?"

"What do you take me for – an imbecile? Of course I was awake."

"But – then – *why*?" I wailed, thinking about the way I had hovered over him, staring, muttering to myself.

"I needed to know if you would try to gain your freedom by killing me," he said, as if it were the most reasonable thing in the world. He didn't take his eyes off his sword and kept rubbing away at the stubborn stain. "I also found out that you were willing to go against every instinct of self-preservation in order to help two women you'd never met. That you're brave enough to face a man twice your size with nothing but a hunting knife, and fast enough to nearly kill him with it. That even when you were so afraid you couldn't speak, you kept your promise not to run. That's what I've learned about you today."

I couldn't think straight. I shook my head, trying to tumble his words into an order that made sense. "What does any of that matter? You know what I am. I told you about the curse. You know about the Wolf."

"Frost." He looked up from his sword at last, and I felt my own eyes widen as I met his. There was no trace of disgust or fear. Or even pity. Only kindness. "You don't have to be afraid of me."

The priests had looked kind, I reminded myself. Compassion was not the same as mercy. There was no way he could let me go. "What are you going to do with me?" I asked.

Sadness crossed his face, darkening the golden lights in his eyes, like a cloud passing over the sun. He slid his sword swiftly back into its sheath and slung it over his shoulder once more. Then he leaned down, opened his pack and drew out a large, lumpy parcel wrapped in sackcloth. He held the parcel out to me and waited patiently until I found the courage to take it. The weight pulled my arms down sharply as soon as he let go. The parcel was heavier than he had made it look.

"Open it," he said.

As I fumbled with the hairy twine that held the wrappings in place, he stood and shouldered his pack again. The wind swept over the hillside and stirred the leaves behind him into a silvery-green cloud. Fine strands of pale hair drifted around his face.

"I don't know what you expected to happen next," he said, "but it's obvious it was nothing good. So listen to me now. I'm going to make you an offer that you are free to accept or refuse as you will."

My fingers stilled on the package. "What offer?"

"Join us. Join me. Become a hill guard."

I felt my mouth drop open. "You – you can't mean that. I've already attacked you once. I'm not safe to be around normal people. I'm cursed."

"I don't believe in curses," he told me, eyes fierce. "I don't believe in magic, or demons. I believe in choice. Whatever you've been told, whoever has hurt you, whatever past haunts you, you can choose to leave it behind. I know it, Frost. I saw who you are today. Your bravery saved those women."

I began to shake my head, but he held up his hand, silencing me. "With some training I believe you could be a great warrior. I can teach you to channel this battle rage that affects you. I can teach you to fight your fear and overcome it. But it can't happen until you take control of your own life. You have to *choose* to stop running. You have to *choose* to believe in me." He smiled, and my breath caught in my throat. "I already believe in you."

"You don't know me. You don't know … what I've done."

"I don't know you very well *yet*," he corrected. "I saw enough today to know that you're a remarkable woman. Decent, kind and brave. I don't accept that you've done anything truly wrong. I don't think you could."

I looked away, clenching my jaw. He had no idea how wrong he was. Yet it still meant so much to hear someone say they believed in me – in my goodness. My own mother would not have made such a claim on my behalf.

I heard the rustle of cloth and the squeak of leather, and suddenly he was kneeling before me, showing me the golden brown and silver-blonde streaks on the top of his head as his long fingers brushed mine aside on the forgotten parcel. He swiftly unknotted the twine, peeling back a layer of sackcloth.

I sucked in a shocked breath as I saw what lay neatly packed beneath it.

My pack. My hunting knives. My snares. My water-skin and dried meat.

My father's axe.

Everything I owned in the world. Everything I had thought lost forever.

Trembling, I closed my fingers around the cold steel and smooth wood of the axe haft. "You found it."

"I've been wanting to return it to you. Other things kept coming up," he said. I felt heat rising in my cheeks as I remembered my repeated escape attempts. "Now you know I mean what I say. You can go if you want and never see me or my men again. I won't stop you. It's up to you, Frost."

His hand closed around mine for the second time and our fingers entwined. It was so natural that I did not question it. I met his strange, dark eyes.

Everything went still. My breath caught. The wind seemed to die as the late afternoon sunlight wrapped me up, trapping me in a veil of warmth. A songbird trilled, and the noise stretched out endlessly, rippling in the stillness. The blue-gold fire in Luca's gaze shivered through my body, altering all it touched: every speck of dust and drop of blood. *Forever.*

Then it was over. His hand released mine. He stood up and was towering over me again. I gazed down at my tingling, trembling fingers.

"You know where to find us," he said. "I'll be waiting."

I strained to hear his footsteps move away, but there was only the voice of the wind. Still, I knew that he had gone.

I sat there for a long time, alone among the gently stirring trees. Something stirred and shifted in my chest too, unfolding beneath my breastbone. It ached, but the pain was sweet. Pain meant life. Something I had no name for was coming alive inside me. Something like hope, or happiness, or belief – none of those things, or all of them. I had thought such a feeling lost forever, just like my father's axe. And just like my father's axe, it had been returned to me. By Luca.

He didn't believe in curses. He believed I could fight the Wolf. He had seen me go berserk and yet he still thought I was decent.

It struck me for the first time then, a realization so obvious that I choked on a laugh.

I was not in Uskaand any more.

There were no priests of Askaan or priests of the Other here. There was no one to pronounce my fate and order the fires lit. No one who knew what I had done or who I had been. No one who even knew my real name. In Ruan I could be a new person. I *could* choose to leave the past behind. If I could bring myself to believe what Luca had said.

Fight my fear. Channel my battle rage. Help people

instead of hurting them. Find a place and keep it, instead of always running, always looking over my shoulder. I didn't know anything about Luca or this country. I didn't know if what he offered was really possible. But I had to choose, like he said. I had to choose whether I believed in him. Whether I believed in myself.

When I held my hand up to my cheek, the skin Luca had touched was still warm.

I stowed my things neatly in my pack, folded the sackcloth on top, and secured my father's axe. Then I shrugged the straps over my shoulders and stood, nodding respectfully to the graves of Nicu and Abhay.

The light deepened from honey to amber as I walked through the rustling leaves, and then faded to blue as the sun sank beyond the mountains. I stopped once to eat and drink. Stars began to bloom in the sky, and the wind turned frosty.

I heard singing.

I stepped out of the trees. A sentry moved swiftly towards me, and I braced myself, lifting my hands to show I held no weapons. I could feel his eyes raking over me, although it was too dark to see his face. Then he nodded, pointing towards the centre of the camp. Towards the glow of firelight.

A few torches flamed here and there, not enough to truly illuminate the camp. The stars seemed to hover just above the tents: constellations like handfuls of luminous silver sand scattered on a low ceiling of blue cloth. The same deep, beautiful voice I had heard the night I escaped beckoned me on, singing that same, haunting song. The melancholy wood flute rose up to join him.

I came out from between two tents and found a group of people – twenty, twenty-five, maybe more – crowded around a sunken firepit. Some sat on long, stripped logs that gleamed white in the dark. Others sat in the grass. Their faces danced with flame colours; expressions masked. I didn't recognize anyone. If Luca was there, I did not see him.

Blue and orange sparks spiralled up into the sky like new suns being born. The people lifted up their faces as they sang, watching the sparks disappear. Even at this distance I could feel the heat of the fire radiating through the ranks of singers and warming my chilled cheeks and hands.

> *"Goodbye, my love, remember well,*
> *My shadow on your door;*
> *I leave my heart, my love, farewell,*
> *And pray you cry no more…"*

I knelt down, unnoticed, at the edge of the gathering, and sang with them.

I cannot feel my toes any more. I use my hands to drag me up the hill; nails splitting, skin breaking as I claw through the thin layer of snow to the stony ground beneath. My vision swims and blurs and my heart seems to choke me. I force myself on, heading for the rocks that jut up at the crest of the slope. If I can only reach them, maybe I can hide. Maybe I can escape.

The wolves' persuading voices have fallen silent now. Their paws crunch rhythmically through the snow behind me. Closer, closer, ever closer. Low, panting breaths. Sharp eager whines. The night is still, save for the sounds of their pursuit.

They know when their prey is at its limit.

Ten

Word of what had happened in my old village spread across Uskaand like ice spreads across a well in the winter: swiftly and inexorably. For a time, everyone had a story to tell of the wild wolf-girl who roamed the land with sharp, hungry fangs and glinting silver eyes. Few gave credence to the tales, though children gasped and giggled over the idea of such a creature, wondering if she might be hiding in the dark forest, or on the bleak loneliness of the plains. But never, of course, in a village very much like their own.

It was four years before the Wolf ascended again. Four years of running, of struggling to find work in tiny villages where the people could barely afford to pay Ma for her services. Of giving false names. Of staying quiet. Staying out of trouble. And never, ever fighting.

Many of the people we met in that time assumed I was simple in the head; I spoke so little, and met no one's eyes.

And I was always "falling down". So clumsy for such a strong, strapping girl.

They gave mother their condolences in hushed whispers. What a shame the daughter of a healer should be enfeebled! An illness no healer could ease. But at least I was quiet and obedient. At least I wasn't … violent.

The ice around my mother's heart grew colder each time we were forced to move on: fleeing in the night like criminals whenever the villagers grew friendly enough to ask questions about where we had come from, whenever my unusual eyes provoked curiosity, whenever people began to suspect I was not such a clumsy idiot, after all. We became experts at packing our worldly possessions at a moment's notice and discarding anything that was not essential. I lived in fear that one day Ma would abandon me too and I would wake to find myself left behind in one of those nameless villages, cast off like a broken stool or a worn-out blanket, alone in the world forever.

But no matter what she felt about me, no matter how she flinched whenever I came too near, or how often I heard her sobbing harshly in the night, she never tried to escape without me. She never even threatened to. She never let me go cold or hungry when she wasn't colder or hungrier herself. She never beat me hard enough to kill me.

Or to break the skin.

My poor ma. Perhaps by the time I was twelve she had begun to believe that we were safe again. That the Wolf was gone. Perhaps she was just too tired to keep running through *another winter. Either way, that year she made the decision to stay in a little village on the edge of the mountains until spring came. It was a decision we were both to regret.*

I clawed my way out of the familiar misery of the memory-dream, jackknifing into sitting position with a choked gasp. My hand fumbled for the reassuring lump of the wolf tooth resting over my heart as I looked around with sleep-blurred eyes.

I was used to waking up in a different place every time I opened my eyes – especially lately – but this … this was something different.

I was sitting on a thick pile of rugs. Layers of black, grey and white-spotted furs lined with bright silks were piled over me. They were as soft as the down on a baby chick and finer than anything I had seen in my life, let alone touched. A wooden screen, decorated with enamel panels that made a forest of gold and silver trees, curved around my sleeping place.

Where am I, Father?

I heard a muffled footfall, and the screen drew back to reveal a tall woman with untidy grey hair, a tattoo on her face and uncomfortably sharp eyes. Memories fell into place with an almost physical thud.

Livia.

"Are you all right?" Her voice was less brisk than I re-membered it, almost hesitant. "You were … calling out."

"Calling out?"

"For your mother."

My face flooded with heat. "Just dreaming. It was nothing."

I fidgeted under her look of barely concealed pity and peered past her at the rest of the space. The roof was peaked canvas and the wooden poles holding it up were hung with glass oil-lamps. The richly embroidered tapestries on the walls depicted mythical creatures – flying horses, fire-breathing lions, three-headed serpents – in faded shades that showed they must be very old. Underfoot, there were layers of rugs, just as fine as the wall-hangings. I saw a low table as long as I was tall, legs deeply carved with strange patterns. The surface was strewn with papers and books, quills and ink. There were chairs and even a proper wooden bed, neatly made with a deep blue coverlet. Only a very sharp eye could make out the tell-tale shapes of the hinges that allowed such luxurious items to be folded for travel. If this was a tent, it was fit for a prince.

Or a nobleman sent into the wilds by his king.

"This is Luca's tent, isn't it?"

Livia nodded, draping her arm casually around the top of the screen. "He carried you here last night. You fell asleep, sitting up, at the gathering place. You must have been exhausted." She paused for a second. "He was pleased to see you."

"Oh." I looked down at the mottled grey fur that covered my knees. "Where is he?"

"He had to go out on a patrol. He asked me to wait until you woke up and to then show you around; help you to settle in."

Something – panic, probably – must have shown in my face. She added, "He'll be back by tonight."

I thought of smooth grey river stones, attempting to keep my expression blank. "I'm sorry to trouble you."

She smiled and pushed the screen back a little further, gesturing at the untidy table. "Not a bit of it. I was taking the opportunity to amend my records. When I try to do it in my own tent I get interrupted every two minutes. I can't even eat without someone running to me needing attention. And speaking of food, Luca left you some breakfast. You must be starving."

I shuffled to the edge of the pile of rugs and disentangled myself from the fur wrapped around me. "I ... you said Luca carried me here. I didn't stir at all?"

"Not a murmur," Livia said, clearing off a space on the table and moving a wooden tray onto it.

I had been a light restless sleeper since I was a child. Habit and necessity would have made it so, even if my nights weren't plagued with dreams of running and howling and sharp white fangs. But Luca had held me in his arms, and I had not woken. My cheeks burned.

I hurried over to the table and sat down on one of the

chairs, busying myself by taking the lids off all the covered bowls on the tray. There was a cup of milk, a bowl of round fluffy pastry things, some sort of egg dish and small stuffed flatbreads that looked crispy and golden, as if they had been fried. When I popped one in my mouth, the flatbread turned out to contain spiced roots and onions. The pastries were sweet: flavoured with nuts and honey. The eggs tasted of green leaves – like spinach, but stronger – and peas, and more onions. The food was very spicy, setting fire to my mouth, but very good. I tried to slow down, but I had only eaten one stingy, tasteless meal the day before and my belly would not let me. I was used to stuffing myself when I could, to make up for the times when meals were poor or even non-existent. Besides, if my mouth was full, I didn't have to speak.

Not that Livia seemed to expect me to. She was scribbling away at her papers, dripping ink everywhere, sneezing whenever she tapped her nose with her quill. Her relaxed posture and the concentration on her face were reassuring, as if there was nothing strange or awkward about sitting here with me. Yet, the last time she had seen me I had been locked up in a cell. Then I had escaped, and the hill-guard captain himself had gone after me. And now I had spent the night in the captain's tent. What must she be thinking?

As I washed down the last spicy crumbs with the last mouthful of milk, Livia put aside her quill and went to a chest at the end of the bed. She drew out a large, folded drying cloth and a bar of soap, and offered them to me. As I stood to take them, I noticed for the first time that Livia was taller than I was – by at least an inch. That was rare enough in men, back in Uskaand. The Sedorne seemed to be a long-legged people.

"I'm supposed to get you outfitted with a uniform and everything else you need today, but I think you should clean up first." She added some clean clothes to the pile in my arms. "These are mine, just for the moment."

"Do I smell that badly?" I asked, mortified.

"You don't stink, but I can tell you've been sleeping on the forest floor for a while. I'm afraid we don't have a bathhouse. I'll walk you down to the river."

"I've never been to a bathhouse," I admitted. "At home we had hot springs."

"Well, that's a relief. If I have to listen to one more new recruit bellyaching about the lack of hot water, I might brain them. I don't understand why they sign up if they want luxury."

"Is that what I am?" I asked tentatively. "A new recruit?"

The hare in Livia's tattoo seemed to leap as she frowned in thought. "Seems like it. I suppose you'll do. Can't say you're lacking in gumption, anyway. And I never knew him to be wrong about anyone before."

As I turned over her words in my mind, she pushed back the tent flap. I followed her outside into early morning sunlight and a businesslike swarm of people.

By day the hill-guard camp was a different place. My head nearly swivelled off my shoulders as I struggled to take in everything that was going on. I followed Livia through the centre of the camp, past a cleared circle of ground where around thirty men and woman were going through some kind of battle-drill, swords rising and falling in perfect synchronization. Near by a pair – one man and one woman – were sparring hand-to-hand, their movements a blur of kicks and punches. Others sat peacefully, polishing armour, repairing tack, sharpening weapons. I glimpsed a man pegging out washing on a line strung between tents. Elsewhere, a woman sat on the ground, a cloth wrapped around her shoulders, while another carefully snipped her hair.

It felt less like a campsite and more like a small town. The tents ranged in size from ones that would easily fit two dozen men inside to others that were clearly meant for only one or two people. As we went past the firepit at the back of the camp, I glimpsed wooden structures – the prison cells where I had been held. Where Birkin was probably being held now.

I hoped that they hadn't put him into my cell. Not that Birkin would fit through the gap I had made.

The variety of skin and hair colours among the camp's inhabitants was bewildering. At home, nearly everyone had the same coppery brown skin and dark hair as me;

the same wide, broad cheekbones and flattish noses. In Southern Uskaand, where I had grown up, even the slight variation of my grey eyes had been enough to mark me as an outsider, the next worst thing to a foreigner, although I knew that in the North, both grey and blue eyes were common.

Among the hill guard, hardly any two people shared the same looks. I saw a man who would have caused whispering and stares in Uskaand, with his round face and button nose and skin so pale it looked positively unhealthy, especially against the fiery red of his hair. The man was talking to a woman who had skin that shone a dark bluish-black and a cloud of hair that stood out around her head like dark thistledown. She had a flat nose like me – yet her cheekbones and chin were pointed and sharp.

And there were so many *women*! I had assumed that the soldiers would be mostly male, as in the army at home, with the odd female cook, or healer, like Livia. But here it seemed around half the soldiers were women, and while I was glad that I wasn't the only female recruit, it was strange to see all the camp dwellers, regardless of sex, in the same clothing – plain shirts and breeches – with weapons strapped to their bodies.

Many of the people we passed stared at me unabashedly, pausing in their tasks to watch as I walked by. I did not meet anyone's eyes. Hostility, wariness and suspicion were all too familiar to me.

"Never mind them," Livia said, hooking her arm casually through mine. I tried my best not to flinch from the unexpected contact. "Some wild tales have been flying around camp ever since the captain and Arian first brought you back. People will soon get used to you."

I tried to smile. It would have been nice to accept her kindness without forcing myself to look for hidden motives – but I still wasn't sure I believed her. No one had ever accepted me. No one had ever got used to me.

Luca wants me here, I told myself, squaring my shoulders. *Livia thinks I'll do. I'm good enough. I will be good enough.*

Livia led me to the edge of camp, where trees began to encroach again. The passage of many feet had worn a trail down the high, moss-furred bank to the wide river bed. The water was a deep, mysterious green, glassily smooth on the surface. There were other women already bathing there, laughing and splashing each other.

"The men wash at night, and the woman in the morning. No mixing, unless by – er, prior arrangement." Livia cast me a sidelong look and I felt my cheeks heating up again. She laughed. "There's a strict no-peeking policy too, so you're safe."

One of the women in the water caught sight of me. She nudged her nearest companion. I couldn't hear their voices over the sound of the river, but the immediate flexing of fists and crossing of arms was all too obvious. They didn't want me there.

"I'll leave you to it, then," Livia said, apparently oblivious, as she began to walk away. "When you've finished, come back to Luca's tent and I'll take you to the seamstress."

The whole group of women was now staring up at me, their relaxed poses hardened into wariness. If I got into the water, would they leave? Or would they attack me? What if I hurt someone? The goatherd would have an excuse to carry out his threat, after all. Or, worse, Luca would realize he'd been wrong, and send me away.

Stay quiet. Don't fight. Stay out of trouble.

I tried to force the familiar refrain out of my mind, but the sensation of coldness lodged. Hugging the things Livia had given me to my chest, I made my decision and turned from the river towards the shelter of the trees. I felt the women's eyes on my back every step of the way.

As the sounds of the camp faded away behind me, my ears were filled with birdsong and the busy muttering of water. Golden clouds of pollen danced in the shafts of sunlight and made my nose itch. I tramped over trailing roots and mossy rocks, struggling for balance on the steeply sloping ground. Sweat sprang up on my face, and I began to pant a little. I also began to feel guilty. Livia had known what she was doing, taking me to the river. She probably expected me to brazen it out, introduce myself and make friends. Instead I had run away again. So much for my "bravery". The further I got from those women and their watchful eyes, the more the knots in my neck and shoulders loosened.

I found a narrow goat-track and followed it, looking for a place where I could climb down to bathe. But the trail curved away from the barely seen glint of the water, and the river sounds grew fainter. I thought of turning back, but … the women might still be there, waiting.

I cursed myself for a coward and tramped on. The trail curved sharply. Finally I heard the roar of water again, ahead of me now, and much louder than before. The trees opened up to reveal a pool of clear green water rippling and glinting in the sun. I gasped at its beauty.

The pool was fed by a thin waterfall that splashed down a rocky cliff-face. Vivid yellow saplings and bluish ferns sprouted from the rocks. A dry crescent of smooth river pebbles edged the pool. I was about to run forward and explore when I saw the man.

His back was to me as he waded from the water to a neat pile of clothes on the dry pebbles on the opposite bank. Unsurprisingly, he was naked. Heavy muscles clenched and shifted smoothly under warm brown skin as he began to dry off.

I had seen naked men before. Uskaand is a land of icy rivers and hot springs, where it is common for men and woman to swim together. The polite thing would have been to simply look away until the man had finished dressing himself.

But I didn't.

His back, shoulders and buttocks were a mess of scars. Long, straight scars that looked as if they had come from a whip. Thick, uneven welts that must have been caused by burns. Thin, silvery marks left by some weapon with a cutting edge. The wounds were long since healed, but some were still livid. I realized I was looking at the result of months – *years* – of abuse. I couldn't imagine how anyone could endure so much pain.

As he pulled on his breeches, I began to back away into the trees. This man, who took such care to bathe in a private place when no one else was around, must never know that he had been seen.

A sharp snap rang out above the sound of the waterfall. I looked down to see that my boot had broken a branch in two. I cursed under my breath – but it was too late to run away without being spotted. Shirt still unfastened, the man was already turning.

"Back early, Luca?" he called. He was smiling, and the look transformed his face so utterly that for a moment I barely recognized him.

It was the goatherd. Arian.

We stared at each other, both shocked and unmoving.

Then he swore, low and vicious. He lunged forward across the pebbled shore to seize my arm. His fingers bit into my flesh, and he shook me hard. Although we were the same height, he almost wrenched my feet off the ground. "Get an eyeful, did you? Now I suppose you'll run back and tell everyone?"

"No! I'm s–sorry!" I stammered, my bundled-up things dropping to the ground as I fought to keep my balance on the shifting river stones.

His free hand twitched up, as if to strike me. "Luca was mad to drag trash like you here—"

Anger and panic combined in a fiery burst and I brought my closed fist down on his wrist. "Let *go*!"

He released me with a grunt of pain, and I used both hands to shove him back. "How was I supposed to know you'd be here? Does this p–place belong to you? Does it?"

"You followed me here – you spied on me."

"Why would I do that? Why would I want to be any-where near a horrible bully who keeps threatening me?" I shoved him backwards again, too incensed now to be cautious. It had been such a long time since I'd lost my temper. "You're not the only one in the world with scars, you know! They're not *that* interesting."

He let out something dangerously close to a snarl. "Get out of here! Before I do something you'll regret!"

"I'm not leaving," I ground out between gritted teeth. "I didn't do anything wrong. All I wanted was a b–bath, and you've already finished. You go!"

He took a slow, careful step back. When he spoke again, the words were low and flat, as if he were spend-ing all his energy to restrain himself. "Listen carefully.

Pick up your things now and leave. Go back to camp. Get away from me."

"Or what?" I demanded, the heady mix of fright and rage driving me on. "Like hurting unarmed women, do you? Your mother must be so proud!"

He flinched visibly, turning ashen before my eyes. I went still, my feverish temper cooled by the sudden look of icy despair in his face. Before I could think to apologize, or ask what was wrong, he had spun around and was walking away, forging a path straight into the trees. In less than a heartbeat, he was gone.

"What did I say?" I whispered.

But I wasn't sure I truly wanted to know.

Eleven

Scrubbed to within an inch of my life, half-dry hair fluffing up around my face, and with the seams of Livia's slightly too small clothes itching at my shoulders, I slunk back towards camp. I felt as if I had been tested twice this morning, and failed both times. First by running from those women when I should have stood my ground, and then by arguing with Arian when I ought to have walked away.

I half-expected to be greeted with drawn swords when I emerged from the trees after my bathe, but no one paid any attention to me. I kept it that way by scurrying around the edges of the camp, eyes down, shoulders hunched.

"Oh, dear," Livia said, as I arrived in Luca's tent. "You look like a whipped dog. What happened?"

"I had a run-in with the g – er – with Arian."

She laughed, pulling a face. "Don't let it worry you. You'll soon find that the only person in the hill guard who manages to get along with Arian is Luca. For the rest of us, it's like trying to be friendly with a–a rock. I'm not sure he has feelings, other than the urge to smash anyone who gets in his way."

I thought about the horrified look Arian had given me just now. The man clearly did have feelings. *But*, I cautioned myself, *that doesn't mean it's safe to feel sorry for him. It just means he's capable of hating you all the more.*

"I'll keep away from him in future," I said, mostly to myself.

"That's what I try to do," Livia agreed cheerfully as she creaked to her feet. "Right, to the seamstress with you."

Once again the healer strode straight through the centre of the camp when I would have stuck to the outskirts. After walking beside me for a minute without speaking she suddenly whopped me hard in the centre of my back. My shoulders shot back as the air *ooph*ed out of my lungs.

"That's better," she said. "You stand out more when you hunch over, you know."

I noticed people grinning at this exchange. *Well, at least they're not glaring. Or laughing.*

The camp seamstress, Atiyah, was a short, round woman with masses of dark hair, and tattoos of cotton flowers covering the bridges of both cheeks.

"Oh, this is the new one, then? She doesn't look so fearsome," she said, snapping a long measuring tape between her hands. I jumped at the sound, and she let out a surprisingly girlish laugh. "Don't worry. I won't bite if you won't."

Livia reeled off a long list of instructions for Atiyah that had apparently come from Luca. I discovered that I was to have "special" armour – lightweight boiled leather that would cover my vulnerable points: gauntlets, vambraces, a neckguard and helm. The seamstress, rather than being annoyed at the extra trouble, as I had feared, seemed intrigued. She measured me quickly and efficiently, peppering Livia with questions all the while, and finally said that she would have to speak to Luca about materials as soon as he got back. Once Livia had extracted a promise that I would have at least one basic uniform to wear by tomorrow, she took me on to the weapons tent. There I was measured again and given a practice sword made of blunt, soft metal, and a wooden stave capped in brass at both ends. When I protested, pointing out that I had my axe, the weapon's master laughed in my face. "You can't train with that!" He snorted. "You'll kill someone, probably yourself."

"How am I going to learn to fight better with the axe by training with a sword and quarterstaff?" I asked Livia, as we left the armoury.

She pursed her lips. "Talk to Luca about it when he gets back. Here we are – your new home."

I looked up to see a long, thin tent, its flap pegged open to reveal dozens of bedrolls lined up neatly on each side, with a few inches between each one. Only one or two people were sleeping within now, but the air that wafted out of the entrance was stuffy and humid with the smell of warm bodies. I could imagine how it would be at night, with the women packed inside like potatoes jostling one another in a sack. How did they *breathe*?

I backed away, shaking my head. "No. I'm sorry, I can't. I can't sleep in there."

Livia's brow furrowed. "This is where all the women sleep."

"Do you?" I challenged.

"Well, no – I stay in the healer's tent. In case of emergencies."

"Then not all the women sleep here. I won't be any trouble. I'll put my bedroll outside; that's what I'm used to anyway. I couldn't even close my eyes in there, let alone sleep." I shuddered.

"We can't let you sleep outside! What if it rains?" Livia said, appalled. "I'd offer to let you stay with me, but I need to keep the space clear for patients. Let's just leave you in Luca's tent for now. He can decide where you should go when—"

"He gets back," I echoed, thinking that it seemed to be the standard reply for all the tricky questions around here.

"Yes," she said, cheerful again. "Now I'm starving. It must be nearly time for a midday meal."

She hooked her arm through mine again – ignoring my instinctive flinch – and towed me towards the largest tent in the camp. Spicy smells drifted my way, making my mouth water and my stomach gurgle.

"This is the mess," Livia said. "They provide three meals a day, although you can normally coax food out of them in-between times if you missed eating because of duties. It's permitted to carry a tray of food away if you wish, but you must bring your plates and utensils back to be washed. And smashing them doesn't count."

I ground my teeth. Was I ever going to live that down?

One side of the tent was pegged out with long poles, creating a sort of canopy where people sat on blankets or the grass, eating and laughing. The interior was filled with long, roughly hewn tables and low stools. At one end of the tent there was a counter covered in plates and trays and dishes, and behind that, men and women laboured over metal cooking pots, moving through clouds of steam and smoke.

By the time Livia and I had reached the canopy, everyone was staring at us. Laughter and chatter had died away, replaced by low whispering.

"Maybe I should just—"

"Not a chance," Livia said flatly. "You might've got your way about sleeping quarters for the moment, but I'm not letting you hide from everything that makes you uncomfortable. We're not ogres. We're your new family, your comrades-in-arms. You need to get to know us and we need to get to know you – which will never happen if you keep running away."

Her wiry arms turned out to have surprising strength. She almost dragged me over to the counter.

Turning my back on the whispering people, I tried to concentrate as she showed me where the wooden trays were stacked, and selected various cold dishes from the covered bowls that waited on the counter.

"You can just ... take it?" I asked incredulously. "As much as you want? Don't they run out?"

I bit my tongue when pity showed in Livia's eyes again. Livia cleared her throat, then leaned over the counter and asked for several bowls of hot food from one of the cooks. She added the extra dishes to our trays and jerked her head towards the tables.

"Find us a seat, then. *Not* that one," she snapped, as I instinctively headed towards an empty table in the far corner. She relented a little as she saw my hunted expression. "Oh, all right. Small steps."

We sat at the empty table and I busied myself with taking the lids off the bowls, releasing pungent smells that made my stomach rumble all the harder. It gave me an excuse to avoid looking at the healer. Her eyes were too sharp for comfort.

"Frost," she said after a moment, stirring thoughtfully at a fragrant green dish of what I thought was lamb. "Do you know what the hill guard is? Really?"

"Luca said you're here to keep people in the mountains safe from the rebels."

"That's our job, not what we are. What we *are* is scraps."

"Scraps?" I frowned, confused.

"When Luca was given the task of creating a force to police these mountains, he didn't choose troops from the regular army. He said they were too used to following orders, and fighting in squares and straight lines and enemies that play by the rules. He knew people like that would be no good. So he gathered together all the scraps. Leftover bits and pieces of resistance groups that survived the war. People who wanted to fight, but couldn't find a place because they had trouble with being told what to do. People who didn't fit into their families, or had lost their families. We're all damaged in some way."

She stared down into her cup of tea. Her face was grave, but not sad. "I come from a very rich, very important Sedorne family. They used to be favourites of Mad Abheron's, and that tells you all you need to know about them. They married me to another of his favourites. He was a wicked man. I ran away once or twice in the early years, but in Sedra a woman belongs to her husband, no matter how vile he might be. I was always dragged back. My family made sure of it.

"After my husband brought me to Ruan I took my chance and ran away from him for the last time. I knew better than to seek refuge with my family by then, but I had no money, no friends, no skills. Nowhere to go. I lived on the streets of Aroha, and I did whatever I had to in order to survive. Eventually, the Order of the Mother found me and took me in. They taught me to heal, and I turned out to be good at it. Years later I assisted when the reia had her son, which is how I came to know Luca, and how I came to be one of his ... scraps."

She nodded at the table next to us. "See that boy there, that handsome boy with the red scarf? His name is Dinesh. His family were killed in a Sedorne border raid when he was five. He was the only survivor. He lived feral in the woods until he was ten, when a wandering namoa – that's the name for a holy man or woman who follows the Mother – found him. He still hardly speaks. And that woman beside him? She's Adela. One of Mad Abheron's serving girls from the age of twelve to sixteen. I can't imagine the horrors she must have seen. We might look official in our nice neat uniforms, but there's not one of us who doesn't know what it's like to be on the run, or lost, or in hiding. That's why we can get into the minds of the rebels we're fighting like no one else. And that's why – no matter where you came from, or what you've done in the past – there is a place for you here. If you can bring yourself to accept it."

Now it was my turn to stare into my cup. I felt honoured that she had confided in me. But it was so hard to believe. So hard to hope. It was maybe the most frightening thing I'd ever done.

"You just think about it," she said, after a minute. "And eat up. I'm putting you to work this afternoon."

Twelve

"You know, I think I preferred it where it was in the first place. Can you put it back over there for me?"

I held in a groan as I shifted the table for the third time. Even lightly built travelling furniture grew heavy when you'd been heaving it around for a whole afternoon.

A shrill whistle sounded outside the healer's tent, and I jumped, nearly dropping the table on my foot.

"It's the signal that Luca and his patrol have come back, safe and sound," Livia said, through a cloud of steam. She was scrubbing the bowls that she used to grind herbs in a bucket of scalding water. "You'll grow to love that whistle in time."

Safe and sound.

Something tugged sharply in my chest.

There was a pause. Then Livia said, "Well?"

I saw that she was grinning.

"What?"

"Aren't you going to welcome him back?"

"He's barely arrived," I said, hoping my voice passed for calm. "He won't want to be bothered with me. I'm just a new recruit."

Her voice was tart as she said, "For the Mother's sake, girl. You don't have to fling rose petals at his feet and sing a stirring song. Just go and say hello. He'll like it."

"You ... don't think he'd mind?"

"I think you should stop worrying so much about what other people think and do what you want. You might shock yourself."

She made me sound like a weak-willed fool. I gritted my teeth, pushed the tent flap back and marched outside.

I hadn't realized how much time had passed while I was helping Livia. It was twilight, and someone had already lit the torches in the camp. The sky was deep blue, with the dark shapes of storm clouds moving over the trees. The cold air and darkness acted like a slap to the face. I stopped in my tracks. I had let Livia bait me, but my concern was valid, after all. Why *would* Luca want to be bothered with me? I refused to let the memory of what had happened on the edge of the farmstead influence me. That, my ma would have said, was the way to come home by weeping cross. Luca probably made everyone feel like that.

He wasn't like me. He was beautiful, and strong, and ... and *good*. That goodness shone out of him, like the golden lights in his eyes. Luca was bound to be valued and respected wherever he went. I was sure he wouldn't deliberately upset me or lead me astray, but he couldn't possibly know how much his words, his casual actions, had meant to me. I wasn't the first scrap he had collected. I would not be the last.

Well, in that case, a little voice inside me argued, *it can't do any harm to go and sneak a glimpse at him. Just to make sure he really is safe and sound. If he looks busy you can slip away without being seen. He won't even notice you.*

I couldn't resist that tempting logic. I followed the sound of voices. A crowd had gathered near the centre point of the camp, where the white stone firepit and the stripped logs glowed in the flaring light of the torches. I could barely see Luca. Only the top of his blonde head, bent to listen, was visible among the people jostling around him. They were all talking at once, bombarding him with questions. I was reminded of a litter of piglets fighting over the best place at their mother's belly. I even saw Atiyah there, waving some pieces of paper – probably wanting to consult him about my armour.

Talk to Luca about it, Livia had said whenever she could not answer a question herself. Apparently everyone did. It was a wonder he ever got a moment's peace.

Luca's head came up. His forehead creased and his gaze flicked over the waiting crowd, searching for someone. I wondered who he wanted. Arian, probably. Then he saw me hovering in the background a little way from the others. The lines on his face smoothed away. He smiled.

The sharp, painful tug in my chest eased, turning smooth and sweet, like warm honey, as I realized that Livia had been right. He was happy to see me.

Several people noticed his smile and turned to stare at me, their voices falling silent. For once I didn't care. I was content to smile back.

In the quiet, a harsh voice rang out.

"For the Mother's sake – you're like a bunch of vultures at a carcass. He's only just got back! Get on with your work and leave him be!"

Arian.

Luca's eyes left me and his smile turned to a grin as his lieutenant ploughed through the waiting people. "You're in a bad temper. Who flicked your nose this time?"

Again, several of the crowd – I recognized one as a woman who had been bathing in the river this morning – turned to look at me. I cursed mentally. Of course – those women would have seen Arian walk past them to bathe and then seen me head off in the same direction, and shortly afterwards Arian had stormed back to camp again. The women had drawn the obvious conclusion and placed the blame on me. And they were right.

"I'm not in a bad temper," Arian said grimly, as if even he didn't believe it. "I'm just stunned that certain people are so rude they didn't let you clean up before they started demanding that you fix their problems. Did anyone even think to bring you any food?"

"I'm not hungry," Luca said, his gaze seeking me out again. I noticed that there was a long streak of dirt on his neck. His clothes were muddy, as if he'd rolled down a hill in the rain. "And our mission was a success, so I'm in a good mood, no matter how grumpy you are. What I want to do is thank the Mother and talk to my men. Any objections?"

There was a collective *whoop*, and before I knew what had happened, a fire was crackling up in the white pit. It spread incredibly quickly, burning with those strange blue-green and purple flickers.

The smell of sunshine and honeysuckle drifted to me in the first waft of woodsmoke, and I looked up to see Luca approaching. A warm, strong hand closed around mine. "Come and sit by me," he said.

I allowed him to tug me towards one of the stripped logs; I kept my eyes on the ground, even though I could barely see my own feet in the gathering darkness, because I didn't quite dare to look at him. We sat, and Luca's thigh pressed against mine. Lightning struck my body. I jolted and nearly toppled off the log as I hastily tried to put distance between us.

Luca caught me and pulled me back, laughing. "What are you doing?"

I shook my head, still staring down. I was so embarrassed I would happily have crawled into the fire and turned into a puff of smoke.

"Frost? What is it?"

I forced my head up and met his eyes. He was still laughing. Embarrassment, tension, apprehension – all of it vanished as thoroughly as I had wished it to a moment before. I laughed too, shaking my head at my own silliness.

"That's better," he said, as people took seats around us. "How has your first day been? I'm sorry I wasn't here. We had to go back and collect Birkin. As much as I'd have liked to leave him there for the bears, the man's entitled to a trial."

"But I thought you said you'd send someone to collect him yesterday?"

"Ye–es." He drew the word out sheepishly. "Well, I may have become a little distracted and..."

I laughed again. "You forgot about him?"

"Only for a few hours. I was up at first light to fetch him, I promise. Only by then he'd managed to work his way out of most of the ropes, and he wasn't happy about being collected."

"Is that how you got covered in mud?"

"No, that was the leopard."

"What?"

"I'll tell you another time," he said. His fingers

contracted in two quick little squeezes around mine, as if to secure my attention. "You still haven't answered my question. How have you fared today?"

"I–I'm not sure. Some parts have been strange. Some parts have been interesting. I like Livia a lot."

Luca opened his mouth, but before he could say anything more, someone cleared their throat loudly. We both looked up to see a circle of interested faces. Arian was sitting directly opposite me, his arms folded across his chest so that his arm muscles bulged threateningly. His face was hard and expressionless; his eyes were fixed on my knee, where Luca's hand rested, joined with mine.

There was an awkward silence. People glanced at Arian, then at me, and away. I could tell something was wrong, but not what it was. I tried to slip my fingers from Luca's, but his grip tightened again as he looked down at me. "In Ruan, when we gather like this around a fire, we believe that the Mother can hear our voices," he said gravely. "We send our thanks to Her, our wishes and prayers, our dark thoughts and bright hopes, in the music we make. She draws it all from us, forgives us, and heals us in our hearts. It's considered an honour to lead the song. I think you should have that honour tonight. You can sing anything you want – it's the feeling that matters, not the words. But you don't have to if you don't want to. I can't force anyone to do anything they don't like."

That last remark seemed aimed not at me, but across the fire at Arian.

I hesitated. The hungry snarling of the fire seemed very loud, but the waiting silence was louder still. I had been tested twice today, and twice I had failed. Now everyone was waiting to see how I would handle this challenge.

There is a place for you here, Livia had said.

You have to believe, Luca had said.

I took a deep breath. "Do you know the 'Fox's Lament'?"

A few of the people around the fire nodded.

"I think I've heard of it," Luca said encouragingly. "You start and we'll follow along."

I took another couple of deep breaths. The hill guards waited with no signs of impatience – apart from Arian, who tapped his fingers against his arm. *Just get on with it!*

I began to sing. My voice rang out, low and a little hoarse with nerves, through the night's stillness.

> *"Said her lover, your hair is like,*
> *The coat of the russet fox, my dear,*
> *Red with passion, red with blood.*
> *Said her lover, your hair is like,*
> *The falling leaves, my dear,*
> *Bright with smiles, bright with tears…"*

After a moment someone pulled out a wood flute and

joined in, and slowly others began to sing too, catching the words. Luca hummed tunelessly.

The white-hot heart of the blaze fluttered, the blue glints deepening, stretching. I almost felt I could see things within it ... living things, moving in the flames. Shadows almost like faces. Shapes almost like hands. Long fingers, reaching out, beckoning with a slow, hypnotic pulse.

My eyes did not want to leave the light. *I* did not want to leave the light.

The fire roared and crackled and whispered. I imagined leaning closer, falling forward into the dancing blue, feeling its warmth embrace me... Somewhere in the night, a wolf howled. An icy shiver trickled down my spine like a melting icicle.

I wrenched my eyes from the fire, my voice drying up into a croak. No one seemed to notice. My gaze darted down to my hands. My left hand, clasped with Luca's, still felt warm. I could still see the colours of the fire. I tried to calm my panicked breath. *It's all right. It's all right.*

The last note of the flute lingered on in the darkness, and the centre of the fire suddenly flared up. The faces around it were transformed with glowing blue and turquoise and green – colours I had never seen in any fire before. A great rush of blue and purple sparks exploded out of the pit and spiralled up into the sky.

It was beautiful, but I watched nervously, my wonder tainted with fear. Did those sparks truly carry the hill guards' prayers with them, as Luca had said? What if the fire called to other things – other forces that dwelled in the night?

The blue fire ebbed and died down. There was a collective sigh.

"She was here," someone said softly.

"She is always here," said Luca.

A scream rang through the night. It was a woman's voice, somewhere close by. Almost as soon as I heard it, it was drowned out by a male roar of rage. Luca was on his feet instantly, letting my hand drop.

"Captain! Help!" someone shouted.

Luca was already running. We followed him. People pushed and crowded around me, forcing me back. I put on a surge of speed and broke through the crowd to see the dark shape of the prison building directly ahead. A familiar-looking female hill guard sat in the grass before it, clutching her head. Blood streaked down one side of her face, and she was pressing a folded handkerchief to the wound. Another soldier – I realized with a shock that it was Dinesh, the boy with the red scarf, the boy Livia had pointed out to me in the mess tent earlier – stood over the large, crumpled form of ... of *Birkin*.

The huge bandit was whimpering like a wounded

animal, curled up in a feeble attempt to defend himself from the vicious kicks Dinesh was aiming at him. Birkin's hands were chained behind his back. His face was a bloody mess; both eyes were nearly swollen shut.

Luca caught Dinesh by the shoulder, whipping him around so hard that the boy slipped and nearly fell. Dinesh raised one fist as if to strike out, then blanched when he saw that it was Luca who had dragged him away.

"He attacked Adela!" he blurted out. "When she went to take him his food, he headbutted her and tried to escape."

"So you thought you would kick him to death while his hands were tied behind his back," Luca said, his voice low and dangerously quiet.

The defensiveness and anger faded from the young hill guard's face. A visible shudder travelled through his body. "I … I saw Adela and I…"

"I didn't ask you to," the female hill guard said, her voice sharp.

Dinesh's face crumpled. Luca let go of him and bent down to look at Birkin. The bandit wasn't making noise any more. I thought he must be dead.

"Someone get the healer!" Arian snapped.

"I'm here, I'm here!" Livia's voice called. Panting a little, she pushed past me and knelt down beside the bandit, laying her hand on his throat. "He's alive. Help me get him to the healer's tent."

Two hill guards hurried forward to hoist the unconscious bandit up. Meanwhile, Arian was murmuring to Adela. The injured woman wobbled to her feet and followed the procession bearing the bandit. The crowd parted and then closed silently behind them.

Luca stared down at the ground. Finally he straightened and fixed his eyes on Dinesh. "Do you realize what you almost did? This would have been murder. Nothing more or less."

Dinesh shook his head. I thought there were tears in his eyes. "I'm sorry," he whispered.

"I know you are," Luca said. His voice was tired, but he reached out, hand steady, to clasp the younger man's shoulder. "You're a good man. We're all good men and women here. That's why doing this job, day after day, is so dangerous for all of us. But you can't become like them. Like him. Not even a soldier any more, but a killer. I don't want that to happen to you."

Luca turned to look at those of us still standing silently in the flickering torchlight. "I don't want it to happen to any of you. We're fighting to restore justice and safety to these mountains, in the name of the king and the reia. The moment we forget that, the moment we're just here to kill and inflict pain, then we'll have become exactly what we despise. Just another bunch of thugs. We have to be better than this, my friends. We have to be better than them."

Thirteen

I lay on the pile of rugs and furs behind the screen in Luca's darkened tent, stomach churning, fretfully turning my wolf tooth over and over in my hand. Birkin's smashed-up face wouldn't leave my mind. I went over the scene again and again, remembering Luca's painfully steady hand reaching out to Dinesh, and the terrible anxiety I had seen in Arian's eyes as Luca had gently led Dinesh away. Something very bad had happened. Not just what Dinesh had done. The way it had affected both him and everyone else.

Violence was an infection, and once it took root, it spread its black tendrils through everything that was good in people, and killed it all. Happiness, trust, love. Dinesh had tried to save Adela, and instead he had turned her against him, perhaps forever.

Just as I had done, with my own mother.

But Dinesh was only human. A normal human boy who had lost control of his normal human temper. Any human might make such a mistake, and repent, and be forgiven. I was not human, not truly. It wasn't my own temper that I threatened to let loose upon the world, but the insatiable appetite of the Wolf, who hungered only for death.

If the Wolf had turned on Birkin, it would have ripped his throat out with *my* teeth. If Luca had caught hold of my shoulder as he had Dinesh's, the Wolf would have turned on him too. There was no limit to the damage I could do to the people I ... cared for.

If I had forgotten all this for a little while, then the sight of Birkin ought to have reminded me. I knew that I should be packing right now, planning to run away from this place and these people, to escape the violence by moving on as I had always done.

But I wasn't. I didn't even want to.

The strength and determination in Luca's voice when he told his men that they were good had woven around my heart, forming an intangible armour against the doubts that tried to send me fleeing. Luca believed what he had said; believed it utterly. And somehow I felt – I *knew* – that the sheer force of that belief could make his words true.

Would make his words true.

The canvas tent flap lifted with a rustle, and a cool finger of night air explored my face. I sat up.

"I know you're there," Luca said.

"I know you do. I was waiting for you."

There was a pause. I heard no movement, but I imagined him walking across the tent. I was proved right by a scratch of flint, a spark and a flare of light. As Luca lit the oil lamp that hung from the wooden post in the centre of the tent, tiny bubbles and imperfections in the blown glass cast starburst patterns on the canvas walls and on Luca's face, turning it into a mask of gold. I forced my gaze away, blinking.

Luca moved to sit on the edge of his bed. I knuckled the water out of my eyes and looked at him again. The illusion was gone. He looked tired. More than tired – exhausted. Worn out.

"I suppose you're wondering what you've got yourself into," he said. His voice showed his exhaustion even more than the deep line between his brows and the strain around his mouth. "I said I could teach you to control your rage. I boasted and bragged. And on your first day here, you see *this*. Proof that I haven't taught my own men that lesson in over a year of working with them." He let out a bitter laugh. "I don't know why anyone would believe I could help them after witnessing that."

I wanted to offer him some kind of reassurance, but making up comforting sayings wasn't something I had ever practised. "You said you believed in choices, not curses," I said slowly, working it out as I went. "That hill guard, Dinesh – he had a choice, didn't he? And he made the wrong one. What happens here when you make the wrong choice? Will you punish him and send him away?"

Luca's head jerked up. "No! He's a good soldier. What happened tonight was – it was too much for him. He loves Adela. He has loved her for a long time, even though she doesn't care for him, and he knows it. He just lost control."

"He won't do it again?"

Luca shook his head. "He's so ashamed of himself he was sick when he got back to the barracks."

"Then you've answered your own question."

"What question?" He rubbed his forehead, blinking tiredly.

"You did help Dinesh. You stopped him before it was too late; you made him see that he had done wrong. You comforted him, and you'll let him stay and make up for what he did. What more could you have done?"

His words came out slowly, haltingly. "Yes, I–I suppose you're right."

"Luca, I didn't come here because I expected you to … to snap your fingers and make me better. I just want someone to help me, the way you helped that boy. You said yourself that you can't force people into things. They have to make their own choices and live with them. Have a bit of respect for Dinesh's free will – and mine. We're neither of us children."

A tiny puff of laughter, genuine laughter this time, escaped Luca's lips. "Point taken. No, you're not children. And that'll teach me to wallow in self-pity."

I opened my mouth quickly, distressed that he had taken my words as a rebuke – then clamped my lips shut when I saw that the dancing gold light had come back into his eyes. I had managed to say something right. Best to shut up and not ruin it.

"Er..." Luca went on. "Please don't take this amiss, but may I ask why you are lurking in my tent at this time of night, handing out common sense?"

"Because I don't have anywhere else to go," I said, a hint of defiance creeping into my voice. "I–I'd rather sleep in a *cave* than in the women's tent with all those people around me breathing and muttering and snoring. Livia said you'd find me a place."

"Hmmm. Are you sure you can't make do with the women's tent? You might get used to it."

I shook my head emphatically, mentally promising myself that I would sneak off and sleep in a tree if Luca tried to insist.

He must have seen the stubbornness in my face because he sighed. "What about with Livia, then? It sounds as if the two of you are getting on quite well."

"She said no. The beds have to be kept free for emergencies."

"That's a good point," Luca said, his face darkening.

I was sure he was thinking about Birkin and Adela. He paused and then said, "I've plenty of room here. You slept well in that little corner over there last night. You could stay with me."

I stiffened instinctively, an icy shadow of fear brushing through my body. I shook my head again – a quick, wary jerk. When he moved, I flinched. But he was only clasping his hands on his knee, the long fingers entwining tightly. His eyes stayed on mine, even and patient. The shadow of the past slipped away and instead of being afraid, I felt guilty and ungrateful. Luca had already had a hundred chances to hurt me. But he hadn't. He wouldn't. He was … one of the good ones. And now I had insulted him. Why did I always get everything wrong?

I'd hesitated too long. Luca nodded resignedly. "All right. I can see you're not happy with that idea."

"I don't – it isn't—" I stumbled over the words, nearly choking on them. "I trust you Luca. I do. But … there's a reason why the men and women's tents are separate. What would people think if I slept in here?"

Luca blew out his breath, sending silky strands of golden hair flying. His cheeks suddenly looked a little ruddy. "Frost, whatever you're worried they might think, they're most likely already thinking it."

I couldn't look at him. "They are? Bu–but why?" I touched my hot cheek with one hand. "What did I do?"

"You didn't do anything. You didn't have to. They're

soldiers. They gossip, they make wild guesses, they come up with dirty songs. Usually all at the same time."

"About me? About you?"

"About everyone. I'm sorry. I ought to have warned you. It's not bad-natured, and none of them are judging us – it's just how they entertain themselves. You'll get used to it."

I was definitely not going to get used to it. "Maybe if you talked to them..." My voice trailed off. "That would just make it worse, wouldn't it?"

"Yes. And since there's nothing you or I can do about it now, it's senseless to allow it to influence your decision. If you're not comfortable bedding down here, I'll figure something else out. Otherwise, my tent is your tent." He bowed from the waist, waving his hand in an exaggerated, foppish movement.

I fiddled with my wolf tooth, still avoiding his gaze. "Well. Well, I... All right, then."

Luca tilted his head until he caught my eye. His quirked lips invited me to share the humour of the situation. Even though I wasn't sure I found it at all funny, my mouth curved upwards, and when Luca let out a soft laugh, I snorted.

The tent flap lifted. Arian walked in, face grave and concerned, mouth already open to speak. He stopped dead when he saw Luca's slightly flushed, grinning face, and his eyes shot to me.

The emotion that wrote itself on his face in that moment was so clear it made me ache. Arian had come to comfort his friend – but Luca did not need comfort. Luca did not need Arian. An eye-blink later the hurt and jealousy were gone, wiped away by his normal blank look. But it was too late. I had seen. And he knew it.

"What is she doing in here?" he asked, voice hard.

Luca's smile faded a bit. "Why shouldn't Frost be here?"

"For the love of the Mother, Luca!" Arian burst out, making me jump. "Why is she in this camp at all? She's not even pretty!"

Luca looked first astonished at the petulant remark and then furious. Again, I thought I saw an emotion – shame? – flicker over Arian's face for a second before he managed to hide it.

"We're not – it isn't like—" I stood up. I didn't want to be the reason for their anger and unhappiness. I had already caused far too much of both in my life. "I think I should go."

"You don't have to defend yourself, Frost," Luca said as he too got to his feet. "And you don't have to go anywhere. Arian, you're being incredibly rude. Even for you."

Arian shook his head in disbelief. "This is just like that time you decided to run the rope bridge over the waterfall. And the time you swore to me that hornet's nest was empty. And the time you promised me the old merchant was harmless. You have no concept of self-preservation at all! You act like you're immortal, like nothing could ever bring you down—"

"Not this again," Luca muttered.

"You don't know who this girl is! She's dangerous! She near as dammit killed both of us! She dug her way out of her cell with a spoon, led you a merry dance up and down the mountain—"

"And risked her life to save you and two innocent civilians."

"That doesn't mean you should bring her home with you! Why on earth would you want a half-mad foreign farm labourer with no training and no experience in the hill guard?"

"Because she's special," Luca said simply. "Before she even knew you, she twice put herself between you and a bandit, just because it was the right thing to do. 'People shouldn't have to be asked,' she said. That's the kind of potential you don't let slip away."

My face was on fire. I looked longingly at the door.

"You are not responsible for every stray that wanders across your path," Arian growled.

When Luca spoke again his voice was a whisper. "You're really going to stand there and tell me that? Where would you be right now if I hadn't taken responsibility for you?"

I waited for Arian to come back with another reminder

of how dangerous I was, but Luca's words seemed to have ended the argument. Arian's throat worked, and he looked down. Then, to my surprise, he turned his head towards me. With his eyes fixed firmly on the tent wall, he said, "I'm sorry. I was wrong to speak as I did."

I nodded hesitantly, accepting the apology.

"I know you're only trying to look to out for me," Luca said gently. "You've always looked out for me. But please stop worrying, my brother."

Brother? My curiosity twinged – could they really be brothers, looking as different as they did? Why hadn't anyone mentioned it? But I wasn't the slightest bit tempted to interrupt and ask questions. I felt as if a hurricane had swept into the tent and very nearly carried me off. Without Luca's intervention, it would have.

Arian clasped Luca's forearm. Then he walked towards the tent flap and pushed it up again. He stopped there, looking back at me.

I realized he was waiting for me to follow him out. My cheeks, which had just been starting to cool, throbbed with fresh heat. I was ready to go after him just to end the excruciating embarrassment when Luca said meaningfully, "Good night, Arian."

Arian nodded a curt "good night" to Luca and stepped outside. Luca stared at the tent flap for a long moment. Then his expression lightened. He turned to me, a mischievous glint in his eye. "Want me to see if I can charm a late dinner out of the cooks? We can have a night picnic and talk about your training."

Despite my embarrassment, I couldn't help grinning at his look of boyish glee. The cares that had weighed him down when he had first returned to the tent seemed to have vanished. "Lead on, Captain," I said.

We had only been in the new village a few days when I realized that the boy was following me.

I couldn't say how I knew. He never tried to talk to me, and only ever looked at me from the corners of his eyes. Yes, he always seemed to be wherever I was, but half the time he had already been at the grain store or the well before I arrived, and after all, it was a small village. People were bound to bump into each other.

The boy's name was Werrik. He was eighteen, a man grown by most people's standards, even with his long, awk-ward limbs and blemished face. Yet Werrik did no work. He laboured at no trade. The men did not take him with them hunting, nor did he till his rich, widowed mother's fields. She hired others for that. The women of the village twitched their skirts aside as he passed and whispered behind their hands – but the whispering always stopped as soon as Ma or I came near.

We were newcomers, practically foreigners, for all that Ma tended them and healed their children, and they would not share their secrets with us. It was not worth the chance that their words might get back to Werrick's mother who paid so many of their husbands' wages.

They watched me with pitying eyes, and said nothing.

I tried to tell myself that I was imagining things. I knew very well that I was plain, stocky and drab. Why would anyone follow me? Look at me, even? I could not bear to see the fear and worry in Ma's face, to force her to move on again when nothing had happened. So I kept the fear and worry for myself. And I prayed – not to the god of my people, the god who had forsaken me – but to my father's memory.

We stayed.

That day – a crisp, winter's day, frosty and clear, six weeks after we had come to the village – I had been sent out to pick a certain tree moss for one of Ma's chest poultices. The task was urgent. The miller, who was one of the village elders and the second richest person there after Werrik's mother, had been taken ill and begun coughing blood. There was a lot of money in it for Ma if she could ease him.

I kept to the outskirts of the wood, with the village in sight, and kept my eyes and ears sharp. But Werrik knew the forest far better than me. By the time I sensed him close by he was already upon me.

I do not want to remember.

I see it in my mind as a series of flashes, jumbled and disconnected, each one limned in darkness. Like fragments of a shattered pot whose edges will never fit together properly again, no matter how skilfully they are glued. Maybe this is the only way I can bear to have the memories in my head.

There is a flash of terror as I see the hungry shine in Werrik's eyes.

Keep quiet.

There is a flash of blurring trees and sudden pain lancing through my forehead as I try to dodge past him and he catches me and pushes me face down on the ground.

Keep out of trouble.

There is a flash of hands, boy's hands, thin and soft and bony, but strong as a man's, closing around my throat. Bruises throbbing on my skin. The shrill ripping noise of my shawl. The stink of sweat.

Don't fight.

There is a flash that fills my ears with the sound of my own screaming, that crushes me with the weight of Werrik on top of me, that makes my face go numb as he cracks my nose into the dirt. Blood spilling down my face.

And then my father's voice. There are no words in it this time, only a howl of rage.

Ice, tearing through my body, a flood of power and cold fury.

The Wolf took me.

I was glad. I was glad. I was glad.

Until the Wolf left me again. Left me there crouching over Werrik, my hands soaked in blood that was not mine, my torn dress scattered with white flecks of bone and other things, worse things.

Until I looked down at Werrik. At what was left of Werrik's face.

And it was too late then. Too late to say I had only wanted to stop him, to defend myself, to get away. Too late to take it back.

Fourteen

"What I want you to think about," Luca said, as he folded himself into a cross-legged position on the grass in the clearing behind his tent, "is the space around you. Try to think of it as … a bubble. A sphere, just large enough that, if you stretch out your arms, you can touch it with the tips of your fingers."

I pulled my legs more tightly underneath me and looked around at the clearing. The sky was overcast, and the day was humid. Sweat made me feel sticky and un-comfortable, even though all I had done so far was to walk out here and sit down.

"Are you ignoring me already?" Luca asked. "We haven't even started yet!"

"No – I'm trying but – I don't really understand this. How it will help me, I mean."

Luca's eyes narrowed thoughtfully. I tried not to fidget

under his piercing stare. "Your wolf, the 'curse' that you have, it stirs when you're wounded, yes? When you see your own blood."

I nodded reluctantly.

"Then the obvious course of action is to make you stronger, faster – a better fighter – and so less likely to shed blood in battle."

I nodded again, more eagerly this time.

"But that, on its own, won't deal with the real problem. We need to get to the root of what the wolf is, and why it responds that way to your blood. Maybe first – before we start work – it would help if you told me more about the wolf. What do you know about it? How exactly does it work?"

I sat silently for a little while, struggling to find words to explain the beliefs I had lived with all my life. "In– in Uskaand there are two gods," I began hesitantly. "The first is Askaan. The god of light and justice. He is the one they build temples to, the one they worship, the one they pray to. His domain is the world of humans and their spirits. He decides which children shall be born, and when everyone should die. The Other god is … is not a true god. That's what the Askaanian priests teach in their temples. They say he is the opposite of Askaan. A being not of divinity, but of darkness. Most towns have a priest of the Other, but they're there as a sort of … safeguard. To keep the Other out. No churches are built for the god of the Other. People don't pray to or worship him. They fear him. His name is never spoken. He is the god of wild creatures, of miscarried children, of disease and suffering. Some people call him the 'Wolf', because it's said when he comes to his priests in dreams that's the form he takes."

"So you believe your wolf is some aspect of a god? The god of the Other?"

"It sounds ridiculous when you say it like that. I don't know. A demon of the Other, maybe? I think that's what the priests said. But they also called it a curse. I wasn't able to ask any questions."

"I've already told you that I don't believe in curses. I definitely don't believe in demons. I'll tell you what I think. There have always been people who have lost control of themselves in battle. History calls them 'ber-serkers' – and you've used that word yourself, in fact. In the *Book of Rodica*, there's a famous hero called Sedrun. His family was killed before his eyes when he was a child. After that he was adopted into a new family and seemed to be perfectly normal, until a battle when he was in his early teens.

"When he saw one of his adopted kinsmen fall, he went into his first berserk rage. It's said that his face swelled to twice its normal size and glowed red, and his hair stood out around his head like spikes. He slaugh-tered the enemy. More than that, he slaughtered everyone in the enemy camp, even the camp followers, and wounded or unarmed men. He killed their animals and set fire to their tents. His own family didn't dare to go near him until the rage had dissipated. What does that tell you?"

"That he was a monster," I whispered, appalled.

"No," Luca said emphatically. "It tells you that Sedrun was so terrified of watching his family die again that his fear transformed him. Took control of him. He destroyed every person who could possibly have been a threat to the ones he loved. Once he had done that, he returned to himself."

"That doesn't make it all right," I protested. "How could he live with himself? He did such terrible things!"

"Sedrun's family called him a hero. They had been losing, and he saved them. After his display, very few people dared to attack them again. That's not the point, though. What I'm saying is that his berserker rages were linked to fear, to self-preservation. And I think yours are too. You say that the wolf takes control when it sees your blood. For you, the sight of your own blood is the trigger that causes your fear to become overwhelming. We need to teach you to accept that fear and control it. Once you've done that, you will be able to accept and control the wolf."

"But—but I don't *want* that. I don't want to accept the Wolf. It's horrible, it's evil. I want to get rid of it."

"I don't know if that's possible," Luca said gently. "The wolf is a part of you."

My fingers tore at the rough grass under my legs. "It isn't. It isn't a part of me. I'm not like that."

"Listen, there may be others out there who can do more for you, who can … lift the curse, or whatever you call it. You don't have to give up hope of that. But, for the moment, I can try to help you control your berserker rage. That's better than nothing, isn't it?"

I looked up from my handfuls of uprooted grass. He was offering me more help and understanding than any-one ever had. I had to believe in him. "Of course. I'm sorry, I didn't mean to be ungrateful."

He pulled a disgusted face. "I don't want gratitude! I just want you to listen to me and try this. Can you please do that?"

"I can try."

"All right, then. Now, you might not understand the significance of what I'm talking about this minute," he said patiently; "but it is important. I want you to close your eyes. In your mind, create a sphere – the sphere of space surrounding you. Feel it. It's yours. Everything inside it belongs to you, every speck of dust, every breath of air."

A ring of space that enveloped me? Like a shell of light? It would be … bright. A bright, silvery blue, shining like starlight on snow. *Cold.* I shivered. There was a squawk and a flutter – birds fighting overhead. My brain seized on the sound, wanting the distraction.

I took another deep breath and forced myself to focus on the soothing rumble of Luca's voice: "... Breathe in slowly. Now out. Breath in. Out. Feel your breath. Feel your body, the weight and strength of it. Feel the life in your body, the light that lives inside you. Try to see it in your mind."

The light inside me would be like the light of the sphere. Blue, bright. I could almost feel the chill. The sensation was strangely pleasant in the damp humidity of the day.

"... See the light flowing through your veins, in your fingertips, your face, your lungs, your legs. Breathe in. Breathe out."

I imagined myself flooded with the steady silvery-blue light. It felt startlingly real. I almost believed that if I were to open my eyes, I would see the icy glow showing through my skin, lighting me from the inside out.

"You have doubts and fear. They give you a sick, clutching feeling in your chest and stomach, don't they? Those feelings are a shadow inside you, a darkness that muffles the light. Take a deep breath, and suck that shadow, all that darkness, down, deep into the pit of your stomach. Can you see it?"

I nodded. As I breathed in, I could see the long, tangled threads of darkness unravelling from the delicate tracery of veins and bones; I was drawing it away from where it blocked out the silvery light. It gathered in the centre of my body. The negative emotions – anger, fear, sorrow, pain – struggled and fought there, clenching together like a black vaporous fist.

"... Take another deep breath. Now breathe out, long and slow, and imagine that darkness, all those feelings, flowing up out of you, flowing away."

I felt the choking blackness travel up out of my throat with my breath; I saw it fill the air like smoke and burn away, torn to rags by the air and the light. The light flowed into the space left behind and flared with new brilliance. For a moment I saw the rippling colours of the Mother's Fire there: green and purple and vivid turquoise and silver. But the flames had no heat. The silvery-blue light and the peacock shades danced together, beckoning, drawing me in. I wanted to let go, to lose myself in the light…

Another shiver travelled through my body, making my fingers and toes twitch.

My daughter...

My eyes flew open and I slapped my hands flat on the wiry grass. I stared down at them. They were brown. The grass was green. My breath did not cloud in the air. I was safe. I had to be safe.

Please, please, let me be safe.

"Are you all right?" I hadn't heard him move – I never did – but suddenly he was kneeling next to me, one hand coming to rest lightly on my back. "What happened?"

What *had* happened?

It had to have been my imagination again, like last night at the fire. That was the only explanation. I was new at this and I'd become scared and ... and that was all.

"I don't know," I said, truthfully enough. "I saw the light, like you said. It was ... strange."

Luca rubbed my back: an absent, comforting gesture. Instead of shrugging away from that touch, I found I wanted to lean in it.

"That's a good sign," he said. "It means you went deep into yourself. I think you did well, especially for a first time."

His praise brought heat flooding into my cheeks, banishing the chill brought on by the strange trance. I ducked my head and found myself staring at the warm golden skin of his throat, revealed by his carelessly laced shirt. The muscles of his chest and arm bulged against the fine material of the garment. His touch on my back seemed to radiate warmth. Another shiver went through me, but it was not the cold that shook my body this time.

"Frost?"

I looked straight up into his eyes. Everything I was feeling must have shown on my face. I heard his sharp intake of breath.

His hand curled against the curve of my spine, fingertips grazing the bare skin above the waist of my breeches. I shuddered. He repeated my name, and this time ... this time it was different.

His face moved closer to mine. His breath was on my face. Then we were kissing, hot, moist lips clinging together. Unthinkingly, I pressed my body into his. The hand on my back fisted, drawing my shirt tightly across my breasts. I gasped, my own hands clenching on my knees, longing to touch him but not quite brave enough.

He released me so abruptly that I fell back on my heels. "I shouldn't have done that." His voice was low, almost harsh. "It isn't right."

The words fell on me like a sudden downpour of snow. In an instant I was transformed from a living, breathing girl into something frozen and cold. Shame made me feel physically sick; clammy sweat sprung up all over my body.

Oh, Father, what have I done?

"I'm sorry..." I whispered. My voice came out cracked and hoarse.

"Frost – Frost – I didn't mean—" He sounded distraught.

I shook my head fiercely. "I know."

"It's not your fault. I should have known better."

"Don't." I scrambled to my feet.

He rose too, putting out a hand as if to – what? Restrain me? Comfort me? Before his fingers could make contact, there was a conspicuous throat-clearing from somewhere near by. We both jumped. It was the first time I'd ever seen Luca taken by surprise – which only made me feel worse. We both turned to see Arian standing in the shade of the tent, his eyes fixed firmly on his boot-tips.

"Sorry to interrupt," he said, sounding anything but. "Two of the scouts have come back with number-reports for you, Luca. I thought you'd want to speak to them as soon as possible."

Luca seemed to hesitate. He did not look at me. Then he nodded decisively. "You're right. Where are they?"

"I sent them to Livia. They took a tumble down a rock face on the way back. Nothing serious, but they both have some bruises and scrapes I thought it best to have seen to."

"Good thinking. I'll … go then." He turned to look at me. I fixed my eyes on the dirt.

"Could you take over for me here for a while?" I heard him ask Arian. "Test Frost's reflexes, show her some basic blocks?"

There was a pause, then a reluctant, "If you think it would be helpful."

"It would," Luca said firmly. "Frost, we're going to speak as soon as I've dealt with this."

I didn't respond. After a moment I heard him sigh. He walked away, leaving me and Arian alone in the clearing.

The quiet stretched out. Humiliation made my belly clench. Arian must have seen what had happened. He must have. His promise to Luca to teach me was nothing more than a way to get Luca away from me, I was sure. I waited for the sound of his footsteps leaving.

Arian cleared his throat again. "All right. Take up a defensive position."

I raised my eyes from the ground. "Wh–what?"

"Do you have cloth for ears? Get ready to defend yourself."

The look in his glacial eyes was annoyed and impatient, but there was no trace of gloating or – worse – pity. He was serious. Slowly, my limbs stiff and heavy, I arranged myself with feet braced a shoulder-length apart. Arian moved to stand opposite. He looked at me critically and then grunted in what could have been approval or disparagement.

"Block!" His fist shot towards my face.

I jerked back just in time, arms wheeling for balance.

"I said block, not dodge," he snapped.

"I d–don't know how." I held my hands up in protest. My emotions were already in turmoil and I was mortally afraid I was going to cry.

He spun, one leg flying out in a lethal, fluid movement.

I darted away again. "I said, I don't know how!"

There was no mistaking the contempt on his face now. "I'm not Luca. You can drop your lost, helpless little girl act."

"What are you talking about?" I edged warily away from him.

He followed. "I haven't forgotten how you fought in that valley, even if he has. I know how strong and fast you are. I've no intention of standing here pretending to teach you what you already know."

Luca had not told Arian the truth about me and the Wolf then. I didn't know whether to be grateful for his discretion or worried that he'd kept my curse a secret from the man who he called his brother. Maybe he was already regretting asking me to come here.

If wasn't before, I bet he is now. I had made both of us ridiculous, practically throwing myself at his feet when he had only meant to be a friend to me. *Oh Father, when did I get so stupid?*

Arian lunged at me again and my thoughts scattered in alarm. I turned to run.

He grabbed me from behind, wrapping both his tree-trunk arms around my midriff and pinning my hands to my sides. His breath panted against the side of my face. I tried to shrug him off, but his grip on my forearms only tightened.

Stay quiet. Don't fight. Stay out of trouble.

"Break my hold," he growled in my ear. "Go on. Show me what you can really do."

A worm of panic squirmed through me. "This is stupid. Just let me g–go."

"Your play-acting doesn't impress me. If you want me to let go, make me."

I stamped on his foot and heard his pained wheeze as I ground my full weight down on his toes. But his grip didn't loosen.

"You'll need to do better than that."

I snapped my head back. He shifted just in time to avoid a broken nose.

"That's more like it," I heard him say distantly. There was a hint of warmth, maybe even satisfaction, in his voice now, and that sent my fear surging to a new peak. He was enjoying this. His grip tightened; his lower body was pressing into mine. For an instant I felt as if were on the ground, a heavy body crushing me. I tasted stale sweat on my tongue.

Don't fight.

No, no, not again, not again.

My last thread of control snapped. I thrashed and kicked, throwing my weight forward, head whipping from side to side. I thought I felt him shifting a little, bracing himself against my struggles. I thought I heard him speak. But I was too far gone to take note.

Stay quiet. Don't fight. Stay out of trouble.

I screamed.

Arian's grip loosened at the exact moment that Luca and Livia walked around the corner of Luca's tent. I fell to my knees and scrambled away from Arian, images from my past flashing before my eyes and mixing dizzily with the present.

The blood.

Livia's flushed, furious face, her voice raised, the words running together with anger.

The blood in my mouth. In my hair, on my dress. Flecks of bone, of wet, grey matter. All over me. I could taste it. Father, Father, please help me.

Luca leaned over me, reaching out, and I cringed away from him. His face went white, eyes turning into dark holes of rage. He stalked across the clearing to where Livia faced Arian, drew his fist back and knocked Arian down with one blow.

My hands. My hands were covered in blood. I scrubbed them down the front of my dress, but the dress was sodden too. It wouldn't come off. Too late. Too late to take it back.

I didn't mean to.

"Frost?" That was Livia's voice, quiet now, and gentle. I looked up, blinking away the vision of red, to see her crouched before me. "You're all right. It's all right. No one's going to hurt you."

"I don't know what happened," I heard Arian say, low and shaken. "I just … I don't know…"

Arian was sat on the ground. Luca towered over him, hands fisted. Arian's hands were open, held out in front of him, and he was staring at them as if they didn't belong to him.

As if they were covered in blood.

He looked up at me. He seemed as shocked as I felt.

"Just ignore him," Livia said, helping me up. "Luca will deal with him. You come with me. You'll feel much better after a cup of tea."

Behind me, I heard Arian's whisper, "I didn't mean to."

I stared down at my own hands. They were clean, faintly stained at the tips with green grass sap, but I could see the blood. I could still feel the blood.

I didn't mean to...

Fifteen

Livia has turned Luca from her tent four times. On the first and second occasions I had still been shivering, wrapped in a blanket despite the heat and clutching a strong mug of aniseed tea in shaking hands. She hadn't even asked me, had just driven him off with a few forceful words.

By the third time Luca came, it was late afternoon. I had shrugged out of the blanket and was sitting cross-legged on the floor, half-heartedly sorting dried herbs into muslin bags. Livia gave me a quick, questioning look, and took my fierce head shake as all the encouragement needed to oust him again.

When I heard his voice outside the tent the fourth time, it was coming on to evening and the light was fading. Before going to the tent flap, Livia reached out very slowly and carefully, and touched my hand. "You'll have to face him sometime, if you're to stay. You don't have to worry that he'll make excuses for Arian – he just wants to apologize for allowing that situation to occur. And you might feel better for hearing it."

I shook my head once more. Livia sighed, but didn't argue. She stood outside the tent talking to Luca for some time. I guessed she wouldn't be able to get rid of him so easily again. He was getting concerned.

Livia had understood immediately what had happened to me in the clearing, and won my gratitude by holding back the questions that were obviously burning her tongue. I guessed that she had just as many shadows in her past as I did, and Arian had managed to blunder into those too, at some point. It had been clear from the first that she disliked and distrusted him. She probably thought I was refusing to see Luca because I was still shaken and angry with him for leaving the two of us alone together like that. Angry about his failure to control his friend and lieutenant. But in truth, I had shed the fear caused by Arian's actions shockingly quickly. Maybe it was because I had long practised forcing such memories back into that tangled knot of darkness under my ribs.

Or maybe it was because I had seen Arian's devastated face after Luca had knocked him down and the way he stared at his own hands, as if they belonged to someone else.

He hadn't meant to hurt me. He had meant to challenge me. He thought of me as a rival, a dangerous unknown who had somehow come too close to his brother – maybe even too close to Arian himself. I could see why. In almost no time I had succeeded in surprising him in his vulnerable state at the forest pool and caused an argument between him and Luca. Then he had seen that scene between Luca and me, and it must have seemed like I was already causing Luca pain. Who knew what damage I might do if I was allowed to stay any longer? His remarks had made it clear that he was sure I was hiding my true self. He had meant to force me – the snarling, powerful wolf he believed was me – out into the open. I don't think it ever occurred to him that he had the power to frighten me, that I was weaker than him, that I could not fight back even if I wanted to.

By the time he saw that he was wrong, it was too late. He couldn't take it back.

I, of all people, knew how that felt.

Arian might be dangerous. In fact, I was sure he was. But he was not sadistic. No one who took pleasure in hurting others could have looked so shocked and ill when he realized what he had done to me. He might not ever be my friend, but I thought I understood him a little now – and in understanding, I could let go of the fear.

The real reason I made Livia send Luca away was far less worthy.

I had kissed him, and he had recoiled from me. Just now, I never wanted to face him again.

Livia was right, though. If I was to stay here, I *would* have to face Luca, and soon. Anything else was cowardly, and too foolish for words. I had made an idiot of myself – but the very fact that Luca kept coming back to the tent meant he must have forgiven me for it. The trust and friendship that had sprung up between us when we had gone after those bandits, when he had given me the chance to run and I had followed him instead, couldn't just be thrown away. I couldn't destroy the first real hope I'd had in years.

I still believed in him.

I had to push those treacherous feelings down, knot them up with the dark memories and ignore them so that no one, especially not Luca, ever suspected they were there.

When the singing started outside, I saw the torn, longing expression on Livia's face. "You can go if you want. I'm all right," I said.

She gave me a considering look, the expression exaggerated now by the lamplight's black shadows. "Why don't we both go to the gathering? You know you're welcome."

"I'm not really in the mood for singing. And I'm not going to run off if you leave me alone, so don't worry."

Her eyes flicked away guiltily, and I knew I had got it right. Luca must have made her promise to keep an eye on me.

"I'm going to Luca's tent to wait for him. You're right. I need to get it over with. Thank you," I said, climbing to my feet, "for being so kind."

She got up too and placed both hands on my shoulders, leaning forward to plant a motherly kiss on my cheek. It took an effort to hold myself still, but less of one than before. I was getting used to Livia.

"No thanks necessary," she said. "Now, off you go."

I forced a smile for her as she extinguished the lamp. Then we both left the tent. She headed towards the centre of the camp and the flickering lights and voices lifted in a sweet, cheerful song about a maiden setting impossible challenges for her beloved. A part of me wanted to change my mind and follow Livia, to envelop myself in that warmth and cheer. But I had no warmth or cheer of my own to offer. I didn't belong there.

Before I could take the first step towards Luca's tent, I felt a tingle of awareness lift the fine hairs on the back of my neck. I was being watched. I turned, searching the slope of the hillside above me. There was a dark shape there. A man was standing on the crest of a rock that jutted out from the trees. The distinctive, square lines of his back and shoulders were silhouetted against the emerging stars.

Arian.

I stared up at his shadow in the night sky. He was determinedly solitary and self-contained, isolated like me, by choice, from the flickering light of the Mother's Fire and the happy babble of voices there. Yet, just like me, something kept him from leaving. Something forced him to prowl the outskirts of life with the hill guards, never quite part of it, but never straying too far.

Luca bound Arian to this place and these people, exactly as he bound me.

I argued with myself as I turned away from the camp and began to walk towards the hillside.

Just because you think you understand him doesn't mean he feels the same about you.

You know he's dangerous, you know he acts without thinking. He's threatened you three times now.

He clearly wants to be alone. What do you think you'll achieve?

What are you even going to say to him?

The voice of common sense raged. I kept walking. I lost sight of Arian as soon as I entered the trees, but I didn't lose track of where I was going. It was as if the sheer loneliness of his self-imposed solitude drew me towards him: an exiled wolf, howling in the night.

As soon as I stepped from the trees that surrounded the outcropping of rock, I could see I had been mistaken about some things. He wasn't standing on the rock, but sitting. The height of the stone had misled me. His shoulders and back were slumped in an attitude of defeat, head bowed, just as it had been after Luca had knocked him down. The steadily brightening starlight showed me that he was sitting on his hands.

I didn't mean to...

I stared up at him, not quite daring to approach, but still feeling there was something I needed to do here. I didn't even know if he had seen me arrive. Should I call out?

"What do you want?" His gravelly question made me jump.

"To talk to you," I managed to say, with a fair assumption of calm.

"If you had any sense at all you'd stay far, far away from me."

The words were probably supposed to be threatening, but instead they reminded me of the sulky mutterings of a child who knows he has done wrong but can't think how to apologize.

I began to climb the rock, feeling carefully for the footholds in the dark. I pulled myself up, with a grunt of effort, to sit about a foot away from him, legs dangling over the edge of the rock, so that I could gaze down at the white and grey muddle of tents below and the pulsing glow of the Mother's Fire. From the corner of my eye, I could see him leaning away from me, the glint of starlight betraying his wide eyes.

"You make a lot of threats," I said. "Do you really enjoy frightening people that much?"

"No!" he snapped. He took a harsh breath, as if to say more, but the silence drew out, and when he spoke again, his rough voice was quieter. "I didn't mean to scare you. I know it's no excuse. But … I won't come near you again."

"Because Luca made you promise not to?"

"I'm not a monster." One hand came out from under his leg and rubbed at his forehead as if his head hurt. "Do you think he would have me here, have me anywhere near him, if I was? You ought to think better of him than that."

"Then why did you act that way earlier?"

I thought I'd guessed the answers, but I wanted to prod him to admit it.

"I don't *know*," he said, words like pieces of jagged rock grinding together. "I despise men who— I feel sick about what I did and I'm sorry. You won't believe it, but I am. My whole life I've tried to protect people, to make up for… My mother, she was only fourteen when I was born. A Sedorne raiding party had attacked the village. One of the men – some disgusting thug – raped her. Got her pregnant with me. Childbirth killed her. Heartbreak killed her. I have to live knowing that. I would never, never hurt a woman – hurt anyone – like that." He stopped, breathing ragged. Then he repeated, "I'm sorry."

I swallowed hard, feeling petty and cruel for goading him to confide in me. His past clearly hurt him very much. But at the same time I was glad. I had been right about him. It took me a minute to be able to answer. "I do believe you."

There was another long pause before he muttered gracelessly, "Thank you."

"Will you help me? Please?"

He lifted his head. "Help you how?"

"I want to learn how to defend myself."

"Luca's going to teach you that. He's the best teacher you could ever have."

"I want you to teach me things he can't. I'm tall for a girl, and I'm strong, but I know that I'm ... vulnerable. When I panic, my instinct is to run. Always to run..." I shook the memories away with difficulty. "And that's going to get me into trouble. It has in the past. I need to be stronger than that. Quicker, faster, and better prepared. I want you to push me, show me the dirty tricks – all the ways to bring someone down that Luca wouldn't need to learn."

He sounded almost amused when he said, "You assume I know dirty tricks?"

"You said yourself that Luca is honourable. He can afford to be, because he's so strong, so good. He fights fair. I won't always be able to. I don't think you've always been able to, either. Am I right?"

He sighed. "Seems like it. Bloody Luca."

Before I could ask what he meant, he rose to his feet, a square shadow against the stars again. He held out his hand to me. I hesitated for a second before taking it. His hand was harder than Luca's; the fingers that closed around mine were rough and square and blunt. He heaved me to my feet with no apparent effort, and let go of my hand immediately.

"Are we friends, then?" I asked.

"Comrades," he corrected. "Less likely to stab you in the back."

When I arrived at Luca's tent a little while later, he was already there waiting for me, sitting on his bed. He had clearly been to the river before coming back. His hair, dampened to the amber gold of good cider, hung loose around his shoulders and down his back. A fresh shirt was only laced halfway up, exposing a smoothly muscled chest, and his feet were bare.

He looked at me anxiously, concern and regret clearly visible in his face.

"I'm glad you came back. I was starting to get worried." There was no reproof in his voice, but I felt the need to apologize anyway.

"I went for a walk, to clear my head."

"Frost, about what happened earlier—"

"I've spoken to Arian. He's sorry, and it won't happen again. I think things will be all right from now on."

Both Luca's eyebrows shot up. "You've spoken to him? When?"

"Just now, when I was out walking."

"That's good," he said slowly. "I don't want you to

have to go through that again. But that wasn't the only thing I wanted to talk about."

"Please don't." I forced my face into a smile, and tried to make the words sound smiling too. "I know what you're going to say; I don't need to hear it. It was a strange moment, one that shouldn't have happened. I'm not here for that, and your … your friendship is very important to me. If it's all right, let's just forget it happened."

Something moved in the deep blue of his eyes – relief, or something else? – and was veiled immediately. He looked away. "Of course. Thank you. Then we'll start training again tomorrow?"

I nodded. "I'd better get some sleep."

Without waiting for an answer, I retreated behind the carved-wood screen and pulled it out so that it concealed me completely. I waited until he had called good night and put out the lamp. Then I buried my face in one of the furs he had given me, and cried.

Sixteen

My life with the hill guard – as *one* of the hill guard, albeit a trainee – settled into a routine very quickly. Every now and again I would stop what I was doing, suddenly breathless, to look around in disbelief at how suddenly my life and all that I knew had changed.

There were other times when everything that had come before – the lifetime of hunger, hurts and hard scrabble – seemed like nothing more than the sore scratchiness of a fading nightmare.

I couldn't decide which sensation disturbed me the most.

I was surprised, and happy, to find that Arian did not try to shirk on our deal. He would have had reason enough. Although the hill guards' main mission of capturing the rebel leaders – including Luca's brother, about whom I had still learned nothing – was in temporary abeyance while they waited for reinforcements, Arian was just as busy as Luca. Sometimes more so, since he was responsible for more of the day-to-day running of the camp. It was him who collected the reports, sent out the scouts, marked maps, organized sentry and other duty shifts, and ordered supplies. But most days he would appear at some point, dragging me away from whatever I had been doing to put me through drills that were far less formal and much more stressful than the ones Luca had devised for me.

"And if I grab you here, what's your first instinct?" Arian asked, his right hand taking a firm hold of my left forearm.

"I would ... hit you," I said hesitantly, trying not to look at the small crowd of hill guards who had gathered around the sparring area to watch.

Arian rolled his eyes up to the sky, as if begging for guidance. "Hit me *where*?"

I made my right hand into a fist and mimed punching Arian's right arm, just above the bony point of his wrist.

"Good. That's better than trying to twist your arm away. But if you hit me here or here" – he took my fist with his free hand and guided it to a point on the inside of his arm, just above the elbow, and then to another point next to the round ball of muscle at the top of his shoulder – "you would make my whole lower arm go numb. I'd be forced to let you go, and my hand would be useless for a couple of minutes at least. Try it."

"Really hit you?" I asked, appalled. Someone in the crowd snorted with laughter.

"Yes, *really* hit me," Arian said, with surprising patience. "How else will you learn? Go on."

I blew out a breath, drew my fist back and shoved it gingerly at the place Arian had shown me. Before the blow could connect, he seized my hand again.

"Too slow," he said. "Because you hesitated, you lost the chance to get free from me simply and easily. What do you do now?"

I tugged hard on my arms, testing. In this situation, Luca would have let go immediately; Arian's grip tightened, not enough to hurt but enough to make it clear that I wasn't getting away.

"I'd kick you," I said decisively. "I'd aim … you know … between the legs. Most men panic when you do that."

"Good. Try it."

"Really?"

"Frost!" Livia's exasperated cry came from somewhere in the crowd. I jumped. I hadn't realized she was among the watchers. "Do you know how many people in this camp would kill for a free shot like that? Just do what he says!"

As the other hill guards dissolved into laughter, I braced myself and kicked out, aiming my boot at the junction of Arian's thighs.

Quick as a flash, he shifted and instead of connecting with him, my foot hit only air. Suddenly he was right up against me, his feet between mine, my arm folded up behind my back.

"Once again you hesitated and lost your chance. Now what?" he asked.

I concentrated on keeping my breathing slow and even as panic squirmed in my chest. *This is why you wanted him to teach you*, I reminded myself. *You need to learn to deal with this.*

"Should I tell you, or just do it?" I asked, surprised that I didn't stutter.

"Do it," Arian said.

I nodded – and jerked my head forward. Arian jumped out of the way just in time avoid the headbutt, releasing my hands. The watchers applauded. Livia let out a piercing whistle.

Arian's expression didn't change, but his eyes lit up with approval, like a smile that didn't reach his lips. "Good. But you've only got me to let go for now. I'm going to keep coming at you until you put me down."

He reached for me again. I jumped to the side, avoiding his hands, and stamped, intending to crush his foot. But his foot wasn't there any more. He pivoted and grabbed me from behind, wrapping his arms around me in a bear hug. His body pressed against my back. It was the same position that had made me panic before.

"All right?" he asked, too quietly for anyone else to hear.

I nodded. My heart had sped up, but for the moment I had control.

"Then show me how you would break this hold."

My upper arms were pinned to my sides, but my fore-arms and hands were free. It took another deep breath for me to gain the courage to squirm around until I could get one hand behind me and—

Arian let go instantly and leaped back. His eyes had gone wide and his mouth was agape.

Under cover of the hooting and applause from the other hill guards – Livia was doubled up, choking with laughter, face bright red – I said, "Didn't think I'd dare, did you?"

"I'm just thankful you didn't have a knife," he said, folding his arms. "The lesson here is supposed to be that you have to avoid getting caught by a stronger fighter. Use your speed. Use your wits. Just make sure they don't get hold of you. If someone does, aiming for the ... uh ... sensitive areas is a good strategy. Let's start again."

"Can I interrupt?"

I turned to see Luca standing on the edge of the spar-ring ground.

Arian's arms dropped to his sides. He nodded at Luca wordlessly and walked away. I watched him go with re-gret as the rest of the crowd dispersed, still catcalling and laughing. There was a stiffness, a distance, between him and Luca. They still weren't comfortable with each other. It was my fault, but I couldn't figure out how to fix it.

"What do you need me for?" I asked Luca, trying to sound cheerful, normal.

He grinned mischievously, taking me by surprise. I couldn't help smiling back, and my own internal tension eased a little.

"I've got a surprise for you."

"What kind of a surprise?"

"It would hardly be surprising if I told you, would it?" he said. "Come and see."

He led me back to his tent, and held the flap open for me to enter. "Notice anything ... new?"

I looked around. My little corner was as I had left it that morning: furs and blankets neatly piled up, screen drawn back. Luca's bed was carefully made as normal. The chairs, the rugs, the tapestries, were all as they had been. The table...

There was an axe on the table. A wooden axe.

I stepped closer, fascinated. It was fashioned from some light, nearly grainless wood that had been sanded until it was smooth and shining. It was almost the same shape as my father's axe, which Luca had taken away from me on the first day I had begun training with a practice sword. The wooden axe's curved blade and sharp pick had been cushioned with wrappings of cloth. It looked like something you would give to a child. A very big, very *violent* child.

"I–is this for me?"

"You've been progressing well in the drills with sword and staff, but I know you love your axe. This way you can practise without risking your – or anyone else's – safety."

"I don't know what to say." My hands reached out, but hovered just above the object.

"You can touch it," Luca said, stepping past me and picking it up with one hand. He held it out for me to take.

I nearly dropped it. The thing was at least three times as heavy as Da's axe, and that was made of oak, with steel blades and reinforced with iron.

"It's weighted," Luca said.

"Oh? I hadn't noticed!" I grunted, heaving it back up with both hands this time.

"We made the stave hollow, and filled it with lead. It will help to develop your fighting muscles and increase your speed – for when you use your real axe," Luca said. "Don't you … I mean – do you like it?" I thought there was the faintest trace of disappointment in his voice.

Happiness broke through the surprise and I turned to look at him, cheeks aching with the width of my smile. "Of course I do. I just – I can't believe you went to so much trouble! Can I practise now?"

Luca laughed, relief clear on his face. "I don't see why not."

After that, axe practice was added to the sword and staff drills that I did with the rest of the hill guard. It was the most demanding of all the training I did. At first, five minutes wielding the weighted axe was enough to leave me gasping, arms trembling and weak, back on fire. But I was used to hard work, and with good food and plenty of rest each day I adjusted with nearly unnatural speed. If some of that was the Wolf's doing, I tried to ignore it.

My shoulders and upper arms had began to bulge against the fabric of my uniform shirts. The second morning that Luca heard me cursing and muttering as I strove to pull breeches on over legs that had become solid with muscle, he took me back to Atiyah and had her measure me again. Her cursing and muttering as she realized she would need to adjust my special suit of armour put mine to shame.

"Too slow!" Luca said, his wooden practice sword knocking lightly against my collarbone. He always pulled his blows so as not to hurt me, but still, the impact made me grunt.

Droplets of sweat flew everywhere as I shook my head. "I can't get that pass right. I don't know why. I always hesitate on the upswing. I feel as if I'm going to lose the axe."

"You need to have more confidence," Luca said. He raised his arm, the muscles revealed by his sleeveless tunic bunching as he wiped a thin sheen of moisture off his forehead. His hair was drawn back into a high horse-tail today, to keep it off the nape of his neck. The skin on his shoulders, the bridge of his nose and his cheeks was burning a deeper gold under the midday sun. Summer was coming, and the heat had driven off all the spectators to our sparring, even Livia, who tended to hover around as if I were a baby chick that might be crushed at any moment.

"The problem is that you're holding yourself back. You won't lose control of the axe – you just need to *believe* that. Start again, slowly this time. Follow the pattern, let your movements flow."

I shrugged my shoulders resignedly, then stepped forward to began the drill again.

Axe diagonally across the torso to counter Luca's overhand swing. Twist sideways to avoid a body kick. Axe down to deflect a gut thrust. Spin to gain momentum for a neck blow. Turn again when the neck blow is deflected, this time jabbing at the face with the head of the axe. Catch Luca's practice blade on the pick of the axe. Shift weight to the back foot and *heave*—

Luca's sword went flying.

"Keep going!" he shouted as I froze, staring at the fallen sword in disbelief. "Finish the pattern."

I gulped, swinging my axe in a double-handed crescent cut that, even with the wooden blade, would have the power to break Luca's neck. I stopped the blow an inch from connecting, and brought the axe back to guard position.

Luca grinned. One arm snaked around and caught my shoulder, tugging me towards him for a brief hug. I turned sideways to avoid poking him with the axe and ended up mashed awkwardly into his chest, the tip of my nose brushing the soft fair hair at the base of his throat. The smell of honeysuckle and warm skin made my breath stop in my throat.

"That's how it's done," he said, voice rumbling through me.

Then he let go. I allowed the head of the axe to drop and stared down at it, pretending a fascination with the cloth-wrapped pick as I muttered, "I need to speed up."

"Eventually, but if you can get it right slow, then getting it right fast is just a matter of practice. You know what I'm going to say now, don't you?"

"Yes." I felt the heat in my cheeks fading as we went back to safe, businesslike talk. I brought the axe back up into guard position as Luca bent to get his sword. "Start again from the beginning."

"Good girl," he said. "You're learning."

In addition to the rigorous physical training, I spent at least an hour every day sitting in the clearing behind Luca's tent, slipping into the strange trance-like state that Luca thought would allow me to gain control of the Wolf. This soon became my least favourite part of the day.

"Your body is full of light," Luca said. "Imagine it pushing out through your pores, drifting in the air around you, filling the sphere. Can you see it? Nod if you can."

I nodded. I could *feel* the light pressing through my skin, silver filaments, fine as hair, piercing the air around me like rays of icy starlight. I shivered. Any moment now—

Saram. My daughter.

I had learned not to gasp, not to snap my eyes open and check for colours. I blocked out the inner voice by concentrating on the itch forming at the small of my back, where sweat was starting to dampen my new uniform shirt. On the tiny strand of hair that had worked free of my braid and was tickling my face. I listened for noises in the camp, sorting through the distant voices and putting names to the ones I knew. My awareness of the silver-blue light faded, and the Wolf's traitorous, lying voice faded with it.

I peeked under my lashes at Luca and saw that he was staring at me, brows furrowed. I hadn't noticed when he had stopped talking. I squeezed my eyes shut again.

"I think that's enough for now," he said, after a moment. "Come back."

I opened my eyes, feeling guilty as I blinked and yawned, pretending I really was waking from a deep trance. Luca sat in silence as I stretched out my arms and legs, then he asked, "Did you see or hear anything today?"

I concealed my startled jump with another yawn. "Hear anything? Hear what?"

"I don't know. I hoped that some inner part of you would start to make itself known. That you would feel or sense or *remember* something that would help us to understand your berserk rage."

Don't let him see it. Don't let him see the lie…

"All I see is light," I said, a little stiffly, filling my mind with thoughts of smooth grey river stones to try and keep my face blank. "Just bright, silvery-blue light, like before. I don't hear anything."

Luca stood, offering me his hand. The day was hot, but my skin was icy cold, so I acted as if I had not seen the gesture and hopped to my feet unaided. By the time I was upright, he had dropped his hand, and was giving me that same searching look.

"If you do remember, or feel anything, no matter how odd or frightening it might seem, you will tell me, won't you? Even if it seems foolish. It's important."

I hesitated for a second, wanting more than anything to spill out my worries to him. *It's the Wolf I see and hear. It's the Wolf that's making itself known. I'm afraid we're making things worse.*

But I couldn't do it. Luca honestly believed that this was the way to help me. How was I supposed to confess to him that when I went into myself, the Wolf was all I found? I didn't even want to admit that to myself. The Wolf was a curse. A demon. A killer. Every bad thing that had ever happened to me and my mother had been the

Wolf's doing. It was not a part of me. It couldn't be. If it was, then I ought to have burned nine years ago.

I was learning how to fight, and getting stronger and faster every day. My special armour, which would leave no chink for an enemy to penetrate and spill my blood, was nearly ready. For the first time I felt like I had a place, a good place, that was mine. If the price of keeping that place was faking my way through these sessions with Luca, then it was a price I was willing to pay. So I nodded, refusing to meet his eyes.

He sighed. "Maybe tomorrow."

Seventeen

Arian stood at the top of the steep, rocky slope, quarterstaff in hand. His eyes were narrowed against the sun, and his shoulders were tense with determination.

I looked down at my hands, clad in a pair of soft, flexible doe-skin gloves. The backs of the gloves, down to the wrist, have been reinforced with an elongated triangle of fine chainmail, and then covered in more leather. Atiyah had explained that this would allow me to deflect a blow without risking the skin beneath the leather. The knuckles had been reinforced with metal caps, padded on the inside. Leather vambraces, splinted with metal strips, buckled onto my forearms. Over the top of these I had a leather tunic which laced up at the sides and covered me to the elbow. The shoulder parts were made of many thin strips of leather; each had been reinforced with metal and curved, so that when I moved my arm they slid back.

At my throat, I wore a wide leather collar, strengthened with small metal studs. My trusty old boots, which had come with me from Uskaand, were the only thing of my own fit to be part of this outfit, and even they had been polished and oiled and fitted with new buckles.

Atiyah had washed the armour in a substance made of charcoal and oil, which gave it a bluish sheen, and tooled designs of frost and stars, intricate and spiralling, onto the breast-piece and vambraces. "The frost is for you. The stars are for good luck," she had explained. "The Mother watches over her own."

It would have been rude to point out that I was not one of the Mother's own. I hadn't taken part in a single one of the gatherings since the evening that Luca asked me to sing. Those strange, cold-looking flames unnerved me. Like Luca's teachings, they made me feel the Wolf's presence too keenly.

The armour was comfortable, surprisingly so, but it was heavy. Six weeks ago I would barely have been able to stand in it and even now I didn't know if I would be able to move fast enough to dodge Arian's stave.

Luca, who was seated cross-legged on top of a large boulder near the middle of the slope, noticed my apprehension. "We need to find out if there are any problems with the leathers, if they restrict or pinch you in a fight. And watching you spar with Arian will help me pinpoint any weaknesses in your technique, too. The object here is to disarm him without getting hurt."

"Are we standing around all day, or are we fighting?" Arian called from the top of the slope. "Come on! I promise not to break any bones."

"Yours or Frost's?" Luca called back, laughing. The two of them seemed to be getting back to normal, and I was glad. "Start whenever you want."

I took a deep breath, and began walking up the uneven ground towards Arian. I could feel his eyes tracking me: a leopard stalking a deer.

Suddenly he let out a battle roar and leaped downhill. The staff jabbed at my face. I spun sideways and the staff touched only air. Arian flipped the stave overhand. I ducked. He swept the staff at my legs two-handed. I leaped over the blow, landed on one leg, pivoted and finished up behind him. The ground slid and crunched underfoot, and dust clouded around us.

"Good!" Luca called. "Always try for the higher ground. But be more aggressive! You can only dodge for so long; get some hits in!"

Arian had already turned. Again he swiped at my legs with the stave. I jumped into a roundhouse kick, aiming for his head. He dodged back just in time. I landed on my other foot, ducked under the sweep of the staff and then kicked out sideways.

My boot thudded into Arian's stomach. He grunted and stumbled, struggling to find his balance as the dry ground slid away underfoot. I threw a punch, clipping him on the jaw. His head snapped back, but his staff came up. The metal cap drove into my stomach.

I reeled back with a grunt. My heel hit a hollow in the ground. I went down, sliding on my backside, a cascade of earth and small rocks rolling down the hillside ahead of me. Arian hastily got out of the way. I slapped both hands on the ground, rolled and came up plastered in dry earth that stung my eyes and clogged my throat.

"One each," Arian said. His eyes were shining – the look I had learned to think of as a kind of hidden smile. He was enjoying this. In a strange way, I was too.

I coughed up some dust and managed to gasp, "Wrong. Two for me."

"That little nudge with your fist doesn't count. You pulled it."

"He's right. One each," Luca shouted. "Less talking, more fighting."

Arian spun the stave one-handed, shifting his weight back onto his left leg. I watched warily, guessing he was about to try a jump-kick. I braced to move to the right. Then he charged, swinging his weapon overhand. Caught off guard, I hesitated a second too long to dodge. Instinctively I brought my left arm up to shield my head.

The staff hit my lightly armoured wrist with a thud.

The impact resounded through leather and metal into bone. I yelled, and my cry of pain, blurring in my ears, stretched out into a long, piercing howl. My right hand shot up without my leave. My fingers closed around the stave. I felt a pulse of cold.

Arian's weapon snapped in two with an echo like a lightning strike. The splintered pieces fell from his fists.

We both stood motionless. I stared at the broken staff on the ground and shivered. Slowly and fearfully I lifted my eyes to Arian's face. He was smiling, revealing a deep dimple in his left cheek that I had never noticed before. "Luca's been teaching you his tricks."

"I d—don't – um – what? You're not angry?"

His eyebrows knotted. "Why should I be?"

"B—because" – I took a quick breath – "I ruined your staff."

"I can always get a new one. Are you smashing rocks yet?"

"No." My legs were wobbly and my head was thick and stuffy. I couldn't make sense of his words. "Why would I try to do that?"

"Because I can," Luca said, walking up the slope towards us. "If I want to. Which I don't very often, because it's silly. What you did to Arian's staff was all part of the technique I've been teaching you, Frost. When you concentrate your body's energy, focus it and channel it, you can do extraordinary things." He gave me a brilliant, happy look. I could see the relief in it. "You've progressed further than I realized. I was worried ... but never mind now. Let me have a look at your arm."

"You don't have to—"

Arian cut me off. "That was a nasty blow. It needs checking."

Luca took my forearm between his hands and unbuckled the vambrace, easing off my glove. His long fingers deftly manipulated my hand, bending it back and forth. He stopped when I winced, and stroked his thumb carefully over a deep red mark that would no doubt be a spectacular bruise later. My breath caught. I hoped that he hadn't noticed.

"No sharp pain or grinding," he said at last. "We'll get Livia to give you some of her bruise salve, but other than that, the armour worked."

"Good. Then I can scrub this dust away," Arian said, as he bent to pick up the two halves of what had been his weapon. Dust billowed off him, and he shook his head and made a sound of disgust. "Whose idea was it to fight up here? Some person who thinks he's terribly clever?"

Luca slapped Arian cheerfully on the back. More dust flew. "Oh, stop complaining. You're worse than a cat. As soon as you get a new staff..."

The two headed down the hill. I followed slowly, grateful to have a moment to think about what had happened without either of them watching me.

I clenched and flexed my injured hand. The pain in the joint was already fading, along with the red mark.

I turned over the glove I had been wearing. There was a thin coat of moisture on the leather. Sweat? If I had checked sooner, would I have seen frost there?

My teeth ground together. *No.* It was impossible. There hadn't been any blood.

At that moment, Luca glanced back over his shoulder at me. His smile banished the chill of fear.

"Hurry up," Arian called. "My back is one big itch."

Father, help me to control the Wolf. I have to.

Half an hour later I stood waist deep in the river, watching soap suds turn grey with rock dust and float away. A couple of other women were washing near by – they sent me friendly smiles, which I returned absently. I wasn't in the mood to talk, but it was nice to feel that I could, if I wanted to. I ducked under the water to rinse my hair, and emerged just as a shrill whistle rang out. Three short bursts. The other women started wading quickly towards the bank.

"What does it mean?" I called out.

"It's the sentry alert," one of them shouted. "Large body of strangers approaching."

I splashed after them, all three of us gaining the bank at the same time and running to where we had left our clean clothes. I yanked on my breeches as the other women fumbled with theirs.

"The rebels?" I asked breathlessly, shoving damp feet

into my boots. I didn't wait for an answer but pulled on my leather jerkin, seized the wooden bucket someone had left there – not a perfect weapon, but better than nothing – and raced up the bank.

I bolted past the wooden outbuildings and the mess tent. The other hill guards were drawing weapons, grabbing armour. I should be doing the same, but I needed to find Luca first. If the camp was under attack I knew he would be right at the front, leading his men into battle, with Arian beside him. And the ones at the front were always the first to die.

"All clear! Stand down! Stand down!"

That was Luca's voice. I skidded to a halt. All around me I heard sighs of relief and the silken sliding noises and soft snicking of blades going back into sheaths.

Luca was leading a group of men and women – Rua and Sedorne, some of them on foot, others leading horses laden with bulging saddlebags – into the camp. They were dressed in plain, hard-wearing clothes and a coat of travel dirt. I had never seen any of them before in my life, but they somehow had a familiar look, both cheerful and formidable.

The men and women of the hill guard ran forward to greet the newcomers, calling out names and embracing the strangers like long-lost friends.

Luca's reinforcements had finally arrived.

Eighteen

Looking around me, I guessed that there were at least fifty new soldiers joining the hill guard. Our numbers had been strengthened by a full third. Luca must be overjoyed. He certainly looked it. He stood, grinning and laughing, right in the middle of the crowd of new arrivals. I felt the familiar warm tug in my chest, a reaction I couldn't seem to control. I opened my mouth to call out – and froze as I saw that he was embracing a woman.

She was short and dark-skinned, with a tattoo covering most of the left side of her face; her hair was braided in dozens of zigzagging rows. A wide, beautiful smile lit her face as she drew back from Luca's hug and rose on tiptoes to kiss him hard on the lips.

The wooden bucket fell out of my hands. I jerked my gaze down, my chest tightening agonizingly. I wheezed around the pain and turned away so that I could run from the scene. Before I could take a step, Luca called my name.

I tried to arrange my expression into something blank, neutral. *River stones. River stones.* I looked up to see him coming towards me, his arm around the shoulder of the dark-skinned woman. I remembered times when he had held me in just such a way, and how it had made me feel. Did she feel the same way now? What about him? He had not flinched away when *she* had kissed him.

Of course not. She was not an exile, a homeless wanderer, a raggy scrap picked up out of pity. She was beautiful.

Please, oh, please, Father, don't let any of this show on my face.

"Frost, this is Hind," Luca said. The happiness in his voice made me feel as if I had been kicked by a mule. "She's the leader of this motley band the king has sent us. Hind, this is my – Frost. She's only just joined us, but she's going to be one of our best. Say hello."

I made a little bow, then forced myself to hold my hand out to the other woman politely in the way that I had seen other hill guards greet one another. "Nice to meet you." My voice was barely above a mumble, but the hubbub around us was so loud, I hoped she wouldn't notice.

The woman – Hind – stepped away from Luca to take

my hand. I noted miserably that her hand was very small compared to mine. Delicate, but strong. Her clasp was firm. She was slender, compactly muscular. I felt hulking and awkward next to her, like a carthorse that had decided to get up on its back legs and don human clothes.

"It's nice to meet you too," Hind said. Her eyes travelled slowly up and down my body, assessing me. "My, but you're a big one, aren't you? What's your weapon of choice?"

"None of that," Luca interrupted, his smile fading abruptly. He caught Hind's hand and pulled her back, making her release me. "Let me introduce you to Adela. You two will get on very well. I'll see you later, Frost — stay out of trouble."

Luca plunged into the crowd, dragging a clearly reluctant Hind after him. Hind winked at me. I dropped my gaze again. The deep ache was spreading. Every part of me throbbed with it. I wanted to sink down onto the grass and curl up into a ball. *Why does it hurt so much? Why does it have to hurt?* I rubbed roughly at my breastbone, flicking the wolf tooth out of the way.

Finally I realized that I was standing conspicuously in the middle of the joyful, babbling crowd with my hair fluffing up around my face, dressed in hurriedly pulled on damp clothes. I bent down to pick up the dropped bucket and the chunk of soap that had bounced out of it, intending to retreat to Luca's tent and hide.

A blunt, callused hand got to the soap before me.

I stared at Arian blankly, blinked, then took the soap. "Thanks."

"You're welcome."

We both straightened up. I nodded at Arian and began to move past him. He made a restless gesture, as if he meant to catch my arm, then thought better of it. I halted, surprised.

He opened and closed his mouth. Finally he spoke: "He's known Hind for years. They're friends. That's all."

Before I could even try to think of a reply, he had walked off, leaving me speechless, my face burning.

The hill guard greeted Hind and her men like long-lost members of the family. The normal chores and activities of the day were cast aside. Tents were thrown open. Cook-fires were stoked up. Jars of ale and barrels of the potent honey-and-apple drink which the hill guard ordered by the cartload were brought out and uncorked. Food was carried from the mess tent, along with stools and blankets and boxes and anything else that could be used as a seat. As the light began to dim, a great blaze was built in the central firepit, and the musically inclined gathered around it. They played lively reels and jigs on drum, flute, spike-fiddle and bone-harp. Those hill guards who played no instrument pulled the new arrivals up to dance with them.

The clearing was filled with laughter and singing and the perfume of woodsmoke. Everyone was occupied with old friends. Livia, with whom I would normally have sought refuge, was seated near the fire in deep discussion with the new healer the reinforcements had brought – a tiny Rua woman who didn't look old enough to bake bread, let alone stitch up people's wounds. I found myself sharing a blanket with Luca, Arian and Hind. Hind and Luca talked and laughed, completely at ease, as they gossiped about people I had never heard of and Luca's old life at the palace. Even Arian, drinking ale for the first time since I had known him, put in an occasional comment or question.

I clutched at my wolf tooth and pretended that I was too interested in the music to talk. This was supposed to be a happy time. Everyone else *was* happy. But the sound of Luca and Hind's mingled laughter and the sight of Hind's hand resting casually on Luca's calf made me so angry and sad – and so ashamed of those feelings – that I felt sick. Just when I had begun to rely on things to stay the same, it was all changing.

Stupid. Things never stay the same. And you can't rely on anything. Luca let out a shout of laughter at something Hind had said and gave her one of his casual, one-armed hugs. *Or anyone.*

"Who's going to sing next?" Razia – a young hill guard that I knew slightly – cried out, staggering as she jumped up. "I know! Frost! You haven't sung for weeks. Come on, it's your turn now!" She rushed over to me and grabbed my hands, trying to heave me to my feet. I shook my head wordlessly, pulling my hands away.

"Frost!" Livia shouted from her place near the bonfire. "They're going to play 'The Falling Night'! That's your favourite, isn't it?"

I was surprised and pleased that Livia had noticed such a small, silly thing about me, but I shook my head again.

"*I'd* like to hear it. That's one of my favourite songs too," Hind chimed in. Something must have shown on my face; she back-pedalled quickly. "Oh, but not if Frost doesn't want to, of course."

"She's just a bit shy around strangers," Luca said, throwing me a smiling, conspiratorial glance, as if we were in on some joke together. For once I felt no temptation to smile back. Luca didn't seem to notice – he was looking at Arian now. "Arian and Frost should sing together."

Arian choked on his swallow of beer and turned a fulminatory look on Luca. Arian lifting his growly voice in a sweet love ballad like "The Falling Night"? No wonder he was glaring.

Luca ignored Arian's look and turned back to me. "You wouldn't be shy if you didn't have to sing alone, would you? You've never heard Arian sing, either. He's very good."

"He used to sing!" Razia said. "He sang for us at the Mother's Fire all the time before Frost…" Her voice trailed off.

There was an awkward silence. I felt as if a skin of ice were forming around me, separating me from everyone else. I looked down at my tightly clenched fists, certain that all the hill guards must be staring at me, either with pity or accusation. *Before Frost came*, Razia had been going to say. Hind cleared her throat as if to say something. I hunched my shoulders.

Arian sighed. "All right."

He reached out and took one of my hands. The rough skin of his calluses scraped against my palm and, with a powerful heave, he pulled me to my feet. There was no chance of resisting him as I had Razia. His fingers squeezed mine for a second before he released me. "They'll never shut up otherwise," he said. "You take the first verse, I'll take the second, and we can sing together in the chorus."

A slightly drunken cheer went up, as if that settled everything. Luca grinned. I let out a miserable huff of breath as I realized that continuing to refuse would only draw even more attention to me. Better to just get it over with. I followed Arian to the fire. Razia tottered after us and sank down next to the new healer. Livia gave me an encouraging wave.

We sat. I clasped my hands nervously between my knees, keeping my eyes away from the firepit. The flames

crackled and popped, red and yellow, like normal flames
– but I no longer trusted fire in this country. I fixed my
attention on the dancing shadow-shapes that the flames
cast on Arian's face. "You didn't have to, you know," I
mumbled to him.

A tiny smile twitched one corner of his lips. But his
voice was his normal flat, brusque growl when he spoke.
"Stupid. It's only a song." He nodded to the musician.

The man lifted his wood pipe and began to play the
first sweet, high trills of the love song.

I swallowed hard, cleared my throat and forced out
the first lines of the ballad.

> *"The falling night has cast your eyes*
> *In lights of blue with far-off stars.*
> *And in the dark, your arms are mountains*
> *To shelter me from the rising storm..."*

Another of the camp's musicians came in with a lute as
the chorus began, and a beautiful, deep voice took up the
words of the song, harmonizing perfectly with mine. It
was a voice I had heard before. The voice that had made
me hesitate as I had escaped from the hill-guard camp
that first night. The voice that had welcomed me when I
had found my way back. Arian's voice?

I gazed at his face as our voices entwined in the simple, beautiful words.

"Sweetling, storms may chase me
Snowflakes fall
But I will be safe in your heart.
Lightning crash
Waters flood
Yet I will be safe in your heart."

I closed my mouth with a snap and Arian carried on, moving into the second verse with the accompaniment of the lute and wood flute.

"The falling night has hid your bright hair
And stole away your shining smile.
But in the dark I feel your heart
And know it beats for me alone."

Arian nodded at me and I sucked in a breath – not even realizing that I had held it while he sang – and joined him in the chorus. *"Sweetling, storms may chase me…"* The flute rose in a final bright curl of notes as we fell silent, and the lute died away.

"You should sing together again," one of the musicians said, his voice hushed. "You suit each other."

There was a rustle of movement as Arian leaned towards me. "Frost…"

Luca appeared beside us, smiling. "You were wonderful. Come on. Quiet, everyone! I have an announcement!"

Taking me by the hand, he pulled me to my feet and lead me away from the fire. I glanced back once. Arian had stayed behind on his stool, staring into the flames.

The hill guards fell silent around us. Torches had been lit on the edges of the clearing now, and the faces around me flickered enigmatically with firelight.

"Weeks ago," Luca continued, raising his voice so that everyone could hear, "when Frost came here, she laid down her axe and traded it for practice weapons. I told her that she wouldn't be allowed to use it again until I felt sure she wouldn't hurt herself or anyone else with it."

There was a small ripple of laughter, which Luca ignored. He looked at me now, his dark eyes full of pride and warmth as he continued: "That axe had belonged to her father and to his father, and it was a noble weapon. I know that it took an immense leap of faith for Frost to put it to one side. But she did. And today, standing before us, we have a warrior who is fit to handle any weapon. I present Frost to you now, no longer as a trainee, but as the newest hill guard."

The hill guards whooped and clapped, stamping their feet.

Luca let go of me to reach behind him for a sackcloth bundle. He held it out, letting the rough material fall to the ground. "We've spruced her up a little. Sharpened her blades, replaced the rusting langets. Given her a polish. I hope you don't mind?"

I shook my head wordlessly. My hands reached out of their own volition, fingers curling slowly and reverently around the smooth wood of the stave. The newly gleaming wood felt as natural and familiar to me as my own arm or leg. Light moved across the twin blades, iridescent as ice on the surface of water. The weapon moved lightly in my hands, weighing nothing to me now. I spun it smoothly and then brought it diagonally across my body into guard position. A singing sense of rightness filled me. I had been parted from a piece of myself. Now I had it back, and it felt wonderful.

"Don't kiss it," Hind said teasingly. She had her arm around Adela. "Luca'll get jealous."

I frowned at the other woman, on the verge of deciding to seriously dislike her. But Luca distracted me by shouting, "I think this calls for more drinks!"

With a roar of approval, several hill guards hurried off to fetch out the last of the ale. Under cover of the renewed noise, Luca stepped closer.

"Frost..." He cleared his throat, suddenly unsure. Then his face cleared, as if he had found the answer to a puzzle. "Do you realize you're still covered in rock dust?"

I put one hand up to my face self-consciously. "Where?"

"It's in your hair, all over your face and neck – did you even bother bathing?"

"Of course I did! The alert sounded while I was in

the river." I ran my fingers over the quick and careless braid that I had pinned around my skull. Dust drifted down past my face and when I looked at my hand it was streaked with grey. I had dunked my head in the river, but the dust must have clung to my thick hair, and started flaking off as it dried. "Why didn't anyone tell me?"

"Maybe they thought you were ageing prematurely and didn't want to hurt your feelings," Luca said innocently.

I narrowed my eyes at him.

He laughed. "Come back to the tent and I'll help you brush it all off."

By the time that I, carefully carrying my axe, had reached the tent, Luca had already lit two lamps inside and was rummaging in the chest at the foot of his bed. I laid my axe carefully on my pile of furs. When I turned, I saw that Luca had laid a drying cloth on the floor next to the low table, and had a silver-backed bristle brush in his hand. Such a fine item had never been near my shaggy mess of hair before.

"This will get it out," he promised. "Come and sit on the cloth, and that way the dust won't get all over the rugs."

I smiled as I went to sit cross-legged on the edge of the towel.

"What?"

"Nothing. Only ... sometimes you can be a little ... motherly."

There was a long pause. I glanced over my shoulder at him. He was still by the bed, mouth hanging open. *"Motherly?"* he repeated.

I couldn't tell from if his voice if he was angry or just shocked. I shrugged, taking a little petty satisfaction in having wrong-footed him for once. "Sometimes. Can I have the brush now?"

"No," he almost snapped, coming to kneel behind me. "You can't see where the dust is."

A tiny laugh escaped my lips. I put my hand over my mouth. After a second I heard him laugh too, if reluctantly.

"Any more jokes like that and I'll make you go and dunk in the river again – and it's cold at this time of night, believe me. Here, hold this." He shoved the brush at me over my shoulder, and as I fumbled to catch it I felt a series of quick tugs at my hair. My braid uncoiled from around my head, falling down my back in a puff of rock dust.

"How did you know how to do that?" I demanded.

"How do you think? My hair's longer than yours. I pin it under my helm all the time. Give me the brush now, and no more funny comments, please."

He tugged the tie from the end of my braid. Feeling him comb gently through the long wriggles of hair with his fingers, I abruptly lost the urge to tease him. My breath left me in a long, shuddering sigh. Mortified, I pressed my lips together, but I could do nothing about the goose pimples springing up on my skin.

"Lean back," he murmured, tilting my head. His fingertips brushed the curve of my ear. My teeth bit into my lip.

The brush made a soft shushing noise as he ran it through the thick, fluffy layers, parting the hair gently to get at all of the dust. I felt myself slumping back further towards him – I couldn't help it – and I put out a hand to steady myself. My palm landed on the leg he had stretched out beside me.

The firm, warm bulge of muscle above his knee tensed under my fingers. The brush paused mid-stroke. I froze.

He cleared his throat. "Tell me if your neck gets stiff." The brush began to move once more. His other hand slid under the weight of my hair to curve supportively around the nape of my neck. Unwilling pleasure crackled down my spine, glowing bright, like the orange sparks that flew up out of a wood fire in the wind.

"I think that's it," he said. The hand on my neck eased me up into a proper sitting position. I realized my hand was still on his thigh and removed it quickly, hiding my tingling fingers in my lap.

Luca pushed the bulk of my hair forward, so that it

hung over my left shoulder, and brushed my back, presumably to direct the dust onto the cloth. Then he shifted to my right. "Turn your head towards me."

Reluctantly, I obeyed. Luca didn't meet my eyes, for which I was pitifully grateful. He had a smaller, folded cloth, which he carefully ran across my forehead and down my right temple to wipe the dust away. His other hand came to rest against my face, holding me still as he stroked the cloth under my jaw and then along the curve of my neck.

"There," he said; "that's the last of it."

He put the small cloth down. I held my breath, longing for and dreading the moment when his hand would drop away from my face.

It didn't come. His eyes suddenly focused on mine.

"Your heart is beating so fast," he said softly, the words barely more than a whisper. "I can feel your blood humming under my hand. Are you frightened of me?"

I swallowed dryly, instinctively whispering too as I replied, "No."

As Luca moved closer, the light from the lamp overhead filled his eyes with a thousand tiny golden suns. His hand slid around the nape of my neck again, fingers spearing carefully through my hair. There was a beat of stillness as we stared into each other, searching, waiting…

We both moved at the same time.

Nineteen

His free arm curled around my back, grasping my hip. He pulled me against him, and my breath huffed out into his lips. I could taste the ale he had drunk in his mouth – honey and apples – and that same wild, heady flavour I remembered from before, but had no name for. I felt soft and weightless, pliable, as if I were not made of flesh but of some warm, golden substance that shaped itself to his touch. Tentatively, I lifted one hand to explore the shape of his jaw, brushing through strands of soft, silky hair, tracing the strong tendons of his warm throat, the vulnerable, bony point of his collarbone. His stubble scraped my chin, breath ghosting across my cheek.

I felt him shift, starting to move back, and I clung instinctively, the fingers that had been wandering over the lines of his shoulders curling into his shirt to hang onto him.

No, no, not yet. Not like last time.

He lifted his face from mine. His breath was fast and slightly raspy, and I squeezed my eyes shut, waiting to be put aside again.

"I've wanted to do that for the longest time."

My eyes snapped open. "Bu–but before – you s–said it was a horrible mistake."

Having spoken, I was immediately conscious that I was still clinging to him, and I snatched my hands away from his shoulders, trying to put some distance between the warm bulk of his body and mine. His arms tightened, then loosened, but only enough to let me get to my knees. He kept his palms flattened against my back.

"I never said it was a horrible mistake," he contradicted. "I said it was *a* mistake. It was. You were a trainee who had just arrived in camp, and you were vulnerable and upset. I had no business kissing you at all."

Pain at the blunt words sheared through me, and brought the clean relief of anger. "Then why do it again?" I demanded. "I'm not a t–toy that you can pick up and put down as it suits you! If you're with H–Hind then why – why ever kiss me at all?"

Unbelievably, he laughed, his face suddenly alight. He dragged me back against him, burying his face in my hair. "You're jealous, aren't you? Thank the Mother! I thought you didn't care one way or the other."

"What are you talking about?"

"I'm in love with you."

I went still. Then I put both hands against the hard planes of his chest and shoved. "No you're not!"

"Yes I am."

"No, you're *not*!"

"Yes I – Frost, for Fire's sake!" He was laughing again. "We could keep this up all night. Just listen to me."

I tried to scramble away, shaking my head furiously. "You don't want me. I'm … I must be hallucinating or—"

Luca caught my wrists. "I am in love with you. I've been falling in love with you ever since you promised me not to run away in order to save those kidnapped women, and kept your promise even when I gave you every chance to make a run for it. I thought then that you were the bravest girl I'd ever met, and nothing that's happened since has changed my mind. I'm in love with you! You're awake and it's real. I'm real. So are you going to give me an answer or aren't you?"

I stopped struggling. "An answer?"

"How do you feel about me?" His voice quavered ever so slightly. He coughed, then said more strongly, "Do you like me?"

I let out a long, slow sigh, slumping. "Of course I – Luca, I like you *so much*. And it's horrible! It hurts, and it makes me happy and sad at the same time, and sometimes

I want to hit you and other times I… And I can't stop."

Luca relaxed, his fingers caressing my arms. "That's good enough for me."

"But you were right the first time," I said quickly. "This is a mistake."

"No it isn't."

"Yes it is."

"No it's not, and if you say it again, I am just going to have to distract you until you forget to be stubborn…" he said, voice turning husky as he lowered his face towards mine.

"Stop!" I turned my head away, more because the look in his eyes was making me feel weak and shivery than because I thought he would force a kiss on me. "You're the one that's being stubborn. You haven't thought this through! You've forgotten what I am, what lives inside me. I'm still cursed. I'm not safe for anyone to love. I … I haven't told you everything."

"Then tell me now," he said simply.

I opened my mouth and then closed it. How could I say that I wanted to keep him safe from me without damaging his faith in me? That I feared if I told him everything he really would cringe away from me, and I didn't know if I could bear it?

I couldn't say that, because it was pure cowardice. If I cared for him, I had to tell him the truth.

I tugged my arms out of Luca's hands and gripped the

wolf tooth through my shirt. *Father, give me the strength to do this.*

"A–all right. I ... I didn't know this myself until last year. Ma didn't tell me until she was dying. I don't know if she even meant to tell me then. Her mind was wandering with fever.

"My father was a wolf hunter. A f–famous one. He roamed from place to place in Uskaand, ridding villages and towns of their local wolf packs and selling wolf pelts. My mother travelled too, selling her remedies and nursing the sick. After he and my mother met, they travelled together, a perfect match. When my mother was far gone with me, my father was called to a large town on the edge of one of Uskaand's great forests. There was a lone wolf haunting the town. They said it was a massive creature, black as night, with eyes like stars. At first it had only ravaged the local farms. The elders ordered traps set – the animal avoided them. They left poisoned meat – the wolf ate it and lived. The beast began to encroach into the town itself. The elders sent hunters and dogs out. The dogs came back mad, foaming and snarling at any human they saw. The hunters did not come back at all. The town was in a panic. People began to say that it was more than just an animal. That it was possessed, or cursed, or ... or sent by the Other god. It became known as the Demon Wolf. Ma told me that when she heard these tales, she begged my father not to go after such an unnatural creature, but my father only laughed."

I paused, a cold shiver working down my spine. Luca tucked a fluffy hank of hair behind my ear, his hand brushing my cheek. I couldn't resist leaning into that touch.

"What happened?"

"My mother waited for him to come back. For three days, she waited. On the night of the third day, a terrible storm blew up. Snowflakes the size of a man's hand fell and a raging wind shook the walls. In the storm, my mother heard a wolf howl – a terrible howl that made her put her hands over her ears to try and block it out – and she knew my father was dead. Knew it, she told me, as if she had been able to hear words in the wolf's cry. And in that moment the birth pangs began to come on her. All night long she laboured alone in the middle of the blizzard, and when I was born…" I stopped. This was the worst part.

"When you were born?" Luca prompted.

"The birth cord had wrapped around my neck. I was dead." I heard Luca's sharp intake of breath. I didn't look at him. "My mother had assisted at many births. She knew there was nothing to be done for me. But when she saw her first and last child blue and withered and still, she cursed the god Askaan. She cursed him for letting her husband die. She cursed him for taking her baby from her before it had even drawn a breath. She called to the god of the Other, and begged him to take the child – to take me – as his own, if only he would give me breath. If only I would live."

"She offered you to the Wolf?"

"Yes." I smiled bitterly. "I can't even imagine what she must have been feeling in that moment. So much sorrow and pain, so much loss. All she wanted was what any mother would have wanted – to save her baby. It was madness… But somehow, it worked. The wind raging around the house rose up so that it deafened her, and the windows and doors burst open and snow filled the room where she lay until she couldn't see a thing. There was a vicious snarl, as close to her as you are to me, and her baby's body was jerked from her arms. Then … she heard a child begin to cry. The storm died down just as suddenly as it had come, and there in the fallen snow, I lay. Alive."

I touched the curling white mark on my face. "There was blood on me – fresh, red blood, as if from a wound. But when my mother cleaned it away there was no wound there, only this scar. In the morning, the townspeople brought my father's body home, and with it the body of the Demon Wolf. They found them locked together, the wolf's teeth in my father's neck, my father's axe buried in the wolf's side. They had to cut them apart – as if in death they had become one creature. That's how I became what I am. My mother made a bargain with the darkness to save me, and paid a heavy price for it."

"Not as heavy as you," Luca said gravely. He traced one finger carefully along the curving mark on my cheek.

"I can *see* the tooth marks."

"It isn't the end of the s–story." I could feel my muscles tensing into hard, knotted bands as I waited for the moment when Luca would understand what I was telling him, when he grasped what I truly was and pushed me away, just as my mother had.

"Ma left the town where I was born and settled in a village far away. She watched me closely, always looking for signs of the Wolf in me, praying that somehow the curse she had called down had not taken root. Then when I was eight, some local boys decided it would be fun to tease me. They threw rocks at me. One of them cut my face, I think, I can't really… Anyway, I saw b–blood. The Wolf came. The villagers had to pull me away and put me in chains to stop me. They were only children, and I nearly killed them."

"You were a child too," Luca said. "If they were stoning you, they could just as easily have seriously hurt you. It seems to me that the wolf – whatever it is – is a kind of guardian to you. He protects you."

"You're wrong," I said. "It *uses* me as a portal into life, into this world. It uses me to bring d–death. That's all it wants."

"You can't know that," Luca said, gently easing my hand from its death grip on the wolf tooth, and taking it between his. "I may not believe in demons, but I know that gods exist, and that their motives aren't readily understood by anyone. In the past, the wolf has emerged to defend you whenever you were bleeding and in danger, but now you can defend yourself. You're learning to control your fear, and I believe once you've done that, you will be able to control the berserk rage. You're not alone with this any more."

I remembered all the times I had faked the trances in front of him and felt overwhelmed by guilt and weariness. He didn't understand. He couldn't. Still, I tried again. I had to. I cared about him too much not to try.

"Luca, you don't know if I'll ever be able to control the Wolf. All it takes is one drop of blood and I lose myself. I feel – I feel as if every time the Wolf possesses me, it becomes stronger. I can sense it all the time now, like ice under my skin. Sometimes I know it's close to surfacing – waiting, watching for the right moment. I hear its voice. I have dreams where it calls to me. One day ... one day I might disappear forever."

Luca pressed his lips sweetly to the corner of mine. The tugging sensation in my chest got worse, pushing at my ribs until they seemed to creak and expand – and I realized, abruptly, that it was my heart I was feeling. My heart that jumped whenever Luca came near. My heart that felt as if it were swelling now. After all that I had told him, he still wanted to kiss me. He didn't fear me. He feared nothing.

"Never," he said, and his voice and eyes held the same

conviction that had spellbound me and convinced me to follow him back to the hill-guard camp. "Frost, your bravery, your kindness, the things that make you, you – those are yours, no matter what. No one can take them away. That's why humans can choose to worship gods or reject them – why they can't force us. They might have powers we don't, but we have something they can't ever touch. A soul. The wolf may borrow your body, but he can't take your soul."

I made one last attempt to warn him off. "I don't know if I even have a soul, Luca. My mother might have given it up when she offered me to the Other. I–I'm a monster. Trusting me could get you killed."

"Trusting anyone can get you killed," Luca said with sudden grimness. "Listen to me now. You've told me your story and I'm honoured that you did. It doesn't change my mind or my heart. You're not a monster, and I won't listen to you say that again. I know what monsters are. I've seen their work. I've *lived* with one."

I looked into the darkness of his eyes. "Y-your brother?" I whispered.

"Did you ever know a child that delighted in pain? A child that captured butterflies to rip their wings off? One who drowns kittens for the sheer fun of watching them die?"

I nodded slowly, shivering. Luca tugged me closer, and I leaned into him, unsure if I was comforting him or myself. "Yes," I said. "I've known boys like that."

"That's what my brother, Ion, was like. He was ten years older than me. I don't know if my parents spoiled him before I was born or if he was just made that way but … you see, he was so charming. So clever, and handsome. He could smile at you so that you barely noticed the blood on his hands. My mother and father tried to excuse the way he acted by saying it was just boyish silliness. My uncle and aunt lived with us then, with my cousin Sorin – King Sorin, as he is now – and they tried to tell us, tried to warn us what he was like but we didn't want to see." Luca paused for a second, his gaze fixed on something far away.

After a moment he seemed to shake himself, and went on. "By the time Ion was eighteen, he couldn't be trusted with any living thing. He rode his horses to death, strangled a hunting dog that snapped at him, harassed the servants, male and female. And I knew all that, hated it, but … but with us, with *me*, he was different. He never hurt me, or teased me. He was patient and kind. He used to lift me up and put me before him on his saddle, sneak me sweets, take me out fishing. At dinner, he would tell us stories, silly stories that made my mother and father laugh until they cried. He was the best big brother in the world. I never feared him. Not for a second. And then…"

I waited while he gathered himself, dreading his next words.

Finally he went on. "My father adopted Arian and brought him into the house. He was like a little wild animal at first, so eager for any scrap of kindness. So hungry for love. We all cared for him so much and wanted to show him that he was worth something – that he could trust us. Ion was away at the time. But the moment he came home I knew. I saw the way Ion looked at Arian. By the next day there were already bruises all over Arian. The hunted look was back in his eyes. I went to my father and told him; I bullied Arian into showing him the marks. Father didn't want to believe it, but he loved Arian too, and that love forced him to face the truth. He called Ion to him, and told him to stop. Just that. I will never forget the look Ion gave me then. It was rage and betrayal, yes, but hurt too. It had never occurred to him that I would take Arian's side over his. To Ion, Arian was just another helpless creature to torment for fun. He wasn't one of us. He didn't matter. No one had ever dared to confront Ion about what he did before, and that we did it now, over an outsider … I think it broke Ion's heart. If he had one to break. He screamed and raged at my father and me, smashed things, terrified us all. The next day he was gone. He went to Aroha, to King Abheron's court."

"The Mad King?"

Luca nodded. "Ion become one of his favourites almost immediately. Apparently his antics … entertained Abheron." His voice trailed off. I felt his chest heave against me as he took a deep breath. "Six months later King Abheron sent men, his own men, in the guise of mercenaries, to Mesgao. To kill us all."

I bit my lip to muffle the gasp that wanted to escape.

"Had Ion complained about the way my father had treated him? Had he let slip a little too much about my father and uncle's opinions of Abheron's sanity? I don't know if he betrayed us, or if Abheron merely acted against us because it amused him.

"My father and uncle were in the midst of constructing a stone fortress in Mesgao, but it was incomplete, and we were living in a wooden structure attached to the back. Abheron's men set fire to it. That was his favourite method of murder. My cousin – Sorin – wasn't there. He had ridden out a few days earlier to visit friends. Arian woke in the night and found the house in flames. I was already unconscious. Somehow he found the strength to drag me out. He realized that whoever had set the fire would be waiting for survivors to run out, so he dragged me into the fortress and hid me behind the piles of stone blocks. He tried to go back, to save my parents and the rest, but Abheron's soldiers caught him on the way. They broke his arm and his nose and cracked most of his ribs, but he never told them where I was hidden. They left him for dead and the house in ashes. My cousin returned a day or two later and found … the remains. He took us away. We were the only survivors."

Luca's voice choked suddenly. His muscles, under my hands, had turned to stone. I turned in his arms and wrapped myself around him, rubbing his back the way he always did for me when I was upset or hurt. He drew his legs up on either side of me and rested his head against mine, as if trying to envelop me, or lose himself in me.

"That's why you made the hill guard," I whispered.

"When the king proposed it, I leaped at the chance to take charge. It seemed like fate. Knowing that Ion was lurking here in the mountains, free, still preying on people ... it was unendurable. I thought if I became captain I could finally make amends for Ion's actions, bring him to face the king, and justice. I've imagined it so many times. What he must look like by now, how he'll react when he sees me. If he'll be sorry." Luca shook his head, hugging me fiercely. "My point is this: I know what evil looks like under the surface. No matter how beautiful the exterior, how good the lies, I don't fool myself, not any more. You carry a terrible burden that no one – not even me – can really understand. But that doesn't change who you are, Frost. You're a good person. And I love you."

"I wish ..." My voice cracked. "I wish I could believe in that."

Luca brushed the dishevelled strands of hair away from my face again and looked into my eyes. "It doesn't matter. I'll keep saying it until you do."

Sometimes as I run, I wonder why I don't give up. Why I don't do as the wolves urge me. Lie down in the snow. Let them finish me off. The chase would be over, and at long last I could rest.

But I can't. My aching arms and legs, my frantically beating heart, my gasping lungs, won't let me. Somewhere deep inside, I know there are worse things than death. If the wolves catch me they will take more than flesh and bones.

They will take my soul.

Twenty

My eyes snapped open in the dark. I lay on Luca's bed, on top of the covers, where I had fallen asleep after Luca and I had finally finished talking, sometime after midnight. His face was a pale smudge beside me in the shadows. His eyes were closed, and his breathing peaceful. I knew the sound well. I had been listening to it every night for the past six weeks. Tonight it was just another reminder of how vulnerable Luca was, without ever knowing it. Panic, stirred by the dream, clutched at my heart.

What if I can't protect him, Father? What if I can't keep him safe from me?

The enclosed space of the tent – the quiet and the shadows – was suffocating. Even Luca's hand, curved protectively around my ribs, felt like a weight too heavy to bear. I couldn't stand it. It took all my self control to ease from under Luca's hand instead of flinging myself violently away from him. Even so, the bed creaked, and Luca grumbled quietly.

I stood over him for a moment, almost panting, trying to make sense of my tangled feelings. Caution stirred in the back of my mind, warning me that something was wrong, but I couldn't heed it. I couldn't breathe. I needed to get out. I had to get away. Now.

Outside the wind had risen, making tent walls billow, stirring the trees into hissing, secret conversations. My shirt flapped around my waist, and my unbound hair fluttered and blew into my face. The sky was filled with great drifts of swiftly moving silver clouds. They formed strange shapes as they rippled and reformed across the stars. The great fire had died out. The singing and revelry was finished, and the camp seemed deserted.

I hesitated again, vaguely disturbed. But something drew me on, away from Luca's tent, towards the deep shadows of the forest. Tossing boughs closed overhead. Leaves danced in the air and flittered past my face. Trees and undergrowth parted before me to form a narrow, whispering tunnel.

After a while, light began to gleam through the gaps between the trees. I felt soft, cold touches against my cheeks and hands. They left tear-trails on my skin. It was no longer leaves drifting around me, but snowflakes. My panicked breath clouded up before my face. Yet I could not stop or turn back. Whatever force had tugged me from Luca's bed had control of me now and my legs would not stop moving.

The last of the trees fell behind me. I stared out over a great plain of snow, lit by a cloudless sky of brilliant stars. At the edge of the plain, so far away that I could barely make them out, sheer cliffs thrust up out of the snow, and beyond them, the jagged shapes of mountains.

A deep growl split the night. Against my will, I turned.

Silver eyes glowed like twin stars in the black wolf's immense skull. His fangs gleamed, tongue lolling redly between them. Steam rose from his mouth and nostrils and from where his great paws were planted in the snow.

I forced words out from between numb lips. "Why have you brought me here?"

I did not. I followed you. I have always been following you.

The creature's voice was the eager, joyous howling of a hunting pack, the sound that had haunted my dreams for half my life. It was the desolate cry of the lone wolf. It was ice cracking, carrion crows squawking, and the final whispers of dying men. And it was my father's voice, the voice that I had always known was his, even though he had died before I was born. The sound of it smote my ears. I cringed, crying out. "What do want?"

You know already. You have spent all your years fighting me, but soon that must stop, Saram. Soon a storm will come. You will need me then.

"I won't. Please. All I want is to be normal."

If you were normal, you would already be dead.

"I—I know that. But … the bargain was not of my making. My mother was the one who called you, and she is dead now. Why won't you leave me alone?"

You are my daughter, and I love you. How can a father abandon his own child?

I put my hands over my ears and ran. The voice seemed to deepen with sorrow as it called after me.

Soon, my daughter. Soon you will summon me, as your mother did. And I will come.

The ice cracked and crunched underfoot as I fled, hands still clapped over my ears, tears streaming down my face. I didn't know when the trees sprang up around me again, but somehow I was running through them, and the wind was back, buffeting and swirling. I stumbled out of the forest…

And opened my eyes in the still darkness of Luca's tent, curled warm and safe in his arms.

The hill guards rose before dawn the following day. Bleary-eyed and grumbling after the excesses of the night before, they picked reluctantly at breakfast while Luca and Arian gave a short tactical briefing. I sat in the corner of the mess tent with Livia, staring unenthusiastically at my own tray of food. My excuse was not too much ale, but too much thinking. Last night's dream sat in my belly like a rock.

"All right, everyone." Luca – a dozen vellum and parchment maps pinned to the canvas wall behind him – held up a hand for silence. "Those of you who've just joined us, or anyone who's been on scouting or messenger duty for a while, should pay special attention. This is what we know. Our enemy's permanent base is at the ruins of the House of God. They may have been there since they first arrived in the mountains, since apparently they've refortified the broken section of the outer wall and have effective defences in place. That is bad news. The more firmly they've established themselves, the harder a time we're going to have digging them back out of there.

"Now, we believe that the splinter group led by Birkin" – he flicked me a smiling glance – "was the last one loose in the hills, which is one piece of good news. But it's likely that once Constantin realizes his roving warrior bands have all been disposed of, he will send out more, and while each time we pick off one of these groups it weakens him, we can no longer spend our whole attention on them. The primary mission was always to find and capture the rebel ringleaders and bring them to justice, especially Constantin. That's what I intend for us to do now."

There was a muted cheer. Luca let everyone get it out of their systems before he waved the noise down again. "We have several obstacles to overcome. We still have no true idea of the enemy's numbers or level of weaponry. The bandits we've taken had nothing but battlefield lootings, but that isn't to say that Constantin doesn't have – or hasn't forged – much better equipment in his permanent base. It's vital to gather more information. We need to break camp here and move into enemy territory. We must learn every cave, crevice and hiding place they may be utilizing. By now they will know that location like the back of their hands, so we need to as well. After that we'll formulate a detailed plan which will cut off their supplies and resources, force them out of the House of God, and channel them to a battleground of our choosing. Remember, the enemy has the high ground and a secure location. Any attempt at a frontal assault on their own terms would be suicide. We need to play to our strengths, be faster, cleverer and more ruthless than them, or there will be no chance of success."

Luca took a long, slow look around the room, seeming to weigh up his troops. His eyes were warm, glowing with belief. "I know that I can rely on you all."

I could feel the response in the air, the sense of pride and determination his look had brought to life. After a moment he stepped aside, waving his arm at the maps. "Arian has been gathering together all the scout reports into a cohesive whole and is going to share more detail on the enemy's circumstances."

My attention wandered as Arian stood and began pointing out features and locations on the maps. I had already read these reports over Luca's shoulder and studied the maps for myself.

I was supposed to be a hill guard now. A real warrior. I was going to war under Luca's command. The outcome of this conflict meant something to everyone here, and everything to Luca. He was willing to put me in the middle of it all because he believed in me.

I was deathly afraid that he was wrong.

Please, Father. Let me be the soldier, the warrior *that he needs me to be.*

Please keep the Wolf prisoner.

Last night's kisses and confessions seemed like a dream: less real than the horrific vision that had followed them. But whenever Luca's eyes rested on me I realized anew – with a shock of mixed terror and joy – that I was loved. Truly loved, for perhaps the first time in my life. I didn't feel worthy of Luca or his feelings. Yet deep inside, where before there had only ever been ice, there was now a flickering warmth that even the fear could not touch.

Soon you will summon me, as your mother did...

Never, I vowed. *Never.*

As soon as it was light enough we broke camp, folding tents, loading horses and locking up the wooden buildings we would be leaving behind. I bid a sad farewell to the place I had come to feel was my home.

It was a hard trek up the mountain. The higher we climbed the less hospitable the terrain became. Green trees shrank away to stunted grey shrubs, shrubs to blue moss and orange lichen, until there was barely a patch of vegetation to be seen. I had been this way before, but I had been in a daze of hunger and desperation then, and had observed very little. I had not remembered the cold. Although the ruins of the House of God were nowhere near the snow-clad upper slopes, after half a day's march up the mountain it was already noticeably colder. I huddled into my new leather jerkin, grateful for the extra layers of clothing.

"We're headed for that ridge?" I asked Luca, peering up at what looked like nothing more than a black, horizontal streak on the mountain's flank.

"Beneath it," Luca said, shielding his face from the sun with one hand. He didn't seem to feel any of my awkwardness or worry, and, as always, his confidence was infectious. "Razia reported an area of level ground suitable for a camp. We might have to clear some rocks, but it will be worth it."

I nodded, forcing my eyes away from his face. I looked for Arian, and found him at the very back of the slowly moving column of soldiers. He was helping to redistribute the packs on the back of one of the shaggy mountain-bred horses. The animal was jigging restively and tossing its head, while the hill guard in charge of it looked on helplessly. Arian's square, competent hands soothed the beast into stillness so that the other man could finish moving the packs.

"He always did have a way with animals," Luca said, a smile in his voice.

I worried at my lip with my teeth. The bond between the adopted brothers was clear to anyone with eyes – but Arian's past and the events that had turned him into such a complex, difficult man were still opaque. Although Luca had shared his own story with me last night, he had said nothing that had accounted for the history of abuse written on Arian's back. Despite the time we had spent training together, I felt I knew Arian no better now than I had when I first walked into camp.

Would Arian ever be able to accept someone else coming into Luca's life? Especially someone who would be important to Luca, close to him, in a way that Arian never could? The jealousy and protectiveness Arian displayed made it painfully clear that Luca was all Arian had – all he cared about. For a long time, with Luca's cousin Sorin keeping both of them hidden away, to protect their lives from the Mad King, Arian had been the only person Luca could trust and rely on as well. But now Luca was making room in his heart for me. Would Arian feel pushed out? Forsaken? If so, what on earth should I do to fix it?

"What are you worrying about?" Luca asked, breaking into my thoughts. "If you frown any harder you'll turn me to stone."

"I'm completely lost," I said, forcing a smile. Now was not the time to burden him with my fears. "Where are we in relation to the House of God?"

"By the time we reach the ridge we'll be a little more than half an hour's march away," Luca said. "Let's get to the head of the column, and I can show you the trail we'll need to follow."

We moved quickly along the line of soldiers, who, burdened as they were with all the rolled-up tents and pieces of furniture that would not fit onto the backs of the sturdy mountain horses, were walking slowly. People waved in a friendly way as we walked by.

The earth beneath my feet was less like earth and more like sand – a fine, silver sand that caught the sunlight and made my eyes smart and water. The path was littered with a tumble of grey and white rocks, from tiny bits of shale that shifted and turned underfoot to massive boulders nearly the size of the house I had lived in as a small child.

On one side of the doggedly trudging hill guards the ground fell away sharply: a sheer cliff, it plunged straight into the River Mesgao, about thirty feet below. We were closer to the heart of the mountains here and the river had taken on a different character. The water no longer ran green and placid in a wide channel but was a sharp, icy blue that crashed and churned along the narrow ravine. On the other side of the hill-guard column, the jagged mountain towered, brown and black against the sky.

Luca passed the front line of soldiers and sprang effortlessly onto a rock. He pulled me up after him, turning to point out the shadow of the forest far below. "We've come around the side of the mountain here, you see. Where before we needed to climb to reach the ruins, now we'll be going downhill. It will make it harder to keep blocking the rebels' supplies – we'll need to send more patrols out – but hopefully it will throw Constantin off."

"You know the route by heart, don't you?"

"I've stared at the maps often enough. When I was little, I always told my family I would explore these mountains one day. They used to laugh at me. Yet here I am."

I squinted up at him, suddenly finding it very important to try and read the expression on his face. "I think they'd be proud of you for remembering your dream like that."

Luca didn't answer straight away. Then he sighed. "My parents were great people. They weren't like a lot of the Sedorne who came here after the occupation and only wanted to fight and steal. They were peaceful and compassionate, and they tried their hardest to help the

Rua and to repair some of the damage that Abheron had done. They built schools and infirmaries, travelled the farms and villages of their territory, brought healers and supplies. They made friends wherever they went, even with people who hated the Sedorne. I don't think I've turned out the way they would have expected. They always intended me to follow in their footsteps – to take the title of Lord Mesgao and concern myself with helping people to build lives."

"You do help people. You save lives all the time," I said, surprised.

"But I'm not a man of peace, am I?" He lifted his hand, which had been resting comfortably on the hilt of his sword. "I'm a warrior. That's the last thing they would have wanted for me."

I thought carefully before I spoke. "This isn't forever. One day you'll be free of Ion and the past. When you've done what you set out to do here, you'll still have your whole life to live as you wish. What will you do then?"

Luca gave a strange little laugh. "You know, I've never really thought about it. I've spent so long chasing his shadow—"

He broke off, turning his head sharply. I heard the rattle of stones tumbling downhill and, following the line of Luca's gaze, saw a plume of dust rising from the rocks above us.

My body went icy cold. Every tiny hair on my skin

raked up. I met Luca's eyes for an instant that felt like an hour and saw Luca's lips frame the word. *"Ambush!"*

There was a shout from the rocks. The air filled with arrows.

I saw two men at the front of the hill-guard column go down and I lunged at Luca, knocking him off the boulder. He hit the ground beneath me with a grunt and then rolled, flinging his larger body over mine as a shield. An arrow shot past and buried itself in the ground an inch from Luca's face.

The arrows hit the trail with a sound like hailstones, almost drowning out the thundering feet, the yelling, the clash of weapons.

"Get up! Get off!" I screamed, struggling to push him away. His back would be a perfect target for the archers.

He leaped to his feet, snagging the front of my jerkin to haul me with him. The enemy had risen from the rocks above the track and sliced through the hill-guard column. Abandoning their packs and baggage, our soldiers were running helter-skelter into battle. Horses kicked and whinnied as they tried to escape the fray. Rock dust rose in clouds around the fighting. It was chaos.

"Holy Mother," Luca whispered. He rushed forward.

A rebel in dented plate armour dropped down from the rocks directly behind Luca. The rebel swung his sword at Luca's back.

A howl of rage erupted from my throat. In one

movement I wrenched my father's axe from its sheath and brought the weapon scything sideways at the rebel's neck. Hot droplets of blood spattered my face. The man fell, pulling the axe out of my hands.

I staggered backwards, staring at what I had done. I barely noticed Luca stepping over the fallen rebel, until he carefully wiped the drops of blood from my face with the back of his gauntlet. He hesitated, clearly wanting to speak – but a scream from downhill forced his attention away.

"Thank you." He nodded at me gravely, then turned and ran towards the fray, gesturing at me to follow him as he drew his sword.

I took a deep breath, giving my stomach a moment to settle. Then I reached out to grip the axe stave. Bone grated against metal. I was forced to plant my boot on the man's back before I could drag the weapon free. I shook the blood off my blades, then ran after Luca.

He was halfway up the slope. He had taken a new sword from somewhere and was fighting with a weapon in each hand, movements a deadly blur of flashing silver and gold that forced the rebels back. Livia and the Rua healer were at the bottom of the slope, a circle of hill guards around them. On the edge of the trail, where the path turned, Arian did battle with Razia at his side, the two of them forcing rebel warriors over the edge of the cliff or onto the blades of those behind them.

Below me, the hill guards were surging steadily downwards, fighting to break through the wall of rebel soldiers at the bottom of the trail. We were outnumbered two to one, but Luca's training was holding strong. Slowly but steadily, we were winning ground and forcing our way out of the trap.

Someone – it might have been friend or foe – shouted, "Bows!"

Another hail of arrows flew down into the battle. There was a piercing scream. I saw Razia crumple, falling almost at Arian's feet with a long white arrow lodged in her chest. Arian dropped his sword, eyes filling with sorrow as he bent over her.

An enemy soldier closed in on him from behind. There was a metal club in the rebel's fist, raised to strike. The ground turned to air under my feet as I raced towards Arian, screaming warnings. Arian jerked upright – too late. The rebel's club thudded into the back of his skull.

His eyes rolled back in his head. For a moment he hung there, balanced on the very edge of the trail, above the river. Then he tumbled over the edge.

I skidded to a halt before the soldier who had clubbed Arian and despatched him with one sweep of my axe. This time I felt no remorse. Razia's eyes were already clouding over. It was too late to help her.

"Frost!" Luca yelled. I turned and found his blue eyes

burning into mine. "He can't swim! Go after him!"

I hesitated for a split second as I looked down over the edge of the trail. The river heaved below. I could see no sign of Arian. If I tried to climb down the rock face, I would never reach the river in time to help him.

I jammed my axe into its sheath and jumped, feet first, over the edge.

Twenty-one

The wind screamed around me as I fell, tearing at my clothes and hair. I had one moment to realize how stupid I had been, to think about hidden rocks, whirlpools, shallow beds. Then I hit the river.

The water closed over my head with a deafening crash. I plunged deep, white clouds of bubbles churning around me, blinding me and pounding against my ears. My skin caught fire with the cold. The axe was a dead weight strapped to my back, dragging me down. I squirmed in the water, like a moth trying to break free of its chrysalis.

Arian is out there. He's out there and he can't swim.

I flailed my cramping limbs, forcing them to move. Lungs aching with the effort of keeping breath in, ribs creaking, I kicked and clawed at the water, praying that I still knew up from down.

I broke the surface in a shower of foam and sucked in a deep breath, choking and coughing as the spray hit the back of my throat.

"Arian!" I screamed. *"Arian!"*

A fallen branch rushed at me, frighteningly fast. I gasped and ducked under the surface. Spiny twigs dragged across the top of my head as the branch passed by. I surfaced again with a yell of pain. The current was sweeping me forward, and my joints ground together with the effort of trying to resist. "Arian! Answer me!"

The water dragged me under again, curling over my head. I came up once more, gasping, head turning frantically as I searched for any sign of him. My vision was too blurry. Then, a little way ahead, I saw something. I blinked water from my eyes, trying to focus. A body floated on the river's surface, unresisting as the current tossed it about. Dark hair drifted in the water like a thundercloud.

I dived forwards. My lungs made hollow wheezing sounds, like punctured bellows, as I fought to reach him. The river lifted me, then sucked me backwards. Arian's arm trailed past me. I stretched out, and my gloved fingers clamped down on his wrist.

Another swell broke over us. I choked on a mouthful of water, sculling with one hand and my legs. I couldn't go under again. I would take Arian with me. I waited for the next swell to bring him closer and then heaved him back, wrapping my other arm around his chest and under his arms. His head lolled onto my shoulder. I pulled him up, trying to keep his nose and mouth out of the river.

Once I was sure of my grip I used my other arm to steer us, kicking strongly with my legs and shielding Arian's body with mine. His face was grey and immobile, without a flicker of life. The gloves prevented me from feeling for blood beating under his skin. I couldn't tell if he was breathing. The thought that I was clinging to his dead body was too awful. He must be alive. Arian was a fighter – he wouldn't give up this easily.

All I could do was hang onto him and try to keep him afloat by pushing him up whenever the river closed over us. I scanned the towering cliffs on either side of the channel, looking for an inlet, an island in the river – anywhere I might have a chance to pull Arian out of the icy water and make sure he was alive.

There was nothing.

Deadly tiredness began to creep over me. The water was too cold, the current too strong. Without my even realizing it, my legs had almost stopped kicking. Soon I had to use both arms to hold onto Arian's limp body, afraid my hands would slip and I would lose him. My throat was as raw as if I had drunk acid.

When the river burst out from the narrow ravine, the violence of the waves sucked us under again. My desire to live flared up once more. I clawed my way back up to the surface, clinging to Arian's arm – to find the water smoothing out around us, deepening to a peaceful green.

It was easier now. Instead of being dragged, pounded and splashed, we drifted. The water began to feel almost warm. I hoped that was because we had reached the lower slopes of the mountain and not because the cold was killing me. The river was still boxed in by walls of rock on either side that would have been impossible to climb even if I hadn't had Arian to look after.

Gradually, the cliffs began to slope down, becoming steep banks. I saw plants and trees growing on their tops. When the banks became tumbled rocks that edged the river with the great conical shapes of pines beyond, I lay back in the water and thrashed my legs, spending what felt like the last of my energy to drag Arian with me.

The current seemed to clutch at us. Panic made my fingers dig into Arian, my breath catching. If we didn't get out of the water soon we never would. I kicked harder, drawing on reserves I didn't know I had. With one last mighty kick, I broke free of the current. We were propelled sideways, towards the bank. The movement spun us around. Arian slid down and I quickly thrust my arm under his neck to keep him from being swamped. His eyes were still closed, and his lips had a grey, clay-like look.

Please, Father. Let him be alive.

I craned my neck back; the water gently lapped at my face. We were floating in an inlet. There was a small bank of yellow sand, almost hidden beneath the overhanging vegetation: a cave. If we could reach it, we would be safe.

I paddled slowly towards the bank, legs too tired now to do more than flap about in the water. Slowly, dry land inched closer. My foot hit the river bed and stuck in deep, squelching mud. I toiled on, still towing Arian. Finally, I reached the tiny strip of sand and began dragging him under the green overhang. Out of the water, my sodden clothes and axe were heavy enough to crush me. Gasping and grunting with effort, back screaming, eyes swimming with black dots, I got Arian into shelter.

I flopped down beside him, too weak even to sit up as I fumbled to pull off my right glove, and reached out for his neck. His skin was wet and chilly, like the scales of a freshly landed fish. I found the hollow under his chin where his blood should be beating.

I couldn't feel anything.

I squeezed my eyes shut, trying to keep my hand steady. It was there. It had to be there.

"Please, Father," I whispered.

A tiny, trembling movement under the pad of my index finger.

I pressed my face to the front of Arian's jerkin. His chainmail dug into my forehead, but I barely felt it. The discomfort of soaking clothes, heavy leather armour, the weight of the axe pressing down on my back – none of it was enough to stir me. A handful of minutes might have passed, or an hour. I didn't know or care. I'd done it. I'd got him out alive.

Something warm trickled down the chilled skin of my face. I lifted my head, blinked, and saw a dark spot land on the chainmail under my cheek. Blood. The branch had got me. Lucky it hadn't been an enemy's blow that had opened my skin – I had more than enough to deal with now without the Wolf rearing its ugly head.

I pushed myself away from Arian and creaked into a sitting position. We were both sodden and chilled through, but the air was mild. If I could get us dry, we'd start to warm up. I shucked off my other glove, my vambraces, the axe harness, the leather jerkin and the leather choker from around my throat. My linen undershirt was also sodden. I took it off, leaving myself clad in only a breast-wrapping. The boots and breeches were clammy and very uncomfortable, but if I removed them too they might shrink as they dried, and leave me nothing to wear. I would just have to put up with it. I spared one moment to examine the blades of Da's axe, pleased to see that they had taken no harm from the rough journey in the river. Then I thrust all the wet things into the corner of the cave, and began the slow and difficult process of divesting Arian of all his leather and chainmail.

In the dim green light of the overhang and with hands that wouldn't stop shaking, it seemed to take forever to get the armour off. I lifted Arian as carefully as I could – he was so heavy, the effort made me pant – and propped his head and neck on my thigh so that I could unlace and remove his soaked undershirt, too. Then I eased him back down onto the sand.

I rubbed my hands together until they felt dry and warm, then I began to chafe Arian's arms, hands and chest, wiping away droplets of river water. My tanned, scarred hands looked pale and fragile against the massive width of his chest. His skin was as soft as kidskin, despite the hard, corded muscles beneath. The fine hair on his body tickled my palms as it dried.

"Arian," I whispered. "Arian. If you can hear me, open your eyes."

Not even a sigh or a twitch of an eyelid. I tested the pulse at his throat again. It was still there, but I knew enough of healing to worry that it was so faint and so fast.

I eased my hand around to the back of his neck, and felt for the wound that had felled him. There was a lump the size of a quail's egg at the base of his skull. At least it wasn't bleeding. But he was still chilly. I lay down next to him again, hooking my leg across his, so that my torso covered his chest and I could press as much of my warm flesh to his cold skin as possible. I slid one arm carefully under his neck and tucked my face into the hollow of his shoulder under his chin.

I had expected to have to fight off a panic at his closeness, as I had with every male since I was twelve, except

Luca. But, maybe because he was unconscious, or maybe because we had sparred and grappled with each other so often in the past six weeks, I found that I was surprisingly comfortable. Physically, at least.

I couldn't stop turning over all the events of this terrible day in my mind. Arian was injured, and we were far from any possible source of help. Razia was dead. I had left Luca – and all of the hill guards – in the middle of battle, heavily outnumbered. We had seemed to be winning, but who knew how the tide of a battle might turn?

The look in Luca's eyes after he saw Arian fall haunted me. He would be horribly worried about his brother. About both of us. What if that slowed him down? Put him in danger?

Who would watch his back with Arian and me both gone?

Twenty-two

Outside, afternoon became evening, and evening, night. The light turned dusky and faded away, leaving our hiding place engulfed in shadows as thick and black as pitch. I couldn't make out Arian's face, or even the movement of my own hand any more.

After an hour or so a faint silver light began to creep into the cave, slowly gaining strength. The moon was rising. Its pale light reflected from the surface of the river, marking it with long grey ripples as it lapped at the sand. I watched the water with weary, sleepless eyes. Arian lay beneath me like the stone Livia had once called him. My hand clasped his wrist tightly – the faint pulse of his blood against my palm was the only reassurance that he was not already gone. He barely seemed to be breathing.

When at last he stirred, my first thought was that I had imagined it. The faint sigh could have been a sound from the water, or the sand settling around us, or a night creature burrowing. Then, after an endless moment, a soft, complaining grumble vibrated through Arian's chest. The shoulder under my face twitched.

Moving slowly, holding my breath, I unwound myself from his body. Bracing my hands on the sand on either side of his head, I peered down at him. Faint glints of light showed me that his eyes were open. I stared into his dimly lit face, watching those tiny glints move as his gaze circled the dark place where we lay, then moved across to the water, and finally shifted back to me.

"Arian?" I whispered. Would he recognize me? Would he even be able to speak?

There was a long pause. Then he whispered, "You're bleeding."

I sighed, relief making my body flush with warmth. "Never mind that. Do you know who I am?"

He swallowed, coughed and leaned sideways, as though trying to sit. I held him down with one hand.

"Let... Let me up," he said, his tone a mixture of confusion and annoyance.

"No. You were injured; you need to lie still."

"You're bleeding. I have to look at your head."

I took my hand off his chest to touch my face, and found a long streak of gore. It had dried along my cheek and chin, and flaked off under my fingers. "It's nothing. My scalp got scratched, that's all."

"Let me up," he said more strongly. "You'd call it a scratch if someone stuck you through with a pike."

"I'm all right," I said, exasperated, as I pinned him down again. "Stop struggling or—"

He went rigid. Then his chest heaved. I got hastily out of the way as he rolled onto his side and began to retch. He brought up what seemed like a gallon of river water, and then flopped back with a muffled groan.

"I told you," I said softly, smoothing the sweaty hair back from his forehead with no more thought than if he were a child. I scooped up a couple of handfuls of sand to throw over the mess he had made, then rinsed my hands in the river. "You were hit in the head hard enough to knock you out for hours. Chances are you'll be sick for a while."

"What happened? Where are we?"

"You don't remember anything?"

He made an impatient gesture with his hand, then covered his face with it. "I remember ... an ambush. Arrows. Razia?"

I hesitated for a second. "I'm sorry. She was dead before you went into the water."

"I went into the— I did what?" He took his hand away from his face.

"One of the rebels clubbed you. You fell over the edge of the cliff and into the river."

"Why aren't I dead?"

"Luca and I saw you fall. He shouted that you couldn't swim and told me to go after you. So I jumped in."

"He ordered you to jump off the cliff into the *river*?"

I shifted sheepishly. "I think he probably expected me to climb down and try to pull you out. But I couldn't see you and I thought I would be too late."

He covered his face with his hand again. "We should *both* be dead."

"Well, we aren't. Say, 'Thank you, Frost.'"

"Thank you, Frost." His tone sounded more grumpy than grateful. "Now help me up."

"I don't think—"

"No, you don't, but I'll overlook it this once. Lying here is making me feel worse. Help me up."

I was tempted, just for a second, to fold my arms and watch him struggle. But I was sure that he would keep on trying until he hurt himself, and that wouldn't do either of us any good. I knelt up and slid my arm under his back, feeling the ridges of scar tissue there drag against my skin. I held my other arm above him. "Grab my arm."

He obeyed. With an effort that made my stomach muscles cramp, I managed to get him upright. Some more pushing and manoeuvring arranged him so that he could rest against the back wall of the cave. He hissed a little when his bare back touched the mossy earth, and I picked up his thin undershirt, which was more or less dry now, and draped it behind him.

"Put yours on too," he said gruffly. Something about the angle of his head made me think that he had averted his eyes. "You'll freeze to death."

"I'm all right," I said. But his words had made me conscious of how little I was wearing. I picked my shirt up and pulled it on over the breast-wrapping.

"Can you tell me where we are?" he asked.

"Not really. The river dragged us downstream a long way, then the channel suddenly widened and we floated for a while until the cliffs disappeared."

"Then we might not be on the River Mesgao any more," he said. "We could have been sucked into a tributary. When it's light I'll climb up and see if I can recognize anything that might help us guess our location."

"You shouldn't be climbing anywhere so soon. You stay here and I'll go out—"

"What would be the use in that? You've already said you have no idea where we are."

"I didn't mean to reconnoitre," I snapped. "I meant to gather firewood and forage for food. You can't even move without wanting to vomit. Who do you think will have to drag you back here if you faint and fall in the water? Show some common sense."

To my surprise, instead of ripping back at me, he laughed. The low, husky noise filled the dark cave, and I sat back, shocked. I had never heard him laugh like that before. I didn't think I'd ever heard him laugh at all.

"What? What did I say?" I demanded.

"Nothing, really," he said, sighing. "I appreciate your advice. But we can't stay here. We need to get to the others."

"We don't know where they are."

"We'll go back to the old campsite. I'll wager anything that that's where Luca and the rest are by now."

I didn't want to say it, but the words wouldn't be contained. "If Luca's still alive. If any of them are."

There was a heavy silence, then Arian said, "Of course Luca is alive. We were winning. I remember that much."

"We were outnumbered. Two to one, at least. And more rebels were coming. We were in retreat. Anything could have happened. We weren't there. I wasn't there—" I managed to stem the flow of words, breaking off with a gasp.

"You followed your captain's orders," he said quietly. "That's all any soldier can do. He sent you to save me, and you did. You should be proud of yourself, not blaming yourself for things you have no control over."

I pressed my lips tightly together. Finally, I said, "A lot of them are going to be dead, aren't they?"

Arian hesitated. "Death is part of a soldier's life. There's no shame in surviving."

I scooted over and leaned back against the cave wall beside him. "But you said you were sure Luca is alive."

"He is," Arian said firmly. "I would know it if anything had happened to him. I've always been able to tell when he was in trouble. He's fine. I promise."

My eyes went back to the slow grey ripples on the water. "Is that how you were able to save him from the fire?"

I knew it wasn't my imagination that Arian's voice had chilled when he said, "Did Luca tell you about that?"

"Yes. You don't have to talk to me about it if you don't want to. Only ... I hope we're friends now, aren't we?"

"I acknowledge that Luca was right about you. You're a valuable member of the hill guard." His tone was flat.

"That's not what I meant, and you know it."

"You don't have to pretend to like me, just to be polite. You can be a friend to Luca and still hate my guts. Everyone else in camp manages it."

"I don't hate you!" I twisted around, trying to see his face. "You're rude, mean, stubborn, and as bad-tempered as a mule, but I like you anyway. The rest of the hill guards would too, if you would only let them. The way you treat people, it's as if you do it on purpose, like you almost want them all to dislike you..."

Arian turned his head away. My mouth dropped open.

"It's true, isn't it? You have done it on purpose. Why? Why do you want people to despise you?"

He laughed again, but this time the sound was bitter.

"They would anyway. It's easier if they loathe me because I've chosen it."

As I stared into the shadows that surrounded Arian,

I saw in my mind the terrible scars on his back.

Who hated him so much? Who convinced him he would always be hated, no matter what he did?

"What were you just saying to me, Arian? About not feeling guilty over things you can't control? That there's no shame in surviving?"

His breath was loud in the darkness. "Don't throw my words back at me. You don't know me."

"Well, that's not my fault! You've never told me – or anyone in the hill guard – a single thing about yourself," I retorted. "Come on, then. What's your big secret? What's so important that you think it justifies acting like a wounded boar all the time?"

"I should never have been born," he said, spitting out the words like rocks. "I've already told you that. I killed my own mother. And every day when my grandfather looked at me and saw these eyes – these Sedorne eyes – he saw the man who destroyed his daughter living in his house, eating his food. Breathing, when she would never breathe again. He punished me for that soldier's sins. And when he got too old and feeble to punish me himself, he let the other villagers do it. I was everyone's whipping boy. I was lucky to survive to the age of nine, and I doubt I'd have made it to ten. Do you know how Lord Petru found me? Did Luca tell you that?"

"No." My hands had doubled up into fists, but I kept my voice steady. I was sure that the faintest hint of pity would shut his mouth up like a bear trap.

"He was visiting the village where I lived. Luca was with him. Lord Petru was talking to the elders, my grandfather was among them. Luca wandered away from the meeting and found me at the river. A group of boys were ducking me. Holding me under until I passed out, then dragging me up, letting me come round, and ducking me again. Luca tried to make them stop and they turned on him and beat him too, not realizing who he was. The commotion fetched everyone, including Lord Petru and my grandfather. Lord Petru saw the scars and bruises and my bony ribs sticking out, and he pitied me and took me away and tried to make me one of his family. Instead I was the end of their family. I ruined everything, drove Ion to the Mad King and triggered the events that caused the fire—"

"Stop it!" I interrupted. "It wasn't the way you're making it sound. Luca told me what really happened. You were a child and Ion was insane. It wasn't your fault."

"He didn't tell you that," Arian said flatly. "He didn't tell you it was Ion's fault. Luca never blamed him for what happened. He blames himself. And that's my fault too. They were happy before I came and afterwards they were dead. None of it would have happened if it weren't for me. So forgive me if I don't want to make friends with anyone new. I've already destroyed enough people."

His logic was familiar. Horribly familiar. Every word

of self-loathing he spoke was one I had used to punish myself in my own mind. And yet, when I heard it from him, it seemed wrong. Why should he take the blame for Ion's actions? Why should he blame the child he had been for things that were out of that child's control?

"You're not the only one, Arian," I said slowly. "Not the only one who was unwanted. Not the only one who had to live with a curse like that. When I was eight years old my village wanted to burn me."

"They – what?"

"You heard me. Village boys attacked me and I fought back. When the men dragged me off their sons they hit me with sticks until I was half dead and threw me in a barn and bolted the door. They thought I was possessed by a demon. I was stuck there for three days with broken ribs and no food or water, listening to them debate setting fire to the building, listening to my mother beg for mercy. I licked the wet mould on the walls to stay alive. By the time I escaped I wished I *had* died."

"Demons?" The bitterness was gone from his voice now. "That's barbaric. No one with a grain of sense believes in demons. You were just a little girl. They ought to have been beating their sons, not you."

"But their sons hadn't gone insane and started snarling and howling like a wolf, had they?" I said wearily. "You've seen me when the battle rage takes me. It's not natural. It's a curse. The villagers wanted to burn me because they were terrified of me. And they were right to be scared. My mother and I ran away, and found another place to live, but the same thing happened again. One of the village boys tried to—" I broke off, shaking my head fiercely as if I could shake the memories away. "He was six years older than me. There was no way I could fight back. But when he hit me he drew blood. And the Wolf came again. It beat him until his face was gone. I can still remember the way his skull cracked under my fists. Coming back to myself, hands and clothes all covered in blood and bits of bone."

"Frost…"

"The boy's family wanted me killed. They were going to drown me that time. My mother begged for mercy again and in the end the elders banished us. It happened every time. *Every time.* Because we were alone and vulnerable, there was always someone who wanted to hurt us. Then the Wolf would come, and when it was done we took the blame. We ended up in a tiny, tumbledown village in the middle of nowhere, where everyone was half-starved. My mother was ill. She was so tired, so worn down, that she couldn't practise her trade any more, and we had no money for food. I went out to hunt for us, and the village women promised that if I brought them some of the meat they would care for her while I was gone. But when I got back she was dead. They were too afraid to enter the house. I don't know if they were more afraid of catching her fever, or my curse. The rumours had followed me, you see. Ma died alone, and cold, and without anyone to hold her hand. Because of me."

Arian growled, "Those women were cowards. They lied to you. How could that possibly be your fault?"

"Arian – you don't make any sense. If what happened to my mother wasn't my fault, then how can what happened to Luca's family be yours?"

He drew in a sharp breath. "It's completely different."

"Yes, it is different," I said, hearing bitterness in my own voice now. "The reason your people hated you was far less reasonable. They hated you for being born. For having green eyes. They hated you just because you were there. You never hurt anyone – not like me. And I'll tell you another thing that's different between your story and mine. Someone found you, Arian, in the midst of your suffering. Lord Petru and Luca saw the goodness in you, and gave you a different life. And even if Lord Petru is gone now, at least you have Luca. He knows everything about you and he loves you anyway, loves you like family. I've never had that. My own *mother* was terrified of me. She used to flinch if I moved too suddenly. At night, every night, I heard her crying because of me, and what I had done."

"*No.*" He sounded almost desperate, as if my story had sickened him as much as his had sickened me. "Don't say that."

"Why not?" I demanded. "You've never forgiven yourself. Why should I?"

There was silence in the little cave for a few minutes.

"All right," he said tiredly. "All right. You're like a landslide when you get started, you know. First the tiny stones, then the pebbles and rocks, then the boulders, raining down on you until you're squashed flat and all you can do is give up."

I let out a tiny, slightly mad laugh. "I'll try to count that as a compliment."

"I shouldn't if I were you." His voice had gone back to its normal dry tone. "Come here. You're shivering, and if we're to get a good night's rest we need to keep warm."

At his insistence, I helped Arian to lie flat again. I thought it might make him sick for a second time, but after some deep, slow breaths through his nose he gestured at me to lie beside him. He seemed surprised when I fitted myself against his side without hesitation.

"This seems … familiar," he said cautiously.

"I was keeping you warm earlier too," I admitted. "While you were unconscious."

He muttered something under his breath.

"What was that?" I asked, wondering if he could really have said, *Just my luck.*

"Nothing, nothing," he said. "Shut up and go to sleep."

It is the end of the nightmare that I dread most. I can never escape it, no matter how long or hard I run. Always, it comes to this.

The steep, jagged rock face towers over me, and my hands cannot find purchase for even one hold. Sobbing and wheezing, I scrabble uselessly at the rocks with bleeding fingers, searching for a crack, a crevice, something, anything, that will allow me to keep running. There is nothing. I can go no further.

The howling of wolves rises, echoing from the rocks that will become my tomb, filling my ears. I turn to face them as they pour over the snow towards me. Without hesitation the first one leaps, teeth bared and flashing in the starlight. I scream...

And in the same moment my scream becomes a snarl; my screaming mouth a muzzle of sharp fangs. I fall upon my weakened prey, tearing into warm flesh, iron-sweet blood splattering and smearing across my fur.

When my hunger is satisfied, I raise my dripping face to the moon and share a howl of victory with my brothers.

We are the Wolf.

Fear us.

Twenty-three

I propped myself up on one elbow and leaned over Arian. Even in sleep his face was grey and exhausted. He had made light of his injuries last night – but if anyone had the sheer stubbornness to start an argument when he was hovering at death's door, it was Arian. I was sore and bruised and my brain was fuzzy from the previous day's ordeal and the lack of food, and no one had even hit me on the head. And I knew that the Wolf was working away to heal me. Arian didn't have that blessing, mixed as it was. He needed rest.

Dawn had only just broken. Light was glinting off the river, but it was still dim in the little cave. I could sneak out and gather firewood without waking him. Once I'd got a fire going, he might be willing to wait for me to find food to cook over it. That would keep him still for a few more hours at least...

"I can feel you staring," he said, turning his head.

Abruptly we were nose to nose. Arian gulped audibly. I eased back, carefully wrapping my shirt around myself, hoping my cheeks weren't too red.

"Sorry. I didn't mean to wake you."

"I have to get up sometime," he said, eyes fixed determinedly on the roof of the cave.

"Not right now. I'm going to look for firewood and to see if I can find something for us to eat."

"Do you know anything about the edible plants and fungi of this country?" he asked, still looking at the roof.

I pulled a face. "It can't be that different from Uskaand. Or I could try to catch a fish."

Arian sighed, then rolled onto his side and cautiously pushed himself up into a sitting position. He made no sound, but his clenched jaw and the film of sweat that sprang up on his face made it obvious how much effort the movement had cost him.

"Idiot. You'd poison both of us in your efforts to distract me. We're not staying here, so put it out of your mind."

"Do you have any idea how terrible you look? You won't make it a mile in this state – and it might be fifty back to the old campsite. Why can't you just be sensible?"

"I'm fine. I've survived a lot worse than this little bump."

"I know," I said grimly.

Instead of growling at me as I'd half expected, he gave me a wry smile. "Yes. So try and be sensible yourself for once. We need to find the others. We don't have any hunting gear, or any food, and neither of us can forage well enough to keep us going for many days. I'm not going to get any better lying here until I starve to death. The first step is for me to try and figure out where we are. Then we can decide what to do next. Agreed?"

"Agreed," I said grudgingly.

"Good. Now let's get moving. The sooner we get out of this cave the better."

"Bossy, bossy," I muttered, crawling out from under the overhang onto the open sand.

"Says the woman who was pinning me to the ground last night," Arian called after me.

The sun was coming up into a long bank of thin, hazy clouds, and I was grateful for its warmth on my aching flesh. My stiff, damp breeches and boots would soon dry out properly. I laced my shirt and rolled up the sleeves, then knelt creakingly down to drink from the river. I heard shuffling noises and a couple of swear words as Arian dragged himself out of the cave behind me. Then there was a splashing as he followed my example, drinking and then splashing his face with handfuls of the icy water.

"How's your head?" he asked. "I never did look at it."

"A bit sore," I admitted.

"Your hair is full of blood. You ought to try and wash some of it out. It'll attract insects."

"*Eugh.*" Suddenly unravelling my damp, knotted hair seemed like much less of a bother.

After a few minutes of vigorous and painful scrubbing, I wrung out the thick rope of hair and bent my head forward for Arian to examine my scalp. His blunt fingers probed carefully. A memory of Luca brushing my hair drifted through my mind, filling me with such confused emotions that I could barely separate pleasure from worry and embarrassment.

You are all right, aren't you, Luca? Father, please let him be all right...

"There are some nasty deep scratches," Arian said, breaking into my thoughts. "You need these cleaned out as soon as possible. Livia will probably want to stitch one or two of them. Can you rebraid your hair over the top? Then the flies won't to be able to get in."

I shuddered. "Yes. I can definitely do that."

When I'd achieved a braid that pulled my wet hair over the worst of the scratches, I retrieved my axe, gave the blades – washed clean of blood by the river – a quick rub with the loose tail of my shirt and then put on my still clammy armoured jerkin and the axe-harness, which had only warped a little. The weight of the weapon made my back ache, but there was no chance I was leaving it behind. Lastly I buckled my vambraces and put on the gloves, which, though still damp, were wearable. My leather choker was almost completely dry, but it had shrunk and cracked and the metal studs were popping out. I reluctantly discarded it. Meanwhile, Arian was fastening his shirt and carefully pulling on his own jerkin. I resisted the urge to help. He wouldn't appreciate it.

I approached the bank that curved around the little inlet, took two handfuls of the thick, coarse vegetation that grew over the edges, dug the tip of my boot in for traction, and heaved myself up onto the top. I tested the solidity of the ground with a few stamps, then leaned down and held my hands out to Arian.

He followed my path, grabbing my hands for the final pull that got him up over the edge. He was breathing heavily when he straightened up, and as he let go he made as if to touch his head, but checked the movement. Once again, I suppressed the urge to scold. I'd already seen that it made no difference. Instead I turned away to study the landscape that now lay before us. The bank sloped up for about a hundred yards before being hidden in the trees, and behind them I could see the shapes of the mountains. They didn't look as far away as I'd expected.

"Any thoughts on where we might be?" I asked.

"We've been lucky. I'm sure this is still the Mesgao. I recognize that ridge, and I'd say we're only a day's hard tramp from the campsite. We might even meet the others on the way."

"Then I suppose we should get going," I said.

I chose to walk on Arian's left and slightly behind him; I kept a careful eye on his gait so that if he staggered or fell I could at least try to catch him. The bank was not steep compared to most of the trails in the mountains, but by the time we reached the trees Arian's breathing was uneven.

"I just need to hit my stride," he said, without looking at me, as we moved into the shade of the forest. "Stop fussing."

I rolled my eyes and pushed ahead of him, tramping down the undergrowth and holding back branches as unobtrusively as possible. He gave me a couple of annoyed looks, but didn't ask me to stop, and that added to my worry. It was a steady uphill climb through the trees. Within an hour or so the rising sun had made the air humid and sticky and Arian's face had taken on that worrying ashen look again.

I wanted to urge him to stop and rest, but I was sure if I suggested it he would shrug it off and walk faster just to prove he could. I began to listen for the sounds of a brook or stream. Drinking was a reason to stop that he wouldn't be able to ignore.

By my reckoning it was nearly another hour before I picked up the sound of water ahead. Arian's progress had slowed more and more – he had begun to walk with his hands slightly extended in front of him, as if he expected to fall. The tiny brook bubbled up swiftly out of a rocky fissure in the side of the hill, and as soon as we reached it Arian sat down on one of the sun-warmed rocks near by. That more than anything told me how exhausted he must be.

"Stubborn, prideful fool," I muttered under my breath as I stripped off my gloves and hung them from my belt.

I examined the fissure, reassured by the coloured lichen and moss growing on the rocks. This was a sign that the water was good. I picked a large, waxy leaf off one of the bushes that were thriving around the brook and rolled it up into a tight cone shape, then let some of the water flow into it. Once I had filled the leaf I sniffed the water, dipped my finger in and tasted it. No strong metallic taste or residue on my tongue. Good.

I carried the water back to Arian. "Try to drink."

"Not an invalid," he said shortly. But he took the leaf and drained it in two gulps.

"More?"

He nodded. I refilled the leaf cone and brought it back. Again he gulped the water down. After a moment he laid back, putting his forearm over his eyes. I sat on the ground and leaned on the rock, pillowing my cheek on folded arms. Arian's wheezy breaths seemed to even out, and I thought there was a hint of healthier colour in his face now.

"I can feel you watching. Again."

"It's not often I get the chance to look at such a rare pig head," I said, trying to keep the anxiety out of my voice. "I'm making the best of it."

"It's a good thing you've got those eyes," he muttered a little sleepily. "Otherwise your mouth would scare all your lovers away."

I snorted. "It's a good thing you've got a skull like a rock, or your soft brain would have been beaten to a pulp by now."

"It's a good thing you're here," he said softly. "Or…"

"Or?" I said, after a minute had gone by.

A tiny snuffle answered me. He had fallen asleep.

I leaned my forehead on my arms, closing my eyes, and let myself drift for a few minutes. Then one of Ma's sayings drifted into my mind. If someone had a head injury and kept falling asleep, it could be a bad sign. I lifted my head and squinted at Arian's face. He looked peaceful enough, but how were you supposed to tell a natural sleep from something more sinister?

I stood up, leaning my hip against the edge of the rock as I gently pressed his shoulder. "Arian. Wake up."

Reassuringly, his eyes blinked open at once. He focused on me without difficulty. "Did I…? Sorry." He sat up carefully, rubbing the back of his neck.

"If you're really tired then you should sleep, but we need to find somewhere with better cover," I said, feeling guilty.

Arian opened his mouth as if to deny that he was the slightest bit tired, but apparently something in my eye warned him against it. He shrugged. "I suppose I'm not as young as I used to be."

"Oh no, old greybeard. It must be a struggle to keep up with us youngsters, as ancient as you are."

"I'm twenty," he said, with dignity. "When I was your age I'd have shaken that blow off like a bee sting."

"Of course you would," I agreed calmly. "And you could sprout wings to drop rocks on your enemies' heads as well. You knocked me out handily the day we met, and it took me two days to recover. And ... I've an advantage you don't."

"Advantage...?"

I sat down on the rock next to him when his voice trailed off. "The Wolf."

"You called it that last night. Is that how you think of your battle rage?"

I nodded silently. I didn't intend to confide the full story of my curse to him, not here and not now. The truce between us still felt fragile, and only Luca could have accepted my mad ravings about gods and demons with barely the blink of an eye.

Arian was right when he said that Luca acted as if he were immortal.

I had a sudden vision of Luca falling, hurt, blood seeping onto his uniform. My chest seemed to contract.

I had to gasp quietly for breath as panic tried to over-whelm me.

Arian frowned at me. "What's the matter?"

I tried to laugh. The sound was feeble, and more tell-tale than a sob. "No, nothing. I was – I was thinking about Luca and about what you said before – that he ... he has no fear. He needs us there, to remind him that he's human. And we're here instead. I can't – what if—" My voice cut off.

Arian said softly, "I've been trying to keep him safe for years. Sometimes it feels as if I'm working *against* him, because the confidence he has, the faith ... after every-thing he's been through, it's almost frightening."

"He's not like us, is he?" I said, staring down at my rough, scarred hands. "It's as if people – normal people – are made of silver. Shiny to start with, but tarnished by time, by ill-treatment. Luca ... Luca is gold. Nothing in the world could ever make him shine less brightly."

"You understand him," Arian said, sighing. "That's good."

Was it? Was it really good for me to know just how wide a gap lay between Luca and me, how mismatched we were? Could any love survive that great a disparity, even the love of a person like Luca? Because I wasn't nor-mal. I wasn't silver. I had never been bright and shiny and clean.

I was base metal.

What if Luca wore himself out trying to turn me into gold?

Arian shifted closer to me on the rock, as if offering reassurance. "Frost ... don't *worry* so much all the time. You'll wear yourself out."

I laughed again, a better laugh this time. Grateful for the distraction, I turned to look at him. "You're the last one in the world who should be giving that advice!"

He was closer than I had realized. I could see the tiny brownish-grey flecks in his eyes, and the dark green ring around the iris, and for the first time I realized that they were beautiful. Arian was beautiful. Perhaps in his own way as beautiful as Luca.

In the next moment his big, rough, fingers cupped my face. He brought our lips together, taking possession of my mouth. Shock – and something else, something guilty and excited that made me squirm – thrilled through me. I put a hand up blindly, and my palm found his heart. I could feel its fast, erratic rhythm. He was shaking.

I pushed at him. He resisted, fingers tightening on my face. Instantly fear overwhelmed shock. I smacked both my hands against his chest, bracing myself to struggle in earnest.

He released me.

I stared up at him. He was breathing hard, but his expression was indecipherable. I couldn't tell if he was angry, embarrassed or disappointed. I couldn't tell if *I* was angry, embarrassed or disappointed.

Disappointed?

Before either of us could say anything, a strange voice called out: "Well, well – it looks like we're interrupting something!"

Twenty-four

I jerked away from Arian and scrambled to my feet on the rock. Da's axe seemed to leap into my hand with a will of its own. I turned to face the speaker.

It was a man. A Sedorne. He stood on the hill above the brook, one hand casually propped on his sword hilt. He was about thirty, I thought, and tall, with a slim, well-muscled frame. He seemed familiar. Something about the shape of his face? Or his confident, graceful posture? It made me want to relax, as if he were a friend.

Until I met his eyes. They were a striking, clear, grey-ish blue, emphasized by the severe way his pale hair was braided back from his face. Something dark – no, more than just dark, *gleeful* – lurked behind those eyes. I had seen that look before. In Ulem's eyes. In Werrick's. This was no friend of mine. A long, cold shudder worked down my back.

As I watched, more Sedorne soldiers began to appear through the trees, ranging themselves beside the first. Four, five, six... I counted twelve, thirteen including the speaker. A stealthy rustle in the vegetation behind me told me there were others too. We were already surrounded. Surrounded while I had been letting Arian kiss me. Why had he *done* that? Why on earth had I let him, even for a second?

Father, forgive me for being so stupid.

These men had to be rebels. They were all paleskinned and mostly light-haired; although they were cleaner, better armoured and better armed than the ones I had seen before. There were two crossbows aimed at us. Or rather, I realized, aimed at Arian, who still sat motionless on the rock behind me.

The man with the wicked eyes laughed. It was a bubbling, infectious sound, one that would have made me want to laugh too, if I hadn't been rigid with fear.

"Finally found yourself a lady-love, Arian?" he said. "I never thought I'd see the day. Not when you've been following Luca around like a lost puppy for so long. Why don't you introduce me to her? Or better yet, why don't you tell me where dear Luca is?"

They know each other. I flicked a quick glance at Arian. His face was utterly blank, eyes as glacial as the first time I had seen him. Slowly he eased himself to his feet and stood beside me, breathing raggedly.

"You're not fit to speak his name," he said acidly.

"More fit than a dirty half-breed bastard," the Sedorne man said, still smiling. "But it doesn't matter. I've been hunting my little brother up and down this mountain for months, and today I am going to find him. Catching you is an unexpected bonus which I fully intend to enjoy. And won't *that* break his heart?"

A cold sweat sprang out over my body. Out of the corner of my eye, I saw Arian's hands curl slowly into fists.

Little brother.

Ion Constantin turned his bright gaze on me again. "I've no grudge against you, however. You can make it easier on yourself by telling me where you're going. I'll find out anyway, you know, but the less annoyed I am when I do, the less you'll suffer."

His tone made it clear that I was going to suffer anyway. Not because he really wanted or needed information, but because he would enjoy it.

I looked helplessly at the crossbowmen. We were so grossly outnumbered. Arian was barely able to walk, let alone fight. He didn't even have a knife. All that stood between him and death was me.

I could feel my breath speeding up; my heart starting to jump. Fear heightened my senses to an almost painful pitch.

We're going to die. There's nothing I can do.

Father, what now? How am I supposed to save him?

Ion was still staring at me, awaiting an answer. Finally, he shrugged and turned his attention back to Arian. "A little slow in the brain, is she? That would explain why she was cosied up with you, I suppose. If she understands Rua, you should tell her to put her axe down now, before I take it from her."

A howl rang through the woods.

Ion was still speaking, saying more poisonous things to Arian. I could barely make out his voice. The Wolf's cry grew louder, louder, vibrating through my bones. But I was the only one who could hear it.

Icy cold was seeping into my veins. I blinked, and the clearing was painted in shades of black and silver.

I haven't seen blood. This shouldn't be happening.

Ion's face was eager and triumphant now; his voice was raised. The rebels were moving forward, closing in around us.

Struggling against the rising cold, I managed to catch Arian's eye.

"Run." The word broke and twisted, turning into a deep, rumbling growl.

Arian stared at me for a second, then threw himself down off the rock, out of my way. I felt a surge of relief that he had understood – and in that instant lost my grip on my body.

The ice flowed up and surrounded the part of me that was Frost, the part that Luca had called my soul, trapping hopes and thoughts and heart deep inside, where they could only watch without reaching the surface.

The Wolf awoke.

Sound flooded the Wolf's ears and its lips curled back into a sharp grin as it spun the axe in its hands, surveying the group of enemies that approached it. This body knew how to use the axe properly now. This body was stronger and faster than it had ever been.

The Wolf was going to enjoy this.

"Put your weapon down like a good girl," the man — some part of the Wolf knew he was the primary enemy — called from his place above the brook. "It'll hurt less that way."

The Wolf threw back its head and let out a deep, mournful howl. The men advancing on it hesitated, exchanging looks of surprise and doubt.

The Wolf leaped off the rock to meet them.

The leap became a flying roundhouse kick that downed the first enemy. A single slice of the axe ended the man's life. Blood splattered the Wolf's face and it breathed in the powerful hot-copper smell and growled. Another man charged. The Wolf ducked the blow and jabbed the metal langet of the axe into his belly. The man doubled over, retching. The Wolf took his head, then whipped the axe back to block a sword blow aimed at its neck.

As the sword skidded off the axe blade the Wolf spun,

grabbed the attacker's sword hand and kicked out at his sternum. There was a loud pop as the man's arm dislocated from his shoulder. He screamed. The Wolf snapped his wrist with a flex of its hand and kicked again, at his side this time, listening for the snap of breaking ribs.

The leader of the enemies shouted: "Bows!"

An arrow whizzed past the Wolf's head. It ducked again, using its victim's body as a shield, and the second arrow thudded into the enemy's chest instead. The Wolf dropped the dead man while he was still twitching.

The Wolf sensed movement behind it. It fell to one knee, and as the sword pierced the air where it had stood, it wrenched the arrow from the dead enemy's torso and stabbed the swordsman in the thigh. By the time the man hit the ground, yelling in agony and clutching at his leg, the Wolf was on its feet again. A well-placed kick to the throat finished the yelling.

Another arrow landed in a tree next to the Wolf. It snarled, then turned and charged directly uphill towards the crossbowman, spinning the axe.

The bowman backed away, desperately fumbling a fresh bolt into the notch and ratcheting the bowstring – before he could pull the trigger, the Wolf had brought him down. Leaving the axe buried in the man's chest, the Wolf seized the crossbow. It turned, tracked the path of the second bowman, who was running for his life downhill, and planted an arrow in his skull.

As the man fell, the Wolf howled again, a cry of triumph. It dropped the crossbow and wrenched its axe free, finally fixing its attention on the primary enemy – the man standing alone at the top of the hill. The man drew his sword and made a beckoning gesture with his hand.

The Wolf ran to meet its challenger.

"You're formidable," the man said warily, edging backwards. "Wasted in the hill guard. Soft-hearted Luca can't possibly appreciate you—"

The Wolf swept the axe up at the man's head. The blade rebounded from the man's sword with a deep clang, and the Wolf growled. It turned the recoil of the axe into a spin, ducked under the man's next blow and aimed the pick at his side.

Again the enemy wrenched his sword down to block just in time. The axe met the blade with a screech and a shower of metal sparks.

Then a new voice cried out: "Here they are! *Attack*."

The hidden fragment of consciousness that was still me stirred, recognizing Livia's voice.

The Wolf snarled as the clearing filled with more men and women, these in a different uniform. They began to attack the remnants of the first group.

"Time for me to be going, I think," the primary enemy said, disengaging his sword and taking a hasty step back. "Men! To me!"

The Wolf felt the blow coming for its back and whirled.

It spun the axe in a massive arc, carving through the new attacker's chest and pushing him off the axe blade with a powerful kick.

The Wolf turned again to see the primary enemy fleeing into the woods, his few surviving men right behind him. The Wolf let out an infuriated bark, and turned to face the new people – the ones who had balked it of its desired prey.

Trapped deep inside, I struggled wildly. Through the Wolf's silver-painted vision, I could see the hill guards streaming through the trees, faces friendly and relieved. They were sheathing their weapons. They thought the danger was past, their enemy gone.

Stop, Wolf! Stop!

"Did you and Arian account for all these, Frost?" Livia called out as she jogged toward the Wolf, looking at the rebels' bodies strewn between the trees. "To think we were worried about you! Are you all right?"

"Livia, get away from her!"

I heard Arian's warning shout and screamed silently, thrashing and kicking against the cold bonds that held me a prisoner in my own body. *No, no, not Livia. No!*

The Wolf lifted its axe and lunged at the grey-haired woman.

Livia narrowly dodged the blow and jumped back, face clearly showing her shock. "Frost, calm down," she said in a slow, coaxing voice. "It's me."

"What's wrong with her?" someone else called out breathlessly. Through the Wolf's eyes I saw others hurrying towards us, worry darkening their faces.

"Get back!" Arian shouted. He was struggling up the hill towards us, keeping to his feet by grabbing the trees for balance as he passed. "She's in a battle rage; she doesn't recognize you."

Livia had backed away a little, turning her head to listen to Arian. The Wolf sensed its enemy's distraction and ran forward, aiming the axe pick in a vicious arc towards her neck.

Livia turned just in time to save her life. The slender blade sliced along the side of her shoulder, opening up a long, deep cut. She screamed with agony, stumbled backwards, and fell to her knees. The other hill guards were racing up the slope, yelling.

NO!

Suddenly my right arm was my own again. My weak, human fingers tightened around the haft of the axe and I held on with all my might as the Wolf tried to bring the blade down on Livia again. The axe shuddered, jerking up, then back, as I fought against the force that controlled my body. The Wolf's lips curled over its teeth. It snapped and growled in frustration.

No. No. No.

Bright threads were bleeding back into my vision. I stared at Livia, who had slumped onto the ground.

Blood – a glowing red that hurt my colour-starved eyes – was streaming through her fingers as she tried to apply pressure to her own wound. She was deathly pale, her breathing shallow.

My fingers, flushed with human warmth again, were sweating and slippery. The axe haft slid in my grasp. The Wolf's lips peeled back on a snarl. The rest of the hill guards were nearly upon us now, drawing their weapons as they converged on the friend who had gone mad and attacked one of their own.

"She can't help it. Let me through. Get out of the way. Let me through!" Arian was shouting. He was too far away.

The axe slipped from my fingers. The Wolf's arm ripped the weapon away and drew it up. Livia cringed back, closing her eyes.

A streak of gold and blue burst through the trees and hit the Wolf, almost knocking it from its feet. A warm hand closed on the icy fingers that held the axe.

"Frost. Frost," Luca whispered, burying his face in the Wolf's – in my – hair. "I know you're there. I know you can hear me. It can't take your soul."

The ice that held me shivered. The fingers that clutched at the axe went slack. Gently Luca eased the Wolf's arm down. "Come back. I know you're in there. Come back to me."

The Wolf growled in disgust … and faded.

The axe dropped from my hand and landed in the grass. I sagged against Luca. He eased me down, supporting me around the shoulders as I slid bonelessly to the forest floor.

I shivered, muscles twitching and cramping. But that pain was nothing – *nothing* – compared to the memory of what the Wolf had done.

I stared up at Luca, feeling tears well up and trickle down my face. "Livia..." I whispered, voice coming out hoarse and broken.

"Rani!" Luca snapped the Rua healer's name, turning his head. "How is she?"

"She's losing blood fast," Rani said, her soft voice cracking. "Quick, someone give me a belt! I need to make a tourniquet. Keep your hand there!"

"See," Luca said. He stroked the tears gently from my cheeks. "Rani is taking care of her. It will be all right."

I turned my eyes to the circle of grim-faced hill guards that stood above me. "No. It won't."

Twenty-five

I stared at the shabby, patched walls of the tent where I'd been sleeping for the past three days. The space was cramped, and the roof leaked when dew formed on it in the mornings. But Luca's large tent, along with the fine tapestries, rugs and furniture that had once filled it, had all been left behind in the desperate scramble to escape the ambush.

I wished more than anything that was all we had lost.

My fingers clenched on the strap of my pack.

Put it on. Put it on, get up, and walk away. Do it now, before he comes back.

Do it now, before you end up hurting him too.

Footsteps sounded outside the tent. Deliberate, heavy footsteps, from a man who never normally made a sound. It was Luca's way of giving me privacy since there was no screen to hide me any more. Hastily I shoved the pack out of sight under a stool and sat down on it.

The flap opened and Luca poked his head in. His tired face brightened when he saw that I was dressed and out of my bedroll. The tenderness in his eyes was a punch to my stomach. I hunched over, fixing my gaze on my hands.

"You're looking better. How do you feel?"

I gritted my teeth. "I'm fine. I'm always fine. How's Livia?"

There was a short pause.

"She's a little bored. Rani's practically having to sit on her to make her rest. She wants to be up and doing. I imagine she'll escape the infirmary by tomorrow."

"What about her arm?"

Another pause.

"It's healing."

"Will she be able to *use* it?"

Luca let out a long sigh. From the corner of my eye, I watched him duck under the flap and come all the way into the tent. The fact that the captain had been hovering in the entrance of what was supposed to be his own living space made me grit my teeth again. He came towards me and dropped down onto the other camping stool before speaking.

"Rani doesn't know yet. Livia can move her fingers, which is good. There's some weakness, which might easily get better."

"Or it might not."

I remembered Livia's immense kindness to me, even when I had been a prisoner in a cell. The way she had bared her own painful history to make me feel comfortable here. I remembered her strong, competent fingers picking through herbs, writing notes. I remembered the way her face shone with determination and pride as she worked.

All gone now, maybe forever. Because of the Wolf. Because of *me*.

"It wasn't your fault," Luca said into the silence. "You have to stop punishing yourself."

"Livia may spend the rest of her life suffering for what I did. Some guilt is a light payment compared to that."

"She doesn't blame you. I don't blame you. No one blames you, except you." There was a trace of impatience in Luca's tone now. He had already repeated these words to me many times. I resisted the need to look at him, keeping my gaze down. Every glance at Luca hurt me now.

"I explained the battle rage to everyone. I told them it was my decision to have you fight despite that. I told them you couldn't help it. It was my responsibility."

"You mean you lied to them. You didn't tell them about the curse. About the Wolf, and the people I've hurt before."

"What would have been the point of that? They don't believe in curses. Neither do I."

"They have a right to know how dangerous I am."

"They've already seen that for themselves. What you

want isn't to give them fair warning, it's to turn them all against you so that you have an excuse to run away."

My head snapped up.

Luca's eyes met mine squarely, and I felt shamed heat rushing into my cheeks – the only heat anywhere in my chilled body.

"I'm not blind, you know," he said, the hurt clear in his voice. "I can see that pack you're sitting on."

I felt my face crumple. I tried to turn away, but Luca was there, kneeling before me, putting strong arms around me and enveloping me in warmth. His summer, honeysuckle scent made me sigh. "I'm not letting you go," he whispered, lips against my forehead.

"This isn't fair," I protested weakly. I was already going soft, my whole body trembling with the need to lean into Luca and let him take my weight. Take my burdens.

The Wolf is my burden.

I straightened up with a jerk, forcing myself out of Luca's arms and onto my feet. I turned in a tight circle, pacing backwards and forwards like an animal in a cage.

Luca rose to his feet.

I warded him off with one hand. "You can't fix this. You can't fix me. No one can. The Wolf is getting stronger. It doesn't need my blood any more. I could go mad at any time and attack anyone. Including you. I can't take that risk. Be the captain I know you are and admit you can't either."

"I don't need you to lecture me on my duty," Luca said, low and strained. "Do you have any idea what I've been dealing with while you've been hiding in this tent refusing to see anyone? We lost twenty-two men in the ambush. Twenty-two of our own, dead. There are some in the infirmary who still might not pull through. Hind almost lost her eye. I'm responsible for *all* of that, and somehow I have to figure out our next move and decide if we have any chance against the rebels now. I need you, Frost. I need you with me, helping me through this. I don't need you threatening to leave."

For the first time I felt I could almost hate Luca. Why couldn't he ever just give up? I wanted to turn on him, to rage and shout at his stupid, courageous optimism, at his refusal to acknowledge that his grand plans for defeating the Wolf had failed. Now I knew why Arian had flown into a fury at him, that second night I was in camp, when Arian had found me in Luca's tent. It hadn't been about me at all. It had been about the fact that Luca had no regard for his own safety, and one day it would get him killed.

But I couldn't break. I had to keep those emotions tamped down, pressed into that tight, black ball of despair that lurked under my ribs. I couldn't afford to lose control now, even for an instant.

"I can't help you," I said, as quietly and calmly as I could. "I can't help anyone. Not even myself."

"Why?" Luca demanded. "I understand if you don't feel you can fight any more, but that doesn't mean you have to abandon us. You're still one of us, aren't you? You said yourself this isn't forever, that one day we'll succeed in capturing Ion and have the rest of our lives ahead of us. Don't you believe that any more?"

My neck and shoulders, all the bones in my head, were aching with tension – with the effort it took to resist Luca's words. "I care for you, Luca. More than for anyone I've ever met in my life. I would do anything for you. I'd die for you."

Surprise, happiness and confusion passed across Luca's face like clouds moving over the sun. He reached out for me.

I backed away. "That's why I have to go. Here, with you, I've changed. My emotions are like water pushing against a dam. The moment I give into them, I open the door to the Wolf again. I can't stay with you. Not without putting you and everyone else here in danger."

The happiness died out of Luca's face, leaving it weary and drawn. "Where are you going to go, Frost? Where can you possibly run to be safe from yourself? If you don't face this now, you will spend the rest of your life running. Too scared to fight. Too scared to love. You'll be your own prisoner. And you'll never be free."

The words rang through my bones with the awful weight of a prophesy. I stared at him in despair.

A familiar voice broke into the tense silence, singing the first lines of one of the traditional Mother's Fire songs.

Arian.

"They must have given up on me." Luca sighed, rubbing his forehead tiredly. "I came to fetch you. We're having a gathering at the firepit to honour the fallen. Will you come? Please?"

Other voices were joining Arian's now, and instruments. Just like the first time I had heard it, I was drawn to the music. But it wasn't for me. It never had been. I shook my head. "They won't want me there."

"I want you there." Luca held out his hand, the lines of sorrow on his face making him look years older.

My fingers twitched, hand yearning to reach out to him. I lifted it – and closed it around my wolf tooth. The sharp tip dug deeply into my palm. I welcomed the pain.

We both stared at his still extended hand. Slowly his fingers curled into a fist and dropped.

"You can't always have what you want," I said.

"No. But you can hold onto what you have," he said softly. "Don't try to leave while I'm gone, because I will come after you. We haven't finished yet."

I nodded shortly.

"Say it."

I ground my teeth together, trapped. "I promise."

"That's good enough for me." He gave me a tight,

unhappy smile, a mere echo of his normal golden grin, and left the tent.

I let out a shuddering breath. Damn him. Now I was trapped here for another night at least. Trapped where no one wanted me to be, not even myself. No one except Luca.

Arian's voice echoed through the thin canvas walls, mingling with the mournful wood pipe, the slow beat of the drum. I even thought I could hear the crackling and whispering of the flames, though that should have been impossible. The sound called to me, beckoned to me. But I knew what I would see if I gave in. Friends' eyes, full of hatred and distrust. Beloved faces, turned into masks of loathing. My own comrades flinching away from me.

I would not see family. I would see my own exile.

I paced up and down, trying to ignore the call of the flames and the singing voices. A dozen times my eyes turned to my half-hidden pack, and I jerked my head away. I couldn't break my promise. But I wanted to. Oh, how I wanted to.

> *"Farewell, my love, our time has come,*
> *Long though I might to stay…"*

I went still as the achingly familiar melody of that song filled my ears.

My resolve shattered.

Barely knowing what I did, I pushed open the tent

flap and stepped outside into the gathering dusk. The light of the Mother's Fire flickered between tents, and the singing voices filled my ears, drawing me onwards as I drifted through the deserted camp towards the firepit.

"Our time has come, my one true love,
The world calls me away..."

A belated sense of caution sounded just before I arrived at the fire. I stopped next to one of the big tents, peering through the gap at the people gathered around the white firepit. The stripped logs were empty tonight, though the space was crowded, packed with every hill guard who could stand. My eyes searched for Luca and found him and Arian side by side, their shoulders almost touching. Somehow despite the difference in their looks they seemed alike in that moment – sternly upright, faces grave as they sang, eyes filled with fire.

Hind was on Luca's other side. Even in the golden flicker of the firelight she looked pale and ill. A thick bandage was wrapped around her face, covering one eye. She leaned into Luca's arm as if she needed his support.

I tore my eyes away from the sight of Luca's hand gently gripping Hind's waist, and realized that Rani was nearly opposite me. She would see me if she looked up. I drew back warily into the shadow of the tent, thankful for the gathering darkness that hid me. The Rua healer looked almost as drawn and weary as Hind; she was staring into the blaze as if she were searching for answers. There was a conspicuously empty space beside her. The space that should have been Livia's.

My wolf tooth felt like a shard of ice against my palm.

I did not try to sing. There was no place for my voice in this music, in this song of power and mourning, a prayer to a goddess that I still did not understand. I fixed my gaze on the deep blue centre of the fire, where colours rippled and danced, more like water than flame.

Their flickering slowed, the pointed tongues of flame elongating, rich blue bleeding into white, into silver, until they resembled a crown of icicles, burning icy-hot within the pit. A warning chill brushed my spine. Instinctively I started to look away, to turn from the flames.

Running from my fear, just as I always had.

Where are you going to go, Frost? Where can you possibly run to be safe from yourself?

For the first time, I had a life that I did not want to leave behind. I had friends. I had love. I had … myself. All I had ever wanted. I didn't want to run this time. I didn't want to look away. My grip on the wolf tooth tightened desperately. I felt my skin split with a sharp sting, and the trickle of blood on my palm.

Father. Please. Help me.

The lonely cry of the Wolf rose up in the night, a cry that only I could hear. I trembled with the desire to flee.

You will spend the rest of your life running. Too scared to fight. Too scared to love.

The Wolf's howl was louder now. Closer.

Father, why don't you answer me? Why is the only time I hear you in my nightmares?

Father?

Was Luca right? Did I have a choice? Did I have a soul? Did I have the right to pray to his goddess and hope for an answer? My need had never been greater than now. I couldn't go on like this any more. If I had to leave Luca, I would leave behind any hope of happiness, or a normal life. I would leave behind belief, and love, and hope. I might as well die.

My breath clouded in the air before me, and I could feel the tickling as the blood on my palm began to freeze. Ice crystals scattered from my hair as blue sparks drifted up from the fire and spiralled towards the emerging stars. Towards the Mother.

You'll never be free.

In a single movement I tore the wolf tooth from around my neck and threw it. Droplets of blood glittered in the firelight as it flew, carrying the dark, seething knot of my despair with it, carrying all the fear and anger I did not dare to express. With a quiet sizzle, it landed in the fire.

Take my message. Hear my prayer.

The singing faltered as people turned to see where the missile had flown from, and noticed me standing there.

An angry murmur rushed through the crowd. Luca's face brightened as he caught sight of me. Arian frowned, his expression worried. I ignored them all.

Please, Mother. Holy Mother. I lay myself at your feet. I offer my life into your hands. I beg you. Please.

Help me.

A voice of overwhelming power, crackling and spitting and dangerous, and yet somehow kind, too, spoke in my mind. I cried out, involuntarily clapping my hands over my ears.

ꟽy daughter. You only had to ask.

Before me, the fire exploded, sucking in air with a great, hollow *whoomph*.

The closest hill guards fell back with cries of wonder and alarm as the flames lashed out like the tendrils of an unearthly plant. Fire hooked itself onto the air and swarmed upwards, unfurling, tangling, growing. Strange colours – colours I had never seen before, and had no name for – pulsed within it, making my eyes water. Within a moment the firepit had become a fiery column, roaring and whirling as it stretched up towards the stars.

The Wolf's howl was nearly deafening me now, sending darts of pain through my skull. Frost was blooming on my skin, a thick, crackling layer. Every instinct I had told me to turn and run. Run before the Wolf took control. Run, before everyone saw what I was. Run before I hurt someone again.

I forced myself to step forward. The hill guards that were still on their feet parted before me, faces awed and frightened. I kept moving until my boots rested on the smooth white stones edging the pit.

"Frost, no!"

Luca's voice cut through the snarling of the Wolf and the roar of the fire. Stiffly, the movement sending flakes of ice showering off me, I managed to turn. Luca was reaching out to me, eyes anguished. Arian and another hill guard were clinging to the back of his jerkin, as if to stop him plunging after me.

"You can't!" he cried. "It's madness – just a legend. You could die. You could burn. You might never come back!"

I wanted to say *I'm sorry*, but my lips wouldn't move. I tried to tell him with my eyes instead. *I can't run any more. I can't run from you. This is the only choice I have left.*

It's this – or nothing.

Still staring into his eyes, I let myself topple backwards into the fire.

Twenty-six

Half-burned logs crunched and disintegrated as I landed, sending black ash and glowing sparks spinning around me like living creatures. I felt no heat. Only a pleasant warmth beating against my cheeks, my belly, my hands. The thick coating of ice on my skin sizzled softly and began to evaporate.

Then the column of fire closed, trapping me within.

White heat engulfed me. I shrieked, writhing in agony. My skin blackened and cracked open and then vaporized. I became a long, screaming streak of flame within the blaze. For a blink of time I could hear Luca screaming too, somewhere beyond the fire, but the heat had taken my sight. I could not see him. I couldn't see anything.

Hush, wolf-child...

Everything went white.

It took me a moment to realize that I was still alive. My lungs were working like bellows. My head rang with the sound of my own screaming. I could feel my heart beating. If my heart was beating, then my body wasn't burned away.

Experimentally, I moved one hand, expecting pain to rip through me. But my arm shifted smoothly. I peeled my eyes open to look. The skin was brown and whole, unmarked. I blinked. Blinked again. The whiteness hadn't been in my mind. I was lying in a hollow, surrounded by banks of snow.

Am I dreaming this?

Cautiously, I rolled over and sat up, examining my body. There wasn't a scorch mark on me. Not so much as a smudge of ash on my clothes. And when I put one hand on the snow and pressed down, the crust did not crack or give beneath the warmth of my skin. It wasn't even cold.

Slowly, I climbed to my feet and looked around. I was in a forest like the ones at home. A winter forest of black, spiny branches and hard azure skies.

I climbed down from the bank of snow – the ice was as hard and steady beneath my feet as steps of stone – and saw that, near by, there was a small wooden house. Icicles hung from the low eaves, but the path and doorstep had been swept. A winter bird trilled sweetly, hidden somewhere in the wood. As I moved closer to the house the door swung open. I stopped in my tracks.

A couple emerged to stand on the scrubbed stone doorstep. They didn't appear to notice me, even though I was close enough to count the freckles on the woman's nose.

The woman had straight, dark hair coiled around her head in a thick braid. Her nut-brown eyes were full of life and happiness as she looked up at the man. Her belly, swelling the front of her simple blue gown, showed that she was far gone with child.

The man was much taller than her, with powerful shoulders and light brown hair that curled wildly around his face. His eyes were grey. He looked a few years older than the woman, perhaps in his mid-thirties. He turned to face her and cupped her neck with one big, blunt hand. His fingers lay on the vulnerable skin gently.

"Stop worriting," he commanded, his voice a deep rumble.

I stiffened as I recognized the voice.

"I wish you would stay home. I do not want my husband searching for a Demon Wolf," the woman said. But she was teasing, not anxious. "We've enough coins saved, Garin. Stay in the warm with me."

"You tempting lass," he said, laughing as he dropped a kiss on her cheek. "I've promised to do a job, and I must do it. Now, can I go without fearing I'll arrive home to find you mending the roof, or scrubbing the floors? Tell me true."

The woman sighed. "Very well. I'll rest as you ask." She turned away and drew out a long, heavy coat made from a luxuriant black-edged silver pelt that I recognized immediately as a wolf fur. She held it out to the man and he took it and shrugged it on over his thick, padded doublet. He picked up a heavy leather pack, from which pieces of curved metal with vicious teeth dangled. Wolf traps. A double-headed axe, its shaft reinforced with iron langets, was bound to the top.

"Don't make supper for me," he said. "If I must stay out a day or two, I must. But I shall be home to take you into town on church day, don't fear."

The woman smiled, clasping his free hand, but now a shadow of concern darkened her eyes. "You will take care? The tales they tell in the town…"

He laughed, drawing their joined hands down to touch her belly. "Superstition and fear, my lass. A wolf is a wolf. A canny and dangerous beast, to be respected, to be hunted with care, but never feared. There is no wolf that can outface Garin Aeskaar."

He kissed her again and stepped off the doorstep. He waited until she had closed the door and the key could be heard to grind in the lock before turning towards the bleak, spiny cover of the trees. As he went his carefree smile disappeared, and his face grew hard and determined.

"No wolf," he muttered to himself. "No mortal wolf."

He passed right by me, the soft fur of his coat

brushing my hand. Then he disappeared into the forest. I stood frozen, staring after him.

Garin Aeskaar was my father. That woman was my mother. Before I was born. This ... this was the last time she had ever seen him alive.

Go with him. The voice of the flames spoke into my mind. **You must see what happens next**.

Trembling with excitement, I obeyed, following the man – my father – into the woods.

Between one blink and the next night fell. I emerged from the trees and found myself in a clearing, looking at a hide of sturdy stripped branches and oilskins. My father sat in the shelter, the wolf-fur coat around his shoulders. A little pot bubbled merrily over a tiny fire. The smell of stewing meat and herbs reached my nose and made my stomach gurgle.

As I appeared, the fire flared up beneath the pot, flames tinged with blue and yellow and green. My father did not seem to notice. He began to sing, his voice soft, as he stirred the pot.

> *"Farewell, my love, our time has come,*
> *Long though I might to stay;*
> *Our time has come, my one true love,*
> *The world calls me away—"*

A vicious, rumbling growl broke into the song. Garin

Aeskaar stiffened, easing slowly into a crouch. I could see his eyes flicking back and forth rapidly, searching the darkness. The growl came again, and Garin seized a branch and thrust it into his fire, holding it there until it caught, his other hand closing over the handle of his axe.

In the shadows, a pair of icy silver eyes glinted.

A coal-black wolf, at least seven feet from the tip of its nose to its hindquarters, emerged into the clearing. Its muzzle was peeled back on a snarl. The Demon Wolf. The beast that my father had slain. It was the same beast that had hunted me through my dreams all my life.

My father lifted the burning branch from the fire and rose slowly to his feet. The wolf flinched back as Garin waved the branch, but it did not run. Hackles raked up along its back as it edged closer, circling the small fire.

"All right, then," Garin said grimly. "Let's be done with it."

The wolf snarled, its great hindquarters bunched to spring.

I squeezed my eyes shut.

You must look.

I could not ignore that voice. Quaking, I forced myself to open my eyes. But the scene before me had changed. The clearing was lit with the sickly pale light of dawn. Garin's hide was smashed and broken, his fire out. Blood spattered, dark and half frozen, in the snow. Two bodies lay together at the edge of the clearing.

I gasped when one of the figures stirred feebly. "Edel…" he whispered. My mother's name. "Saram…"

"That's my name!" I cried, trying to step forward. "Can he see me?"

The air solidified around me, holding me still. He is speaking to his unborn child, said the voice of the flames. He picked that name for you when you lay in your mother's womb. Your first movements inside her reminded him of the soft rippling of flame.

"Flame?" I shook my head dazed. "But my name doesn't mean— It means sorrow."

So the young men of your village said, as they taunted you. They thought it came from the word "sarm", meaning grief and loss. But your father came from the far North, and there "saram" is a word that means fire, and warmth. You were never named "sorrow", child.

Tears sprang up in my eyes as I stared at my father – my da, who had loved me before I was born, and named me for fire – dying in the snow. No wonder my ma had hated my nickname. No wonder she had refused to call me Frost. If only she had told me!

Look.

Above the two bodies, something writhed and churned. A clear, silvery light struggled with blackness, like starlight fighting to break through deep cloud. The silver light danced with shapes, like curls of frost or falling snow. The dark was absolute dark, and nothing could be seen within it. The air was filled with a wolf's howling, and sharp claps of what sounded like thunder. It was beautiful and terrible at once.

"What is it?"

It is your father, and the creature he slew. That wolf was no ordinary beast. Your priests of the Other would have recognized it, for it was a favourite of their god. The wolf had lived nearly a century before it encountered a hunter strong enough to kill it. But in the moment of their deaths, their spirits have become tangled.

The silver light seemed to surge with new strength, the frost shapes within it burning with white fire. It enveloped the darkness and drew it down within itself, wrapping threads of light around it, until the spirit of the Wolf became a dark knot at its centre.

He has heard your mother calling out in her fear and despair. He wants to see her again, to look on her face one more time. He wants to see his child.

The silvery light exploded outwards. I was blown with it. I heard breaking glass and a scream, and, in the whirling, dancing snow, I saw a silvery shape like a man reaching out to where my mother was huddled in bed clutching a motionless bundle to her chest.

At the centre of the silver man, darkness whirled and raged.

As the man's silver hands touched the baby, the darkness suddenly expanded. The man-shape jerked, lines of darkness threading swiftly through its form like veins of poison. A deep, vicious snarl rent the air and my mother screamed again. The silvery hand that touched the baby's head pulled away, but the darkness had already fallen over the child; the silver spirit's movement only ripped the tiny body from its mother's arms.

Garin Aeskaar's spirit caught the child – caught me – and cradled me. Silver snowflakes and blackness fought around the baby's form. Garin's head bent, as if to kiss the baby's face. On one bluish cheek, a white mark like frost, like a wolf bite, slowly unfurled. The baby kicked and screamed as pinpricks of blood rose on the scar and slowly trickled down its cheek.

"Saram…" whispered Garin Aeskaar's voice. The silvery spirit, still wreathed in darkness, carefully placed the baby down on the edge of the bed. Then he seemed to wink out.

Ma snatched her baby – me – up from the snow, tears streaking her face.

"What happened?" I asked. "I–I don't understand…"

Slowly, the sight of my mother sobbing over the baby began to blur and slide, as if seen through tears. Gold and blue seeped up through the blurring image and became flames, dancing in a circle around me, above me, beneath my feet. I stood at the centre of a ball of cool flame.

Your father saved you. He brought your spirit back and sealed it in your body. But in doing so, he also trapped himself, and the Wolf, within you.

"Then my mother never made a bargain with the Other god. She didn't give away my soul. The spirit of the Demon Wolf is inside me," I whispered. "That's what causes the rage. Luca was right; it is a part of me."

"Not only the Wolf. I am with you too, Saram."

I whirled to see a silvery light in the shape of a man stepping through the golden blue flames. Within the shape, a black shadow – the Wolf – shifted and struggled. The dark stain inside the light was larger than it had been in the vision, and the veins of darkness were more like ropes than threads.

But I didn't look at the darkness for long. My hands were reaching out of their own volition.

"Father?"

The silvery shape solidified slowly. Colours and textures – skin and hair, leather and fur – gradually deepened and rippled over the light, clothing the translucent form until it exactly resembled the man I had just seen die.

My father stood before me.

He opened his arms and I went into them, my head coming to rest on his massive chest. One giant hand cradled the back of my neck. He smelled of snow, and sunshine, and wet wolf pelt, and of … of *father*.

I buried my face in the soft fur of his coat and cried.

"I have always been with you," he said, his voice rumbling against my ear. "Always watching over you. But until the Lady spoke to me, I was too entwined with the Wolf to protect you from it. I could not tell where it began and I ended. When I saw blood – my baby girl's blood – through your eyes I could not control myself, or it. I had to fight, had to protect you. And every time I lost control it grew stronger, feeding on my fear and anger. I am sorry. You have suffered so much for my weakness."

I clutched at his coat as if I would never let go. "No," I said, my voice clogged and distorted with tears. "I have lived because of your strength. Thank you, Father. Thank you for staying with me. Thank you for my life."

"Listen now," Garin said, putting me away from him a little. "My Lady has something to say to you."

Twenty-seven

Y ou have a choice to make, the flaming voice – the Mother's voice – said. Your father gave you life, but the price of that life was the curse you bore. For many years now, the strength of the Wolf has been all that allowed your father's spirit to cling to you. I can release the Wolf and return him to his master – but if I do, it will also release your father's spirit. And without that, your body will die.

"No," my father growled.

The other choice is to continue as you have been. In that case, the control of the beast will fall to your father, just as it always has.

I stared up into Da's grey eyes that were almost identical to my own. "What kind of choice is this? If I ask you to break the curse I'll die, and abandon my friends, and everyone I love. But if I ask you to let me live, I will be binding my own father's soul to suffering, and I will still be a monster."

Da's face twisted. "Hush! You are nothing like a monster. The rage isn't your doing, it's mine. The beast feeds on my anger and fear. Perhaps My Lady can help me to be stronger, to control myself better."

"Da, you can't wish to be trapped in this ... this half-life. My mother is waiting for you in the next world. It isn't right."

He hesitated for only a second before he answered. "You are my daughter. It's no torment to be with you."

"You're as bad a liar as I am," I muttered.

How could I choose the fate of another person's soul – my father's soul? How could I choose between life and death? This was a dilemma that no mortal should ever have to face.

I didn't want to die. Never, even in my darkest hour, had I longed for death. I just wanted to live freely, to be like everyone else.

I saw Luca's face in my mind. The beautiful hope and strength in his eyes. The anguish as he had reached out to me before I fell into the fire. When I thought of leaving him like this, wounding him with my death, my heart felt like a ball of ice.

"What if..." I said, finally, speaking to the Mother. "What if you released my father, but left the Wolf inside me? Could I live then?"

The spirit of the Wolf is powerful and tenacious. It would be enough to keep you alive. But you would have to be equally strong. Strong enough to fight it alone.

Garin said eagerly, "I can teach her. I can teach her how to fight the Wolf, if you give us time."

Within the Sacred Flame, there is no time and all time. You may teach your child, Garin Aeskaar. But, Saram, remember this. If you confront the spirit of the Wolf, and lose, the Wolf will suppress your will and take your body for its own. You know what will happen then. Are you sure you wish to take that risk?

I hesitated. There would be no turning back after this. Was there some other way, some less perilous way?

But where had running from my fear ever got me? Where had doubting myself ever got me? I had never been able to run far or fast enough to escape the Wolf. I had one chance to free myself. I had to believe in my own strength, as Luca did.

I took a deep breath. "Yes."

Then go, child, and fight with my blessing.

The blue and gold ring of fire began to sink down, and the solid, comforting weight of my father's arm around me faded with it. I cried out, trying to hang onto him, but he was already gone, slipping through my fingers like mist.

I stood at the centre of a great, frozen plain. The star-gemmed bowl of the sky curved overhead. Wind whistled across the plain and sent up a veil of fine snow. Wolf song echoed through the night.

It was my nightmare.

Terror took hold of me. My mind went blank. I did the only thing I knew how to do.

I ran.

The howling echoed behind me, singing of the hunt, singing of blood spilled on snow, singing of their prey's fear on the wind. I was their prey. And they were getting closer.

The plain blurred past my eyes. The only things standing still were the stars. My heart was agony, punching against my ribs as if it were fighting to escape too. My limbs were already heavy and numb. How much further could I run?

They were gaining on me. I couldn't run fast enough. They always caught me.

They always caught me...

I stumbled to a halt, sucking in a breath that made me choke. My legs quivered with the instinct to flee as I always had. But I could not outrun the Wolf.

I had to stand and fight.

I turned to face the dark shapes that flowed across the plain towards me. "I won't break this time," I said. "I won't run from you any more."

A familiar weight came into my hand. I looked down as my father's axe rippled into being.

"Da," I called, watching as the far-off wolves drew closer, their long black bodies streaking through the snow. "You said you would teach me."

"And so I will," my father said, suddenly beside me. His smile as he looked down at me was proud. "Give me my axe now, Saram."

A little reluctantly, I lifted up the weapon and handed it over. Da took it with a sigh, closing both hands on the haft, then swinging it in a whistling arc through the air. "It's been too long since I held this. Stay behind me, child, and watch what I do."

"But—" I began to protest. Surely I was meant to do the fighting?

Da waved me to silence. "Look!"

The pack of wolves let out a great howl, voices mingling into one. Their dark forms seemed to melt, coalescing, running across the snow like blood. Then there was no wolf pack any more, only one giant wolf, as broad across the shoulders as me.

My Wolf.

Its massive paws sent up a powdery spray of snow as it ran. It raced towards us and began to circle, forcing me to turn to keep it in sight. My father pushed in front of me, axe ready. The Wolf howled again, and as before in my dreams, I heard words in the cry. Words spoken in Garin Aeskaar's voice. It made sense now – how else could a wolf speak, but by borrowing the voice of the

338

human spirit that was tangled with its own?

You have summoned me, daughter. Are you ready to accept my strength at last?

"She is no daughter of yours!" Garin shouted. "This is my girl!"

Deep, mocking laughter reached my ears.

It is my strength that keeps her alive, my spirit that keeps her breathing. You are only mortal. Thanks to me, she is so much more than that. She is as much my daughter as yours.

My father opened his mouth, but before he could speak again, I called out, "You call yourself my father. Why have you brought me such misery, then? Why have you blighted my life, and forced me to run from everything I cared about?"

It is your own weakness that has made you sorrowful. All that matters is the hunt. The kill, and the taste of blood. Drive the weakness from your spirit, and you will be the greatest hunter, the greatest warrior, that ever lived. I will make you so.

"Silence, beast!" Da bellowed, face flushing with rage.

"No, Da!"

It was already too late. My father's temper had overwhelmed him. He lunged at the Wolf, his axe slicing down. The creature seemed to bend its spine in two to avoid the blow. Da's axe buried itself in the snow. The Wolf lunged at his throat.

Letting out a shrill battle cry, I dived forward and tackled the beast, jamming my forearm under its jaw and wrapping my other arm around its powerful shoulders to hold its head away.

The immense body bucked and writhed, trying to escape my hold. The powerful back legs raked at me, opening up lines of burning pain on my belly and sides. Its claws were like iron. We rolled over and over in the snow, the Wolf's hot, copper-scented breath blasting over my face. The great crescent teeth snapped half an inch from my nose.

I managed to wrestle my way on top, digging one knee into the creature's stomach and bracing the other in the snow beside it. Behind me, I could hear my father shouting my name, but he came no closer.

I will devour you, the Wolf snarled. **I will rip you apart with these fangs. I will feast on your human heart, weakling cub!**

My fingers dug into the thick fur like claws. If I let go for an instant, it would be over. I stared down into the Wolf's blazing eyes, focusing every fragment of my will to keep myself from blinking.

"Submit." My voice emerged as a low, vicious growl. "Submit to me."

I am the Wolf.

"Submit!"

The beast began to howl. The eerie sound reverberated through my body, through the plain itself. Distant mountains quaked. The earth rumbled beneath us. From the corners of my eyes I saw the stars flare blindingly and begin to fall, streaking across the sky with tails of white fire.

The wolf struggled more desperately than ever, kicking at my ribs until I was sure they must have snapped. I dug my fingers deeper into its pelt and held on. I did not blink.

"This is my soul! Mine! You do not command me. No one commands me. *Submit!*"

The star-bright eyes flickered away, for just a second.

The Wolf went still beneath me. Then its giant, foam-flecked muzzle lifted up until the moist nose just touched the very tip of mine.

You are my daughter, after all.

The Wolf dissolved in my grasp, and a cloud of darkness curled around me. It caressed me with icy tendrils, like smoke, or black down, or the softest and finest of fur coats. Then it seemed to sink away – sink into me – and disappear. The earth shuddered and trembled, gave one last heave, and settled, like a restive animal that feels the hand of its master.

Da skidded to his knees next to me and jerked me into his arms.

"She held me back," he whispered, hoarse and uneven. I could feel him trembling. "The Mother would not let me help you."

"I had to defeat him myself, Da," I panted. "Don't you see that? I had to know I could do it on my own, or

I would never have been able to live without fear. Power and ruthlessness are all the Wolf respects. As long as he knows I am stronger than him, I will be his master. The moment I give into fear, he will drag me down and crush me beneath his paws."

"My brave girl. My brave little girl." Garin rocked me backwards and forwards, then drew back, looking down at me. "There's something I must tell you, Saram. It's about your mother. I know she wasn't kind to you – and I can't ask you to forgive her for the way she was. But she didn't know the real reason your life was spared. Edel thought that she had given away your soul, and she could not forget it, or ever shake herself free of the fear that she had damned you. The guilt tormented her. She believed everything that happened to you was her fault. It made her hard and cold. It made her hurt you when you were already hurting more than any child ever should. But she did love you, Saram. She did. She would have given up her own soul if it would have saved yours. Remember that. Remember I love you too."

He embraced me again. I leaned on his shoulder. Every part of me was throbbing with exhaustion, bruises and scratches. But I was at peace. Beyond the mountains, the sun began to rise, casting out rays of red and gold into the sky. The falling stars faded one by one.

The arms around me began to glow silver-bright, sending out rays like the sun. I was enveloped in a strange floating sensation as Da's human form began to fade, disappearing into a shape of pure light.

"I will always watch over you," he whispered. "My frostfire. Always…"

There was a gentle, ghostly touch on the frost mark on my cheek. Then the silver light that was my father's soul flowed upwards, stretching thin and pale until it disappeared into the gold of dawn.

Tears dripped slowly down my cheeks.

"Thank you," I whispered. "Thank you for letting me meet him."

The landscape around me began to dissolve just as my father had done: snow and sky becoming gently rippling flames of blue and gold and purple.

After a while – and it might have been a very long while – I realized I was lying on my side in the bottom of the camp firepit, ashes and charcoal gritty under my cheek, with the tranquil peacock flames burning all around me. The moment my eyes focused on them, they died down, leaving nothing but ashes.

"Frost?"

It took me a moment to recognize my name, and another moment to know the voice.

"Arian…?"

I coughed, and then coughed again more violently, as ashes caught in the back of my throat. I tried to push myself upright, but my arms felt like limp pieces of string.

In a sudden panic I squinted down at them, and sagged with relief when I realized they weren't burned to a crisp. I didn't feel much different. There was only one change, other than the fact that I wanted to sleep for a week.

The gnawing, guilty ache of fear that had been my constant companion since I was eight years old was gone. I wasn't afraid any more. What did I have to be afraid of, after all?

I was free.

"Frost?"

Arian's voice was closer now. I forced my head up – I felt as if I wore a crown of lead – and saw him kneeling at the edge of the firepit, hands clasped as if in prayer. He looked terrible. His jaw was unshaven, his hair was standing up in messy peaks; his clothes were rumbled and grubby. He looked as if he hadn't slept or washed in days.

"It's all right," I rasped out. "I'm still Frost. I'm still me."

He carried on staring as if he expected me to start barking like a dog at any moment.

"Arian, are you going to help me out of here or not? It's not comfortable! At least give me your hand!"

His eyes squeezed shut, an expression of profound relief crossing his face. "You got yourself in there on your own," he said, eyes still closed. "Maybe I should make you crawl out by yourself too."

"Then I'll just get Luca to help me," I retorted.

His face spasmed. Uneasiness prickled the back of my neck. I looked around. "Where is he? Where's Luca?"

Arian opened his eyes. The expression there made my stomach turn over.

He said, "I don't know."

Twenty-eight

Arian told me the message had come only an hour after I had toppled into the fire and disappeared from view. As Luca had sat by the firepit in the dark – distraught and fearful, not knowing if I were even alive within the raging blaze – a ragged little Rua boy had run into the camp, begging for help. His sister and mother had been taken by three Sedorne men as they guided the family's small herd of cattle down from their grazing pastures for the night.

Even in the midst of his own sorrow, Luca could not refuse a call for help like that. Within a few moments, he had armed and mounted himself, picked a force of five hill guards to accompany him, and left, ignoring Arian's pleas for caution. He had insisted Arian stay to guard the firepit. To guard me.

The following morning, three of the five hill guards

Luca had taken returned. One of them had died shortly after. The two survivors told Arian that his worst nightmare had come true.

Luca had walked into a trap.

The tracks of the kidnapped women and their captors had led the small hill-guard force not to a bandit group of three, but of over twenty, concealed up and down a narrow valley. Luca had shouted at his men to run. They obeyed. Two fell to enemy swords in the valley, and another had caught an arrow in the back. They hadn't seen what happened to Luca.

Arian had sat by the fire for the next three days, held prisoner by Luca's orders, waiting either for Luca to return or for me to emerge. Under Hind's command, the rest of the hill guards had combed the mountains, searching for any sign of Luca or the men who had ambushed him. They had found nothing.

The captain of the hill guard had disappeared.

"Is he dead?" I asked Arian bluntly as I sat in Luca's tent.

Arian stared at me as if his doubts about my sanity had returned. "I don't know."

"Yes, you do. You said before that you always know if he's in trouble, if he needs you. Does he still need you?"

He let out a long, shuddering breath. "I think so."

"Then he's still alive," I said, fixing my eyes on his and letting the strength of my conviction burn through my voice. "We are going to eat. We're going to pack. Then we're going to go out there and find him – do you understand? We are going to find him."

I watched the terrible lines of strain and worry on his face ease a little as he slowly nodded. "What happened to you in that fire? You're different."

"No. I'm the person I was always meant to be."

"The sun's almost down," Arian said quietly.

"There's plenty of light left," I said, straightening from where I'd been bent over, squinting at a scuffed mark in the dry dirt. I rubbed my stinging eyes with the heels of my hands.

On the hillside above, in the far distance, I could see the dim figures of another party of hill guards moving downhill, probably intending to go back to the camp for the night. I looked past them to search the shapes of the mountains as if they might offer me some clue.

At the core of me, where fear and self-doubt had always lurked, there was ... something new. I didn't have a name for it yet. I didn't really understand it, or its limits. Maybe it was the courage that Luca had always told me was mine, though I didn't feel particularly brave. I just knew it was up to me to find him and bring him home.

"They've already searched here," Arian said, sounding frustrated. "I'm sure they wouldn't have missed anything."

"Maybe not. But look – the ground is rough here,

and there are so many patches of undergrowth and trees, they couldn't have searched all of them. And these landslides were recent. I'm betting all these rocks would be nearly impossible to get over without turning an ankle or taking a tumble."

"I don't understand—"

"If you were Luca, if you knew these hills like the back of your hand, if you were … maybe injured and running from an enemy, you'd come here. This is a perfect hiding place. Come on."

I plunged past him into a stand of thick bushes. Leaves slapped my face, branches tore at my skin. I tripped, and only Arian grabbing the pack on my shoulders kept me upright.

"Luca!" Arian yelled. "If you're here, answer me!"

There was no reply.

"Frost—"

"Just a little longer," I said. "I'm sure we're going to find something."

Arian muttered under his breath, but did not argue. I had the feeling that he didn't dare to. If he argued himself out of hoping, what would he be left with?

A moment later I nearly fell out of the thick cover of leaves. This time Arian didn't catch me in time, and I went down on my knees, hard. I barely noticed. Above us was a towering pile of great, bare rocks that ended in a sheer drop. I could see the midnight-blue glitter of the river below. Above was another thick stand of trees. Perfect cover – and just what Luca would have been looking for as he made for home.

I tried to distinguish marks in the dusty soil, but I could barely see anything now. The red-gold light of the setting sun was shining on top of the rocks, but down here it was twilight.

"Up," I said. "We have to go up."

Arian didn't bother to argue this time. We scrabbled and grunted our way up the thin strip of earth next to the rockfall, sending pebbles and earth cascading down behind us.

"What are we looking for?" Arian asked me, stopping to wipe sweat and dust off his face.

I looked up at him – and froze. My finger trembled as I pointed. "That."

There, on one of the rocks next to Arian's shoulder, was a smear of dried blood. It was the shape of a hand. A large, long-fingered hand.

Arian whispered something under his breath. It might have been a curse, or a prayer.

My eyes skittered over the rocks until I found a gap between two boulders a few steps to Arian's right. I pointed again. Arian fell down on his knees and tried to crawl inside, but he was too broad. "I need light. I can't see anything in there. Luca! Luca, can you answer?"

"Get out of the way." I nudged Arian forcefully aside,

wrenched my pack off my back and squeezed myself into the gap, my shoulders scraping painfully on the rough rock on either side.

"Luca?" My voice emerged as a croak. There was no echo in the tiny, damp space.

I groped through the moist dirt, stretching out my hands blindly. My fingertips fell on cloth, then the unmistakable shape of a muscular wrist.

"*Luca.*"

"What can you see?" The rocks couldn't muffle the urgency in Arian's voice.

"It's him. Help me."

Luca's skin under my hand was ice cold, and the only sound I could hear in the tiny space was my own shallow breathing. I clamped my fingers down and pulled, inching backwards. The angle was wrong. I couldn't get my legs under me. Arian caught hold of my waist and dragged me. I grunted as my joints protested against the strain.

There was a ripping noise. I skidded backward in a cloud of dust as something gave way in the dark space. My burden came with me, sliding out of the cave into the last light of the day.

Arian let go of me and turned away with a deep, hurt noise, one hand slapping against the nearby rock to keep him upright.

It *was* Luca. The fine planes of his face were unmistakeable, even swollen, bruised and caked in blood, even with his glorious golden hair shaved painfully short, so that his scalp glinted through the ragged fuzz.

His uniform was in rags. Deep bruises showed on his arms, chest, and in a choking necklace of fingerprints around his neck. Blistered burn marks formed precise cross-shapes on both of his cheeks. The traitor's mark.

He lay still, limp and lifeless.

Something – a sob, a scream, I did not know what – caught in my throat and choked me. I couldn't breathe. I couldn't move. The world came loose of its mooring in the heavens and wheeled crazily around me as the sun sank behind the horizon, plunging us into darkness.

No.

No.

No.

Luca let out a faint moan.

Air flooded my chest in a dizzying, painful rush. The world steadied. Impenetrable blackness became dusk. "He's alive. Arian, he's alive!"

Arian whipped round, his face a staring mask of disbelief, of hope. Then he scooped up Luca's body, lifting the taller man in one movement, as if he weighed nothing. I leaped to my feet, snagging my discarded pack.

We ran.

The journey back to the camp took an agonizing eternity; moments stretched out into hours. The harsh sound of my own breathing deafened me. I slid and slipped down the slope ahead of Arian, holding back tree limbs, stamping down roots – not for his sake this time, but for Luca's. Whenever I glanced back, I saw Luca's head rolling bonelessly against Arian's shoulder, his face a merciful blur in the dusk. Arian's face was turned down, always. I didn't think he was even looking where he was going.

Finally, I caught sight of the orange flicker of torches through the trees. I pushed through, breaking into the clearing and leaving Arian behind as I pelted through camp to the small tent pitched next to the makeshift infirmary. I shoved up the tent flap.

The torchlight revealed Rani in a tangle of pillows and blankets, with Livia curled next to her. Both healers jerked upright, instantly alert. Livia's hair stood out around her head like a silvery mess of straw.

"What? Who – *Frost*?" Rani's eyes narrowed.

"We found Luca. He's hurt. He needs help."

Rani was flinging back the covers and dragging on a pair of breeches before I had finished speaking. "Light the lamps. Hurry!"

Livia rushed to comply, fumbling with her still-bandaged bad arm. I went to help her, and in a moment the tent was flooded with golden light.

"It's really him?" Livia asked.

I looked up and met her eyes. Whatever she saw in mine made her tanned face go pale.

Before we could say any more, Arian walked in. He

gently laid Luca down on the spare bedroll in the healer's tent. Both Rani and Livia gasped as they saw his face.

Livia ripped open her healer's bag.

"Go outside now," she said, eyes not leaving Luca. "Go out and wait. We need space."

Arian stood motionless, staring down at Luca's bloodied form. Livia jerked her head at me. I caught hold of Arian's hand and tugged at it, and he followed me. Outside, the camp lay still and quiet.

The moment I let go of Arian's hand he folded up on himself, dropping to the ground as if his legs could no longer support him. Slowly, I sank down beside him, drawing my knees up and wrapping my arms around them.

"He's going to be all right," I said, not sure if I was talking to Arian, or to myself. "We got him back. He's going to be fine."

Arian didn't answer. I doubt he even heard.

It seemed like a whole night had passed before Rani finally poked her head out of the tent flap. Arian scrambled clumsily to his feet. I stayed on the floor.

"It's bad," Rani said, without waiting to be asked. "His wounds … they're appalling, but they aren't serious in themselves. They must have wanted to keep him alive. The burns on his face, though … the marks…" She paused, hands clenching on a piece of bloodstained bandage. "They're infected."

"What does that mean?" Arian demanded roughly.

"I don't know if – it's possible he might not make it through the night."

I clutched at my ribs, rocking gently. "He'll make it. He will. He wouldn't leave us like this."

Arian turned silently and walked away into the camp.

"Go after him," Rani said. "There's nothing you can do for Luca now."

She made as if to slip back into the tent, then stopped. Her eyes met mine squarely for the first time since I had attacked Livia. "Thank you for bringing him back. For not giving up. If you hadn't found him, he would probably have been dead by tomorrow. At least now he has a chance."

I sat on the ground for a long time after Rani had gone back inside, trying to deny the stomach-churning pain. Trying to force the feelings away into that dark ball under my ribs like I always had before. But I couldn't. I had changed. There was no empty, cold place where I could huddle up hope and fear within me any more. No way to isolate myself or run away from these feelings to make it easier. I had to accept them, and I had to do it without breaking. I had to, because Luca needed me. He needed me to be the person he had always believed I was. Brave and strong. Strong enough to get through this, and bring him through it too.

Slowly, slowly, I got myself back under control again.

I was able to breathe, to uncurl myself from my tight ball of misery and sit up straight. I got creakily to my feet and just stood there, dazed, for a little while. Then, leaving my pack in the dirt, I went after Arian. Rani was right. Luca wouldn't want his brother to be alone.

I found Arian in Luca's tent. When I pushed the flap open I saw him sat on my bedroll, clutching the bedding to his face. As he looked up, the moonlight silvered the lines of moisture trailing down his cheeks. I let the flap fall closed so that darkness blocked out the sight.

"He's all I have," he whispered, his voice as thin and frightened as a child's. "He's all I've ever had."

Moving through the shadows on memory, I knelt down on the bedroll next to Arian and reached out, embracing him tightly.

"Not any more," I said, staring into the night, dry-eyed. "It's going to be all right, Arian. You've got me now."

Twenty-nine

Arian was gone when I woke.

I sat up in the mess of bedding where we had huddled together in the night, clutching at each other for comfort like the abandoned orphans that we were, and covered my face with both hands. I wanted to scream and sob and wail. But, just as the night before, I could not seem to find my tears. It was as if they had dissolved into my blood along with the overpowering emotions still surging there. My eyes were as dry and gritty as if they were full of sand. There was no relief from the crushing sorrow.

Then I realized: Rani had not called me in the night. Luca was alive.

A starburst of golden exultation exploded inside me. I leaped out of the bedroll – I had fallen asleep fully dressed – and ran outside.

The moment I left the tent, I knew that Livia or Rani

had informed the hill guards about Luca. An air of grim watchfulness hung over the camp. It was long past dawn, but no one made any pretence at following the normal drills or doing chores. Hill guards gathered in groups outside their tents, talking quietly, their faces turned towards the healer's tent. As I passed them I received nods and bows and grave, grateful looks. I nodded back uncomfortably as I hurried to Livia's tent.

Inside, Luca lay with his bandaged hands folded on top of a blanket; the wounds on his face were hidden under layers of white cloth. The rags we had found him in had been replaced by a clean, white shirt, and the dirt had been combed out of his shorn hair so that it glowed on the pillow, like a halo of light. His breath – a dry, almost imperceptible crackle – was the loudest noise in the space. His swollen eyes were fast shut.

Rani was asleep too: a blanket-covered lump in Livia's bed. Arian sat on the floor by Luca, his legs folded up to leave space for Livia, who had taken a low stool near by and was mashing herbs into a paste. They both looked up as I came in. Livia gave me a weary smile. Arian's gaze slid away from mine, and he shifted a little and leaned over Luca, as if to readjust the blanket. The scene was peaceful and normal, and although my heart ached at the sight of Luca's bandages, my joy that he had beaten the odds was enough to soothe it. He was going to be all right.

Then Luca screamed.

The hoarse, agonized cry was so terrible that at first I didn't even realize there were words in it. And as soon as I understood them, I wished I hadn't.

"Ion, no! Please, Ion! *Ion!*"

Luca was staring right at Arian, his bound-up hands scrabbling at the sheets. Arian shot to his feet, almost falling in his haste to get away, as Rani jerked upright in the bedroll. Livia had dropped her pestle and mortar and made no effort to retrieve them. They all stared at Luca in horror, seemingly frozen.

I did the only thing I could think of.

I sat down in the space Arian had left.

"Shh," I murmured, taking one of Luca's bandaged hands in mine. I kissed the tips of his fingers – the only part I could get to – and gently brushed my fingers through the soft remnants of his hair. "Luca, you're safe. You're home. You're home with me."

Luca stopped struggling. He turned towards the sound of my voice, the bruised slits of his eyes falling closed. Tears trickled out, soaking into the bandages on his face. I carried on stroking his hair and talking nonsense until the tension had leached out of his body and he went limp again.

Life in the hill-guard camp continued in a strange repeating pattern. The soldiers drilled and practised, cared for their weapons and armour, and carried out the patrols that Luca had ordered before he went on his last rescue mission. No one suggested leaving, or sending to the king for further orders. No one else offered to take charge. Everyone was waiting. Waiting for Luca to wake.

Three days passed, during which Luca's fever rose and fell, rose and fell again. Rani and Livia worked desperately to coax him to take food and water and medicine, and it seemed to do some good. The wounds in his cheeks stopped seeping and closed over, and finally his temperature broke.

For a little while Livia was jubilant. But Luca still didn't wake. When he did open his eyes it was in terror, shouting his brother's name. At times like that I was the only one who could calm him. I wanted to believe it was because Luca recognized me, but I didn't know how that could be when he didn't even seem to realize where he was.

After that first day, Arian was reluctant to re-enter the tent. He visited several times and hovered, half in and half out, his eyes always fixed on Luca with a look that I couldn't interpret. He came again on the eighth day after Luca's fever broke, while Rani was catching a few moments' sleep. Livia – having assured me with some tartness that she had no trouble carrying a mere food tray – had gone to fetch breakfast. I didn't think it was my imagination that Livia's injured arm was slowly gaining strength. But I could just have been comforting myself again.

"You should take a turn sitting with him," I whispered to Arian, not wanting to disturb Rani's well-deserved rest.

Arian was staring at Luca as if he had never seen him before. "His face...?"

I nodded. "The infection's gone. The only thing that'll make it better now is time."

Rani had removed Luca's bandages the day before. The wounds on his hands and body were closed and pink, the bruises faded to faint yellowish smudges, barely discernable. The swelling of his face was almost entirely gone. Only the burns remained red and encrusted. There was no reason why Luca shouldn't come back to himself, open his eyes and get up.

Unless he didn't want to.

"Rani says Luca might be able to hear our voices," I persisted. "Having you near by would comfort him."

"I'd only frighten him again. It's you he wants." Arian shrugged. "Can't blame him."

He left before I could ask him what he meant.

That evening I persuaded Livia and Rani to go for a walk together after dinner. I told them – and myself – that it was because they were both exhausted by caring for Luca, and they needed some time away from the healing tent. It was only when they were gone that I admitted to myself why I was so determined they should go.

Alone with Luca for the first time since we had found

him, I took up his hand and held it, pressing a kiss to the palm, and then to each of his fingertips. His strong, slender hand felt all wrong, in mine, bony and fragile. It was as if he were shrinking away inside himself, just as Ma had done. I couldn't stand it.

"I miss you so much, Luca. I didn't know I could miss anyone like this. All my life I've been alone. It was only when you made me stay here, when you made me one of your men and one of your friends that I knew what it was to be ... something else. To be something that wasn't frightened and lonely and always looking for a way to escape. I don't want to be that person again. I need you to wake up. Please wake up. Please, Luca. Wake up for me. Because ... because..." – I clutched his hand between both of mine – "I love you."

There was no response. Nothing. His face was as still and lifeless as wax death mask.

The tears came then, at long last. They trickled down my face, almost scalding my cold skin. I hunched over him in helpless, wracking sobs that made my ribs ache. I felt the drift of cold air around the back of my neck, but I didn't register that someone had entered the tent until a hand came to rest lightly on my shoulder. I lifted my face, expecting Livia or Rani, and choked on my tears when I saw Arian standing over me.

"I can't – I can't—" I shook my head frantically, my fingers tightening around Luca's until I could feel my bones grinding against his. Something had come loose inside me. I couldn't stop crying.

Arian folded himself, with difficulty, into the space next to me. He shoved Livia's stool out of the way, and put his arm around my shoulder, pressing my face into the hollow of his neck. He uttered none of the soothing lies that Livia and Rani showered me with. He didn't even look at me at first, though the grip of his arm was tight. I was grateful for that. I leaned against him, accepting his support as I struggled to get myself back under control.

After a moment, he bent his head and kissed me.

It was strangely awkward to start with, that meeting of mouths. Like the fumbling affection of a child who tries to imitate what he has seen adults do. But slowly the warmth of him seeped into me. The comfort of his solid frame allowed me to relax for the first time in weeks and I was able to let go, instead of holding myself painfully up-right, straight and strong. We were jammed into the tiny space, barely able to move, but one of his hands gently traced the shape of my face, and I could feel his fingers trembling, and his shuddering breaths. Unconsciously my lips parted. I sighed into the kiss, aching, longing to just … forget. Forget sorrow, worry, pain and fear. Forget myself.

Forget Luca.

Luca. Whose hand still lay clasped in one of mine. Luca, with his reckless, brilliant smile, and his blue-gold eyes. Luca, with his terrible scars and shaven head.

Luca, whom I loved.

I went rigid. I let go of Luca's hand at once and eased both my hands between me and Arian, pushing him gently but firmly away. We stared at each other in silence. Arian's face, for once free of its icy blankness, was a study in conflict, guilt furrowing his forehead and tightening his mouth.

"Arian ... I..."

Luca's low, even breathing hitched, the rhythm speeding as if with effort. As I turned my head, his eyelids flickered. Then opened.

I knew straight away that this was not like the false awakenings of before. This time Luca was really awake. This time he was *seeing* me. For a long, heart-still moment, we looked into each other, and I saw everything I had ever wanted in those night-sky eyes.

Then a frown moved across his face. His gaze sharpened as it flicked to Arian and then back to me. I realized with a lurch of my stomach how it must look. Arian's hands were cupping the back of my shoulders and mine were resting on his chest. Both our lips were moist and a little swollen. Arian's guilty face was the most telling thing of all.

Luca lifted his hand, fingers shaking as they made contact with the thick, raised scabs on his cheeks.

His eyes squeezed closed and he muttered, voice dry

and hoarse, "Ion told me … he had seen Arian with a girl. With you. Taunted me, when he realized it meant something. I didn't believe him. I didn't believe him." His eyes snapped open, and I flinched from the look of betrayal there. "But it was true."

"Luca, it isn't—"

"Get out!" he yelled, his voice breaking. He rolled over to get as far from me as possible, wrapping his arms around his head. "Get out of my sight!"

I eased to my feet but didn't move, caught between running for help and trying to calm Luca down. Arian hovered beside me. Before I could make up my mind I heard footsteps outside and Rani thrust the flap back to rush into the tent. "What happened?"

"I – he woke up, and for a moment he seemed fine, then—"

"He's still delirious," Arian said, as Livia came in. "He must be. He can't really think—"

"Get her out," Luca's voice cut through ours. "I don't want them in here. I don't want her anywhere near me. *Get them out!*"

Rani got down next to the bed and gave me a look that was a mixture of panic and pleading.

"It's all right," I said, stumbling back. "I'll go."

Arian followed me from the tent, hands reaching out to steady me. I jerked away from him.

"I'm sorry," he said. His voice was low, almost

trembling. "I'm sorry. This – this isn't like Luca. I'll explain everything to him. He'll understand."

I shook my head, my ears still burning with the hatred in Luca's voice. *I don't want them in here. I don't want her anywhere near me. Get them out.*

Livia pushed open the flap. I looked past her. Luca was sat up in the bed now. He was staring at me. I took a step forward.

He turned his face away.

Livia let the flap fall closed behind her. She was white and shaken.

"I'm sorry," she said quietly. "He's really awake this time. He … just doesn't want to see you, Frost."

"Let me talk to him," Arian said.

Livia shook her head. "He doesn't want to see you, either. He said – Arian, he said you're relieved of command. He wants us to bring Hind."

Arian's head snapped back as if he had been struck. His eyes closed, jaw clenching. There was an awful silence.

"He's only just woken up," Livia said. "Maybe he's confused. This doesn't mean—"

"Yes, it does," I said dully. I turned and walked away.

Thirty

The morning bell clanged distantly. All around me the other women in the barrack tent stirred, pushed their blankets back and stretched. On my left, Hind yawned hard enough to make her jaw crack. After a moment's hesitation, she leaned over and touched my shoulder.

"Frost? Are you awake?"

"My eyes are open," I said tonelessly, easing into a sitting position.

Curly strands of hair were working lose of Hind's intricate braids, giving her a wildly curling fringe. Added to the black cloth patch over her eye, it lent her a raffish air that seemed strangely at odds with the quieter, more sober person she had become since the ambush. It was hard to remember that not long ago I had been horribly jealous of Hind. In the wake of Luca's rejection I had finally realized how foolish that was. He would never have betrayed me with Hind, who didn't even like men in that way. He would never have betrayed me with anyone.

Until I betrayed him.

Hind pulled off the patch, worn at night to prevent her from rubbing at her still healing eye, and revealed the livid red scar that bisected her eyelid; the iris was still surrounded by a corona of burst blood vessels. She blinked rapidly as she adjusted to the light. Her other eye, fixed on me, was uncomfortably sharp.

"It will get better," she said. "It's only been a week."

"I know." I pushed the blankets away and stood up. "I know."

We headed down to the river in a sleepy-eyed, chattering crowd. Everyone washed hastily in the night-chilled water before streaming back through camp towards the mess, where warm cooking smells revived us. I let myself be swept along by them, voices, laughter and faces blurring together. As we reached the mess – two smaller tents now, pitched side by side with their backs pinned together to make space enough for everyone – Hind gave me a bracing thump on the shoulder and then peeled off. I didn't look to see where she went.

I sat down at an empty table in the farthest corner, leaning my elbows on the unpolished wood and putting my head in my hands. After a few minutes, Livia and Rani joined me there. Silently, Rani slid three dishes off her own tray towards me, and put a cup of aniseed tea down at my elbow. Both women began to eat while I tried to make sense of the pattern of knots in the wood.

"At least drink your tea," Livia said.

I looked up, meaning to answer – but the words died on my tongue as I saw Luca on the other side of the mess. Hind was on his left. She was eating mechanically, her gaze seemingly fixed on the tent wall, as if she wanted to be somewhere else. I could see why. Arian was there, too. He was talking to Luca earnestly, his hands held out in a gesture that was close to begging. It was impossible to tell whether Luca was listening or not. His eyes were downturned and the layers of fresh white cloth hid most of his face.

Livia and Rani weren't responsible for those bandages. They had been on when Luca had emerged from his own tent the day after he had seen me and Arian together, and they had never left his face since. Not when he ate. Not when he sparred with various members of the hill guard, viciously attacking and defeating one after another until his muscles were visibly trembling and sweat was dripping from his shorn head. Not when he hit Dinesh in the face and broke his nose, and the blood spurted everywhere, soaking the white cloth on Luca's wounds. Not even – the story went – when he went down to the river to bathe. Each morning the bandages were fresh and clean again, but no one had seen Luca so much as touch them in public.

I was staring at the bandages so intently that at first I didn't realize Luca's eyes had lifted from the table.

He was looking at me.

My breath left me all in a rush, and I started up, legs trembling. I could not see what was in Luca's eyes, but this was the first time he had looked at me in a week and surely, please, *please*...

Luca slammed a fist down on the table, knocking over a bottle that was next to his bowl. Clear liquid spilled across the table and dripped off the edge as his finger drilled through the air to point at Arian's face in a gesture that screamed accusation and rage.

Arian stood up jerkily and left the tent. I stayed where I was, awkwardly half-risen, until Rani pushed a plate of steamed brown rice cakes at me, caught my hand, and shoved the cup of tea into it. "Sit. Eat. Drink."

I sank down and sipped the tea obediently. "Livia?"

"Hmm?" The healer gave me an enquiring look, her mouth full.

"Why don't you hate me?"

Livia swallowed hastily, coughed and took a gulp of her own tea before she answered. "You're talking about my arm now, aren't you?"

I nodded miserably.

"It was my own fault, Frost. Arian tried to warn me. He was screaming at me to get away from you, and I didn't listen. That was my own stupidity – I didn't like him, and I didn't want to listen to him, even though I could see something was wrong with you. I brought it on myself and it would be even more stupid to blame you for that."

I hesitated, then looked at Rani. "You did, though. I could tell."

Rani pulled a face, her large, dark eyes shamed. "For a little while. I suppose I ... wanted someone to blame for all of it. Everything that had gone wrong. But even when I was at my angriest I knew it wasn't fair. I'm sorry."

"It's all right," I said, embarrassed. I hadn't been looking for an apology. I had just wanted to understand.

"Besides, if I'd never got hurt, Rani might never have had the courage to tell me that she ... well, that she liked me," Livia said, with a sly, sideways look at the other healer. "So in a way, we should both thank you."

Rani flushed bright red and put her hand over her face. From somewhere, I managed a tiny smile. Just as Rani was opening her mouth to verbally flay Livia, we became aware of an expectant stillness falling in the mess tent.

Luca was standing, with his arms folded across his chest, clearly waiting for silence. The closed, defensive posture hurt me, deep down. Luca had always held his arms open to the world, fearless and laughing, scorning caution and fear. Now he looked as if he didn't trust his own soldiers not to turn on him.

How much of this change was the result of his ordeal at his brother's hands, and how much was the pain he had felt at seeing me in Arian's arms? Did it even matter?

It must seem to Luca that everyone he had ever cared about had betrayed him.

He nodded shortly. "I have important things to say this morning, so listen closely. I won't repeat myself. First, Arian no longer holds the position of my lieutenant."

I already knew this, but it looked like it wasn't common knowledge. A shocked murmur moved through the tent. Luca's narrowed eyes quelled the noise before it could grow.

"From now on you will take your orders from me or Hind. More importantly, from now on we're changing our tactics. We were sent here to do a job – and we have *failed*. Hanging back, skulking in the hills, plotting and planning, giving lectures to the locals. None of that has brought us any closer to our goal. And all this time the rebels have been strengthening their fortress, pillaging the countryside and laughing at us. We were sent here to dig those sons of whores out. I'm sick of waiting. We pack up today and march first thing tomorrow, to take back the House of God. We will attack head on and we will keep coming until we've destroyed them. It's the only way to win."

His eyes flashed around the tent with a glint like a knife blade, as if daring someone to raise an objection.

I hardly dared move. The silence seemed to buzz against my eardrums.

Attack head on? Luca himself had told us, time after time, that the hill guard couldn't possibly succeed in a frontal assault. The rebels had the high ground, the ruins of a massive stone complex riddled with secret tunnels and passageways, not to mention unknown numbers and weaponry.

It was suicide.

I glanced at Livia and Rani, and saw them both looking pale and grave-faced. They knew it too. Why didn't they speak? Why didn't Hind? Where was Arian – why wasn't he here to protest against this? Why didn't *someone* speak?

Why don't you?

I looked down at my hands, clasped neatly on the table in front of me. I swallowed. The tea had turned coppery and thick on my tongue, like blood.

When it was obvious there would be no objections, Luca nodded again. Was it my imagination that his shoulders slumped a little then? It might have been relief or … disappointment? Neither emotion was reflected in his voice when he next spoke.

In the humming quiet Luca outlined his plan for the attack, appointed three squad leaders to help organize the men during the battle, and gave detailed commands as to what equipment would be needed and what should be left behind. We were to take minimal supplies, and no tents. It would be a forced march to the fortress, and we would attack at dawn. There would be no signal for a retreat.

There would be no retreat.

When he had finished speaking, Luca stared at us all, as if waiting for something. Whatever it was, it didn't come. He jerked his head at Hind and stalked out. She followed like someone in a trance.

We sat in frozen silence. Then I jumped up, knocking over my stool, and ran after Luca.

I reached the entrance of the mess in time to see Luca and Hind disappear around the corner of the supply tent. I took one step after them, then froze, unable to go any further.

What was I going to say, or do? Luca wouldn't listen to me. He hadn't let me within ten feet of him since he had opened his eyes and seen that his brother's taunts had held a seed of truth. I was the very last person in the world that could persuade him out of this insane plan. The last person who should try.

"No turning back, then," Arian said. "He really did it."

He was leaning against a tree that overhung the mess, arms folded across his chest. The similarity to Luca's posture made me grit my teeth. If Luca had been avoiding me, I had been avoiding Arian. Trying to forget that kiss, and the way Arian had looked, and how I had been tempted just when I should have resisted. Faced with him now, with the defeat and regret in his once cold eyes, I couldn't bring myself to shun him any longer.

"There's nothing we can do, is there?" I whispered.

"I can't get through to him. I don't think anyone can." Arian bowed his head for a moment, then squared his shoulders. "I need to talk to you."

He went into the trees. I stared after him, then, with a sigh, went pushing through the undergrowth behind him.

"Why can't we talk in camp?" I called.

He made no answer.

We reached a little clearing of soft spring grass and he came to a halt, standing motionless, hunched, with his back to me. The sunlight played over his dark figure in rippling tides of blue-green and gold.

"You know that we have no chance of winning. Are you going to stay?" he asked.

I ran one hand restlessly over the coiled braid of my hair. "You already know the answer."

"Even if leaving is the only sensible thing to do?"

"*You're* not going anywhere."

He was silent. I sighed and shifted impatiently, wishing he would get to whatever the point was. I opened my mouth to snap at him – then closed it, my sense of justice prodding at me.

It wasn't fair to heap all the blame for what had happened on Arian's head. I could have stopped him in the tent, but I hadn't. That was my own burden to bear. Just like Rani, I had needed someone to be angry at, and I had chosen Arian. After battering my way through his defences, calling myself his friend, telling him that he could rely on me as well as on Luca, I had abandoned him to wallow in my own misery. My father would have been ashamed of me.

I stepped a little closer to him, and softened my voice. "I'm sorry. Are you all right?"

He was silent. I was wondering if he had heard me, when he asked suddenly, "What happened to you in the Fire? I knew as soon as you came out that something had changed, but you've never spoken of it. Did you see Her?"

Taken aback, I hesitated and shook my head. "I can't really… It's not something I *can* speak of. It would just sound like fever dreams, or nonsense. She didn't show me Herself. She showed me *myself*. I don't know how much of it was what anyone would call real. I only know it wasn't a dream because if I'd been dreaming I would have burned to death."

"Then you're cured now. You've got what you wanted from Luca. You should go."

I scowled. "I'm not leaving him."

He spun around to confront me, face desperate. "Why not?"

Everything came together in my mind. White-hot fury flared within me, and my fist caught Arian soundly in the jaw. His neck snapped back. The shock sang through my knuckles and the bones of my hand as he staggered, catching a tree branch to stay upright.

"Everything – everything between us – pretending to be my friend, kissing me after the ambush and then again in Livia's tent… You've just been trying to get rid of me! Holy Mother! Are you that desperate to get Luca all to yourself?"

He let go of the branch and stepped forward, bruised jaw thrust out. "No! This isn't about Luca! It's about you. I want you to save yourself before he gets you killed."

"You don't care what happens to me," I snarled.

The anger and frustration drained out of his face and he seemed to slump. "I do care. I do."

I swallowed hard. "What are you saying?"

"I did want him all to myself, you're right," he mumbled. "When you first came here I was so jealous I could barely see straight. I could tell that Luca felt something for you, and I hated you for it. But how could I keep feeling that way once I'd got to know you? The more time I spent with you the more I could… It's the way everything lights up when you smile. The kindness in your eyes. The way you can't stand by and watch anyone suffer, even if it means getting into fights you'll never win or jumping off cliffs into rivers. And when I realized you liked me – really *liked* me – when no one ever has, apart from Luca, I … I couldn't lie to myself any more."

He stared at me despairingly. I stared back, bereft of speech.

Arian – Arian! – cared for me? *Me?* Loved me, even? Dear Mother, he had a strange way of showing it!

Or … or had he? I thought about all the time he had spent with me, patiently teaching me to overcome my fears and fight back. About his singing with me by the Mother's Fire. About how, more and more, I had noticed that strange look in his eyes which I had thought of as a hidden smile. I remembered him awkwardly reassuring me and kissing me before Ion turned up, and how, after I had stepped into the Mother's Fire, he had sat by the firepit day and night, waiting for me to emerge, instead of going after Luca.

I am a fool.

Arian had shown me how he felt in every way possible for a man like him. He had practically shouted it from the rooftops, if only anyone had bothered to listen. If only I had listened…

I was torn between gratitude and sorrow. He must have been suffering so much, and all in silence. There was a part of me that responded to the tortured nature of a love like that, a part of me that wanted the strange mixture of misery and comfort Arian offered. Because he and I were alike. More alike than me and Luca in many ways. We were both lost souls. Luca had caught us, brought us together, made us feel that we were part of something …

and then set us both adrift again. It was natural that we would try to cling to each other.

But that was the problem, wasn't it?

Not long ago, before I had become a hill guard, before I had known Luca's love, before I had found the courage to walk into the Sacred Flame, I would have been so grateful to anyone for such feelings that I would probably have given myself to them. Just like Arian, cold and wary and damaged as he was, had fallen in love with me simply because I didn't hate him. Simply because I was *there*. Isolation and loneliness made a person so vulnerable to even the tiniest scraps of kindness. Hadn't that been why I began to fall in love with Luca in the first place?

But gratitude, which Luca had always scorned, was not the same thing as love. Clinging to a person because they made you feel less alone wasn't love. And what I felt for Arian wasn't love, at least not romantic love. It was affection and understanding, and friendship.

The person I was in love with was Luca.

I had walked into the Sacred Flame for him. Not because he thought I was unworthy – but because he did not. His belief in me had turned me into the person he had always believed I was. I was strong. I was brave. I was decent. And I was good enough for him. Even if Luca didn't want me any more, even if he never forgave me, I was strong enough to be true to myself now. I was strong enough to keep loving him, no matter what.

I took a deep, calming breath and reached out to Arian, hoping to comfort him – but before I could speak, his expression changed. He started forward, reaching out. "Frost, you've hurt your hand."

The punch to Arian's face had split the skin over two of my knuckles and beads of blood had risen to the surface. I recoiled, holding up my good hand to keep Arian away.

"Stay back," I warned him.

He froze.

I was shaking, my muscles twitching with instinctive fear. This was the moment of testing. *Wolf? Are you there?*

There was a swirl of frosty cold in the air around me, and then a sense of weight, a pressure that made me brace myself. For a moment I could feel the great, furred creature leaning his shoulder affectionately into my side, smell his damp pelt, hear the deep, even rhythm of his breath. Something icy and rough swiped across my scar, and I bit my lip to hold in a cry of surprise.

Then the presence faded, leaving nothing more than a faint chill, and a stinging cheek, in its wake.

Thank you, Father. Thank you, Holy Mother.

Thank you, Wolf.

"It's all right," I breathed, exultant. "It's just a scratch."

Released from my command to be still, Arian stepped forward and took my bleeding hand between his. His rough, calloused fingers touched me as gently as if I were made of glass. As gently as if he were still terrified, deep down, that he might hurt me by accident. I knew all too well how he felt, because it was the same fear which had plagued me all my life. I prayed to the Mother that Arian would one day be free of it.

"I'm glad," he said at last. "I'm glad that ... you don't have to be scared any more."

His eyes slowly lifted from my hand to my face. There was hope in his face – the kind that sits on the edge of agony. I turned my hand in his and clasped his fingers.

"I can't," I said softly but firmly. "I can't give up on him."

Arian drew in a hissing breath between his teeth, and I saw to my horror, the sudden brightness in his eyes. His fingers twitched as if to let me go, and I brought my other hand up swiftly to keep him with me.

"Don't. Don't, Arian." A warm tear slipped down my face. "I'm sorry. If I had never met Luca—"

"You'd never have met me either. Or if you had, we'd have ended up killing each other," he said with a choked laugh. "It all goes back to him. Somehow he just ... keeps everything together. He always did."

"Not any more." I whispered. "He's not even keeping himself together now. He's broken. You love him as much as I do, so you tell me – can we keep him from destroying the hill guard? Can we keep him from destroying himself? Is it worth risking everything, even our lives, to try?"

I fixed my gaze on him and looked into him as Luca

had looked into me so many times. I let him see every-thing I felt, and watched as his head came up, as the strength and pride returned to his eyes. I watched as he began to believe again.

"Yes." The word held a trace of his old arrogance.

I smiled through my tears. "Friends, then?"

Arian lifted my hands to his mouth and careful-ly brushed a butterfly kiss to my bleeding knuckles. "Friends always."

I couldn't face the humid enclosure of the women's bar-racks that night. I made my bed in the warm grass, in the shelter of an ancient tree on the edge of camp, where I could hear the faint sounds of the river in the ravine below.

After spreading out my bedroll, I curled up on my side with my hands under my face, careful of the still-healing split on the back of my knuckles. Tomorrow everything would change again. But change no longer frightened me. I had an ally – a friend – who would fight beside me through anything, and no matter what hap-pened, I would never run away again.

It was surprisingly easy to relax beneath the gently whispering leaves and the bright, silent stars. I let the night sing me to sleep.

It might have been minutes or hours later that I felt something touch my cheek. The touch whispered gently along the line of my scar, and my breath caught. I opened my eyes in the darkness.

There was a blur of movement, and something pale flashed away so quickly that by the time my vision had cleared, there was nothing to see. I stared into the shadows, breathing in the faint smell of honeysuckle.

Thirty-one

Dawn came to the mountain at last, bleaching the low, heavy clouds from black to purple. I had to squint as I peered over the top of the boulder where I sheltered with Arian. "Snowlight", Ma would have called this. A sign for those with any sense to get indoors, for a storm was coming.

The rockfall where we had chosen to hide was three hundred yards from the tall wooden gates that guarded the outer wall of the House of God. Hill-guard scouts had reported that a portcullis lay behind the gates, guarded day and night by a pair of rebel warriors who would slam it down the moment anyone attempted to rush the entrance. It was an excellent system. With one weakness.

"Anything moving out there?" Arian asked, low voiced.

I shook my head as I sat back on my heels, absently chafing my fingers. The thin leather of my gauntlets was not much protection against the bitter cold this far up the mountain.

"Aren't you supposed to be Uskaandian? This little chill shouldn't bother you," Arian said roughly. He reached out for my hands.

I drew back nervously. "Arian—"

"Idiot." In a peremptory gesture, he seized my wrists, and shoved my hands into the bends of my knees. "Leave them there. They'll warm up."

There was an awkward pause.

"Um. Thank you."

Arian nodded shortly, not looking at me. Guilt and gratitude made my heart ache. We were huddled less than a foot apart, and yet loneliness seemed to form a dark shroud around him, sealing him away from me. I wished I could somehow comfort him in his pain – but I was the cause of it. I would only make it worse.

After a minute, I said, "In Uskaand we have enough sense to wrap up in the winter. No one leaves their house without a fur-lined coat, boots and mittens. Armour is not the same." I eyed his hands. "You're not even wearing gloves. Why don't your fingers drop off?"

He shrugged. "The village where I grew up was nearly as high as this, and I never had fur-lined mittens. I'm used to it."

"Braggart."

His dimple flashed briefly. "Arch-wife."

Encouraged by this sign of good humour, I had opened my mouth to offer another insult when there was a scuffling noise behind us. My axe appeared in my hand like magic. Arian whipped a long knife from a sheath on his thigh.

We both slumped with relief when a stony-faced hill guard climbed over the tumble of rocks into our hiding place. "Two minutes," she said, voice low. "Get ready."

"Is everyone in place?" Arian barked.

"Yes, S— Yes, Arian." Arian might not be lieutenant any more, but no one had quite become used to that yet. Not even Arian himself.

"Thanks," I said.

She nodded and backed out of sight. "Mother's blessings."

The tension we had tried to dissolve with our bickering flowed into the gap she left.

"Charge the outer wall, get to the courtyard," I mumbled, shoving my axe back into its harness. "Stay with the others. Secure the perimeter."

Arian grabbed my hands and tucked them under my legs. "Just remember that your most important task is to keep yourself safe. You can't help Luca, or anyone, if you're…" He broke off and swallowed. "If you're dead. No picking fights you can't win today. All right?"

"Same goes for you," I retorted, ignoring the nerves that made my stomach jump. "If I see you making any attempts to bravely sacrifice yourself, I'll kick you in the head."

Arian let out a tiny snort of laughter. "Understood."

Light flared overhead and we both got to our knees, watching the point of fire arc across the dark sky, illuminating the outer wall of the House of God. As the light fell I could make out every detail of the wall, the shapes of the stone blocks, the intricate patterns made by spiny mountain vines on the masonry, the small wooden clog abandoned by the entrance.

With a faint tinkle of breaking glass, the light smashed into the palisade, leaving a black smear on the wood that instantly burst into flames. A second light flew, then a third, all hitting the same section of wood. They were glass bottles, each filled with pitch, a burning rag stuffed into their necks.

The fire caught swiftly, red tongues of flame licking up the dry timber. A plume of noxious black smoke billowed up.

Arian made a tiny grunt of satisfaction. "They've used water repellent on the logs. It's helping the fire to spread."

I heard a distant shout of alarm, and a moment later the great wooden gates began to swing open, revealing the slowly rising portcullis behind.

"It's working," I breathed.

Six men, clad in the lacquered armour of gourdin, elite Sedorne warriors, ducked under the portcullis and ran out. Their swords were sheathed. They carried buckets and lengths of cloth. The first of them began to beat at the flames, while the others formed a chain, passing along buckets of water to throw over the blaze.

"They're efficient," I said. The silent, well-organized group bore little resemblance to the shambling, dirty bandits I had fought before.

"Unfortunately for them, you can't put a pitch-fire out with water," Arian said. "Come on, Luca. Come *on*."

One of the gourdin seemed to trip, sprawling headlong on the ground. The man beside him turned to help. This time I saw the arrow sprout from his neck before he fell. The light metal armour the gourdin wore didn't stand a chance against the specially forged metal-piercing crossbow bolts Luca had instructed the archers to use. The rebel soldiers died quickly, and if any of them cried out, I didn't hear it.

As we watched, a dozen hill guards leaped down from the rocks by the outer wall where they had painstakingly hidden themselves the night before. They separated into two groups. One group carried a solid piece of timber, the height of a man, on their shoulders. The other group rushed the entrance, flying through the gates and under the portcullis, weapons already drawn. There was a scream, abruptly cut off, as the advance party found and overwhelmed the two rebels that guarded the gate. The second group reached the portcullis as it began to fall and wedged the timber beneath it, forcing the portcullis back up again. The men turned and waved their swords.

Attack.

I scrambled up over the boulder and leaped forward, ripping my axe free of its sheath as I went. Arian landed beside me, sword drawn. All along the slope, hill guards were rising from the rocks and surging up the slope towards the rebel base in a silent, deadly mass. The only sound was the tromp of boots on the shaly, uneven ground. There would be no war cries today to warn our enemies.

We hit the top of the slope in a wave and flooded through the gates. I was among the first to pass under the portcullis, with Arian a step behind me. Beyond the palisade was the inner wall of the House of God. Just as Luca had warned, it was pocked with gaps and holes, but still far more intact than the outer wall.

This was the truly dangerous moment of his plan. If the rebels managed to respond in time and trap us here in the narrow crescent between the walls, we would be slaughtered without ever breaching the central courtyard of the stronghold. Hill guards were flying through the gaps as fast as they could, their progress still largely silent. I saw no gourdin, apart from the fallen ones by the gate. Nor was there any sign of Luca. I hesitated, turning to search for a glimpse of the captain among the soldiers. Rock dust and pitch-smoke clogged my throat and stung my eyes.

"He's in by now," Arian said, grabbing my free hand to haul me over a pile of fallen masonry. "Come on."

I pulled my hand free. "Stop looking after me. I can manage." I skidded down the stone blocks and jumped through a gap in the inner wall, landing in the courtyard a step ahead of him.

The large, circular area was disconcertingly quiet. All that greeted us were neat piles of rope and timber, and barrels and boxes of supplies stacked against the walls of the former House of God. The building itself was a massive stone structure, with dozens of slit windows and multiple layers of ramparts climbing to a thin, stone tower. The front wall of the building showed signs that it, like the outer walls, had once been undermined and pulled down. Clay bricks had been used to repair the gaps and make the building safe again.

At the eastern edge of the courtyard was a single-storeyed wooden hut with a peaked roof, about twice the size of the hill guards' mess tent. The gourdin barracks.

"Squads One and Two, surround the barracks!" I heard Luca call out, not much louder than his normal speaking voice. He was at the top of the courtyard, bandaged face shining white, bloodied blade in one hand. "Secure the entrances!"

Arian and I exchanged glances. We hadn't been assigned to any squad. With a shrug, I jammed my axe back into its harness and grabbed a heavy barrel, pushing it onto its side and rolling it towards the nearest entrance. If we could block the exits, all the best rebel warriors would be trapped inside. The members of Squads One and Two clearly had the same thought. They ran towards the provisions stacked against the walls and dragged away heavy sacks and pieces of timber to pile against the doors.

"Idiots!" Arian hissed. "We don't have time. *Secure* the doors, don't barricade them!" He surged past us all, sword unsheathed, hand outstretched to seize the door handle. Before he could reach it, the door flew open.

A gourdin charged out. His sword flashed. A young hill guard, who had put away her blade to carry a wooden crate, fell with a scream, clutching at her neck.

"'Ware! 'Ware!" the gourdin yelled. "Men, to me!"

The man went down under Arian's sword, but two more doors had already burst open. More rebel warriors spilled into the courtyard. Some wore full armour, others only shirts and breeches, but all were fully armed. I cursed as I realized we had wasted our chance at a nearly bloodless victory. A glance up at the fortress showed me that the small windows were beginning to flicker with lights as the gourdin's shouts woke the occupants. The time for silence and stealth was done.

The hill guards ran to meet the rebels with battle roars. I drew my axe and flew into the fight. The hours of training took over and my weapon rose and fell, body spinning and kicking, on instinct alone. Arian fought at my back, sword in one hand, a weighted wooden baton in the other. We carved a swathe through the rebel warriors. I saw the fierce hope on the faces of the hill guard around me. *We're winning. We can win. We can defeat them.*

"Frost…" A familiar voice at my elbow brought me spinning around.

It was Hind. Her face was the colour of ash, the front of her tunic soaked with blood. One arm hung uselessly at her side. She sagged, and I caught her around the shoulders before she hit the ground. "Arian! Help!"

Arian dispatched the gourdin before him with a ringing blow to the head and turned, eyes widening when he saw Hind clinging to me. He shoved his sword into its scabbard and the baton into his belt and eased his arm around Hind's waist. Together we dragged her out of the tide of the battle and carefully lowered her to the ground by the wall. A dead gourdin had collapsed there, his face still twisted into an expression of horror. I looked away.

"Luca—" Hind said. "He went in there. I tried to stop him…"

"Luca did this to you?" I whispered, disbelieving.

"Only the arm," Hind said between her teeth. "Punched me in my shoulder. Arm went numb. I couldn't hold my sword. Gourdin got me."

I swore aloud.

"He went into the House?" Arian asked urgently. "Alone?"

"He's going after *him*," Hind said. Her good hand gripped Arian's arm. Her eyes bored into us. "He's not thinking straight. Ion will kill him."

"You need a healer—" I began.

Hind shook her head. "Rani will find me. No time. Go after him."

Arian hesitated, looking at the battle. Then he nodded sharply at me. "Let's go."

Hind closed her eyes as we got up and ran. I prayed that she was right and that someone would find her before it was too late.

We skirted the battle in the centre of the courtyard and headed towards the wooden door set into a new section of bricks at the front of the House of God. A gourdin was blocking the entrance. His massive shoulders nearly touched the frame on each side, and he held a small war-axe in each meaty fist. There were three bodies in hillguard uniforms lying near by. I didn't let myself look at their faces, but none of them had Luca's short, golden hair.

"No further," the rebel warrior said to us, voice rumbling like thunder. "You won't step one foot further into our home."

Arian drew his sword with a metallic rasp. "This isn't your home, Sedorne. This is stolen property. Now move – or die."

Thirty-two

I went in low, swinging at the gourdin's leg. Moving fast for such a bulky man, he brought his right axe down, catching my axe blade on his pick. His other axe flicked up to catch Arian's sword in exactly the same way. The rebel twisted and pulled his axes expertly. I staggered forward a step, fighting to hang onto my weapon.

Arian let go of his sword and leaped away. The sudden release of tension made the rebel lurch off balance. I wrenched at my larger axe. Metal screamed, and the weapon went flying from the gourdin's hand. I bared my teeth in a grin of triumph. One axe down, one to go.

Arian reached under his jerkin and pulled out his weighted baton as the gourdin took his remaining axe in both hands and aimed a side blow at my gut. I got my weapon down just in time, deflecting the blade with the iron langet.

Arian surged into the fray and drove the end of his baton into the rebel's stomach. The rebel went white and stumbled backwards and Arian smashed his baton into the man's knees.

The gourdin bellowed as his legs buckled. He crashed to the ground. At the same moment, I jabbed the iron-bound head of my axe into his temple. There was a crunch as the metal met the rebel's skull, and he slumped to the floor, lying half in and half out of the doorway.

Arian got to his feet and retrieved his sword. Together we jumped over the giant's legs and landed in a large, echoing space, full of shadows.

The room was oddly shaped, with many sides, and was mainly taken by roughly made wooden furniture. It looked for all the world like the hill guards' mess tent. I had braced myself for more enemy soldiers, but the room was empty.

"They left only one man to defend the doorway? That's crazy."

"They didn't believe attackers would get this far," Arian said, his gaze searching the room. "The inbred belief that they were invincible was the reason the Sedorne lost the war. Come on, we need to keep moving."

We searched the room cautiously, keeping our backs to the wall, until we found a doorway. There was no door in it – a rail above indicated a curtain had once hung there, but no more. Arian eased through the gap, still plastered to one wall. I took the other side. The corridor was wide, with a towering ceiling that disappeared into darkness. The only light was from thin window slits high up. I still couldn't hear any movement; there were no voices or footsteps. It was eerie.

Arian was running one hand over the wall. Then he ducked down and seemed to be touching the floor.

"What are you doing?"

"There are sconces here for lamps, but they're empty. And I can feel dust on the floors. I think this part is disused," he said.

"That makes no sense. It's directly off the main room," I said, feeling the hairs on the back of my neck lift. "Can I have your baton? There's no space for an axe here."

"Take the knife instead," he said, handing it to me hilt first. "You're more used to an edged weapon."

We moved forward, weapons ready. I expected to see light at any moment, but instead the place grew darker. It was like venturing into a cave.

"This place is massive," I whispered as we came to a circular chamber with four more empty doorways leading off it. Even lowered, my voice echoed off the walls.

"We're going to have to risk a light," Arian said. "I've got a candle in my belt pouch. Hold this."

He pushed the baton into my free hand, and, after some muttered swearing and scraping noises, a light flickered to life. He took the baton back and let some of the molten wax drip onto the end before sticking the candle to it. Now the baton was a candleholder as well as a weapon. He held the light up high, but the tiny flame didn't offer much illumination – just enough to keep us from stumbling over our own feet.

"Maybe we should go back and try another exit from the main room?" I suggested.

There was a muffled cry from one of the corridors and without another word we both rushed forward.

Almost immediately an acrid stench reached my nose. Urine. Hot fat. Blood.

The flicker of Arian's candle showed us a man's body. A gourdin, fallen across the corridor. He had been carrying a tallow light when he fell. It lay beside him, the flame extinguished by his blood.

"Luca's work?" Arian muttered as we passed into the space at the end of the corridor.

It had once been a large, circular room. Now crude wooden bars divided it into cages. People were huddled at the corners of the cages, revealed by the pale light coming through the high window slits and Arian's candle. The stink of unwashed bodies and the sight of skinny arms and legs poking out of ragged clothes told me that these prisoners had been here for some time. They were all Rua.

"Slaves." The word tasted vile in my mouth.

Arian stepped towards the first cage. A woman, her face so lined with dirt that she might have been eighteen or eighty, was crouched there with a small child. The child let out a tiny whimper and the woman hushed him, the faint glimmer of light in her eyes revealing that she was watching Arian intently.

He yanked his sword from its sheath.

The woman cringed back, her arms going around the child.

Arian sliced through the wooden bolt that held the cage closed and yanked the door open.

"It's all right," he whispered, voice more gentle than I had ever heard it before. "We're the royal hill guard. The king and reia sent us. You're safe now. You can come out."

The woman stared up at him, motionless apart from the panicked panting that made her chest heave. The child whimpered again.

"A man went past just now," the woman whispered, her voice hoarse and dry. "He had a uniform like yours. He killed the guard, but he didn't stop to let us out..." Her eyes travelled over Arian and me again, and she seemed to relax. "He was Sedorne, though. I suppose he didn't care about us."

Burn you, Luca. My jaw ached from keeping the words in. Around the room the other Rua prisoners were beginning to stir, murmuring with fear or sudden hope.

"We're going to let you all out," Arian said firmly.

Working as quickly as we could, we smashed open the locks on the wooden cages. "You're free now," I whispered to each prisoner. "You're free."

"Does anyone here know their way around the fortress?" Arian asked, when everyone was out. "There's fighting outside. I don't want to send you out there."

"I can fight," said a bent old man, peering fiercely at Arian through a fringe of white hair. "I'd like to kill a few Sedorne."

"We don't have weapons to give you," I temporized hastily. "Anyway, some of the Sedorne are on our side. We can't have you killing them."

The old man snorted. Some of the others chuckled tiredly. Most just stared, mute with shock and not sure whether to believe in their sudden release.

"We're the scum," the first woman said. Despite her skinniness she had managed to hoist the little boy – not her boy, she said, but his ma was long gone – up onto her hip. "Ones too sick or young or ugly or old to sell on. They march us out to do the labouring that's too dirty for them. We know our way about. We can hide until the fighting's stopped, one way or another."

"Stay out of sight. We'll send someone to look for you if – when – we win," I said.

The woman nodded and moved towards the corridor, the others trailing more slowly after her. As she reached the doorway she looked back. "That Sedorne boy. He went up those stairs like a rat down a sewer hole. If you're interested."

"We are. Thanks."

"Give him a few lumps for me," the woman said, turning away.

Arian opened his mouth, but I put my hand on his shoulder and shook my head. How could he defend Luca's actions to these people?

Arian went up the stairs first with his guttering light. I followed closely behind him, knife point aimed carefully at the ground so as not to stab him if he stopped suddenly. The foul air of the slave pens clung to my skin.

When we reached the top of the steps we found ourselves in an empty corridor identical to the one that had led to the room of prisoners. There was another set of stone steps directly ahead of us.

"I don't like this." Arian stared at the corridor. "We could wander through this place for hours and find nothing. It's immense. Where is Luca heading? He can't have any more of an idea where Ion is than we do."

"No," I said, shaking my head. "He must have some idea, or he wouldn't have turned on Hind like that. Where would he look for Ion? That's the question. Where is Ion likely to be in a place like this?"

The candle on the baton had burned down while we were freeing the prisoners and the hot wax had hardened into yellow rivulets on the sides of the weapon. As Arian stood thinking, the flame finally went out, leaving us surrounded by shadows. He lowered the baton, and the last of the wax splattered onto the stone flags.

"Luca told me once that Ion always liked to look down on people – to pretend that he was an eagle and everyone else was a mouse."

I nodded, remembering how Ion had stared smugly down at Arian and me when he had caught us by the brook. Even when the Wolf had started slaughtering his men, he hadn't bothered to climb down from his perch and help. "I don't think he really likes fighting much. Not if his opponent can fight back, anyway. I'll bet he's hiding somewhere high up, where he can watch but not get involved. There's a tower here. That would be the first place Luca would look."

"Then we need to keep going up too."

We headed up the next flight of stairs at a run – but as Arian reached the top he stopped dead. I steadied myself on the wall with my free hand, and peered over his shoulder. This corridor was different to the previous ones. There was a long, faded rug laid on the flagstones, and a table with a chipped jug and ewer. An oil lamp burned in a sconce above the table.

People lived here.

We hurried towards the next set of steps. Our tramping footsteps sounded unbearably loud. I turned to keep our backs covered.

"Mama?"

A small girl, her hair standing out around her face in

a dandelion halo of blonde curls, toddled into the corridor. She froze when she saw us, clutching handfuls of her too-long nightdress as her mouth formed a perfect *O* of surprise.

"Go!" I cried.

I heard the little girl wailing behind us as we dashed up the stairs and came out onto the next floor to find a corridor fully lit with oil lamps. A middle-aged man with curling grey hair rushed out from a behind a curtain, buckling on a sword belt. He gaped when he saw us. Then his hand went to his sword.

Arian's baton lashed out and caught the man a solid blow in the temple. Dried wax flew everywhere. The man reeled back through the curtain. A scream – a woman's this time – filled my ears. Arian started to go after the man, but I dashed past him towards the next flight of stairs. Taking them two at a time, I almost ran face first into the wooden door at the top.

An icy blast of air made my eyes water as I wrenched the door open, waiting only for Arian to follow me out side before I slammed it shut behind us.

"Give me your baton!" I snatched it from him and forced it through the iron ring of the door handle, twisting it up so that its handle was jammed into the door frame. No one would be able to come after us now.

I wiped the sheen of cold sweat from my forehead as I looked around. We were standing on top of a rampart

– an immensely thick, curving wall that seemed to form the front edge of the building. Behind us there was a sloping slate roof. And to our left was the tower we had been searching for. A small wooden door, level with the rampart, was set into its base.

From this vantage point, we had a perfect view of the ruined walls of the former House of God and the ferocious fire that was consuming the remains of the palisade, sending out a pall of smoke that hung over everything. Below, it was a twenty-foot drop to the great courtyard where we had left our friends fighting. I could hear weapons clashing, people screaming. I took a step forward to look down at the battle, but Arian put his arm out to stop me.

"Not now. Let's do what we came for and search the tower."

I nodded, pulling my axe out again. I handed the borrowed knife back to Arian, who sheathed it at his thigh and drew his sword. We made for the tower door.

"I should go first," I said. "I don't want to be behind you with my axe."

"Not a chance," he said grimly. "I know you. If Ion's up there you'll end up getting yourself killed."

I ground my teeth. It was like he had become a shorter, grumpier version of how Luca used to be. "You don't have to protect me."

"Well, I'm going to. Squawk about it all you like."

"You—"

I closed my jaws with a snap as we both heard a familiar voice ring out overhead. It might have been a shout of triumph or pain, but it was unmistakeably Luca.

Arian's head snapped back. "He's in there."

The shout came again, and this time there were words in it. Luca was calling his brother's name. I flung open the tower door.

The small chamber beyond was dark and mostly taken up by a set of winding stone steps. Luca's voice was echoing down from somewhere above. Not giving Arian a chance to argue, I pelted up the steps first. He was right behind me. Our footsteps rang through the tower until the entire structure seemed to shake. The tiny slit windows flashing past gave me dizzying glimpses of the courtyard below, of sky, of rooftops.

"... hear us ... coming," Arian said between his teeth.

"Too late now," I gasped, trying to keep my axe blades from hitting the wall. A bad rebound would cut my throat. Arian was having the same trouble. The sound of his sword scraping off the rock made my teeth ache. I looked up and saw wooden planks overhead.

Another twist of the stairs and I reached the top. I stumbled out into a surprisingly large space – not a room but a wooden platform, with the stone blocks of the tower reaching only to waist height. Above that the chamber was open to the elements. Wooden posts held up a conical roof, and a bronze bell hung in the roof space, its thick rope falling down to coil in the centre of the room. The place was a shambles. A chair and table had been overturned, papers, books and pens lay scattered on the floor, ink pooled in glossy puddles over curling parchment maps.

Luca stood with his back to us on the other side of the tower. There was a knife in his hand. The point of the knife was pressed to his brother's throat as Ion leaned back against the low wall of stone, his arms held out on either side of his body to try and keep his balance. If he moved the slightest bit forward the knife would pierce his neck. If he leaned back another inch he would topple over the edge of the wall.

Ion's eyes flicked to us as we made our noisy arrival, but Luca's head never turned. The bandages that were still wrapped around his face showed white through the uneven tufts of growing hair at the back of his head, like bone.

"Reinforcements have arrived," Ion said hoarsely. The movement of his throat pressed the knife a little deeper. A bright droplet of blood slid down his neck. "Don't you want to say hello?"

Luca said nothing, but the knife in his hand seemed to tremble. Then it twisted. The drop of blood became a rivulet.

I stared at his still figure. Luca had been shouting a moment before. The wreckage in the room showed that there had been a fight. And yet now, when he had his knife at Ion's throat, Luca had frozen.

Arian eased past me, his sword still at the ready. "Luca…" he whispered, voice tentative, soft, as if he were speaking to a frightened animal. "It's all right. You don't have to."

Luca's face snapped round, his eyes burning almost black against the bandages. "I don't need your help."

"Look out!" I screamed.

Ion's hand shot up and caught Luca's wrist, wrenching the knife sideways. The tip opened a shallow cut along Ion's jaw. He barely flinched. Luca grunted with pain, though, as Ion twisted his wrist to force him to drop the knife. Luca kicked out at the same moment that Arian surged towards them. Ion caught Luca's boot and shoved him back into Arian, who had to drop his sword to avoid stabbing Luca with it. They both went down.

In a blur of speed, Ion leaped over them and ran at me, clearly intending to make a break for the stairs. I whirled my axe up into attack position. Ion stopped with a jerk, his face registering caution mixed with something I could have sworn was pleasure.

"Well! If it isn't Wolf Girl! Fancy meeting you here."

Before I could react, he seized the white bell rope in both hands, took a step back and leaped over the low stone wall, out of the tower. The bell clanged loud enough to deafen me. I brought my axe down and sliced through the taut rope.

There was a yell from outside. I ran to the opening and looked down. Ion, still clutching the end of the rope, had landed on the rampart below. He straightened, sent me a cheery wave, and then jumped onto the steep, sloping roof. He slid down it and out of sight.

"You let him go." Luca's voice came out as a snarl between gritted teeth. "I had my knife at his throat, and you let him escape."

I turned to see Luca slapping away Arian's hands as Arian tried to help him up. He flipped to his feet unassisted, fury showing in every line of his body.

"You might have had your knife at his throat, but you couldn't do it," Arian said wearily. "Could you? For the Mother's sake, Luca, you couldn't do it!"

Luca looked at him with something like hatred. "You have no idea what you're talking about. I was going to skin him like a rabbit. Now he's running. This place is a maze – he could hide forever, thanks to you."

"Stop it!" I yelled. "This isn't Arian's fault."

"If you hadn't interrupted—"

"Exactly the same thing would have happened," I said angrily, shoving my axe into its sheath. "You'd have stood there until he took the knife from you and gutted you with it. You know it, Luca. I can see it in your face."

Luca made a choked sound. "You can't see anything in this face, you idiot."

He shoved past us and fled down the stairs.

Thirty-three

By the time we reached the bottom of the tower, Luca was already gone, vanished as swiftly as his brother.

"Where now?" I asked.

Arian tilted his head, as if listening for something. Then he took two strides to the edge of the rampart and looked down into the courtyard. He beckoned me.

Below us, a few hill guards were still skirmishing on the east side of the courtyard, but their opponents seemed to be household servants, armed not with swords or axes but kitchen knives. One even held a broom. The hill guards were forcing them back steadily. As I watched, one of the servants at the front tripped over a loop of rope and fell, taking two of his comrades with him. The hill guards swarmed into the opening, and within moments the servants had laid down their weapons and were surrendering.

Almost all of the gourdin lay dead. Those few who were

still alive were trussed up like market-day chickens against the wall of their barracks. Most of the hill guards were engaged in leading out small parties of crying Sedorne women and children, many clad in their nightclothes.

Six Sedorne men – older and better dressed than the others – stood to attention against the inner wall. Were these the rebel leaders, the Sedorne lords who had been too proud to accept exile, and had followed Ion here? They were trying to act proud now, but their lifted heads and scornful faces could not hide the fact that they were bound to one another, hand and foot. None of them looked to be injured either. They had been taken without a fight.

"It worked," I breathed. "Luca's plan really worked. I wish he could see this. I wish he could see what his men did for him."

"I don't know if he cares any more," Arian murmured.

I opened my mouth to disagree. Then closed it again. Finally, I said, "We can't keep chasing him. We've done all we can now. We should go down and help them."

I pulled the baton from the iron ring at the door cautiously, but no enraged Sedorne burst through to attack us. As we headed down to the ground floor I found the house already transformed. Instead of silence and darkness, the long corridors rang with the voices and footfalls of fellow hill guards and shone with the light of their lamps and torches as they combed the place for hidden enemies.

We found Livia in one corner of the strangely shaped room leading to the courtyard. She and Rani were unpacking healing supplies on one of the tables. Someone had put lights in the sconces for them. Several men and women, including two of the Rua prisoners that Arian and I had freed earlier, were lying on blankets on the floor. Some of them only looked to have minor injuries. Others were in a bad way. Hind was among them, her tunic cut away to reveal a bloodstained bandage that covered most of her upper body. She lay quietly, eyelids flickering faintly.

"How is she?" I asked Livia.

The older woman made a troubled face. "She's bled a lot. She kept asking for Luca before she passed out. Where *is* the captain?"

"He managed to corner Ion, but Ion got away. They're both running around somewhere here. Be careful," I said.

Arian asked, "What can we do to help you?"

Livia looked surprised, then offered Arian a genuine, if tired smile. "There are plenty of injured out there, but they're too stubborn to stop for treatment. Some of them will start dropping soon. Could you try and get them to come here? They'll listen to you."

Arian nodded. We headed towards the door. What Livia hadn't said – and I knew all too well – was that there must be plenty of dead out there too. Friends as well as enemies. I braced myself as I stepped outside, eyes quickly scanning the courtyard.

The air was icier than before, the smell of smoke like a tarry coat on the tongue. Tiny flakes of snow were just beginning to fall on the shivering groups of rebel women and children. I counted about thirty grown women, some of them servants, some of them nobles, and around the same number of children, ranging in age from babies to adolescent girls. I saw barely any adolescent boys. Were they among the gourdin, living or dead?

"We can't keep these children out here in those clothes. It's too cold," I said. "Luca should be here organizing this. Could we double-check the empty barracks for weapons and then put the civilians in there, where they can be warm and out of the way?"

Before Arian could respond, there was a stir and a murmur from the hill guards.

It was Luca. He stood atop a pile of boxes at the eastern edge of the courtyard. It was as if he had materialized out of thin air. As we watched, the captain jumped down from the boxes. His movements were jerky, as close to clumsy as Luca could ever be. He drew his sword and stalked through the space without a glance or word of greeting for his men. They parted hurriedly before him.

He reached the gourdin tied up by the barracks, seized the closest one by his bound hands and walked back to the centre of the courtyard, forcing the man to scrabble after him on his knees or be dragged.

"Where is he?" Luca demanded. His deep, commanding voice rang out in the near silence. Even the rebel women and children had stopped crying. "Where is Ion Constantin?"

The gourdin squinted up at Luca wordlessly. I couldn't tell if his face was sullen or just confused. Luca released the soldier's hands and dealt the man an open-handed slap that knocked him sideways. "Speak."

The man shouted something in Sedorne. I didn't know most of the words – but certain phrases are always going to be tossed around in a military camp, and I had learned enough of those to pick out "traitor" and "coward".

I started forward. Arian's hand closed on my upper arm, jerking me to a halt—

Luca stabbed the defiant gourdin through the heart.

The man collapsed without a sound. I didn't need to look at his wide, vacant eyes to know that he was dead. As I stared, frozen with shock, Luca turned away. The captain's glittering gaze lighted on another gourdin. He was much younger, this one, no older than fourteen or fifteen. His face was still soft and round, and he had a sleek braid of honey-coloured hair. He looked ridiculous in the dark, lacquered armour which was clearly a size too large for him, but his expression was defiant.

Luca walked towards him.

"That is what will happen to anyone who refuses to speak to me. Do you understand? You are the prisoners here. You have no rights. You have no one to defend you. If you want to live, you answer me."

He reached out and caught the young boy's braid, jerking it savagely. His sword swung up, splattering droplets of blood across the boy's face. "You look the type to catch Ion's fancy. I'll bet he showed you some of his little hiding places. Or maybe one of your friends knows? Speak up!"

An older woman standing among one of the civilian groups cried out; her heavily accented Ruan was made more difficult to understand by her sobs. "My son is innocent. We do not know where Ion is. Leave us alone, please!"

"Why?" Luca gave the boy a shake, yanking at the long braid until I could see tears springing up in the boy's angry eyes. "Why should I leave you alone? You watched as your men went out of this place each day, to go thieving and murdering and kidnapping in the hills. You've lived happily off the spoils of their crimes for years. How many boys like your son have suffered and died at your husbands' hands? At Ion's hands? You're none of you innocent."

The woman reached out pleadingly. "But he is a child! He has done nothing!"

Luca's face twisted under the bandages. "Someone here knows where your leader has his hiding place. Someone knows, and they're not telling." Luca shoved the boy roughly, knocking him down onto his bound hands and knees. "Perhaps you're more scared of him than you are of me. That is going to change. If someone doesn't speak

413

up in the next ten seconds, I will cut off this boy's fingers. Then I'll take out his eyes and his tongue. And when I'm done with him I will choose another, and another, until I find the right one. The one who can answer me."

Luca began to lift his sword again.

You have to believe in me.

The echo of Luca's words, words he had spoken to me months ago, rang through my bones. The movement of his blade seemed to slow as I watched, drifting up as gently as a feather. The snow hung motionless in the air around me.

If you give into anger you will become the thing that you despise.

I could feel the world sucking in its breath. Waiting. Waiting for history to shift. Waiting for me to choose.

It can't take your soul.

I was the fulcrum on which this moment turned. Only I had the power to stop it. I had made a promise to the Wolf, to my father, to the Holy Mother. I had made a promise to myself. I would never run away again. I would fight for what I believed in.

I believed in Luca.

I shook off Arian's hand and stepped forward. The snow began to fall again. Time sped up. The world let out its breath.

"No."

Luca swung round. Dark droplets scattered from his

sword onto the snow-dusted dirt.

"What?"

"I said no. I won't let you."

Luca barked, "Arian. Get her out of my sight."

I didn't look around. I didn't have to.

"Not this time, Luca." Arian's voice was low, rough with pain. "I can't do what you want this time."

"Someone arrest both of them," Luca shouted. "Now!"

A couple of reinforcement hill guards moved. Hind's shout stopped them. The injured lieutenant was clinging to the open door of the house, a dark stain spreading across her bandage. Rani stood behind her, arms ready in case she fell.

"Stay where you are," Hind called. "No one interfere. This is between them."

Luca gave a hollow imitation of a laugh. "I see. You've planned this together. You've all betrayed me."

"No one has betrayed you," I said. "You proposed suicide and we agreed. You broke ranks and abandoned your men in battle and we still carried out your plan. We've done everything you asked of us, without question. But not this. We're not murderers, Luca. We have to be better than them. You taught us that."

"I was wrong," Luca snapped. "I was *stupid*. Playing nice, preaching honour, where did that get me? They don't follow the rules. They do what they want and then they laugh in our faces. We'll never win that way."

"You have won! You're here, aren't you? We've completed the mission. We've taken back the House of God. What more do you want?"

"I want Ion dead!" Luca roared. "I want him to suffer. I don't care about anything else. You won't stop me!" He whirled around, raising his sword above the boy at his feet.

I wrenched my axe free of its sheath and lunged forward.

Axe blade and sword met with a long, trembling whine of metal as Luca bore down on me and I struggled to force his sword up.

From the corner of my eye, I saw a blur of motion as Arian grabbed the Sedorne boy, flung him over his burly shoulder and darted away. The boy's mother and the rest of the small group of women fled after him.

"This isn't you," I ground out through clenched teeth. "This isn't you, Luca!"

"You don't know who I am," Luca panted. "The person you knew is dead."

"No!" Sparks flew between us as I disengaged and spun away out of range. "You didn't die! We thought you were going to. We searched, and we prayed, and we watched over you, and you *lived*. It was a miracle. You're throwing that away. You're throwing everything away."

"I don't have anything left!"

Luca's desperate, glittering eyes flicked to where the

group of civilians were sheltering against the wall behind Arian.

Arian hadn't drawn his sword, and I knew he wouldn't. *Couldn't*, not against Luca. He would put himself between Luca's sword and whatever victim Luca chose, but he wouldn't fight him. I didn't know if Luca would really cut through his brother, his best friend, but I couldn't take the chance.

I stepped into Luca's line of sight.

"No," I repeated.

"Ion could be getting away right now."

"Then look for him. Take this place apart stone by stone if you want, but leave the civilians and the prisoners alone."

"I can't find him that way!" Luca took a deep, gasping breath, as if he were about to break down. Then he straightened, shoulders going back, chin lifting. "Very well. You've disobeyed my orders. You've betrayed me. If I have to bring you down I will. But this isn't a sparring match, Saram Aeskaar. We'll fight to the death."

"*Frost…*"

I heard Arian's horrified whisper, but it was already too late. I had made my choice. I had to fight – and I had to win.

I was fighting for Luca's soul.

Thirty-four

I stared into Luca's face. The snowflakes drifted gently into his shorn hair. A faint chill that was nothing to do with the snow skated over my skin. The Wolf was stirring. *Go back*, I told him firmly. *I don't need you.*

There had to be something of the old Luca in there. Something of that golden man who had broken through my shell of fear and distrust. The man I had fallen in love with. He couldn't be gone forever. I wouldn't let him be. I just had to get him to listen to me. To see me.

I swallowed hard. Then I whispered, "Begin."

Luca came at me so fast that for an instant he seemed to blink out of sight. I panicked. Pure instinct had me bringing the axe up to block the vicious slice at my side. Luca flicked his sword away into another cut at my shoulder. Again, I whirled the axe round just in time to deflect the blow.

Luca snarled and, whipping his sword round, flew into a spinning kick. I dodged. Luca's boot passed my stomach by less than an inch.

"You can't win if you don't attack," Luca said as he landed. His words reminded me painfully of the many times we had sparred with each other. But this time neither of us held a blunt practice weapon. And this fight wouldn't stop if one of us drew blood.

"I don't want to attack," I said, watching warily as Luca circled me. I shifted to keep him in sight. "I don't want to hurt you."

"That puts you at a serious disadvantage," Luca said, "because right now I don't care if I hurt you."

He lunged, sword aimed at my belly. I skidded sideways to avoid the blade and moved right into a punch. The blow landed squarely on my cheek and knocked me back a step. I ducked hastily to avoid a sword slash that would have laid my face open, and spun my axe in a wide two-handed sweep, driving Luca back.

"You should have let Arian challenge me," Luca taunted, bouncing lightly on the balls of his feet. "At least he'd have had some chance."

My entire face throbbed, and it hadn't even been that hard a punch. I knew that Luca could have knocked me out if he'd wanted to – but only if he didn't mind breaking my jaw. He was holding back. He didn't want to hurt me, no matter what he said.

My Luca was still in there.

"He'd have no chance at all. He'd never fight you for real," I said. "Arian would let you carve him open before he took the risk of hurting you. But you don't care about that any more, do you? You don't care that he loves you, that he'd die for you. All you care about is Ion."

For a second Luca's mask of hatred seemed to flicker. He shook his head fiercely. "Don't tell me what I feel. This has nothing to do with Aria. Don't bring him into it."

"*You* brought him into it. You brought us all into this by bringing us here."

He attacked again. I blocked a lightning-fast slash at my face and a thrust at my chest, spun away from a flying kick, ducked under another punch – and drove my axe forward, hitting Luca squarely in the stomach. He stumbled back with a grunt.

We circled each other, breathing heavily. Sweat was beading on my skin despite the cold.

"Ion must be so proud," I said softly. "I bet he's somewhere here, watching you, absolutely hugging himself with glee. This must be what he's always wanted."

"What? What are you talking about?" Luca edged sideways, his blade lifting as if to shield himself from my words.

"Haven't you figured it out yet? He caught you. He tortured you. And then … he let you go."

"I *escaped*."

"Are you sure about that? I don't think, in the state you were in, you could have escaped from your own bedroll. He was playing with you. He let you go because he wanted to see what you would become. He wanted to see if he could take that brave, kind brother – that golden boy who he must have loved and hated so much – and turn him into a mirror image of himself."

"I am not like him!"

"Look at yourself, Luca," I snapped. "Look at what you're doing. You're trying to kill one of your own men, and when you've finished you're going to start torturing children. Mad King Abheron would want you on his side."

"Shut up!"

Luca flew at me.

The moment our blades met I knew I had been right. Luca had been holding back before. His strength now forced me backwards, my feet skidding in the snow.

"You know it's true," I said, diving sideways to avoid another cut at my face. Luca didn't respond. His eyes were febrile, desperate, as if I had driven him to the edge of madness. He whirled and kicked wildly, teeth bared.

I fell back. I was fighting just to keep on my feet. Luca's sword bounced off the iron langet of the axe and nicked my chin. Blood trickled down my neck as Luca landed a kick that nearly stoved my ribs in. I stumbled, knees going weak. Luca raised his sword.

The Wolf stirred again.

Daughter, it whispered. Its voice was different now – not quite Garin Aeksaar's any more, but something fiercer, something more akin to the snarling, ferocious voice I had heard in my vision. **Daughter. You must fight for your life now, or you will die.**

Then help me, Father. Fight with me.

The wild thing inside me unfolded. A shiver travelled through my body as its powerful limbs infused mine with strength. Muscles tensed, twitched. Frost begin to curl across my skin. My vision sharpened, flickering with silver lights.

I felt the wolf bite blaze into life on my cheek.

My axe flew up, catching the edge of Luca's blade. Luca disengaged, turned and dropped, sweeping his leg out. I jumped it and flew into a two-footed kick. My feet thudded into the centre of his chest. Cold burst through the muscles of my legs, travelling down to my boots.

Luca's metal chest plate buckled. He flew backwards with a hoarse cry of pain as I landed squarely on both feet.

He hit the snow a few feet away, rolling over once before climbing shakily upright. He wavered for a second, then took his sword in both hands. I could hear his breath coming in painful gasps. His face around the bandages was whiter than before.

"You do know it, don't you?" I said mercilessly as I moved towards him. "We stormed this place, defeated our enemies and secured the House of God – and yet somehow, despite all that, he's won. He's won *you*."

"You don't know what he did to me," Luca said. Tears were shining in his eyes. "You have no idea… He took everything. *Everything.* I can't get it back!"

I swung my axe in a great overhead arc that forced Luca's sword up into a defensive position. He disengaged with a hard grunt. I blocked his next blow easily, recognizing the forms of the drill we had practised together so many times. Panicking and in pain, Luca had fallen back on the basic moves.

It was too bad he had taught them to me himself.

I slid sideways to avoid a body kick, bringing my axe down to deflect the sword aimed at my gut, then spun, bringing the axe up for a neck blow that I knew Luca would catch on his blade. I disengaged and used the momentum to whip round, this time jabbing at Luca's face with the head of the axe.

As Luca blocked, I caught his sword on the pick of the axe. I twisted, turning the pick and shifting onto my back foot, dragging with all the Wolf's lent strength.

Luca's sword jumped from his hand.

It skidded through the snow to land at Arian's feet. Arian stamped his boot down on it, meeting Luca's betrayed look without wincing. Luca turned to face me, defiant, clearly waiting for me to strike him down. When I didn't, he charged me.

I dropped my axe with a clang and let him tackle me, using the Wolf's agility to turn us in the air so that we landed with me on top. I closed my hands on his fists and pinned them to the ground. Gloved hands burning icy cold with the power required to resist his struggles, I braced my knees on either side of his body to keep him in place.

"Why didn't you strike?" he demanded, voice ragged, chest heaving. "Burn you! We're supposed to fight to the death. Traitor!"

"Idiot," I said softly, gazing down into his face.

"Don't – don't look at me like that. I'm not that person any more. I'm not the one you loved. I'm not him."

Slowly, cautiously, I reached for the bandages that were wrapped around Luca's face. Luca bucked, legs kicking frantically, but he didn't try to push me off. His newly freed hands clenched at his sides. His teeth ground together as if to keep the pleas inside.

The stained bandages fell away, exposing the livid burns. Tears trickled down the crusted wounds. He tried to turn his head away from me. I stripped off my gloves and caught his face between my cold hands. I kissed his forehead. His mouth. Then, most gently and reverently of all, I kissed each cross-shaped scar.

He went still beneath me.

"You can't," he whispered. "Not after what he did to me."

"I don't *care* what he did," I said, my voice breaking. "Nothing – *nothing* – could take away the feelings I have for you. They're part of me now, part of what makes me, me."

"You don't know," Luca said, his eyes begging me to understand. "I'm not the same. I'm ruined inside, empty. It's too late. I want … I just want to be dead. He took everything I had."

"But you aren't dead, and no one can take your soul. Not the gods, not even Ion. Remember?"

I slid back, taking my weight off Luca's chest and easing into his lap as I pulled him carefully into a sitting position. Resting my cheek against his, I gently combed my fingers through the silky, uneven tufts of his hair. He still smelled the same. I hadn't even realized how much I missed the scent of honeysuckle. "I know you're in there. I know the man I love is still alive. I'll keep telling you that until you realize it's true. Come back. Come back to me."

Something seemed to break free inside him. His arms wrapped around me, squeezing tight, tight. He buried his face in my shoulder. His body shook with hoarse, almost soundless sobs.

Across the courtyard I met Arian's eyes. They were alive with the brilliance of his smile, the dimple showing in his cheek. Whatever pain he felt at seeing me in Luca's arms was hidden – and I realized then that he would never let me, or anyone else, see it again. He was too good a brother. Too good a friend.

He saluted me sharply, then took his boot off Luca's sword. His lips parted as if to speak.

I never found out what he would have said.

Arian's gaze flicked upwards, over my head. His eyes widened. Then he launched himself at me and Luca.

The impact knocked the wind from my lungs. The three of us skidded across the ground, my right knee and elbow grinding painfully into the frozen dirt. I felt Arian jerk. His breath huffed against my neck.

People were yelling: yelling my name, Arian's and Luca's. I heard Ion Constantin's voice spitting out vile curses. Luca was struggling to get out from beneath me and Arian. I tried to help, but I couldn't get my legs under me. Arian was a dead weight pinning me down.

"Arian! *Arian!*" I didn't know if it was me screaming or Luca, or both of us.

His weight was suddenly lifted away. An icy shudder wracked my body as the warmth of him left me. Luca jackknifed upright. I scrambled to my knees. We both turned.

Arian lay prone in the snow. Livia was crouched beside him. There was blood everywhere.

Arian's blood.

Luca groaned. He pulled Arian to his chest, cradling the other man's body in his arms. The healer said nothing, not even a caution to be careful. That would have told me everything I needed to know, even if I couldn't see the wound for myself. A crossbow bolt was buried deep in Arian's side. Dark blood was bubbling out, trickling over his armour, over Luca and pooling in the snow beneath him.

"Oh, my brother," Luca whispered. "Not like this. Not for me."

"Idiot. Not … just for you." Arian gasped the words, breath moving his chest in short, shallow jerks. "Frost…"

I crawled towards them on hands and knees, pressing myself into Arian's uninjured side so that I could help support his weight. His arm lifted, his trembling fingers cupping my neck as he drew me down towards him.

"Gonna … kick me in the head?" he asked, trying to smile. His teeth were streaked with blood.

"I'll let you off this time," I said, struggling to smile back. I laid my hand on his heart, gently touching my lips to his. He tasted of iron and salt. Blood and tears. "Arian, I—"

He shook his head a little, opening his eyes wide, like a child trying to stay awake past bedtime. "Keep … my brother … out of trouble for me?"

"You know I will."

"Yes." His eyes lifted to Luca, dimple flashing again. "You too. Look out for bossy—"

A terrible convulsion rattled Arian's body. His fingers dug into the skin under my ear as he fought to hang on. Luca bent his head, pressing a kiss to his brother's forehead, clutching Arian to him as Arian's limbs spasmed: twitching with the last of his strength.

I felt Luca's fingers brush mine. I reached out, and our hands entwined on Arian's breast. We held him between us in the silence of the falling snow. The only warmth in my world at that moment was the point where our hands met. I squeezed my eyes shut.

Arian's fingers slid limply away from my neck.

"Good riddance to the bastard whore's son!" Ion's strident voice echoed over the courtyard.

On top of the first rampart, two hill guards held Ion Constantin, his hands bound behind his back. The crossbow he had used to kill Arian – that he had intended to use on Luca and me – lay smashed on the ground at the base of the wall. His face was stretched into a joyful grin. "May Ovidiv piss on his carcass!"

Inside me, the Wolf snarled, snapped, and then howled: an unearthly wail of sorrow that made my ears throb, my teeth ache, my back arch. The Wolf could feel my pain.

It wanted vengeance.

Ice exploded across my skin with an audible *snap*. Luca grunted with pain, but clung to my hand, face twisting. "No, Frost! Don't!"

Carefully, I disentangled my fingers from his and climbed to my feet. Everything clouded and rippled around me, the intense cold warping the very air. My hair was working free of its braid, whipping around my face as if in a high wind. Glowing ice crystals formed among the thick strands. The ice crackled at my fingertips, then extended, forming long claws.

"*Ion Constantin.*" It was my lips that moved, but the words came out as a high-pitched, ululating wail, a mixture of human and beast.

I bent my knees and leaped. The earth cracked and dimpled as my feet left it. I caught hold of the top of the rampart with both hands and swung up effortlessly, patterns of ice swirling across the stone as I stood. The hill guards who had been holding Ion released him and stepped back, expressions awed.

"*Ion Constantin,*" I repeated, my voice a wolf pack in full cry. "*This time, you will pay for what you have done.*"

He didn't cringe back. Stiffly, as if it cost him a great effort, he bent his head and spat at my feet.

The saliva froze instantly. My boot crushed it as I caught Ion around the neck. The shards of ice on my fingertips pierced him; blood spurted and then solidified like red flowers around the wounds. I lifted him up so his feet scrabbled uselessly.

"Go on, if you've the belly for it," he said between gritted teeth. Ice blisters crawled across his skin where I held him, and he writhed with pain, but his taunting eyes never left mine. "Go ... on!"

It would only take the tiniest squeeze, just a flex of my fingers, to crush his neck. To close that wicked mouth forever. My fingers began to tighten.

The door to the rampart slammed open behind me. I heard running footsteps.

"Wait!" It was Luca's voice. "Don't kill him! Not like this!"

"Pleading ... for mercy ... for your big brother? How ... touching," Ion rasped.

"Frost, Arian told me what happened to you in the fire," Luca said. "He forced me to listen, even when I tried to ignore him. He was so proud of you. Don't make the same mistake I did. Ion's not worth it, not when you fought so hard to tame your wolf."

Ion struggled weakly in my grip. The blisters covered more than half his face now, scalding the skin yellow and bright red, like a burn. "Great gods ... you're ... spine-less. No brother of ... mine."

"You don't have to do this. Please, Frost," Luca begged. "He just wants to hurt you more, damage you more. That's all he's ever wanted. To see people suffer. I realize that now."

"Snivelling ... *coward*." Ion's hands came up to claw at my fingers as if he couldn't stand it any more. He screamed as his hands stuck to the ice coating my flesh. "You're ... nothing now ... do you hear me, Luca? *Nothing!*"

My fingers opened. Ion dropped heavily to the

rampart, blood oozing sluggishly from his neck and hands. He stared at me in disbelief.

"Luca is something you could never be." My human voice emerged from the Wolf's howl as I spoke. The ice on my skin cracked and drifted away like snow. Icicles fell from my hair, shattering on the stone with musical noises. "He is something you could never understand. Luca is loved."

I turned away from him into Luca's arms.

Thirty-five

"Farewell, my love, our time has come,
Long though I might to stay;
Our time has come, my one true love,
The world calls me away..."

The candle, even protected by the bubble of glass in my cupped hands, flickered and danced. The wind rose and the trees that surrounded the cairn of white stones stirred.

"Goodbye, my love, remember well,
My shadow on your door;
I leave my heart, my love, farewell,
And pray you cry no more..."

The sound of the leaves nearly drowned out my voice as I finished the song. Carefully, I wedged the base of the candleholder between two large stones, watching as the flame stretched long and thin, and then went out. Above, the stars were slowly surfacing from the dark water of the sky.

After a while, my back and knees began to ache from kneeling for so long. But I didn't move. I was waiting.

It had been nearly a month since the battle at the rebel fortress. I didn't know much about what happened after I passed out on the rampart. The Wolf's overwhelming display of power had drained me completely, and by the time I woke up again, I was on my way down the mountain, tucked into a hastily constructed litter, with Livia to look after me. Another group had followed behind, bearing the bodies of the dead hill guards.

We had come back to the old camp and buried the fallen. Arian's body had been given the special honour of this cairn in the clearing on the edge of the site. In Uskaand, they burned the dead on wooden pyres, so that their ashes were carried away on the wind. Watching, dry-eyed, as they had covered the shrouded form of my friend with stones, blocking out warmth and light and air forever, I had wanted nothing more than Luca's arms around me.

But he was not there.

"You don't have to worry about him," Livia had said. "He was tired and grieving and upset but – but he was himself. You brought him back. He wanted you away from that place so that you could recover."

But he didn't want me with him.

Messages came frequently to the camp from the absent hill guards, the ones who had stayed on to secure the House of God and the captured rebels. Livia read the letters to me. The prisoners – including Ion – had been escorted to Mesgao and handed over to the small army garrison there. They would be marched to Aroha to stand trial before the king and reia. The freed Rua were taken back to the villages and farms they had been stolen from.

There were no messages from Luca.

After a fortnight, more hill guards began to trickle back into camp, their tasks completed. Then Rani arrived, bringing all the surviving and wounded hill guards with her, including Hind, who had joked that she was half cat, and was sure she still had three lives left. Rani also brought the news of Luca's imminent return.

"Arian," I said to the stones. "Arian, I don't know what to do."

"He's not here, you know," a familiar voice said from the shadows.

I started to my feet and then faltered, a wave of dizziness sweeping over me. Strong arms caught me before I could fall. The scent of sunshine and honeysuckle teased my nose.

Luca's hands were very warm against my back, making me aware of how chilled I had become. In the starlight, all I could make out of him was the gilt gleam of his shaggy hair and the bluish-gold of his eyes. There were no bandages on his face.

I made a restive movement, and immediately Luca's arms dropped away. I could have cried out at the loss, but it was too late. He was already stepping back.

"I didn't mean to startle you."

I shrugged, words clogging in my throat.

"I'm sorry I've been gone so long," Luca said tonelessly. "Would you sit down with me? For a little while?"

I knelt again. Luca followed suit. We both stared at the cairn. I waited for him to speak, but the only sound was the rustling of the leaves in the rising wind.

"What did you mean?" I asked, after a moment, unable to stand the awkward silence any longer. "By saying that he's not here?"

"I meant … that this place is for us, not him. Warriors, great-hearted men and woman, are embraced in the Holy Mother's mantle of flame. He's with Her now."

"He'll like that." I stared down at my hands.

There was another uncomfortable silence. It felt unreal. We had never been like this with each other. It was as if we were more strangers now than we had been when we had first met. There was so much pain, so many bad memories between us; I had no idea how to fix it.

"You miss him a great deal, don't you?" Luca asked softly.

I turned my head to look at the pale blur of his face in

the darkness. "Don't you? He was your brother."

"He was more than that to you. He was my friend and my brother but he was your ... your..."

I sighed. "Luca, it wasn't like that."

"You don't owe me any explanations," he said, voice strained. "I'm so sorry for the way I reacted before. It was unforgiveable. You never made any promises to me, and—"

"Will you *shut up*?" I demanded, my voice coming out so like Arian's that it brought a lump to my throat. "Arian kissed me twice. I let him twice. That was all. Put whatever else you imagined out of your mind. It's unfair – not just to me – but to him. He knew that I loved you, and he accepted it."

Luca hesitated. When he spoke again his words were so unexpected that it took me a moment to understand. "Do you ... still? Can you feel anything for me after what I've done? I tried to kill you..." His voice cracked. "I broke every promise I ever made to you. Even if you could put up with this face, I'm not exactly a good bargain any more."

I took a deep, slow breath. I had thought we'd put this behind us in the courtyard at the House of God. But I had to remember that even if Luca was better now, he was still a changed man. A man who had been broken and had put himself back together again. He would never be the reckless, care-for-nothing risk-taker he had been before. Caution had been burned into his flesh.

Maybe he would never take anyone's love for granted again. And maybe that wasn't a bad thing.

"When I first met you, Luca, you guessed that I'd been alone for a long time," I said slowly, feeling that the slightest mistake, a single wrong word, could break something irreplaceable. "I had. I'd been in darkness nearly all my life, and you brought light into my existence for the first time. And maybe that's the reason why I started to ... to have feelings for you. You seemed like a dream. Perfect and golden and good, and sure of everything. You made it too easy to believe that you would always be strong, always have all the answers. I think you believed it yourself. But that – that's just infatuation. Hero worship. It's not real. I've learned a lot about love over these last months. And part of what I've learned is that you have to want someone for who they are, not who you want them to be. You have to love a real person, not some dream in your head. Neither of us could have lived that way."

"What does that mean?" he asked quietly. He was twisting towards me – trying to see my face. "What are you saying, Frost?"

I turned, letting the starlight fill my eyes. "I don't want you because I expect you to swoop in and rescue me and make everything all right. I don't want you because you have all the answers. I don't even want you because you're beautiful. None of that matters. You could never be a bad bargain to me, because … you're Luca. And I love you."

I heard the sharp intake of his breath. Then his arms were around me, his heart thundering against my breast as if he had just crossed the finishing line in a life or death race. I felt warm tears streaming down my cold cheeks, and I didn't know or care who they belonged to. I held onto him with everything I had. I would never let go again.

Finally, Luca drew back a little, holding me against him with fearful tenderness. His eyes were great, dark pools, as warm and filled with happiness as they had ever been. I lifted my hand and laid it on his cheek, where the scar marked his skin, and he did not flinch from my touch.

He said, "I didn't know if you could forgive me for everything I put you through, for causing Arian's death. I didn't know if I should even ask you to."

"You didn't cause Arian's death," I said, thumping him lightly on the arm. I had a feeling I would have to repeat these words many times before they really sank in. Luca was too used to taking responsibility for other people to relinquish guilt easily. "Ion shot the arrow, and Arian chose to save us. He would never have blamed you, any more than I would have blamed him if you had died in his place." I glanced at the mound of stones. The candle was alight again, its tiny flame flickering blue and purple and green. My breath caught.

I whispered, "You're the one who taught us both that we had choices. Arian made his. All he ever wanted was for the people he loved to be safe and happy."

"If you stay with me, then he'll have his wish," Luca said. "I think … it might take some time for me to … to be who I was before. I might still be mad for all I know. But come what may, I'll always love you, Frost."

Then he kissed me, and I tasted honeysuckle sweetness and the bitter saltiness of tears on his lips. I tasted his sorrow and his love. I tasted frost and fire.

I tasted forever.

Acknowledgements

It seems to me that life's difficult experiences divide up into two categories. The first is for situations and challenges which seem unbearably hard, even impossible, at the time – but which, looking back, make you smile and think, "Hey, it wasn't all bad." The second is for times so unpleasant that you *avoid* looking back on them if at all possible, and do everything in your power not to repeat them. Writing *FrostFire,* and then completely rewriting it when it turned out not to work, was certainly one of life's challenging experiences for me. But thanks to the following list of people, instead of giving up writing forever and running off to Tibet to herd yaks, I can now smile wryly and say, "Well, it wasn't too bad." My deepest thanks go out to:

My editor, Annalie, and my agent, Nancy, who managed to catch me before I could book passage to the

Himalayas, and persuade me that I was much better cut out for revising than animal husbandry.

The members of the Furtive Scribblers Club, who kept pace with the dizzying changes to my "work in progress" and kept cheering me on, even when they had no idea what gender any of my characters were, or who would live or die.

All the wonderfully talented crew at Walker Books, who make me realize every time I meet them that I really am working with the best publisher in the world.

My crew of Twitter pals, including my adopted mothers Emma Davies and Vivienne Da Costa, the lovely Liz de Jager, Sarah Gibson and Lynsey Newton, Elle and Kate, not-really-stalkers Ashley Benson, Misty Braden and Enna, and fellow writers Kaz Mahoney, Cat Clarke (Ha! Next to each other again!), Jackie Dolomore and Lee Weatherly. And many more, who were always willing to exchange rants or war stories.

My adorable "Dear Readers", who make running my blog and website worthwhile. Special thanks go to Alex, Isabel and Megha, who can be counted on to respond to everything I write with such enthusiasm that I become convinced I'm a genius, for thirty seconds at least.

And finally, to my parents. Just because.

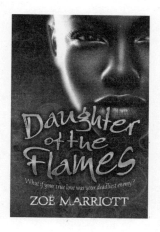

Zira was orphaned when the Sedorne invaded her country. For ten years she has been in hiding, training to become a warrior priestess. Now the time has come to fight back– and nothing will stand in the way of her people's freedom. Not even the man she loves.

Trained in the magical art of shadow-weaving,
sixteen-year-old Suzume is able to recreate herself in any form –
a fabulous gift for a girl desperate to escape her past.

But who is she really? Is she a girl of noble birth living under the
tyranny of her mother's new husband, Lord Terayama, or a lowly
drudge scraping a living in the ashes of Terayama's kitchens, or
Yue, the most beautiful courtesan in the Moonlit Lands?

Whatever her true identity, Suzume is destined to capture the
heart of a prince – and determined to use his power to destroy
Terayama. And nothing will stop her, not even love.

Darkness has fallen across a kingdom
far away. The queen is dead – killed in the
forest by a terrifying beast – and her daughter,
Alexandra, suspects that the new woman in
her father's life is not all that she seems. Exiled
and betrayed, Alexandra must face magic,
murder and the loss of all she holds dear
in a desperate struggle against evil.

 **UNDER COVER**

READ BETWEEN THE LINES

 READ
- Sneak previews
- Author interviews

DISCOVER
- Trailers
- Behind the scenes footage

 WIN
- Review copies
- Signed books

COMMENT

Have your say on the books that you want to read

Scan the code to watch our book trailers*

Discover more at
WWW.UNDERCOVERREADS.COM

* How to scan the code
1 – Download a QR code reader for your mobile phone
2 – Open it up and hold your phone in front of the code to scan
3 – Enjoy our book trailers!